Using the pseudonym **J.D. Robb, Nora Roberts** published her first Robb novel in 1995 and introduced readers to the tough as nails, but emotionally damaged homicide cop **Eve Dallas** and billionaire Irish rogue, **Roarke**.

With the **In Death** series, Robb has become one of the biggest thriller writers on earth, with each new novel reaching number one on bestseller charts the world over.

For more information, visit **www.jd-robb.co.uk**

D0544303

The world can't get enough of J.D. Robb

Have you read them all?

Go back to the beginning with the first three In Death novels.

For a full list of J.D. Robb titles, turn to the back of this book

Book One
NAKED IN DEATH

Introducing Lieutenant Eve Dallas and billionaire Roarke. When a Senator's granddaughter is found shot to death in her own bed, all the evidence points to Roarke – but Eve senses a set-up.

Book Two
GLORY IN DEATH

High-profile women are being murdered by a knife-wielding attacker. Roarke has a connection to all the victims, but Eve needs his help if she's going to track down the real killer.

Book Three
IMMORTAL IN DEATH

With a new 'immortality' drug about to hit the market, Eve and Roarke must stop a vicious and evil drug dealer and killer – before it's too late.

Head to the end of this book for an exclusive extract from the **J.D. Robb** thriller,

FESTIVE IN DEATH

J. D. ROBB

IMMORTAL IN DEATH

piatkus

PIATKUS

First published in the United States in 1996 by Berkley Publishing Group,
a division of Penguin Putnam Inc., New York
First published in Great Britain in 2003 by Piatkus Books
This reissue published by Piatkus in 2010

5 7 9 10 8 6

A CIP catalogue record for this book
is available from the British Library.

ISBN 978-0-7499-5461-1

Typeset in Bembo by Palimpsest Book Production Ltd,
Falkirk, Stirlingshire
Printed and bound by CPI Group (UK) Ltd, Croydon, CR0 4YY

Papers used by Piatkus are from well-managed forests
and other responsible sources.

MIX
Paper from
responsible sources
FSC® C104740

Piatkus
An imprint of
Little, Brown Book Group
100 Victoria Embankment
London EC4Y 0DY

An Hachette UK Company
www.hachette.co.uk

www.piatkus.co.uk

Eve Dallas – Personnel File

Name: Eve Dallas

Nationality: American

Rank: Homicide Lieutenant, New York Police and Security Department

Born: 2028

Height: 5 foot 9 inches

Weight: 120 lbs

Eyes: Golden brown

Hair: Light brown

ID number: 5347BQ

Service:
Began police officer training at the Academy in 2046, aged 18.

Family:
Between the ages of eight and ten, Eve lived in a communal home while her parents were searched for. Eve was found with no ID, no memory, and was traumatised having been a victim of sexual assault.

Why Eve is a cop:
'It's what I am. It's not just that someone has to look, even though that's just the way it is. It's that I have to look.'

The fatal gift of beauty

LORD BYRON

Make me immortal with a kiss

CHRISTOPHER MARLOWE

1

Getting married was murder. Eve wasn't sure how it had happened in the first place. She was a cop, for God's sake. Throughout her ten years on the force, she'd firmly believed cops should stay single, unencumbered, and focused utterly on the job. It was insane to believe one person could split time, energy, and emotion between law, with all its rights and wrongs, and family, with all its demands and personalities.

Both careers – and from what she'd observed, marriage was a job – had impossible demands and hellish hours. It might have been 2058, an enlightened time of technological advancement, but marriage was still marriage. To Eve it translated to terror.

Yet here she was on a fine day in high summer – one of her rare and precious days off – preparing to go shopping. She couldn't stop the shudder.

Not just shopping, she reminded herself as her stomach clutched, shopping for a wedding dress.

Obviously she'd lost her mind.

It was Roarke's doing, of course. He'd caught her at a weak moment. Both of them bleeding and bruised and lucky to be alive. When a man is clever enough and knows his quarry well enough to choose such a time and place to propose marriage, well, a woman was a goner.

At least a woman like Eve Dallas.

'You look like you're about to take on a gang of chemi-thugs bare-handed.'

Eve tugged on a shoe, flicked her gaze up and over. He was entirely too attractive, she thought. Criminally so. The strong face, poet's mouth, killer blue eyes. The wizard's mane of thick black hair. If you managed to get past the face to the body, it was equally impressive. Then you added that faint wisp of Ireland in the voice, and, well, you had one hell of a package.

'What I'm about to take on is worse than any chemi-head.' Hearing the whine in her own voice, Eve scowled. She never whined. But the truth was, she'd have preferred fighting hand to hand with a souped-up addict than discussing hemlines.

Hemlines, for sweet Christ's sake.

She bit back an oath, watching him narrowly as he crossed the spacious bedroom. He had a way of making her feel foolish at odd times. Like now as he sat beside her on the high, wide bed they shared.

He caught her chin in his hand. 'I'm hopelessly in love with you.'

There he was. This man with the sinfully blue eyes, the strong, gorgeous, somehow Raphaelite looks of a doomed angel, loved her.

2

'Roarke.' She struggled to hold back a sigh. She could and had faced an armed laser in the hands of a mad mutant mercenary with less fear than she faced such unswerving emotion. 'I'm going through with it. I said I would.'

His brow quirked, dark and wry. He wondered how she remained so unaware of her own appeal as she sat there, fretting, her poorly cut fawn-colored hair standing up in tufts and spikes, aroused by her restless hands, thin lines of annoyance and doubt running between her big, whiskey-colored eyes. 'Darling Eve.' He kissed her, lightly, once on the frowning lips, then again in the gentle dip in her chin. 'I never doubted it.' Though he had, constantly. 'I've several things I have to see to today. You were late last night. I never had a chance to ask if you had plans.'

'The stakeout on the Bines case went to after oh three hundred.'

'Did you get him?'

'Walked right into my arms – blissed on dreamers and a marathon VR session.' She smiled, but it was the hunter's smile, dark and feral. 'Murdering little bastard came along like my personal droid.'

'Well, then.' He patted her shoulder before rising. He stepped down from the platform into the dressing area where he pondered a selection of jackets. 'And today? Reports to file?'

'I'm off today.'

'Oh?' Distracted, he turned back, a gorgeous silk jacket

3

in deep charcoal in his hand. 'I can reschedule some of my afternoon, if you like.'

Which would be, Eve mused, a bit like a general rescheduling battles. In Roarke's world, business was a complicated and profitable war. 'I'm already booked.' The scowl snuck back on her before she could stop it. 'Shopping,' she muttered. 'Wedding dress.'

Now he smiled, quickly, easily. From her, such plans were a declaration of love. 'No wonder you're so cranky. I told you I'd see to it.'

'I'll pick out my own wedding dress. And I'll buy it myself. I'm not marrying you for your damn money.'

Smooth and elegant as the jacket he slipped on, he continued to smile. 'Why are you marrying me, Lieutenant?' Her scowl deepened, but he was, above all, a patient man. 'Want a multiple choice?'

'Because you never take no for an answer.' She stood, shoving her hands into the front pockets of her jeans.

'You only get a half point for that. Try again.'

'Because I've lost my mind.'

'That won't win you the trip for two to Tropic World on Star 50.'

A reluctant smile tugged at her lips. 'Maybe I love you.'

'Maybe you do.' Content with that, he crossed back to her and laid his hands on her strong shoulders. 'How bad can it be? You can pop a few shopping programs into the computer, look at dozens of suitable dresses, order in what appeals to you.'

'That was my idea.' She rolled her eyes. 'Mavis ditched it.'

'Mavis.' He paled a bit. 'Eve, tell me you're not going shopping with Mavis.'

His reaction brightened her mood a little. 'She has this friend. He's a designer.'

'Dear Christ.'

'She says he's mag. Just needs a break to make a name for himself. He has a little workshop in Soho.'

'Let's elope. Now. You look fine.'

Her grin flashed. 'Scared?'

'Terrified.'

'Good. Now we're even.' Delighted to be on level footing, she leaned in and kissed him. 'Now you can worry about what I'll be wearing on the big day for the next few weeks. Gotta go.' She patted his cheek. 'I'm meeting her in twenty minutes.'

'Eve.' Roarke grabbed for her hand. 'You wouldn't do something ridiculous?'

She tugged her way free. 'I'm getting married, aren't I? What could be more ridiculous?'

She hoped he stewed over it all day. The idea of marriage was daunting enough, but a wedding – clothes, flowers, music, people. It was horrifying.

She zipped downtown on Lex, braking hard and muttering curses at a sidewalk vendor who encroached on the lane with his smoking glide cart. The traffic violation was bad enough, but the scent of overcooked soydogs hit her nervous stomach like lead.

The Rapid cab behind her broke the intercity noise pollution code by blasting his horn and shouting curses through his speaker. A group, obviously tourists, loaded down with palm cams, compumaps, and binoks gaped stupidly at the whizzing traffic. Eve shook her head as a quick-fingered street thief elbowed through them.

When they got back to their hotel, they were going to find themselves several credits poorer. If she'd had the time and a place to pull over, she might have given the thief a chase. But he was lost in the crowd and a block across town on his air skates before she could blink.

That was New York, she thought with a faint smile. Take it at your own risk.

She loved the crowds, the noise, the constant frantic rush of it. You were rarely alone, but never intimate. That's why she'd come here so many years ago.

No, she wasn't a social animal, but too much space and too much solitude made her nervous.

She'd come to New York to be a cop, because she believed in order, needed it to survive. Her miserable and abusive childhood with all its blank spaces and dark corners couldn't be changed. But she had changed. She had taken control, had made herself into the person some anonymous social worker had named Eve Dallas.

Now she was changing again. In a few weeks she wouldn't just be Eve Dallas, lieutenant, homicide. She'd be Roarke's wife. How she would manage to be both was more of a mystery to her than any case that had ever come across her desk.

Neither of them knew what it was to be family, to have family, to make a family. They knew cruelty, abuse, abandonment. She wondered if that was why they had come together. They both understood what it was to have nothing, to be nothing, to know fear and hunger and despair – and both had remade themselves.

Was it just mutual need that attracted them? Need for sex, for love, and the melding of the two that she had never thought was possible before Roarke.

A question for Dr Mira, she mused, thinking of the police psychiatrist she often consulted.

But for now, Eve determined that she wasn't going to think about the future or the past. The moment was complicated enough.

Three blocks from Greene Street, she seized her chance and squeezed into a parking space. After searching through her pockets, she found the credit tokens the aging meter demanded in its moronic and static jumbled tones and plugged in enough for two hours.

If it took any more than that, she'd be ready for a tranq room and a parking citation wouldn't bother her in the least.

Taking a deep breath, she scanned the area. She wasn't called this far downtown often. Murders happened everywhere, but Soho was an arty bastion for the young and struggling who more often debated their disagreements over tiny glasses of cheap wine or cups of cafe noir.

Just now, Soho was full of summer. Flower vendors burst with roses, the classic reds and pinks vying with the hybrid stripes. Traffic droned and chugged on the street, rumbled overhead, puffed a bit on the rickety passovers. Pedestrians stuck mostly with the scenic sidewalks, though the people glides were busy. The flowing robes currently hot from Europe were much in evidence, with arty sandals, head-dresses, and shiny ropes swinging from earlobes to shoulder blades.

Oil, watercolor, and compu artists hawked their wares on corners and in storefronts, competing with food vendors who promised hybrid fruits, iced yogurts, or vegetable purees uncontaminated by preservatives.

Members of the Pure Sect, a Soho staple, glided in their snowy, street-dusting gowns, their eyes glowing and their heads shaved. Eve gave one particularly devout-looking supplicant a few tokens and was rewarded with a beatific smile and a glossy pebble.

'Pure love,' the devotee offered her. 'Pure joy.'

'Yeah, right,' Eve murmured and sidestepped.

She had to backtrack to find Leonardo's. The up-and-coming designer had a third-floor loft. The window that faced the street was crammed with fashions, blots and flows of color and form that had Eve swallowing nervously. Her taste leaned toward the plain – the drab, according to Mavis.

It didn't appear, as she took the people glide up to get a closer look, that Leonardo leaned toward either.

The clutching in her stomach came back with a vengeance as she stared at the window display with its feathers and beads and dyed rubber unisuits. However much pleasure she would get from making Roarke wince, she wasn't getting married in neon rubber.

There was more, a great deal more. It seemed Leonardo believed in advertising in a big way. His centerpiece, a ghostly white faceless model, was draped in a collection of transparent scarves that shimmered so dramatically that the material seemed alive.

Eve could all but feel it crawling over her skin.

Uh-uh, she thought. *No way in heaven or hell.* She turned, thinking only of escape, and rapped straight into Mavis.

'His stuff is so frigid.' Mavis slipped a friendly, restraining arm around Eve's waist and gazed dreamily into the window.

'Look, Mavis—'

'And he's incredibly creative. I've watched him come up with stuff on screen. It's wild.'

'Yeah, wild. I'm thinking—'

'He really understands the inner soul,' Mavis hurried on. She understood Eve's inner soul, and knew her friend was ready to bolt. Mavis Freestone, slim as a fairy in her white and gold rompers and three-inch air platforms, tossed back her curling mane of white-streaked black hair, judged her opponent, and grinned. 'He's going to make you the most rocking bride in New York.'

'Mavis.' Eve narrowed her eyes to forestall another interruption. 'I just want something that won't make me feel like an idiot.'

Mavis beamed, the new winged heart tattoo on her biceps fluttering as she lifted a hand to her breast. 'Dallas, trust me.'

'No,' Eve said even as Mavis pulled her back to the glide. 'I mean it, Mavis. I'll just order something off screen.'

'Over my dead body,' Mavis muttered, clumping her way down to the street entrance, dragging Eve behind her. 'The least you can do is look, talk to him. Give the guy a chance.' She thrust out her bottom lip, a formidable weapon when painted magenta. 'Don't be such a squash, Dallas.'

'Shit, I'm here, anyway.'

Flushed with success, Mavis bounced to the whining security camera. 'Mavis Freestone and Eve Dallas, for Leonardo.'

The outer door opened with a grinding clunk. Mavis made a beeline for the old wire-screened elevator. 'This place is really into retro. I think Leonardo might even stay here after he hits. You know, eccentric artist and all that.'

'Right.' Eve closed her eyes and prayed as the elevator bumped its way upward. She was taking the stairs down, absolutely.

'Now, keep an open mind,' Mavis ordered, 'and let Leonardo take care of you. Darling!' She positively flowed out of the dinky elevator and into a cluttered, colorful space. Eve had to admire her.

10

'Mavis, my dove.'

Then Eve was struck dumb. The man with the artist's name was six-five if he was an inch and built like a maxibus. Huge, rippling biceps mountained out of a sleeveless robe in the eye-searing colors of a Martian sunset. His face was wide as the moon, its copper-toned skin stretched tight as a drumhead over razor-edged cheekbones. He had a small, glinting stone winking beside his flashing grin and eyes like gold coins.

He swirled Mavis into his arms, off her feet, and around in one fast and graceful circle. And he kissed her, long, hard, and in a fashion that warned Eve the two of them had a great deal more going on than a mutual love of fashion and art.

'Leonardo.' Beaming like a fool, Mavis ran her gold-tipped fingers through his tight, shoulder-length curls.

'Babydoll.'

Eve managed not to gag as they cooed at each other, but she did roll her eyes. She was stuck now, without a doubt. Mavis was in love again.

'The hair, it's wonderful.' Leonardo ran loving fingers, the size of soydogs, through Mavis's streaked mop.

'I hoped you'd like it. This . . .' There was a dramatic pause, as though she were about to introduce her award-winning schnauzer. 'Is Dallas.'

'Ah yes, the bride. Lovely to meet you, Lieutenant Dallas.' He kept one arm around Mavis and shot the other out to take Eve's hand. 'Mavis has told me so much about you.'

'Yeah.' Eve slanted a look toward her friend. 'She's been a little light on details on you.'

He laughed, a booming sound that made Eve's ears ring even as her lips twitched in response. 'My turtledove can be secretive. Refreshments,' he stated, then whirled off in a cloud of color and unexpected grace.

'He's wonderful, isn't he?' Mavis whispered, eyes dancing with love.

'You're sleeping with him.'

'You wouldn't believe how . . . inventive he is. How . . .' Mavis blew out a breath, patted her breast. 'The man is a sexual artist.'

'I don't want to hear about it. Absolutely don't want to hear about it.' Drawing her brows together, Eve scanned the room.

It was wide, high ceilinged, and crowded with flows and streams of material. Fuchsia rainbows, ebony waterfalls, chartreuse pools dripped from the ceiling, along the walls, over tabletops and arms of chairs.

'Jesus,' was all she could manage.

Bowls and trays of glittering ribbons, tapes, and buttons were piled everywhere. Sashes, belts, hats, and veils crowded with half-finished outfits of shimmering materials and studded bodices.

The place smelled like an incense farm married to a flower shop.

She was terrified.

A little pale, Eve turned back. 'Mavis, I love you. Maybe

12

I haven't told you that before, but I do. Now I'm leaving.'

'Dallas.' With a quick giggle, Mavis grabbed her arm. For a small woman, Mavis was amazingly strong. 'Relax. Take a breath. I guarantee Leonardo's going to fix you up.'

'That's what I'm afraid of, Mavis. Deeply afraid.'

'Lemon tea, iced,' Leonardo announced with a musical lilt as he came back through a curtain of draping simulated silk with a tray and glasses. 'Please, please, sit. First we'll relax, get to know each other.'

With her eye on the door, Eve edged toward a chair. 'Look, Leonardo, Mavis might not have explained things, exactly. See, I'm—'

'You're a homicide detective. I've read about you,' Leonardo said smoothly, snuggling on a curve-sided settee with Mavis all but in his lap. 'Your last case generated a great deal of media. I must confess I was fascinated. You work with puzzles, Lieutenant, as I do.'

Eve sampled the tea, nearly blinked when she discovered it was full-bodied, rich, and wonderful. 'You work with puzzles?'

'Naturally. I see a woman, I imagine how I would like to see her dressed. Then I must discover who she is, what she is, how does she live her life. What are her hopes, her fantasies, her vision of herself? Then I must take all of that, piece each part of her together to create the look. The image. At first, she is a mystery, and I'm compelled to solve her.'

Unashamed, Mavis sighed lustily. 'Isn't he mag, Dallas?'

Leonardo chuckled, nuzzled Mavis's ear. 'Your friend is worried, my dove. She think I'll wrap her in electric pink and spangles.'

'It sounds wonderful.'

'For you.' He beamed back at Eve. 'So you're going to marry the elusive and powerful Roarke.'

'It looks that way,' Eve muttered.

'You met him on a case. The DeBlass case, correct? And intrigued him with your tawny eyes and serious smile.'

'I wouldn't say I—'

'You wouldn't,' Leonardo continued, 'because you don't see yourself as he does. Or as I do. Strong, valiant, troubled, dependable.'

'Are you a designer or an analyst?' Eve demanded.

'You can't be one without the other. Tell me, lieutenant, how did Roarke win you?'

'I'm not a prize.' She snapped it, then set her glass aside.

'Wonderful.' He clasped his hands together and almost wept. 'Heat and independence, and just a little fear. You'll make a magnificent bride. Now to work.' He rose. 'Come with me.'

She stood up. 'Listen, there's no point in wasting your time, or mine. I'm just going to—'

'Come with me,' he repeated and took her hand.

'Give it a chance, Eve.'

For Mavis, she allowed Leonardo to lead her under and around falls of material and into an equally cluttered workstation on the far side of the loft.

The computer made her feel a little better. Those she understood. But the drawings it had generated, which were pinned and tacked to every available space, made her heart sink.

Fuchsia and spangles would have been a relief.

The models with their long, exaggerated bodies looked like mutants. Some were sporting feathers, others stones. A few were wearing what could have been clothes, but in such outrageous styles – pointed collars, skirts the size of washcloths, unisuits snug as skin – they looked like participants in a Halloween parade.

'Examples for my first show. High fashion is a twist on reality, you see. The bold, the unique, the impossible.'

'I love them.'

Eve curled her lip at Mavis and folded her arms. 'It's going to be a small, simple ceremony, at home.'

'Um.' Leonardo was already at his computer, using the keyboard with impressive skill. 'Now this . . .' He brought up an image that made Eve's blood chill.

The dress was the color of fresh urine, ringed with flounces of mud brown from its scalloped neck to its knife-point hem that dripped with stones the size of a child's fist. The sleeves were so snug Eve was certain anyone wearing it would lose all feeling in their fingers.

As the image turned, she was treated to a view of the back, dipping past the waist and trimmed in floaty feathers.

'. . . is not at all for you,' Leonardo finished, and indulged in a deep belly laugh at Eve's blanched skin. 'I apologize.

I couldn't resist. For you . . . just a sketch, you understand. Slim, long, simple. Only a column. Not too delicate.'

He continued to speak as he worked. On the screen, lines and shapes began to form. Sticking her hands in her pockets, Eve watched.

It looked so easy, Eve mused. Long lines, the most subtle of accents at the bodice, sleeves that came to soft, rounded points just at the back of the hand. Still uneasy, she waited for him to start to add the gingerbread.

'We'll fuss with it a bit,' he said absently, and again turned the image to show a back as sleek and elegant as the front, with a slit to the knees. 'You wouldn't want a train.'

'A train?'

'No.' He only smiled, flicking a glance up at her. 'You wouldn't. A headdress. Your hair.'

Used to derogatory comments, Eve ran her fingers through it. 'I can cover it up if I have to.'

'No, no, no. It suits you.'

Her hand dropped in shock. 'It does?'

'Indeed. You need a bit of shaping. I know someone—' He flicked that aside. 'But the color, all those tones of brown and gold, and the short, not quite tamed style is very good on you. A couple of snips.' Eyes narrowed, he studied her. 'No, no headdress, no veil. Your face is enough. Now, color and material. It must be silk, of a good weight.' He grimaced a little. 'Mavis tells me Roarke will not be paying.'

Eve's back went up. 'It's my dress.'

16

'She's dug in on this one,' Mavis commented. 'Like Roarke would notice a few thousand credits.'

'That's not the point—'

'No, indeed not.' Leonardo smiled again. 'Well, we'll manage. Color? I don't think white, too stark for your skin tone.'

Pursing his lips, he went to his palette key and experimented. Fascinated despite herself, Eve watched the sketch turn from snowy white to cream, to pale blue, to vivid green and a rainbow between. Though Mavis oohed and ahed over several choices, he only shook his head.

He settled on bronze.

'This. Yes, oh yes. Your skin, your eyes, your hair. You'll be radiant, majestic. A goddess. With it you'll need a necklace, at least thirty-inch length. Better yet, two lengths, twenty-four and thirty inches. Copper, I think, with colored stones. Rubies, citrine, onyx. Yes, yes, and carnelian, perhaps some tourmaline. You'll speak to Roarke about the accessories.'

Clothes never meant a damn to her, but Eve caught herself yearning. 'It's beautiful,' she said cautiously and began to calculate her credit situation. 'I'm just not sure. You know, silk . . . It's a little out of my range.'

'You'll have the dress at my cost, and for a promise.' He enjoyed watching the wariness come into her eyes. 'That I will be allowed to design Mavis's dress as your attendant, and you will use my designs for your trousseau.'

'I haven't thought about a trousseau. I've got clothes.'

'Lieutenant Dallas has clothes,' he corrected. 'Roarke's partner in marriage will need others.'

'Maybe we can make a deal.' She wanted that damn dress, she realized. She could feel it on her.

'Wonderful. Take off your clothes.'

She snapped back like a spring. 'Okay, asshole—'

'For the measurements,' Leonardo said quickly. The look in her eye had him rising, stepping back. He was a man who adored women, and understood their wrath. In other words, he feared them. 'You must consider me as you would your health provider. I can't design the dress properly until I know your body. I'm an artist, and a gentleman,' he said with dignity. 'But Mavis can stay if you feel uneasy.'

Eve tilted her head. 'I can handle you, pal. If you get out of line, even think about it, you'll find out for yourself.'

'I'm sure of it.' Cautiously he picked up a device. 'My scanner,' he explained. 'It will measure you very accurately. But you have to be naked for a true reading.'

'Stop snickering, Mavis. Go get us some more of that tea.'

'Sure. I've already seen you naked, anyway.' Blowing kisses to Leonardo, she headed off.

'I have other ideas . . . about clothes,' Leonardo said when Eve narrowed her eyes. 'The underfoundation for the dress, of course. Evening and daywear, the formal, the casual. Your honeymoon is where?'

'I don't know. I haven't thought about it.' Resigned, she took off her shoes, unhitched her jeans.

'Roarke will surprise you then. Computer, create file, Dallas, first doc, measurements, coloring, height, and weight.' After she'd tossed her shirt aside, he stepped forward with the scanner. 'Feet together please. Height, five foot nine inches, weight, one hundred and twenty.'

'How long have you been sleeping with Mavis?'

He rattled off more data. 'About two weeks. She's very dear to me. Waist twenty-six point two inches.'

'Did you start sleeping with her before or after she told you her best friend was marrying Roarke?'

He stopped cold, and his brilliant gold eyes glittered with temper. 'I am not using Mavis for a commission, and you insult her by thinking it.'

'Just checking. She's very dear to me, too. If we're going to deal on this, I want to make sure all the cards are faceup, that's all. So—'

The interruption came in fast, and came in furious. A woman in skintight, unadorned black burst in like a comet, perfect teeth bared, lethal red nails curled into talons.

'You two-timing, back-stabbing, mother-fucking son of a bitch.' She made her leap, rather like a gorgeous mortar locked on target, and with a speed and grace brought on by pure fear, Leonardo evaded. 'Pandora, I can explain—'

'Explain this.' Turning her wrath on Eve, she swiped out, barely missing scooping Eve's eyes out of their sockets.

There was only one thing to do. Eve decked her.

'Oh Jesus, oh Jesus.' Leonardo hunched his huge shoulders and wrung his ham-size hands.

19

2

'Did you have to hit her?'

Eve watched the woman's eyes roll back, then roll forward. 'Yeah.'

Leonardo set down his scanner and sighed. 'She's going to make my life a living hell.'

'My face, my face.' As she teetered back into full consciousness, Pandora scrambled up, patting her jaw. 'Is it bruised? Does it show? I've got a session in an hour.'

Eve shrugged. 'Tough luck.'

Jumping from mood to mood like a crazed gazelle, Pandora hissed through her teeth, 'I'll ruin you, bitch. You'll never work on screen, on disc, and you sure as hell won't get a runway job. Do you know who I am?'

Being naked under the circumstances just added to Eve's mood. 'Do you think I care?'

'What's going on? Damn it, Dallas, he's just trying to fit you— Oh.' Hurrying in with glasses in both hands, Mavis stopped dead. 'Pandora.'

'You.' Obviously, Pandora's supply of venom wasn't running low. She sprang at Mavis, sending glasses crashing, tea flying. In seconds, the two women were wrestling on the floor and tearing at each other's hair.

'Oh, for Christ's sake.' If she'd had a stunner on her, Eve would have used it on the pair of them. 'Break it up. Goddamn it, Leonardo, give me a hand here before they kill each other.' Eve dived in, pulling at arms and legs. She gave Pandora an extra elbow jab to the ribs for her own enjoyment. 'I'll haul you into a cage, I swear to God.' For lack of anything else, she sat on Pandora and tugged over her jeans to get her badge out of the pocket. 'Take a good look, you idiot. I'm a cop. So far, you've got two counts of assault. Want to go for three?'

'Get your bony, naked ass off me.'

It wasn't the order but the relative calm with which it was delivered that had Eve shifting. Pandora rose, brushed her hands meticulously down her black skin suit, sniffed, tossed her luxurious mane of flame-colored hair, then aimed a frigid glare with heavily lashed emerald eyes.

'So, one at a time's not enough for you anymore, Leonardo. You scum.' Sculpted chin lifted, she cast a scornful look at Eve, then at Mavis. 'Your appetite might be increasing, darling, but your taste is deteriorating.'

'Pandora.' Shaken, still wary of attack, Leonardo moistened his lips. 'I said I can explain. Lieutenant Dallas is a client.'

She spit like a cobra. 'Is that what you're calling them now? You think you can just toss me aside like yesterday's news, Leonardo? I say when it's over.'

Limping a little, Mavis walked to Leonardo, slipped an arm around his waist. 'He doesn't need you or want you.'

'I don't give a damn what he wants. But need?' Her full lips curved into a nasty smile. 'He'll have to tell you the facts of life, little girl. Without me, there won't be any show next month for his second-rate clothes. And without a show, he's not going to make any sales, and without sales, he won't be able to pay for all that material, all that inventory, and that nice, fat loan he took from the leg breakers.'

She took a deep breath and studied the nails she'd chipped. Fury seemed to fit her as cleanly as her black skin suit. 'This is going to cost you big time, Leonardo. I've got a busy calendar for the next couple of days, but I'm going to find a way to squeeze in some time to have a chat with your backers. What do you think they'll say when I tell them I simply can't lower my standards to walking the runway in your designs? Inferior as they are.'

'You can't do that, Pandora.' Panic was in every word, a panic Eve was sure was for the glowing redhead like a fix for an addict. 'It'll ruin me. I've put everything into this show. Time, money—'

'Isn't it a shame you didn't think of that before you picked up this little piece of navel lint?' Pandora's eyes narrowed into sharp slits. 'I think I can manage to have lunch with a few of the money men by the end of the week. You've got a couple of days, darling, to decide how you want to play it. Get rid of the new toy, or pay the consequences. You know where to reach me.'

She went out with the exaggerated glide of a model, and punctuated the exit by slamming the door.

'Oh shit.' Leonardo sank into a chair and covered his face with his hands. 'Her timing is perfect, as always.'

'Don't. Don't let her do this to you. To us.' Near tears, Mavis crouched down in front of him. 'You can't let her run your life anymore, or blackmail you—' Inspired, Mavis sprang up. 'It's blackmail, isn't it, Dallas? Go arrest her.'

Eve finished buttoning the shirt she'd pulled on. 'Honey, I can't arrest her for saying she's not going to wear his clothes. I can go haul her in for assault, but she'd be out almost before I closed the door on her.'

'But it *is* blackmail. Everything Leonardo's got is tied up in the show. He'll lose everything without it.'

'I'm sorry. Really. It's just not a police or security matter.' She dragged her hands through her hair. 'Look, she was hot and pissed off. Hopped on something from the look of her eyes. Odds are she'll calm down.'

'No.' Leonardo sat back in the chair. 'She'll want to make me pay. You must have understood we were lovers. Things were cooling off between us. She's been off planet for a few weeks, and I considered our personal relationship over. Then, I met Mavis.' His hand found hers, gripped. 'And I knew it was over. I spoke with Pandora briefly, told her. Or tried to.'

'Since Dallas can't help, there's only one thing to do.' Mavis's chin quivered. 'You have to go back to her. It's the only way.' She added before Leonardo could speak, 'We won't see each other, at least not until after your show. Maybe then, we can pick up the pieces. You can't let her go to your backers and ditch your designs.'

'Do you think I could do that? Be with her? Touch her after this? After you?' He rose. 'Mavis, I love you.'

'Oh.' Her eyes filled, spilled over. 'Oh, Leonardo. Not now. I love you too much to watch her ruin you. I'm going away. To save you.'

She dashed out, leaving Leonardo staring after her. 'I'm trapped. The vindictive bitch. She can take everything from me. The woman I love, my work, everything. I could kill her for putting that look in Mavis's eyes.' He drew a deep breath, looked at his hands. 'A man can be pulled in by beauty and not see beneath it.'

'Does what she says to these people matter so much? They wouldn't have put money behind you if they hadn't believed in your work.'

'Pandora is one of the top models on the planet. She has power, prestige, connections. A few words from her into the right ear can make or break a man in my position.' He lifted a hand to a fantasy of net and stones hanging beside him. 'If she goes public, claiming my designs are inferior, the projected sales will drop away. She knows exactly how to accomplish that. I've worked all my life for this show. She knows it, and she knows how to take it from me. And it won't end there.'

His hand fell back to his side. 'Mavis doesn't understand that, not yet. Pandora can hold that laser beam above my neck for the rest of my professional life – or hers. I'll never be free of her, Lieutenant, until she decides she's finished with me.'

By the time Eve got home, she was exhausted. An added session of tears and recriminations with Mavis had sapped her energy. For now, at least, Mavis was comforted with a quart of ice cream and several hours of videos in Eve's old apartment.

Wanting to forget emotional upheavals and fashion, Eve went straight to the bedroom and fell facedown on the bed. The cat Galahad leaped up beside her, purring manically. After a few head butts brought no reaction, he settled down to sleep. When Roarke found her, she hadn't moved a muscle.

'So, how was your day off?'

'I hate shopping.'

'You just haven't developed the knack for it.'

'Who wants to?' Curious, she rolled over, studied him. 'You like it. You really like to just buy things.'

'Sure.' Roarke stretched out beside her, stroking the cat when it pawed its way onto his chest. 'It's nearly as satisfying as having things. Being poor, Lieutenant, quite simply sucks.'

She thought it over. As she'd been poor once, had managed to lever herself up to struggling, she couldn't disagree. 'Anyway, I think I got the worst of it over with.'

'That was quick.' And the speed worried him, a little. 'You know, Eve, you don't have to settle for something.'

'Actually, I think Leonardo and I reached an understanding.'

Staring up and through the sky window where the sky was the color of old bleach, she frowned. 'Mavis is in love with him.'

'Um-hmm.' Eyes half closed, Roarke continued to stroke the cat and thought about switching the gesture to Eve.

'No, I'm talking the big one.' She let out a long breath. 'The day didn't go exactly smoothly.'

He had the figures for three major deals running through his head. Shuttling them aside, he shifted closer to her. 'Tell me about it.'

'Leonardo – he's this massive, and oddly attractive . . . I don't know. Event. Heavy on the Native American blood, at a guess. He has the bone structure and coloring of an NA, biceps like astro torpedoes, and a voice that has a hint of magnolia. I'm not much of a judge, but when he settled down to sketch, he seemed very focused and talented. Anyway, I was standing there naked—'

'Were you?' Roarke said mildly, and nudging the cat away, he rolled on top of her.

'For measurements,' she said with a sneer.

'Do go on.'

'Okay. Mavis was getting some tea—'

'Convenient.'

'And this woman bursts in, all but drooling at the mouth. A jaw dropper – close to six foot, thin as a laser beam, about a yard of red hair and a face . . . well, I'll use magnolias again. She's screaming at him, and this big bull of a guy cowers back, so she jumps at me. I had to flatten her.'

26

'You hit her.'

'Well, yeah, before she sliced my face with those knife-point nails of hers.'

'Darling Eve.' He kissed her cheek, then the other, then the dent in her chin. 'What is it about you that draws the beast out of people?'

'Just lucky, I guess. So, this Pandora—'

'Pandora?' His head came up, eyes narrowing. 'The model.'

'Yeah, she's supposed to be pretty hot shit.'

He started to laugh, just a chuckle at first that grew and swelled until he had to roll over on his back again. 'You punched precious Pandora in her billion-dollar face. Did you knock her on her pretty ass?'

'As a matter of fact.' Understanding bloomed and with it a surprising and unexpected twinge of jealousy. 'You know her.'

'You could say that.'

'Well.'

He cocked a brow, not so much warily as with amusement. She was sitting up now and scowling down at him. For the first time in their relationship, he sensed a hint of green in the look. 'There was a time – briefly.' He scratched his chin. 'It's all very vague.'

'Bull.'

'It could come back to me. But you were saying?'

'Is there any exceptionally beautiful woman you haven't slept with?'

'I'll make you a list. So, you knocked her down.'

27

'Yeah.' Eve regretted now pulling her punch. 'She's squealing and whining, then Mavis comes in and Pandora goes for her. The two of them are pulling hair and scratching; Leonardo's wringing his hands.'

Roarke tugged her down on top of him. 'You lead such an interesting life.'

'The upshot is, Pandora threatens Leonardo: he ditches Mavis for her or she's going to wreck this fashion show he's counting on. Apparently he's sunk everything into it, borrowed from spine crackers, too. She blackballs the show, he's ruined.'

'Sounds just like her.'

'After Pandora leaves, Mavis—'

'Were you still naked?'

'I was getting dressed. Mavis decides to make the supreme sacrifice. It was all pretty dramatic stuff. Leonardo declares his love, she starts crying and runs out. Jesus, Roarke, I felt like some pervert with surveillance goggles. I got Mavis settled in my old apartment, at least for the night. She doesn't have to be in to the club until tomorrow.'

'Stay tuned,' he murmured and smiled at her blank look. 'The old daytime dramas. Always end on a cliff-hanger. What is our hero going to do?'

'Some hero,' Eve muttered. 'Damn it, I like him, even if he is a pussy. What he'd like to do is bash Pandora's head in, but he'll probably cave. Which is why I thought we could put Mavis up here for a few days if she needs it.'

'Sure.'

'Really?'

'It is, as you've often pointed out, a big house. I'm fond of Mavis.'

'I know.' She gave him one of her quick, rare smiles. 'Thanks. So, how was your day?'

'I bought a small planet. I'm joking,' he said when her mouth fell open. 'I did, however, complete negotiations for a farming commune on Taurus Five.'

'Farming?'

'People have to eat. With a bit of restructuring, the commune should be able to provide grain to the manufacturing colonies of Mars, where I have a sizable investment. So, one hand washes the other.'

'I guess. Now about Pandora . . .'

He rolled her over and tugged the shirt he'd already unbuttoned off her shoulders.

'You're not distracting me,' she told him. 'Just how brief is brief in this case?'

He gave what passed for a shrug and nibbled his way from her mouth to her throat.

'Is it like a night, a week . . .' Her body flashed hot when he closed his mouth over her breast. 'A month— Okay, now you're distracting me.'

'I can do better,' he promised. And did.

Visiting the morgue was a lousy way to start the day. Eve strode down the silent, white tiled halls trying not to be annoyed that she'd been called in to view a body at six A.M.

Worse, it was a floater.

She paused at a doorway, holding her badge up for the security camera, and waited for her ID number to be accessed and approved.

Inside, a single technician waited near a wall of refrigerated holding drawers. Most would be occupied, she thought. Summer was always a hot time for dying.

'Lieutenant Dallas.'

'Right. You got one for me.'

'Just came in.' With the careless cheer of his profession, he moved to a drawer, coded for view. Locks and refrigeration blipped off, and the drawer, with its occupant, slid out with a small burst of icy fog. 'Uniform on scene thought she recognized him as one of yours.'

'Yep.' In defense, Eve drew breath in and out of her mouth. Seeing death, violent death, was nothing new. She wasn't sure she could have explained that it was easier, less personal somehow, to study a body where it had fallen. Here, in the pristine, almost virginal surroundings of the morgue, it was all more obscene.

'Johannsen, Carter. Aka Boomer. Last known address the flop on Beacon. Petty thief, professional weasel, occasional dealer in illegals, and pitiful excuse for a humanoid.' She sighed as she studied what was left of him. 'Well, hell, Boomer, what did they do to you?'

'Blunt instrument,' the tech said, taking her question seriously. 'Possibly a pipe or a thin bat. We'll have to finish testing. A lot of strength behind the blows. Only spent a

30

couple hours at most in the river; the contusions and lacerations are evident.'

Eve tuned him out, let him ramble on importantly. She could see well enough for herself.

He'd never been a looker, but they'd left behind very little of his face. He'd been severely beaten, the nose crushed, the mouth all but obscured with blows and bloating. Bruising at the throat indicated strangulation, as did the vivid broken blood vessels that polka-dotted what remained of his face.

His torso was purpled, and from the way his body lay, she guessed his arm had been shattered. The missing finger of his left hand was an old war wound, one she recalled he'd been rather proud of.

Somebody strong, angry, and determined had gotten to poor, pathetic Boomer.

And so, in that short floating time, had the fish.

'The uniform ran the partial prints he had left for ID, you confirm with visual.'

'Yeah. Send me a copy of the post mortem.' She turned and started out. 'Who was the uniform who connected me?'

The tech pulled out his notebook, tapped keys. 'Peabody, Delia.'

'Peabody.' For the first time, Eve smiled a little. 'She gets around. Anybody asks for or about him, I want to know about it.'

On the way to Cop Central, Eve contacted Peabody. The uniform's calm, serious face floated on screen.

'Yes, Lieutenant.'

'You hauled in Johannsen.'

'Sir. I'm completing my report right now. I can send you a copy.'

'Appreciate it. How did you tag him?'

'I had a porta-ident in my field kit, sir. I ran his prints. The fingers were severely damaged, so I only managed a partial, but the indication was Johannsen. I'd heard he was one of your weasels.'

'Yeah, he was. Good work, Peabody.'

'Thank you, sir.'

'Peabody, you interested in assisting the primary in this case?'

Control slipped for an instant, just long enough to show the glint in Peabody's eyes. 'Yes, sir. Are you the primary?'

'He was mine,' Eve said simply. 'I'll clear it. My office, Peabody. One hour.'

'Yes, sir. Thank you, sir.'

'Dallas,' Eve muttered. 'Just Dallas.' But Peabody had already broken transmission.

Eve scowled at the time, snarled at the traffic, and detoured three blocks to a drive-through cafe. The coffee was slightly less disgusting there than at Cop Central. Fueled with that and with what had probably been intended as a sweet roll, she stowed her vehicle and prepared to report to her commander.

As she rode up in the stifling excuse for an elevator, she

could feel her back stiffening. Telling herself it was petty, that it should have been over, didn't seem to matter. Resentment and hurt left over from a previous case wouldn't completely fade.

She walked into the administration lobby with its busy consoles, dark walls, and threadbare carpeting. She announced herself at Commander Whitney's reception station and was asked to wait by the bored voice of an office drone.

She remained where she was rather than wandering over to look out of the window or to while away time with one of the aging magazine discs. The all-news station on screen behind her had been turned to mute and didn't interest her in any case.

A few weeks before, she had more than her fill of the media. At least, she thought, someone as low on the food chain as Boomer wouldn't generate much publicity. The death of a weasel didn't earn rating points.

'Commander Whitney will see you now, Dallas, Lieutenant Eve.'

She was buzzed through the security doors and turned left into Whitney's office.

'Lieutenant.'

'Commander. Thank you for seeing me.'

'Have a seat.'

'No, thank you. I won't keep you long. I just identified a John Doe floater at the morgue. He was Carter Johannsen. One of my weasels.'

An imposing man with a hard face and tired eyes, Whitney leaned back in his chair. 'Boomer? He used to wire explosives for street thieves. Blew off his right index finger.'

'Left,' Eve corrected. 'Sir.'

'Left.' Whitney folded his hands on the desk and studied her. He'd made a mistake with Eve, a mistake in a case that had affected him personally. He understood she had yet to set it aside. He had her obedience and her respect, but the nebulous friendship that could have existed between them was gone.

'I take it this was homicide.'

'I haven't gotten the post mortem, but it appears the victim was beaten and strangled before entering the river. I'd like to pursue the matter.'

'Were you working with him on any ongoing investigation?'

'Nothing ongoing, no sir. He occasionally fed the Illegals with data. I need to find out who he worked with in that department.'

Whitney nodded. 'Your caseload at the moment, Lieutenant?'

'Manageable.'

'Which means you're overloaded.' He lifted his fingers, curled them down again. 'Dallas, people like Johannsen court disaster, and they usually find it. You and I both know the murder rate rises in this kind of heat. I can't waste one of my top investigators on this kind of case.'

Eve set her jaw. 'He was mine. Whatever else he was, Commander, he was mine.'

Loyalty, he mused, was one of the values that made her one of his best. 'You can shuffle it to the top for twenty-four hours,' he told her. 'Keep it open, in your files, for seventy-two. After that, I'll have to transfer the case to a junior investigator.'

It was no more than she expected. 'I'd like to have Officer Peabody with me on it.'

He stared at her balefully. 'You want me to approve an aide for a case like this?'

'I want Peabody,' Eve returned without flinching. 'She's proven herself excellent in the field. She's aiming for detective. I believe she'll get it quick with some hands-on training.'

'You can have her for three days. If something more vital comes through, you're both off.'

'Yes, sir.'

'Dallas,' he began when she turned to leave. He bit down on his pride. 'Eve . . . I haven't had the chance to offer my best wishes, personally, for your upcoming marriage.'

Surprise flickered in her eyes before she controlled it. 'Thank you.'

'I hope you'll be happy.'

'So do I.'

A bit unsettled, she made her way through the maze of Cop Central to her office. She had another favor to call in. Wanting privacy, she closed her door before engaging her tele-link.

'Feeney, Captain Ryan. Electronic Detective Division.'

She was relieved when his rumpled face filled her screen. 'You're in early, Feeney.'

'Shit, didn't even have time for breakfast.' He spoke mournfully and through a mouthful of Danish. 'One of the terminals springs a leak, and nobody can fix it but me.'

'Being indispensable's tough work. Can you fit in a search for me – unofficial?'

'My favorite kind. Shoot.'

'Somebody whacked Boomer.'

'Sorry to hear it.' He took another bite of Danish. 'He was a shit, but he usually came through. When?'

'I'm not sure; he was fished out of the East River early this morning. I know he sometimes fed somebody over in Illegals. Can you find out for me?'

'Linking weasels and their trainers is dicey work, Dallas. You got to be real security conscious about that stuff.'

'Yes or no, Feeney?'

'I can do it, I can do it,' he muttered. 'But don't bring this back on me. Cops hate to have their files searched.'

'Tell me about it. I appreciate it, Feeney. Whoever did him worked him over hard. If he knew something worth killing him over, I don't think it was one of my ongoings.'

'So maybe it was somebody else's. I'll get back to you.'

She leaned back from the blank screen and tried to clear her mind. Into it floated Boomer's battered face. A pipe or

36

a bat maybe, she mused. But fists, too. She knew what hard, bare knuckles could do to a face. She knew what they felt like.

Her father had had big hands.

It was one of the things she tried to pretend she didn't remember. But she knew how they'd felt, how the blow would shock even before the brain registered the pain.

What had been worse? The beatings or the rapes? One was so mixed with the other in her mind, in her fears.

That odd angle of Boomer's arm. Broken, she mused, and dislocated. She had a vague, hideous memory of the brittle sound of a bone snapping, the nausea that went above the agony, the high-pitched whine that substituted for a scream when a hand was clamped over your mouth.

The cold sweat, and the bowel-loosening terror of knowing those fists would come back, and come back until you were dead. Until you wished to God Almighty that you were.

The knock at her door had her jolting, had her swallowing a yelp. Through the glass she saw Peabody, uniform pressed, shoulders straight.

Eve ran a hand over her mouth to steady herself. It was time to go to work.

3

Boomer's flop was better than some. The building had once been a low-rent hourly motel that had catered to hookers on a budget before prostitution had been licensed and legalized. It was four stories, and no one had ever bothered to put in an elevator or glide, but it did boast a dingy lobby and the dubious security of a surly-faced droid.

From the smell, the health department had recently ordered insect and rodent extermination.

The droid had a tick in her right eye from a faulty chip, but she focused her good one on Eve's badge.

'We're up to code,' she claimed, standing behind cloudy safety glass. 'We have no trouble here.'

'Johannsen.' Eve tucked her shield away. 'Anyone visit him lately?'

The droid's dinky eye hitched and rolled. 'I'm not programmed to monitor visitors, only to collect rents and maintain order.'

'I can confiscate your memory discs and play them back for myself.'

The droid said nothing, but a faint hum indicated she was running her own disc. 'Johannsen, room 3C, has not returned in eight hours, twenty-eight minutes. He left alone. He had no visitors in the last two weeks.'

'Communications?'

'He does not use our communication system. He has his own.'

'We're going to have a look at his room.'

'Third floor, second door left. Don't alarm other tenants. We have no trouble here.'

'Yeah, it's a paradise.' Eve headed up the steps, noting the crumbling wood, well gnawed by rodents. 'Record, Peabody.'

'Yes, sir.' Dutifully, Peabody clipped her recorder to her shirt. 'If he was here about eight hours ago, he didn't last long after he left. Probably no more than a couple hours.'

'Long enough to get the shit beat out of him.' Idly Eve scanned the walls. Several illegal invitations and anatomically doubtful suggestions were inscribed. One of the authors had a spelling deficiency and consistently left the *c* out of fuck.

Still, the message was clear enough.

'Homey little place, huh?'

'Reminds me of my granny's house.'

At the door of 3C, Eve glanced back. 'Why, Peabody, I think you made a joke.'

While Eve chuckled and took out her master code, Peabody flushed scarlet. She had herself back in line by the time the locks disengaged.

'Bolted himself in, didn't he?' Eve muttered as the last of the three Keligh-500s opened. 'And didn't go for cheap.

These babies cost about a week of my pay each. For all the good they did him.' She let out a breath. 'Dallas, Lieutenant Eve, entering victim's residence.' She pushed the door open. 'Damn, Boomer, you were a pig.'

The heat was enormous. Temperature control in the flop consisted of closing the window or opening it. Boomer had opted for closed, and had trapped stifling summer inside.

The room smelled of bad food gone over, stale clothes, and spilled whiskey. Leaving Peabody to do the initial scan, Eve walked into the center of what was little more than a box and shook her head.

The sheets on the narrow bed were stained with substances she wasn't keen to analyze. Boxes of take-out food were piled beside it. From the small mountain of dirty clothes heaped in corners, she assumed laundry hadn't been high on Boomer's list of household chores. Her feet stuck to the floor and made little sucking sounds as she wandered the room.

In self-defense, she fought the single window open. The sounds of air and street traffic poured in like a flood.

'Jesus, what a place. He made decent money weaseling. No way he had to live like this.'

'He must have wanted to.'

'Yep.' Wrinkling her nose, Eve eased open a door and studied the bathroom. There was a stainless steel toilet and sink, a shower stall built for the height disadvantaged. The stench roiled her stomach. 'Worse than a three-day corpse.'

She breathed through her mouth, turned back. 'There's where he put his money.'

In agreement, Peabody joined Eve at a sturdy counter. On it was a pricey data and communication center. Attached to the wall above was a viewing screen and a shelf over-flowing with discs. Eve chose one at random, read the label.

'Boomer was into culture, I see. *Bodacious Boobs of Bimbo Bitches.*'

'That took the Oscar last year.'

Eve snorted and tossed the disc back. 'Good one, Peabody. You want to keep that sense of humor going, 'cause we're going to have to run all this shit. Box up the discs, record number and labels. We'll scan them back at Cop Central.'

Eve engaged the 'link and searched through for any calls Boomer had saved. She zipped through food orders, a session with a video prostitute that had cost him five thousand. There were two calls from a suspected dealer of illegals, but the men had merely chatted about sports, heavy on baseball and arena bash. With some curiosity, she noted that her office number was logged twice in the last thirty hours, but he'd left no message.

'He was trying to get in touch with me,' she murmured. 'He disengaged without leaving a message. That's not like him.' She pulled out the disc and handed it to Peabody to put in evidence.

'There's nothing to indicate he was afraid or worried, Lieutenant.'

'No, he was a true weasel. If he'd thought someone was

going to pin him, he'd have camped on my doorstep. Okay, Peabody, I hope your immunizations are up to date. Let's start going through this mess.'

By the time they were finished, they were filthy, sweaty, and disgusted. At Eve's direct order, Peabody had loosened the stiff collar of her uniform and rolled up the sleeves. Still, sweat rained down her face and had her hair curling madly.

'I thought my brothers were pigs.'

Eve toed aside dirty underwear. 'How many you got?'

'Two. And a sister.'

'Four of you?'

'My parents are Free-Agers, sir,' Peabody explained with twin notes of apology and embarrassment in her voice. 'They're really into rural living and propagation.'

'You continue to surprise me, Peabody. A tough urbanite like you springing from Free-Agers. How come you're not growing alfalfa, weaving mats, and raising a brood?'

'I like to kick ass. Sir.'

'Good reason.' Eve had left what she considered the worst for last. With unconcealed revulsion, she studied the bed. The thought of body parasites scrambled through her head. 'We've got to deal with the mattress.'

Peabody swallowed hard. 'Yes, sir.'

'I don't know about you, Peabody, but I'm heading straight for a decontamination chamber when we're done here.'

'I'll be right behind you, Lieutenant.'

'Okay. Let's do it.'

The sheets came first. There was nothing but smells and stains. Eve would leave them for the sweepers to analyze, but she'd already ruled out any possibility that Boomer had been killed in his own flop.

Still, she was thorough, shaking out the pillow, manipulating the foam. At her signal, Peabody hefted one end of the mattress and she the other. It was heavy as a rock, and with a grunt they flipped it.

'Maybe there is a God,' Eve murmured.

Affixed to the bottom of the mattress were two small packs. One was filled with pale blue powder, the other a sealed disc. She tugged both free. Clamping down on the urge to break open the powder, she studied the disc. It wasn't labeled, but unlike the others, it had been carefully encased to keep it free of dust.

Ordinarily, she would have run it immediately in Boomer's unit. She could stand the stench, the sweat, even the dirt. But she didn't think she could maintain another minute wondering what microcosmic parasites were crawling over her skin.

'Let's get the hell out of here.'

She waited until Peabody carried the evidence box out into the hall. With one last glance at the way her man had lived, Eve shut the door, sealed it, and left the red police security light beaming.

★　　★　　★

Decontamination wasn't painful, but it wasn't particularly pleasant. It had the single virtue of being fairly short. Eve sat with Peabody, both of them stripped to the skin, in a two-seated chamber with curved white walls reflecting the hot white light.

'But it's a dry heat,' Peabody stated and had Eve laughing.

'I always figured this is what Hell's like.' She closed her eyes, willed herself to relax. She didn't consider herself phobic, but closed-in spaces made her itchy. 'You know, Peabody, I used Boomer about five years now. He wasn't exactly the GQ type, but I wouldn't have pegged him living like that.' She still had the smell in her nostrils. 'He was clean. Tell me what you saw in the bathroom.'

'Filth, mold, scum, towels that hadn't been washed. Two bars of soap, one unopened, a half tube of shampoo, tooth gel, an ultrasound brush and shaver. One hair comb, broken.'

'Grooming tools. He kept himself in shape, Peabody. Even liked to consider himself a lady's man. My guess is the sweepers are going to tell me the food, the clothes, the grunge is all about two, maybe three weeks old. What does that tell you?'

'That he was holed up – worried, scared, or involved enough to let things go.'

'Exactly. Not desperate enough to come in and unload to me, but worried enough to hide a couple of things under his mattress.'

'Where no one would ever think of looking for them,' Peabody said dryly.

'He wasn't terribly bright about some things. You got a guess on the substance?'

'An illegal.'

'I've never seen an illegal that color. Something new,' Eve mused. The light dimmed to gray and a beeper sounded. 'Looks like we're clean. Let's dig up some fresh clothes and go run that disc.'

'What the hell is this?' Eve scowled at her monitor. Unconsciously she began to toy with the weighty diamond she wore around her neck.

'A formula?'

'I can figure that out, Peabody.'

'Yes, sir.' Chastised, Peabody eased back.

'Shit, I hate science.' With hope, Eve glanced over her shoulder. 'You any good at it?'

'No, sir. I'm not even competent.'

Eve studied the mix of numbers, figures, and symbols and crossed her eyes. 'My unit's not programmed for this crap. It'll have to go to the lab for analysis.' Impatient, she drummed her fingers on the desk. 'My hunch would be it's the formula for that powder we found, but how the hell would a second rater like Boomer get his hands on it? And who was his other trainer? You knew he was one of mine, Peabody. How?'

Struggling with embarrassment, Peabody stared over Eve's shoulder at the figures on the screen. 'You listed him in several intradepartmental reports on closed cases, Lieutenant.'

'You make a habit of reading intradepartmental reports, Officer?'

'Yours, sir.'

'Why?'

'Because, sir, you're the best.'

'Are you sucking up, Peabody, or bucking for my job?'

'There'll be room when you're promoted to captain, sir.'

'What makes you think I want a captaincy?'

'You'd be stupid if you didn't, and you're not. Stupid, sir.'

'Okay, we'll let that rest. Do you scan any other reports?'

'Now and then.'

'Do you have any clue as to who Boomer's trainer would be in Illegals?'

'No, sir. I've never seen his name attached to any other cop. Most weasels only have one trainer.'

'Boomer liked to diversify. Let's hit the streets. We'll scope a few of his usual joints, see what we turn up. We've only got a couple of days on this, Peabody. If you've got anyone warming the home fires for you, let him know you'll be busy.'

'I'm unattached, sir. I don't have a problem with putting in extra time.'

'Good.' Eve rose. 'Then saddle up. And Peabody, we've been naked together. Drop all the "sirs," will you? Make it Dallas.'

'Yes, sir, Lieutenant.'

It was after three A.M. when she stumbled through the front

door, tripped over the cat who had decided to guard the entrance hall, swore, and turned blindly for the stairs.

In her mind were dozens of impressions: dim bars, strip clubs, the steamy streets where low-level licensed companions plied their trade. All of them ebbed and flowed together in the unappetizing stew that had been Boomer Johannsen's life.

No one knew anything, of course. No one had seen anything. The single corroborative statement she'd gleaned from her crawl through the seamier side of the city was that no one had heard from or laid eyes on Boomer in over a week, possibly longer.

But someone had laid a great deal more than eyes on him. Her time was running low to find out who and why.

The bedroom lights were on dim. She'd already stripped off her shirt and tossed it aside when she noted the bed was empty. There was an instant flare of disappointment, a faint uncomfortable tug of panic.

He'd had to leave, she thought. *He was right now heading toward any possible spot in the colonized universe. He could be gone for days.*

Staring miserably at the bed, she toed off her shoes and tugged off her slacks. Groping in a drawer, she pulled out a cotton undershirt and yanked it over her head.

God, she was pitiful, mooning because Roarke had to take care of business. Because he wasn't there for her to snuggle up against. Because he wasn't there to ward off the nightmares that seemed to plague her with more intensity

47

and frequency as her memories of the past grew to crowd her.

She was too tired to dream, she told herself. Too busy to brood. And strong enough not to remember anything she didn't care to remember.

She turned, intending to go to her upstairs office to sleep when the door slid open. Relief flushed through her like shame.

'I thought you'd had to leave.'

'I was working.' Roarke crossed to her. In the dim light his black shirt was a stark contrast to the white of hers. He tipped up her chin and looked into her eyes. 'Lieutenant, why do you always run until you fall down?'

'I have a deadline on this one.' Perhaps she was over-tired, or perhaps love was beginning to be easier, but she lifted both hands to his face. 'I'm awfully glad you're here.' When he lifted her up and carried her toward the bed, she smiled. 'That's not what I meant.'

'I'm tucking you in, and you're going to sleep.'

It was hard to argue when her eyes were already closing. 'Did you get my message?'

'The elaborate one that said, "I'll be late"? Yes.' He kissed her forehead. 'Turn yourself off.'

'In a minute.' She fought back the edges of sleep. 'I only had a couple minutes to contact Mavis. She wants to stay where she is for a couple days. She isn't going in to the Blue Squirrel either. She called in and found out Leonardo's been by there a half a dozen times looking for her.'

'The course of true love.'

'Mmm. I'm going to try to take an hour personal time tomorrow and swing by to see her, but I may not make it until the day after.'

'She'll be all right. I can go by, if you like.'

'Thanks, but she wouldn't talk to you about it. I'll take care of it as soon as I figure out what Boomer was up to. I know damn well he couldn't read that disc.'

'Of course not,' Roarke soothed, hoping to lull her to sleep.

'Not that he wasn't good with figures. Money figures. But scientific formulas—' She bolted straight up, nearly bashing Roarke's nose with her head. 'Your unit'll do it.'

'It will?'

'I got the runaround from the lab. They're backed up, this is low priority. No priority,' she added, scrambling back out of bed. 'I need an edge. You've got scientific analysis abilities on your unlicensed unit, right?'

'Of course.' He sighed and rose. 'Now, I suppose?'

'We can access the data from my office unit.' Grabbing his hand, she tugged him toward the faux panel that concealed the elevator. 'It won't take us long.'

She filled him in on the basics as they traveled up. By the time he'd coded them in to the private room, she was wide awake and revved.

The equipment was elaborate, unlicensed, and of course, illegal. Like Roarke, she used the handplate for access, then moved behind the U-shaped console.

'You can pull the data faster than I can,' she told him. 'It's under Code Two, Yellow, Johannsen. My access number's—'

'Please.' If he was going to play cop at three A.M., he wasn't going to be insulted. Roarke sat at the controls and manipulated a few dials manually. 'Into Cop Central,' he said and smiled when she frowned.

'So much for security.'

'Anything else you'd like before I focus on your unit?'

'No.' She said it firmly, moving behind him. Manipulating a keyboard with one hand, Roarke drew one of hers over his shoulder, to his lips, to nibble on her knuckles. 'Show-off.'

'It would hardly be any fun if you just plugged me in with your code. In your unit,' he murmured, and switched to auto. 'File Code Two, Yellow, Johannsen.' Across the room one of the wall screens flashed.

Waiting

'Evidence number 34-J, view and copy,' Eve requested. When the formula scrolled on, Eve shook her head. 'See that? It might as well be ancient hieroglyphics.'

'Chemical formula,' Roarke mused.

'How do you know?'

'I manufacture a few – legal ones. This is some sort of analgesic, but not entirely. Hallucinogenic properties . . .' He clucked his tongue, shook his head. 'I've never seen anything quite like it. Not a standard. Computer, analyze and identify.'

'You say it's a drug,' Eve began and the computer went to work.

50

'Most certainly.'

'That fits with my theory. But what was Boomer doing with the formula, and why would someone kill him for it?'

'That would depend on how marketable it is, I'd think. How profitable.' He frowned up at the screen as the analysis began to form. The molecular reproduction circled on the screen in colorful dots and spirals. 'Okay, you have an organic stimulant, a standard chemical hallucinogenic, both in fairly low and nearly legal amounts. Ah, there's the properties for THR-50.'

'Street name Zeus. Nasty stuff.'

'Hmm. Still, it's low wattage. But that's an interesting mix. There's mint, to make it more palatable. I'd say it could also be manufactured, with some alterations, in liquid form. Blend it with Brinock – that's a sexual stimulant and enhancer. In the right measures, it can be used to cure impotency.'

'I know what it is. We had a guy who OD'd on it. Killed himself after what appeared to be the world's record in masturbation. Jumped out of a window in sexual frustration. His dick was swollen like a pork sausage, about the same color, and still hard as iron.'

'Thank you for sharing that. What's this?' Puzzled, Roarke went back to the keyboard. The computer merely continued to flash the same message.

Substance unknown. Probable cell regenerator. Unable to identify.

'How is that possible?' he mused. 'I have an automatic update on this. There's nothing out there it can't identify.'

'An unknown substance. Well, well. That might be worth killing for. What will it give us without it?'

'Identify with known data,' Roarke ordered.

FORMULA EQUALS STIMULANT WITH HALLUCINOGENIC PROPERTIES. ORGANIC BASE. WILL ENTER BLOOD-STREAM QUICKLY TO AFFECT NERVOUS SYSTEM.

'Results?'

INCOMPLETE DATA.

'Hell. Probable results with known data.'

WILL CAUSE FEELINGS OF EUPHORIA, PARANOIA, SEXUAL APPETITE, DELUSIONS OF PHYSICAL AND MENTAL POWERS. DOSAGE OF 55 MG INTO AVERAGE HUMAN OF 130 POUNDS WILL LAST FOUR TO SIX HOURS. DOSAGE OF MORE THAN 100 MG WILL CAUSE DEATH IN 87.3 PERCENT OF USERS. SUBSTANCE SIMILAR TO THR-50, AKA ZEUS, WITH ADDITION OF STIMULANT TO ENHANCE SEXUAL ABILITY AND CELL REGENERATION.

'It's not that different,' Eve murmured. 'It's not that important. We've already got chemi-heads mixing Zeus with Erotica. It's a nasty combination, accounts for most of the rapes in the city, but it's not secret or particularly profitable. Not when any average junkie can mix it up in a porta-lab.'

'Except for the unknown. Cell regeneration.' His brow quirked. 'The fabled Fountain of Youth.'

'Anybody with enough credits can get youth treatments.'

'But they're temporary,' Roarke pointed out. 'You have to go back at regular intervals. Bio peels and antiaging injections are expensive, time-consuming, and often uncomfortable. And standard treatments don't have all the extra punches of this.'

'Whatever the unknown is, it makes the whole works bigger, or deadlier. Or, as you said, more marketable.'

'You've got the powder,' Roarke pointed out.

'Yeah, and this might get the lab to shag their butts a bit. It's still going to take more time than I have.'

'Can you get me a sample of it?' He swiveled in his chair and smiled up at her. 'Not to denigrate your police labs, Lieutenant, but mine might prove a shade more sophisticated.'

'It's evidence.'

His brow lifted.

'Roarke, do you know how far I've already crossed the line getting you to do this?' She blew out a breath, remembered Boomer's face, his arm. 'Hell with it. I'll try.'

'Good. Disengage.' The computer shut down silently. 'Now will you go to sleep?'

'For a couple hours.' She allowed the fatigue to seep back, linked her arms around his neck. 'You going to tuck me in again?'

'All right.' He hitched up her hips so that her legs wrapped around him. 'But this time you stay where I tuck you.'

'You know, Roarke, my heart just flutters when you get masterful.'

'Wait till I get you back in bed. It's going to flutter plenty.'

She laughed, nuzzled her head on his shoulder, and was asleep before the elevator finished its descent.

4

It was dead dark when the 'link beside Eve's head beeped. The cop in her surfaced first, smacked the engage, and reared up.

'Dallas.'

'Dallas, oh God, Dallas. I need help.'

The woman in her caught up with the cop in a snap and stared at Mavis's image on screen. 'Lights,' she ordered, and the room brightened so that she could see clearly. The white face, a blackening bruise just under the eye, raw, bleeding scrapes on the cheek, wild disheveled hair.

'Mavis. What is it? Where are you?'

'You've got to come.' Her breath hitched and snarled. Her eyes were too glazed with shock to allow tears. 'Hurry. Hurry, please. I think she's dead and I don't know what to do.'

Eve didn't ask for location again, but punched in an order to trace transmission. Recognizing Leonardo's address when it blipped on under Mavis's face, she kept her voice calm and firm.

'Stay where you are. Don't touch anything. You understand me? Don't touch anything, and don't let anyone in but me. Mavis?'

'Yes, yes. I will. I won't. Hurry. It's so awful.'

'I'm on my way.' When she turned, Roarke was already up and pulling on his trousers.

'I'll go with you.'

She didn't argue. In five minutes flat they were on the road and speeding through the deepest slice of night. Empty streets gave way to the constant swarm of tourists in midtown, the flash of video billboards offering every pleasure and purchase known to man, then to the trendy insomniacs of the Village who loitered over minuscule cups of flavored coffee and lofty discussions in outdoor cafes, and finally, to the sleepy habitats of the artists.

Other than to find out their destination, Roarke didn't ask questions, and she was grateful for it. She could see Mavis's face in her mind, white and terrified. Worse, much worse, she saw Mavis's hand, trembling. And the smear that had darkened it had been blood.

A high wind that hinted of a brewing storm whipped through the city canyons. It slapped at Eve as she leaped from Roarke's car before he'd stopped completely at the curb. She took the thirty yards of sidewalk in a dead run, smacked the security camera.

'Mavis. It's Dallas. Mavis, damn it.' Such was her state of mind that it took her ten frustrated seconds to realize the unit was smashed.

Roarke went through the unsecured door and into the elevator beside her.

When it opened, she knew it was as bad as she'd feared.

On her earlier visit, Leonardo's loft had been cheerfully cluttered, colorfully disorganized. Now it was viciously tumbled. Long trails of material shredded, tables overturned with their contents strewn and broken.

There was blood, a great deal of it, splattered on walls and silks like a bad-tempered child's angry fingerpaints.

'Don't touch anything,' she snapped at Roarke, out of reflex. 'Mavis?' She took two steps forward, then stopped as one of the billowing curtains of shimmery cloth rippled. Mavis moved passed it, stood swaying.

'Dallas. Dallas. Thank God.'

'Okay. It's okay.' The minute Eve caught her close, the relief poured. The blood wasn't Mavis's, though it was spotted on her clothes, on her hands. 'You're hurt. How bad?'

'I'm dizzy, sick. My head.'

'Let her sit down, Eve.' Taking Mavis's arm, Roarke led her to a chair. 'Come on, darling, sit down. That's the way. She's in shock, Eve. Get her a blanket. Put your head back, Mavis. That's a girl. Close your eyes and just breathe for a while.'

'It's cold.'

'I know.' He reached down, flipped up a ragged piece of glistening satin, and draped it over her. 'Deep breaths, Mavis. Slow, deep breaths.' He flicked a glance up at Eve. 'She needs attention.'

'I can't call the MTs before I know what the situation is. Do what you can for her.' All too aware of what she was likely to find, Eve moved past the curtain.

She'd died badly. It was the hair that confirmed to Eve who the woman had once been. The glorious curling flame of it. Her face, with its stunning, almost eerie perfection, was all but gone, mashed and mangled under cruel, repeated blows.

The weapon was still there, carelessly tossed aside. Eve supposed it was intended to be some sort of fancy cane or walking stick, a fashionable affectation. Under the blood and gore it was a glossy silver, perhaps an inch thick with an ornate handle in the shape of a grinning wolf.

She'd seen it, tipped into a corner of Leonardo's work space, only two days before.

It was not necessary to check Pandora's pulse, but Eve did so. Then she stepped back carefully so as not to contaminate the scene any further.

'Christ,' Roarke murmured from behind her, then laid both hands on her shoulders. 'What are you going to do?'

'Whatever I have to. Mavis wouldn't have done this.'

He turned her to face him. 'You don't have to tell me that. She needs you, Eve. She needs a friend, and she's going to need a good cop.'

'I know.'

'It's not going to be easy on you being both.'

'I'd better get started.' She walked back to where Mavis sat. Her face was like softened wax, the bruise and the scratches livid against the bone-white skin. Eve crouched down and took Mavis's icy hands in hers. 'I need you to tell me everything. Take your time, but tell it all.'

'She wasn't moving. There was all the blood, and the way her face looked. And – and she wasn't moving.'

'Mavis.' Eve gave the hands one quick, hard squeeze. 'Look at me. Tell me exactly what happened from the time you got here.'

'I came . . . I wanted . . . I thought I should talk to Leonardo.' She shivered, plucked at the scrap of material covering her with hands still stained with blood. 'He was upset when he went to the club the last time looking for me. He even threatened the bouncer, and that's not like him. I didn't want him to ruin his career, so I thought I could talk to him. I came, and someone had broken the security unit, so I just came on up. The door wasn't locked. Sometimes he forgets,' she murmured and trailed off.

'Mavis, was Leonardo here?'

'Leonardo?' Dulled with shock, her eyes scanned the room. 'No, I don't think so. I called out, because I saw there was such a mess. Nobody answered. And there – there was blood. I saw blood. So much blood. I was afraid, Dallas, afraid that maybe he'd killed himself or something crazy, and so I ran back into . . . back. I saw her. I think . . . I went over. I think I did because I was kneeling beside her and I was trying to scream. I couldn't scream. It was all in my head that I was screaming, and I couldn't stop. And then I think something hit me. I think . . .' Vaguely she touched her fingers to the back of her head. 'It hurts. But everything was the same when I woke up. She was still there, and the blood was still there. And I called you.'

'Okay. Did you touch her, Mavis? Did you touch anything?'

'I don't remember. I don't think so.'

'Who did that to your face?'

'Pandora.'

A quick spurt of fear. 'Honey, you told me she was dead when you got here.'

'It was before. Earlier tonight. I went to her house.'

Eve took a careful breath to counteract the twisting in her stomach. 'You went to her house tonight. When?'

'I don't know exactly. About eleven maybe. I wanted to tell her I'd stay away from Leonardo, to make her promise not to ruin everything for him.'

'You fought with her?'

'She was jazzed up on something. There were some people there, like a small party. She was nasty, said things. I said things back. We got into it a little. She smacked me, scratched me.' Mavis tugged back her hair to reveal other wounds along her neck. 'A couple of the people there broke it up, and I left.'

'Where did you go?'

'A couple of bars.' She smiled weakly. 'A lot of bars, I think. Feeling sorry for myself. Just hanging. Then I got the idea to talk to Leonardo.'

'When did you get here? Do you know what time?'

'No, late, real late. Three, four o'clock.'

'Do you know where Leonardo is?'

'No. He wasn't here. I wanted him to be here, but she . . . What's going to happen?'

'I'm going to take care of it. I have to call this in, Mavis. If I don't do it soon, it's going to look bad. I'm going to have to put all of this on record, and I'm going to have to take you into Interview.'

'Into – into . . . You don't think I—'

'Of course I don't.' It was important to keep her voice brisk, to disguise her own fears. 'But we're going to clear it all up as quick as we can, as clean as we can. Let me do the worrying right now. Okay?'

'I can't feel much of anything.'

'You just sit here while I start things rolling. I want you to try to remember details. Who you talked to tonight, where you were, what you saw. Everything you can remember. We'll go over it all again in a little while.'

'Dallas.' With a little shudder, Mavis sat back. 'Leonardo. He'd never do that to anyone.'

'Let me do the worrying,' Eve repeated. She glanced at Roarke, and understanding the signal, he moved over to sit with Mavis. Eve pulled out her communicator and turned away.

'Dallas. I have a homicide.'

Eve's life had never been easy. In her career as a cop she had seen and done too many nightmarish things to count them all. But nothing had ever been more difficult for her than taking Mavis into Interview.

'Are you feeling okay? You don't have to do this now.'

'No, the MTs gave me a local.' Mavis reached up, touched

the lump on the back of her head. 'Numbed it good. They fiddled around with some other stuff, kind of snapped me back into focus.'

Eve took a long study of Mavis's eyes, her color. Everything looked normal, but it didn't ease her dread. 'Listen, it wouldn't hurt for you to check in to health center for a day or two.'

'You're just putting it off. I'd rather get it over with. Leonardo.' She swallowed hard. 'Has anyone found Leonardo?'

'Not yet. Mavis, you can have an attorney or representative here.'

'I don't have anything to hide. I didn't kill her, Dallas.'

Eve flicked a glance at the recorder. It could wait just another minute. 'Mavis, I have to do this by the ropes. Exactly. They can bump me off the case if I don't. If I'm not primary, I can't be as much help to you.'

Mavis licked her lips, her tongue quick and thirsty. 'It's going to be hard.'

'It could be really, really hard. You're going to have to handle it.'

Mavis tried for a smile, nearly managed it. 'Hey, nothing can be worse than walking in and finding Pandora. Nothing.'

Oh, yes, it could, Eve thought, but she nodded. She engaged the recorder, recited her name, ID, and officially gave Mavis her rights. Carefully, she took Mavis over the same ground she had covered on the scene, pinning down times as much as possible.

'When you went to the victim's home to talk to her, other people were present.'

'A few. It looked like a small party. Justin Young was there. You know, the actor. Jerry Fitzgerald, the model. And another guy I didn't recognize. Looked like a suit. You know, an exec.'

'The victim attacked you?'

'She popped me one,' Mavis said ruefully, fingering the bruise on her cheek. 'She started out just being bitchy. The way her eyes were wheeling around in her head, I figured she was pumped.'

'You believe she was using illegals.'

'Big time. I mean her eyes were like crystal wheels, and that punch. I tangled with her before, you saw it,' Mavis went on while Eve winced. 'She didn't have that kind of power before.'

'You hit her back?'

'I think I got one in, at least one. She scratched me – those damn nails of hers. I went for her hair. I think it was Justin Young and the suit that pulled us apart.'

'And then?'

'I guess we spit at each other for a couple of minutes, then I left. Went bar crawling.'

'Where did you go? How long did you stay?'

'I went a couple of places. I think I hit the ZigZag first, the joint over on Sixty-first and Lex.'

'Did you speak to anyone?'

'I didn't want to talk to anyone. My face hurt, and I was feeling lousy. I ordered a Triple Zombie and sulked.'

'How'd you pay for it?'

'I think . . . Yeah, I think I just entered my credit account on screen.'

Good. There'd be a record, time, place. 'From there, where did you go?'

'I walked around, bumped into another couple of dives. I was pretty blitzed.'

'Were you still ordering drinks?'

'I must have been. I was pretty drunk when I thought about going over to Leonardo's.'

'How'd you get downtown?'

'I walked. I needed to sober up a little, so I walked. Took a glide a couple of times, but mostly hoofed.'

Hoping to spark some memory, Eve repeated all the information Mavis had just given. 'When you left the ZigZag, which direction did you walk?'

'I'd just had two Triple Zombies. I wasn't walking, I was stumbling. I don't know which way. Dallas, I don't know the name of the other joints I went into, what else I drank. It's all a blur. Music, people laughing . . . a table dancer.'

'Male or female?'

'A guy. Hung, with a tattoo, I think. Could have been paint. Pretty sure it was a snake, maybe a lizard.'

'What did he look like, the table dancer?'

'Shit, Dallas, I never looked above the waist.'

'Did you talk to him?'

Mavis put her head in her hands and struggled to bring it back. Holding onto the memory was like trying to hold a fistful of water. 'I just don't know. I was seriously impaired. I remember walking and walking. Getting to Leonardo's, thinking it was the last time I was going to see him. I didn't want to be drunk when I did, so I took some Sober Up before I went in. Then I found her, and it was a lot worse than being drunk.'

'What was the first thing you saw when you walked in?'

'Blood. Lots of blood. Things knocked over, ripped, more blood. I was so afraid that Leonardo had hurt himself, and I ran back to his work area, and saw her.' This was a memory she could bring back with perfect clarity. 'I saw her. I recognized her because of the hair, and because she was wearing the same outfit as she'd had on earlier. But her face . . . it really wasn't even there at all. I couldn't scream. I knelt down beside her. I don't know what I thought I could do, but I had to do something. Then something hit me, and when I woke up, I called you.'

'Did you see anyone as you were going into the building, on the street outside?'

'No. It was late.'

'Tell me about the security camera.'

'It was broken. Sometimes street punks get a charge out of bashing them. I didn't think anything of it.'

'How did you get into the apartment?'

'The door wasn't locked. I just walked in.'

'And Pandora was dead when you got there? You didn't speak with her, argue?'

'No, I told you. She was lying there.'

65

'You'd fought with her earlier, twice. Did you fight with her tonight in Leonardo's apartment?'

'No. She was dead. Dallas—'

'Why did you fight with her on the previous occasions?'

'She threatened to ruin Leonardo's career.' Emotions flickered over Mavis's bruised face. Hurt, fear, grief. 'She wouldn't let him go. We were in love, but she wouldn't let him go. You saw the way she was, Dallas.'

'Leonardo and his career are very important to you.'

'I love him,' Mavis said quietly.

'You'd do anything to protect him, to see that he wasn't harmed, personally or professionally.'

'I'd decided to get out of his life,' Mavis stated with a dignity that warmed Eve. 'She'd have hurt him otherwise, and I couldn't let that happen.'

'She couldn't hurt him, or you, if she was dead.'

'I didn't kill her.'

'You went to her home, argued, she hit you and you fought. You left and got drunk. You made your way to Leonardo's apartment, found her there. Maybe you argued again, maybe she attacked you again. You defended yourself, and things got out of hand.'

Mavis's big, tired eyes registered puzzlement first, then hurt. 'Why are you saying that? You know it's not true.'

Eyes flat, Eve leaned forward. 'She was making your life hell, threatening the man you love. She hurt you, physically. She was stronger than you. When she saw you come into Leonardo's she went for you again. She knocked you down, you hit your head. Then you were afraid, you grabbed the closest thing at hand. To protect yourself. You hit her with it, to protect yourself. Maybe she kept coming at you, so you hit her again. To protect yourself. Then you lost control, and kept hitting her, and kept hitting her, until you realized she was dead.'

Mavis's breath sobbed through her lips. She shook her head, kept shaking it while her body trembled violently. 'I didn't. I didn't kill her. She was already dead. For God's sake, Dallas, how can you think I could do that to anybody?'

'Maybe you didn't.' Push, Eve ordered herself as her heart bled. Push hard, for the record. 'Maybe Leonardo did, and you're protecting him. Did you see him lose control, Mavis? Did he pick up the walking stick and hit her?'

'No, no, no!'

'Or did you get there after he had done it, after he was standing over her body. Panicked. You wanted to help him cover it up, so you got him out; called it in.'

'No. It wasn't like that.' She lunged up from her chair, cheeks white, eyes wild. 'He wasn't even there. I didn't see anyone. He could never do that. Why aren't you listening to me?'

'I am listening to you, Mavis. Sit down. Sit down,' Eve repeated more gently. 'We're almost done here. Is there anything you wish to add to your statement, or any change you wish to make in its content at this time?'

'No,' Mavis murmured and stared blindly over Eve's shoulder.

'This concludes Interview One, Mavis Freestone, Homicide file, Pandora. Dallas, Lieutenant Eve.' She noted the date and time, disengaged the recorder, took a leveling breath. 'I'm sorry, Mavis. I'm so sorry.'

'How could you do that? How could you say those things to me?'

'I have to say those things to you. I have to ask those questions, and you have to answer them.' She put a firm hand over Mavis's. 'I may have to ask them again, and you'll have to answer them again. Look at me, Mavis.' She waited until Mavis shifted her gaze. 'I don't know what the sweepers will pull in, what the lab reports will say. But if we don't get real lucky, you're going to need a lawyer.'

The color faded from Mavis's face, even her lips, until she resembled a corpse with hurting eyes. 'You're going to arrest me?'

'I don't know if it's going to come to that, but I want you to be prepared. Now, I want you to go home with Roarke, and get some sleep. I want you to try hard, real hard, to remember times and places and people. If you remember anything, you're going to record it for me.'

'What are you going to do?'

'I'm going to do my job. I'm damn good at my job, Mavis. You remember that, too, and trust me to clear this up.'

'Clear this up,' Mavis repeated, bitterness in her voice. 'Clear me, you mean. I thought it was "innocent until proven guilty."'

'That's just one of the bigger lies we live by.' Standing, Eve ushered Mavis into the corridor. 'I'll do my best to close the case quickly. That's all I can tell you.'

'You could tell me you believe me.'

'I can tell you that, too.' She just couldn't let it get in the way.

There was always paperwork and procedure. Within an hour she had Mavis signed out and under voluntary holding at Roarke's. Officially, Mavis Freestone was listed as a witness. Unofficially, Eve knew, she was the prime suspect. Intending to begin amending that immediately, she walked into her office.

'Okay, what's this shit about Mavis whacking some fancy-faced model?'

'Feeney.' Eve could have kissed every rumpled inch of him. He sat at her desk, his ubiquitous bag of sugared nuts in his lap, and a scowl on his wrinkled face. 'Word travels.'

'It was the first thing I heard when I made my stop at the eatery. One of our top cop's pals gets collared, it makes a buzz.'

'She hasn't been collared. She's a witness. For now.'

'Media's picked it up already. They don't have Mavis's name yet, but they've got the victim's face splashed all over the screen. The wife dragged me out of the shower to hear about it. Pandora was a BFD.'

'Big fucking deal, alive or dead.' Weary, Eve eased a hip onto the corner of her desk. 'Want a rundown of Mavis's statement?'

'What do you think I'm here for, the ambience?'

She gave it to him in the cop shorthand they both understood, and left him frowning. 'Damn, Dallas, it doesn't look good for her. You saw them going at it yourself.'

'Alive and in person. Why the hell she got it into her mind to confront Pandora again . . .' Rising, she paced the room. 'It makes it worse. I'm hoping the lab comes back with something, anything. But I can't count on it. What's your caseload like, Feeney?'

'Don't ask.' He waved that away. 'What do you need?'

'I need a run on her credit account. The first place she remembers going into is ZigZag. If we can place her there, or at one of the other joints at time of death, she's clear.'

'I can handle that for you, but . . . We got somebody hanging around the murder scene, bopping Mavis on the head. Chances are there won't be much of a time lag.'

'I know. I've got to cover all the bases. I'm going to track down the people Mavis recognized at the victim's house, get statements. I've got to find a table dancer with a big dick and a tattoo.'

'The fun never ends.'

She nearly smiled. 'I need to find people who can testify she was really ripped. Even with a dose of Sober Up, she couldn't have been clean enough to have taken out Pandora if she'd been drinking her way downtown.'

'She claims Pandora was using.'

'Something else I have to check out. Then there's the elusive Leonardo. Where the fuck was he? And where is he now?'

5

Leonardo was sprawled in the middle of Mavis's living room floor, where he had fallen hours before in a drunken stupor brought on by a full bottle of synthetic whiskey and a boatload of self-pity.

He was surfacing groggily and feared he'd lost half of his face sometime during the miserable night. When he lifted a cautious hand to it, he was relieved to find his entire face in the usual place, only numbed from being mashed into Mavis's floor.

He couldn't remember much. It was one of the reasons he rarely drank and never permitted himself to overindulge. He was prone to blackouts and blank spaces whenever he chugged down a few too many.

He thought he remembered staggering into Mavis's apartment building, using the key code she'd given him when they realized they were not just lovers but in love.

But she hadn't been there. He was almost sure of that. He had a vague picture of himself lurching across town, glugging from the bottle he'd bought – stolen? Hell. Blearily he tried to sit up and pry his pasty eyes open. All he knew for certain was that he'd had the damn bottle in his hand and the whiskey in his gut.

He must have passed out. Which disgusted him. How could he expect to make Mavis see reason if he came weaving into her apartment, babbling drunk?

He could only be grateful she hadn't been there.

Now, of course, he had a raging hangover that made him want to curl into a ball and weep for mercy. But she might come back, and he didn't want her to see him in such a mortifying state. He made himself get up, hunted down some painkillers before programming her AutoChef for coffee, strong and black.

Then he noticed the blood.

It was dried, streaking down his arm, onto his hand. There was a gash on his forearm, long, fairly deep, that had crusted over. Blood, he thought again, stomach jittery as he noted that it stained his shirt, his pants.

Breathing shallowly, he backed away from the counter, staring down at himself. Had he been in a fight? Had he hurt anyone?

Nausea rose in his throat as his mind skipped over huge voids and blurry memories.

Oh sweet Jesus, had he killed someone?

Eve was staring grimly at the medical examiner's preliminary report as she heard a quick, sharp rap on the door of her office. It opened before she acknowledged it.

'Lieutenant Dallas?' The man had the look of a sun-bleached cowboy, from his shit-eating grin to his worn-heeled boots. 'Goddamn, it's good to see the legend in the flesh. Seen your picture, but you're a long sight prettier.'

'I'm all a-flutter.' Eyes narrowing, she leaned back. He was plenty pretty himself, with wheat-colored hair curling around a tan, lived-in face that creased appealingly around bottle-green eyes. A long, straight nose, the quick wink of a sly dimple at the corner of a grinning mouth. And a body that, well, looked like it could ride the range just fine. 'Who the hell are you?'

'Casto, Jake T.' He tugged a shield from the snug front pocket of his faded Levi's. 'Illegals. Heard you were tracking me.'

Eve scanned the badge. 'Did you? Did you hear why I might have been tracking you, Lieutenant Casto, Jake T.?'

'Our mutual weasel.' He stepped all the way in and planted a hip companionably on her desk. That brought him close enough for her to catch the scent of his skin. Soap and leather. 'Goddamn shame about old Boomer. Harmless little prick.'

'If you knew Boomer was mine, what's taken you so long to come see me?'

'I've been tied up on something else. And to tell the truth, I didn't think there was much to say or do. Then I heard Feeney from EDD was poking around.' Those eyes smiled again, with just a touch of sarcasm. 'Feeney's pretty much yours, too, isn't he?'

'Feeney's his own. What were you working Boomer on?'

'Usual.' Casto picked up an amethyst egg from her desk,

admired the inclusions, passed it from hand to hand. 'Information on illegals. Small shit. Boomer liked to think he was big time, but it was always little bits and pieces.'

'Little bits and pieces can build the big picture.'

'That's why I used him, honey. He was pretty reliable for a bust here and there. Couple of times I tagged a middle level dealer on his data.' He grinned again. 'Somebody's gotta do it.'

'Yeah. So who beat him into putty?'

The grin faded. Casto set the egg back down and shook his head. 'Can't say as I have a clue. Boomer wasn't your lovable sort, but I don't know anybody who hated him enough, or was pissed enough, to whack him that way.'

Eve studied her man. He looked solid, and there had been a tone in his voice when he'd spoken of Boomer that reminded her of her own cautious affection. Still, she believed in holding her cards close. 'Was he working on anything in particular? Something different? Something bigger?'

Casto's sandy brow lifted. 'Such as?'

'I'm asking you. Illegals aren't my game.'

'There wasn't anything I knew of. Last I talked to him, hell, maybe two weeks before he went floating, he talked about sniffing out something outrageous. You know how he talked, Eve.'

'Yeah, I know how he talked.' It was time to lay one of her cards down. 'I also know I copped some unidentified substance hidden in his apartment. It's in the lab now, and they're analyzing. So far, all they tell me is it's a new blend, and it's more potent than anything currently on the street.'

'New blend.' Casto's brow creased. 'Why the hell didn't he tip me to that? If he tried to play both sides . . .' Casto hissed a breath between his teeth. 'You think he got whacked over it?'

'That's my best theory.'

'Yeah. Dumb shit. Probably tried to shake down the maker or the distributor. Listen, I'll talk to the lab, and I'll see if there's any buzz on the street about something new coming in.'

'Appreciate it.'

'It'll be a pleasure working with you.' He shifted, let his gaze linger on her mouth for a beat, with a kind of talent that missed insulting by miles and bull's-eyed on flattering. 'Maybe you'd like to catch a bite to eat, discuss strategy. Or whatever comes to mind.'

'No, thanks.'

'Is that no because you're not hungry, or because you're getting married?'

'Both.'

'Well, then.' He rose, and being human, she had to appreciate the way the denim snugged over long, lanky legs. 'If you change your mind about either, you know where to find me now. I'll be in touch.' He sauntered toward the door, paused, and turned. 'You know, Eve, you've got eyes like good, aged whiskey. Sure brings out a powerful thirst in a man.'

She frowned at the door he closed behind him, annoyed at the fact that her pulse was a little quick, a little unsteady. Shaking it off, she dragged both hands through her hair and looked back at the report on her screen.

She hadn't needed to be told how Pandora had died, but it was interesting to see that the ME believed the first three head blows had been fatal. Anything after that had just been indulgence on the killer's part.

She'd put up a fight before the head blows, Eve noted. Lacerations and abrasions on other parts of the body were concordant with a struggle.

The time of death was listed at oh two fifty, and stomach contents indicated the victim had enjoyed an elegant last meal, at about twenty-one hundred, of lobster, escarole, Bavarian cream, and vintage champagne.

There had also been heavy traces of chemicals in her bloodstream which had yet to be analyzed.

So, Mavis had probably been right. It looked as though Pandora was jazzed on something, possibly on the illegals list. In the grand scheme of things, that might or might not make a difference.

But the traces of skin under the victim's nails were going to make a difference. Eve was terrifyingly sure when the lab finished its work, it was going to prove to be Mavis's skin. Just as the strands of hair the sweepers had bagged near the body were going to be Mavis's hair. And most damning, she was afraid, the prints on the murder weapon could be Mavis's.

As a setup, Eve thought and let her eyes close, *it was perfect. Mavis comes in, wrong time, wrong place, and the killer sees a tailor-made scapegoat.*

Had he or she known the history between Mavis and the victim, or had that just been one more stroke of luck?

In any case, he knocks Mavis out, plants some evidence, even adds the master stroke of scraping the dead woman's nails over Mavis's face. Easy enough to press her fingers onto the weapon, then slip out and away with the satisfaction of a job well done.

It wouldn't take a genius, she mused. But it would take a cold, practical mind. And how did that jibe with the rage and the insanity of the attack on Pandora?

She would have to make it jibe, Eve told herself. And she would have to find a way to clear Mavis and find the kind of killer who could batter a woman's face into nothing, then tidy up after himself.

Even as she started to rise, her door burst open. Wild-eyed, Leonardo lurched inside.

'I killed her. I killed Pandora. God help me.'

With that, his wild eyes rolled back and all two hundred and sixty pounds of him thudded to the floor in a dead faint.

'Jesus. Jesus Christ.' Rather than try to catch him, Eve nipped back out of the way of his falling body. It was like watching a redwood go down. Now he was stretched, feet on her threshold, his head nearly brushing the opposite wall. She crouched down, put her back into it and managed to roll him over. She tried a couple of sharp, light slaps, then waited. Muttering to herself, she put her back into that as well and rapped his cheeks hard.

He moaned, and his bloodshot eyes fluttered open. 'What – where—'

'Shut up, Leonardo.' Eve snapped out the order as she rose, went to the doorway, and kicked his feet inside. With the door firmly shut, she looked down at him. 'I'm going to read you your rights.'

'My rights?' He looked dazed, but managed to heave himself up until he was sitting on the floor instead of lying on it.

'You listen up.' She gave him the standard revised Miranda, then held up a hand before he could speak. 'You understand your rights and your options?'

'Yeah.' Weary, he rubbed his hands over his face. 'I know what's going on.'

'You wish to make a statement?'

'I've already told you—'

Eyes flat, she held up a hand again. 'Yes or no. Just yes or no.'

'Yes, yes, I want to make a statement.'

'Get up off the floor. I'm going to record this.' She turned to her desk. She could have hauled him down to Interview. Probably should have, but it could wait. 'You understand whatever you say now is going on record?'

'Yes.' He got to his feet, then dropped into a chair that groaned under his weight. 'Dallas—'

She shook her head to cut him off. After engaging her recorder, she noted the necessary information, then gave him his Miranda again for the record. 'Leonardo, you understand these rights and options, and at this time have waived counsel and are prepared to make a statement?'

'I just want to get it over with.'

'Yes or no?'

'Yes. Yes, damn it.'

'You were acquainted with Pandora?'

'Of course I was.'

'You had a relationship with her?'

'I did.' He covered his face again, but could still see the image that had flashed on Mavis's viewing screen when he'd decided to flip on the news. The long black bag being carried out of his own apartment building. 'I can't believe this has happened.'

'What was the nature of your relationship with the victim?'

It was so cold, he thought, *the way she said it. 'The victim.'* Leonardo dropped his hands into his lap and stared at Eve. 'You know we were lovers. You know I was trying to break it off because—'

'You were no longer intimate,' Eve interrupted, 'at the time of her death.'

'No, we hadn't been together for weeks. She'd been off planet. Things had cooled between us even before she left. And then I met Mavis, and everything changed for me. Dallas, where is Mavis? Where is she?'

'I'm not at liberty to give you Ms Freestone's where-abouts at this time.'

'Just tell me she's all right.' His eyes filled, swam. 'Just tell me she's all right.'

'She's being taken care of,' was all Eve would say. Could say. 'Leonardo, is it true that Pandora was threatening to ruin you professionally? That she demanded you continue your relationship with her, and that if you refused, she would pull out of the showing of your fashion designs. A show that you had invested with a great deal of time and money.'

'You were there, you heard her. She didn't give a rat's damn about me, but she wouldn't tolerate me being the one to pull back. Unless I stopped seeing Mavis, unless I was her lapdog again, she would have seen to it that the show was a failure, if it ran at all.'

'You didn't want to stop seeing Ms Freestone.'

'I love Mavis,' he said with great dignity. 'She's the most important thing in my life.'

'And yet, if you didn't accede to Pandora's demands, you would in all probability be left with enormous debts and a stain on your professional reputation that would have been intolerable. Is this correct?'

'Yes. I put everything I had into the show. I borrowed a great deal of money. More, I put my heart into it. My soul.'

'She could have wiped that all out.'

'Oh yes.' His lips curled. 'She would have enjoyed it.'

'Did you ask her to come to your apartment last night?'

'No. I never wanted to see her again.'

'What time did she come to your apartment last night?'

'I don't know.'

'How did she get in? Did you let her in?'

'I don't think so. I don't know. She would have had my key code. I never thought to get it back from her or to change it. Everything's been so crazy.'

'You argued with her.'

His eyes glazed over, went blank. 'I don't know. I don't remember. But I must have. I would have.'

'Recently, Pandora came into your apartment uninvited, threatened you, attacked your current companion physically.'

'Yes, yes, she did.' He could remember that. It was a relief to be able to remember that.

'What was Pandora's state of mind when she came to your apartment this time?'

'She must have been angry. I would have told her I wasn't giving Mavis up. That would have infuriated her. Dallas . . .' His eyes focused again, and desperation shone in them. 'I just don't remember. Any of it. When I woke up this morning, I was in Mavis's apartment. I think I remember using my key code to get in. I'd been drinking, walking and drinking. I rarely drink because I tend to lose time, black holes in my mind. When I woke up, I saw the blood.'

He held out his arm where the wound had been poorly bandaged. 'There was blood on my hands, on my clothes.

Dried blood. I must have fought with her. I must have killed her.'

'Where are the clothes you were wearing last night?'

'I left them at Mavis's. I showered, and I changed. I didn't want her to come home and find me looking like that. I was waiting for her, trying to figure out what to do, and I turned on the news. I heard – I saw. And I knew.'

'You're saying that you don't remember seeing Pandora last night. You don't remember having an altercation with her. You don't remember killing her.'

'But I must have,' he insisted. 'She died in my apartment.'

'What time did you leave your apartment last night?'

'I'm not sure. I'd been drinking before. A lot. I was upset, and I was angry.'

'Did you see anyone, speak with anyone?'

'I bought another bottle. From a street hawker, I think.'

'Did you see Ms Freestone last night?'

'No. I'm sure of that. If I'd seen her, if I could have talked to her, everything would have been all right.'

'What if I tell you Mavis was in your apartment last night?'

'Mavis came to see me.' His face brightened. 'She came back to me? But that can't be right. I couldn't have forgotten that.'

'Was Mavis there when you fought with Pandora? When you killed Pandora?'

'No. No.'

'Did she come in after Pandora was dead, after you'd

killed her? You were panicked then, weren't you? Terrified.'

There was panic in his eyes now. 'Mavis couldn't have been there.'

'But she was. She called me from your apartment, after she found the body.'

'Mavis saw?' Beneath the copper tone, his skin went pasty. 'Oh, God, no.'

'Someone struck Mavis, knocked her unconscious. Was it you, Leonardo?'

'Someone hit her? She's hurt?' He was up, out of the chair, dragging his hands through his hair. 'Where is she?'

'Was it you?'

He held out his arms. 'I'd cut my hands off before I'd hurt Mavis. For Christ's pity, Dallas, tell me where she is. Let me see if she's all right.'

'How did you kill Pandora?'

'I – the reporter said I beat her to death.' And he shuddered.

'How did you beat her? What did you use?'

'I – My hands?' Again he held them out. Eve noted there was no sign of bruising, no tears or abrasions on the knuckles. They were perfect, as if they'd been carved from rich, glossy wood.

'She was a strong woman. She must have fought back.'

'The cut on my arm.'

'I'd like the cut to be examined, as well as the clothes you say you left at Mavis's.'

'Are you going to arrest me now?'

'You are not being charged at this time. You will, however, be held until the results of the tests are complete.'

She took him over the same ground again, pushing for times, for places, for his movements. Again and again, she bumped up against the wall blocking his memory. Far from satisfied, she concluded the interview, took him to holding, then made arrangements for the tests.

Her next stop was Commander Whitney.

Ignoring his offer of a chair, she stood facing him as he sat behind his desk. Briskly, she gave him the results of her initial interviews. Whitney folded his hands and watched her. He had good eyes, cop's eyes, and recognized nerves.

'You have a man who has confessed to the murder. A man with motive and opportunity.'

'A man who doesn't remember seeing the victim on the night in question, much less bludgeoning her to death.'

'It wouldn't be the first time a perp confessed in such a way to make himself seem innocent.'

'No, sir. But I don't believe he's our killer. The tests may prove me wrong, but his personality type doesn't fit the crime. I was a witness to another altercation where the victim attacked Mavis. Rather than attempting to stop the fight, or showing any signs of violence, he stood back and wrung his hands.'

'By his own statement, he was under the influence on the night of the murder. Drink can and does induce personality changes.'

'Yes, sir.' It was reasonable. In her heart she wanted to pin it on him, to take his confession at face value and run with it. Mavis would be miserable, but she'd be safe. She'd be cleared. 'It's not him,' she said flatly. 'I recommend holding him for the maximum amount of time, reinterviewing to try to jog his memory. But we can't charge him for thinking he committed murder.'

'I'll go along with your recommendation, Dallas. The other lab reports should be in shortly. We'll hope the results will clear everything up. You understand they may further incriminate Mavis Freestone.'

'Yes, sir, I understand that.'

'You have a long-standing friendship with her. It would be no blot on your record to withdraw as primary on this case. It would, in fact, be better for you, and certainly more rational if you were to do so.'

'No, sir, I will not withdraw as primary. If you pull me, I will take leave and pursue the case on personal time. If necessary, I will resign.'

For a moment, he rubbed his joined hands against his brow. 'Your resignation would not be accepted. Sit down, Lieutenant. Damn it, Dallas,' he erupted when she remained standing. 'Sit. I'll make it a fucking order.'

'Yes, Commander.'

He sighed, reined in his temper. 'I hurt you not long ago with a personal attack that was neither appropriate nor deserved. Because of that, I damaged something between us. I understand that you no longer feel comfortable under my command.'

'You are the best commander I've ever served under. I have no problem with you as my superior.'

'But no longer friends – not even remotely.' He nodded, accepting her silence. 'However, because of my behavior during your investigation of a case that was very personal to me, you should be aware that I fully understand what you're going through on this one. I know what it is to be torn between loyalties, Dallas. While you may be unable to discuss your feelings in this case with me, I strongly suggest that you do so with someone you can trust. My mistake in the other investigation was in not sharing the burden. Don't make the same one with this.'

'Mavis didn't kill anyone. No amount of evidence will convince me otherwise. I'll do my job, Commander. And in doing it, I'll find the real killer.'

'I have no doubt you'll do your job, Lieutenant, or that you'll suffer for it. You have my support, whether you choose to use it or not.'

'Thank you, sir. I have a request to make on another case.'

'Which is?'

'The Johannsen matter.'

This time he sighed, long and deep. 'You're like a damn terrier, Dallas. You never let go.'

She couldn't argue the point. 'You have my report on what was found at Boomer's flop. The illegal substance has not been fully identified. I've done some research of my own on the formula we discovered.' She took a disc out of her bag. 'It's a new blend, highly potent, its effects would probably be fairly long term as compared to what's found on the street. Four to six hours for an average dose. Too much more at one time would be, in eighty-eight percent, fatal.'

Lips pursed, Whitney turned the disc over in his hands. 'Personal research, Dallas?'

'I had a connection, I used it. The lab is still working, but they have identified several of the ingredients, and their ratios. My point is, this substance would be enormously profitable, as it takes only a small amount to produce results. It's highly addictive, and produces feelings of strength, delusions of power, and a kind of euphoria – not tranquillity, but a sense of control over self and others. It also contains some sort of cell regenerator. I've calculated the results of long-term addiction. Daily use for a period of five years will, in ninety-six point eight percent, result in a complete and sudden shutdown of the nervous system. And death.'

'Christ Jesus. It's poison?'

'Ultimately, yes. The manufacturers certainly know this, which makes them guilty not only of distributing illegals, but of premeditated murder.'

She let him chew over that a moment, knew the headache it would cause if and when the media dug its claws into the data. 'Boomer may or may not have known about this aspect, but he knew enough to be killed for it. I want to pursue the case and, as I'm aware, I'm distracted by other matters, so I request that Officer Peabody be assigned as my aide until the matter is resolved.'

'Peabody has little experience in illegals or homicide, Lieutenant.'

'She makes up for it with brains and sweat. I'd like her to assist in my coordinating with Lieutenant Casto of Illegals, who also used Boomer as a weasel.'

'I'll see to it. As to the Pandora homicide, use Feeney.' He lifted a brow. 'You already are, I see. Let's pretend I've just ordered it, and make it official. You'll have to deal with the media.'

'I'm getting used to it. Nadine Furst is back from leave. I'll feed her what seems best. She and Channel 75 owe me a few.' She rose. 'I have some people to talk to. I'll contact Feeney and take him along.'

'Let's see if we can get things cleared up before your honeymoon.' Her face was such a study of contradictions, embarrassment, pleasure, and fear, he roared out a laugh. 'You'll live through it, Dallas. I can guarantee it.'

'Sure, when the guy who's designing my wedding dress is in holding,' she muttered. 'Thank you, Commander.'

He watched her walk out. She might not have been aware that she'd dropped the barrier between them, but he was.

'The wife's going to love this.' More than content to let Dallas handle the driving, Feeney leaned back in the passenger seat. Street traffic was light as they headed toward Park Avenue South. Feeney, a native New Yorker, had long since tuned out the bellows and echoes of the tourist blimps and sky buses that crowded overhead.

'They told me they were going to fix it. Those fuckers. Hear that, Feeney? Do you hear that goddamn buzzing?'

Obligingly, he focused on the sound coming from her control panel. 'Sounds like a swarm of those killer bees.'

'Three days,' she fumed, 'three days in repair, and listen to it. It's worse than it was.'

'Dallas.' He laid a hand on her arm. 'You may have to face it, finally, learn to deal with the simple fact that your vehicle is a piece of garbage. Requisition a new one.'

'I don't want a new one.' Using the heel of her hand, she rapped the control panel. 'I want this one, without the sound effects.' She got caught at a light, tapped her fingers on the wheel. The way the controls sounded, she wouldn't be able to trust automatic. 'Where the hell is 582 Central Park South?' Her controls continued to buzz, so she slapped them again. 'I said, where the hell is 582 Central Park South?'

'Just ask nice,' Feeney suggested. 'Computer, please display map and locate 582 Central Park South.'

When the display screen popped up, the holographic map highlighting the route, Eve only snarled.

'I don't baby my tools.'

'Which may be why they're always breaking down on you. As I was saying,' he continued before Eve could snap at him, 'the wife's going to love this. Justin Young. He used to play this stud on *Night Falls*.'

'Isn't that a soap?' She shot him a glance. 'What are you doing watching soaps?'

'Hey, I tune in the Soap Channel for a little relaxation like everybody. Anyway, the wife was nuts about him. He does the movie thing now. She hardly goes a week without programming one of his movies on screen. Guy's good, too. Then there's Jerry Fitzgerald.' Feeney smiled dreamily.

'Keep your little fantasies to yourself, pal.'

'I tell you that girl's built. Not like some of the models who have their bodies honed down to bone.' He made a sound like a man anticipating a large bowl of ice cream. 'You know one of the best things about working with you recently, Dallas?'

'My charming ways and rapier wit?'

'Oh sure.' He rolled his eyes. 'It's being able to go home and tell the wife who I interrogated today. A billionaire, a senator, Italian aristocrats, film stars. I tell you, it's done wonders for my prestige.'

'Glad I could help.' She squeezed her battered police issue between a mini Rolls and a vintage Mercedes. 'Just try to control your awe while we do the third degree on the actor.'

'I'm a professional.' But he was grinning as he climbed out. 'Just look at this place. How'd you like to own a place in here?' Then he chuckled and shifted his eyes away from the glossy faux marble facade of the lofty building. 'Oh, I was forgetting. This is slumming for you now.'

'Kiss ass, Feeney.'

'Come on, kid, loosen up.' He slung an arm around her shoulder as they headed toward the doors. 'Falling for the richest man in the known world isn't something to be ashamed of.'

'I'm not ashamed of it. I just don't like to dwell on it.'

The building was choice enough to have a live doorman as well as electronic security. Both Eve and Feeney flashed their badges and were admitted into a marble and gilt lobby accented with leafy ferns and exotic flowers in huge china pots.

'Ostentatious,' Eve muttered.

'See how jaded you're getting?' Feeney moved out of range and approached the inner security screen. 'Lieutenant Dallas and Captain Feeney, for Justin Young.'

'One moment, please.' The creamy computer voice paused while their identification was verified. 'Thank you for waiting. Mr Young is expecting you. Please proceed to elevator three, request your party. Enjoy your day.'

6

'So, how do you want to play it?' Feeney pursed his lips, studied the tiny camera in the corner of the elevator on the way up. 'The standard good cop/bad cop?'

'Funny how it always works.'

'Civilians are easy marks.'

'Let's start with the sorry to bother you, appreciate your cooperation sort of thing. If we get a sense he's playing games, we can shift gears.'

'If we do, I want to be the bad cop.'

'You're a lousy bad cop, Feeney. Face it.'

He gave her a mournful look. 'I outrank you, Dallas.'

'I'm primary, and I'm better at bad cop. Live with it.'

'I always have to be the good cop,' he muttered as they stepped into a well-lighted hallway with more marble, more gilt.

Justin Young opened the opposing door with perfect timing. And, Eve thought, he'd dressed for the part of the well-to-do yet cooperative witness in casual, expensive, buff linen slacks and a drapey silk shirt of the same tone. On his feet were trendy sandals with thick soles and intricate beading over the instep.

'Lieutenant Dallas, Captain Feeney.' His beautifully sculpted face was in serious lines, the killer black eyes sober and a dramatic contrast to a wavy mane of hair the same color as the gilt in the hallway. He offered a hand adorned with a wide ring studded with onyx. 'Please come in.'

'Thank you for agreeing to see us so quickly, Mr Young.' Perhaps her eye had become jaded, but Eve's initial scan of the room left her thinking, *Overdone, overwrought, and over-expensive.*

'It's such a tragedy, such a horror.' He gestured them in toward a huge L-shaped sofa jammed with pillows in wild colors and slick fabrics. Across the room, a meditation screen was programmed to a tropical beach at sunset. 'It's almost impossible to believe she could be dead, much less that she died in such a sudden and violent way.'

'We're sorry to intrude,' Feeney began, prepping for his good cop role while he struggled not to gape at all the tassels and stained glass. 'This must be a difficult time for you.'

'It is. Pandora and I were friends. Can I offer you something?' He sat, elegant and slim, in a wing chair that could have swallowed a small child.

'No, thank you.' Eve tried to wiggle her way back among the mountain of cushions.

'I will, if you don't mind. I've been living on little more than nerves since I heard the news.' Leaning forward, he pressed a small button on the table between them. 'Coffee, please. One.' Settling back, he smiled a little. 'You'll want to know where I was when she died. I've done a number of police vehicles in my career. Played the cop, the suspect, even the victim in my early days. With my image, I've always been innocent.'

He flicked a glance up as a domestic droid, dressed, Eve noted with horrified amusement, in the classic French maid's uniform, carried in a glass tray topped with a single cup and saucer. Justin took the cup from it, used both hands to bring it to his lips.

'The media hasn't stated exactly when Pandora was killed, but I believe I can give you my movements for the entire evening. I was with her, at a small party at her home until about midnight. Jerry and I – Jerry Fitzgerald – left together, and went to have a drink at a nearby private club. Ennui. It's very in right now, and it pays for both of us to be seen. I imagine it was one or so when we left. We considered doing a bit of club hopping, but I confess, we'd both had enough to drink, and enough socializing. We came here, stayed here together until about ten the next morning. Jerry had an assignment. It wasn't until she'd left and I was having my first cup of coffee that I turned on the news and heard about Pandora.'

'That certainly covers the evening,' Eve said. He'd recited it all, she thought, as though it was a well-staged play. 'We'll need to speak to Ms Fitzgerald to verify.'

'Certainly. Would you like to do so now? She's in the relaxation room. Pandora's death has left her a bit rattled.'

'Let's let her relax a bit longer,' Eve suggested. 'You said you and Pandora were friends. Were you lovers?'

'Now and again, nothing serious. It was more that we ran in the same circles. And to be brutally honest at such a time, Pandora preferred men who were easily dominated, intimidated.' He flashed a smile as if to show he was neither. 'She preferred affairs with those who were striving rather than those who had attained success. She rarely enjoyed sharing the spotlight.'

Feeney picked up the rhythm. 'Who was she involved with, romantically, at the time of her death?'

'There were a few, I believe. Someone I think she'd met on Starlight Station – an entrepreneur, she called him, but with a sarcastic tone. This up-and-coming designer Jerry tells me is brilliant. Michelangelo, Puccini, Leonardo. Something of the kind. Paul Redford, the video producer who joined us that night.'

He took a sip of his coffee, then blinked. 'Leonardo. Yes, it was Leonardo. There was some sort of tiff there. A woman came by the house while we were there. They fought over him. An old-fashioned catfight. It would have been amusing if it hadn't been so embarrassing for everyone involved.'

He spread his elegant fingers, looked mildly amused despite his statement. *Well done,* Eve thought. *Well rehearsed, good timing, lines professionally punched.*

'It took Paul and I both to separate them.'

'The woman came to Pandora's home and attacked her, physically?' Eve asked in carefully neutral tones.

'Oh no, not at all. The poor thing was devastated, pleading. Pandora called her a few vile names and hit her.' Justin demonstrated by making a fist, jerking it. 'Really socked her. The woman was small, but she was game. Scrambled right up and plowed in. After that it was wrestling and hair pulling, scratching. The woman was bleeding some when she left. Pandora had lethal nails.'

'Pandora scratched the woman's face?'

'No. Though I'm sure she was going to have quite a bruise. It was her neck as I recall. Four long, nasty scratches on the side of the neck where Pandora raked her. The woman, I'm afraid I don't know her name. Pandora just called her bitch, and varieties of the same. She was trying not to cry when she left, and told Pandora, quite dramatically, that Pandora would be sorry for what she'd done. Then I'm afraid she ruined her exit by sniffling and claiming that love conquers all.'

It sounded just like Mavis, Eve thought. 'And after she left, how did Pandora behave?'

'She was furious, overexcitable. That's why Jerry and I left early.'

'And Paul Redford?'

'He stayed; I can't say how long.' With a sigh that signaled regret, Justin set his coffee aside. 'It's unfair to say anything negative about Pandora when she can't defend herself, but she was hard, very often abrasive. Cross her, and you paid.'

'And did you ever cross her, Mr Young?'

'I was careful not to.' He smiled charmingly. 'I enjoy my career and my looks, Lieutenant. Pandora was no threat to the first, but I'd seen and heard of her doing some damage to faces when annoyed. Believe me, she didn't wear her manicure like knives just for fashion.'

'She had enemies.'

'Plenty of them, most of whom were terrified of her. I can't imagine who might have finally snapped and struck back at her. And from the news reports I've heard, I can't believe even Pandora deserved to die so brutally.'

'We appreciate your candor, Mr Young. If it's convenient, we'd like to speak with Ms Fitzgerald now. Alone.'

He lifted a slim, elegant brow. 'Yes, of course. No co-ordinating stories.'

Eve only smiled. 'You've had plenty of time to do that already. But we'd like to speak to her alone.'

She had the pleasure of seeing his smooth facade shaken a bit by her statement. Still, he rose and walked toward a connecting corridor.

'What do you think?' Feeney muttered.

'I think it was a hell of a performance.'

'We're on wavelength there. Still, if he and Fitzgerald were ripping up the sheets all night, it keeps him in the clear.'

'They alibi each other, it keeps them both in the clear. We'll get the security discs from building management, check what time they came in. See if they went out again.'

'I never trust those, not since the DeBlass case.'

'If they diddled with the discs, you'll see it.' She glanced up at the sound of Feeney sucking in his breath. His hangdog face had gone terrier bright. His eyes were glazed. After a glimpse at Jerry Fitzgerald's entrance, Eve wondered why Feeney's tongue wasn't hanging out.

She was built, all right, Eve mused. Her lush breasts were barely covered with ivory silk that dipped nipple low, clung, then halted briefly a few millimeters below crotch level. One long, shapely leg was decorated beside the knee with a red rose in full bloom.

Jerry Fitzgerald was definitely blooming.

Then there was the face, soft and slumberous as though she'd just climbed out of sex. Ebony hair was razor straight and curved to perfection, framing a round, feminine chin. Her mouth was full and wet and red, her eyes dazzling blue and edged with spiky, gold-tipped lashes.

As she glided to a chair like some sort of pagan sex goddess, Eve patted Feeney's leg in support – and restraint.

'Ms Fitzgerald,' Eve began.

'Yes,' she said in a voice like sacrificial smoke. Those killer eyes barely flickered on Eve before they latched like limpets on Feeney's homely and dazed face. 'Captain, it's just so awful. I've tried the isolation tank, the mood elevator, even programmed the hologram for meadow walks, as that always relaxes me. But nothing I do gets all of this out of my mind.'

She fluttered, lifted both hands to her unbelievable face. 'I must look like a hag.'

'You look beautiful,' Feeney babbled. 'Stunning. You look—'

'Get a grip,' Eve muttered and jabbed him with an elbow.

'We appreciate how upset you are, Ms Fitzgerald. Pandora was a friend of yours.'

Jerry opened her mouth, closed it, smiled slyly. 'I could tell you she was, but you'd find out quickly enough we weren't friendly. We tolerated each other as we were in the same business, but frankly, we couldn't stand one another.'

'She invited you into her home.'

'That's because she wanted Justin to be there, and we're very close right now. And Pandora and I did socialize, we even did a few projects together.'

She rose, either to show off the body or because she preferred to serve herself. From a cabinet in the corner she took out a decanter in the shape of a swan and poured its sapphire blue contents into a glass.

'Let me say first that I am sincerely upset about the way she died. It's terrifying to think that anyone could hate so much. I am in the same profession, and as much in the public eye. A kind of image, as Pandora was. If it happened to her . . .' She broke off, drank deeply. 'It could happen to me. One of the reasons I'm staying here with Justin until it's all resolved.'

'Take me through your movements on the night she was killed.'

Jerry's eyes widened. 'Am I a suspect? That's almost flattering.' She came back to the chair, drink in hand. After she sat, she folded up her exquisite legs in a way that made Feeney vibrate beside Eve. 'I never had the guts to do more than give her a few verbal shots. Half the time she didn't even know I was zinging her. Pandora wasn't exactly a mental giant and never understood subtlety. All right then.'

She sat back, closed her eyes, and told basically the same story as Justin had, though she had, apparently, tuned in more closely on the altercation between Pandora and Mavis.

'I have to admit, I was cheering her on. The little one, not Pandora. She had a style to her,' Jerry mused. 'Odd, memorable – somewhere between a waif and an Amazon. She was trying to hold her own, but Pandora would have mopped the floor with her if Justin and Paul hadn't stopped it. Pandora was really strong. She was always in the health club working on muscle tone. I once saw her literally throw a fashion consultant across the room because the poor sap had mislabeled her accessories before a showing.'

She waved that off, opened a drawer on the brass table beside her, and located an enameled box. She took out a glossy red cigarette, lighted it, blew out perfumed smoke. 'Anyway, the woman started off trying to reason with Pandora, make some sort of a deal with her over Leonardo. He's a designer. My take was Leonardo and the waif were an item and Pandora wasn't ready to cut him loose. He's got a show coming up.'

She smiled that cat's smile again. 'With Pandora gone, I'll have to throw him my support.'

'You weren't involved in the show before?'

'Pandora was headlining. I said Pandora and I had done a few projects together. A couple of videos. Her problem was, she had looks, even presence, but when she had to read someone else's lines or try for charming on screen, she was an oak. Wooden. Just awful. But I'm good.' She paused to let more smoke stream through her lips. 'Really good, and I'm concentrating on my acting work. But . . . stepping in on this show, with this designer, will be a nice boost for me mediawise. That sounds callous. Sorry.' She shrugged. 'It's life.'

'Her death comes at an opportune moment for you.'

'When I see an opportunity, I take it. I don't kill for it.' She moved her shoulders again. 'That was more Pandora's style.'

Now she leaned forward, and her bodice gaped carelessly. 'Look, let's not play games. I'm clear. I was with Justin all night, didn't see her after about midnight. I can be honest, tell you I couldn't stand her, that she was certainly a professional rival, and that I knew that she'd have liked to lure Justin away from me just for spite. And maybe she could have done it. I don't kill over men, either.' She warmed Feeney with a glance. 'There are so many charming ones out there. And the simple fact is, you couldn't fit all the people who detested her into this apartment. I'm just one of the crowd.'

'What was her mood on the night she died?'

'Razzed and jazzed.' In a quick change of mood, Jerry threw back her head and laughed lustily. 'I don't know what she'd been knocking back, but it sure as hell put a glint in her eye. She was on fast forward.'

'Ms Fitzgerald,' Feeney began in slow, apologetic tones, 'you believed Pandora had ingested an illegal?'

She hesitated a moment, then moved her alabaster shoulders. 'Nothing legal makes you feel that good, honey. Or that mean. And she was feeling good and mean. Whatever it was, she was chasing it with champagne by the bucket-load.'

'Were you and the other guests offered illegal substances while you were there?' Eve asked.

'She didn't invite me to share. But then, she knew I didn't use. My body's a temple.' She smiled as Eve's glance focused on her glass. 'Protein drink, Lieutenant. Pure protein. And this?' She waved her slim cigarette. 'Veggie, with a lace of perfectly legal calmer, for my nerves. I've watched a lot of the mighty fall, taking a short, fast trip. I'm in for the long haul. I allow myself three herbal smokes a day, an occasional glass of wine. No chemical stimulants, no happy pills. On the other hand . . .' She set her drink aside. 'Pandora was a champion user. She'd gulp down anything.'

'Do you know the name of her supplier?'

'Never thought to ask her. Just wasn't interested. But at a guess, I'd say this was something new. I've never seen her so powered up, and though it pains me to say it, she looked better, younger. Skin tone and texture. She had, well, a glow on. If I didn't know better, I'd say she'd had a full treatment, but we both use Paradise. I know she wasn't in the salon that day, because I was. Anyway, I asked her, and she just smiled and said she'd found a new beauty secret, and she was going to make a pile on it.'

★   ★   ★

'Interesting,' Feeney commented when he plopped back down in Eve's car. 'We talked to two of the three people who last socialized with the victim. Neither of them could stand her.'

'They could have done it together,' Eve mused. 'Fitzgerald knew Leonardo, wanted to work with him. Simplest thing in the world to alibi each other.'

Feeney tapped his pocket where he'd slipped the security discs from the building. 'We'll run these, see what we find. Still seems to me we're missing motive. Whoever took her out didn't just want to kill her, they wanted to erase her. We've got a powerful kind of rage here. Didn't seem to me either one of those two would work up a sweat.'

'Push the right buttons, everybody sweats. I want to swing by ZigZag, see if we can start pinning down Mavis's moves. And we need to contact the producer, set up an interview. Can you put one of your drones on the car companies, Feeney? I can't see our heroine taking the subway or a bus downtown to Leonardo's.'

'Sure.' He took out his communicator. 'If she took a cab or a private transpo service, we should be able to nail it down in a couple hours.'

'Good. And let's see if she made the trip alone, or if she had company.'

ZigZag didn't do much hopping in the middle of the day. It lived for night. The sunlight crowd were mostly tourists or the harried urban professionals who didn't much care if the decor looked tawdry and the service was surly. The club was like a carnival that glittered at night, and showed its age and its flaws in the harsh light of day. Still, it maintained that underlying mystique that drew crowds of dreamers.

There was a steady drone of music, which would be cranked up to ear-splitting once the sun set. The open, two-level structure was dominated by five bars and twin revolving dance floors that would begin their circuit at nine P.M. Now they were still, stacked one over the other, the clear floors scarred from the beatings of nightly feet.

The lunch offerings ran to sandwiches and salads, all named after dead rockers. Today's special was peanut butter and banana on white, with a side of vidalia onions and jalapenos. The Elvis and Joplin combo.

Eve settled with Feeney at the first bar, ordered black coffee, and sized up the bartender. She was human rather than the usual droid. In fact, Eve hadn't noticed any droids employed in the club.

'You ever work the night shift?' Eve asked her.

'Nope. I'm a day worker.' The bartender set Eve's coffee on the bar. She was the perky kind, one who looked more like the front woman for a health food chain than a drink swiller at a club.

'Who's on the ten to three who notices people, remembers them?'

'Nobody around here notices people, if they can help it.'

Eve took out her badge, laid it on the bar. 'Would this clear somebody's memory?'

'Couldn't say.' Unconcerned, she shrugged. 'Look, this is a clean joint. I've got a kid at home, which is why I work days and why I was fussy about where I took a job. I checked this place out through and through before I hooked up. Dennis, he runs a friendly club, which is why you've got servers with pulses instead of chips. It might get a little wild, but he keeps the lid on.'

'Who is Dennis, and where do I find him?'

'His office is up the twisty stairs to your right, behind the first bar. He owns the place.'

'Hey, Dallas. We could take a minute for some eats,' Feeney complained as he walked behind her. 'The Mick Jagger sounded worth a try.'

'Get him to go.'

The bar wasn't open on this level, but obviously Dennis had been alerted. A mirrored panel slid aside, and he stood there, a slight, ascetic-faced man with a pointed red beard and a monk's circle of raven black hair.

'Officers, welcome to ZigZag.' His voice was whisper quiet. 'Is there a problem?'

'We'd like your help and cooperation, Mr . . .?'

'Dennis, just Dennis. Too many names are unwieldy.' He ushered them inside. The carnival atmosphere ended at the threshold. The office was spartan, streamlined, and quiet as a church. 'My sanctuary,' he said, well aware of the contrast. 'One can't enjoy nor can one appreciate the pleasures of noise and crowds and tangling humanity unless one experiences its opposite. Please sit.'

Eve took a chance on a stern-looking, straight-backed chair while Feeney eased himself into its mate. 'We're trying to verify the movements of one of your customers last night.'

'For?'

'Official reasons.'

'I see.' Dennis sat behind a slab of high-gloss plastic that served as his desk. 'And the time?'

'After eleven, before one.'

'Open screen.' At his order, a section of the wall slid open to reveal a viewer. 'Replay security scan five, begin eleven P.M.'

The screen, and the room, erupted with sound and color and movement. For an instant it dazzled the eye, then Eve focused. It was an overview of the club in full swing. A rather lordly view, she mused, as if the watcher soared quietly over the heads of the celebrants.

It suited Dennis down to the ground.

He smiled, judging her reaction. 'Delete audio.' Abruptly, silence descended. Now the movement seemed unworldly. Dancers gyrated on the circling floors, lights flashed over their faces, catching expressions, intense, joyful, feral. A couple at a corner table snarled at each other, body action clearly demonstrating an argument in progress. At another, a mating ritual with soulful looks and intimate touches.

Then she spotted Mavis. Alone.

'Can you enhance?' Eve rose, jabbed a finger to the center left of the screen.

'Of course.'

Frowning, Eve watched Mavis brought closer, clearer. It was, according to the time display, twenty-three forty-five. There was a bruise already darkening under Mavis's eye. And when she turned her head to brush off an advance, the signs of raw scratches on her neck. But not her face, Eve noted with a sinking heart. The bright blue drape she wore was torn a bit at the shoulder, but it was still attached.

She watched Mavis flick off a couple of other men, then a woman. She downed her drink, set the glass down beside a matching pair of empty ones on her table. She listed a bit as she rose, balanced herself, then with the exaggerated dignity of the greatly impaired, Mavis elbowed her way through the crowd.

The time was twenty-four eighteen.

'Is that what you were looking for?'

'More or less.'

'Disengage video.' Dennis smiled. 'The woman in question comes in the club from time to time. She is usually more sociable, enjoys dancing. Occasionally she will sing. I find her a different sort of talent, and certainly a crowd pleaser. Do you need her name?'

'I know who she is.'

'Well then.' He rose. 'I hope Miss Freestone isn't in any trouble. She looked unhappy.'

'I can get a warrant for a copy of that disc, or you can give me one.'

Dennis lifted a bright red eyebrow. 'I'll be happy to give you one. Computer, copy disc and label. Is there anything else I can do for you?'

'No, not at this time.' Eve accepted the disc and slipped it into her bag. 'Thanks for your cooperation.'

'Cooperation is the glue of life,' he said as the panel slid shut behind them.

'Weird-o,' Feeney decided.

'An efficient one. You know, Mavis could have gotten into a tussle while she was club hopping. She could have gotten her face scratched, her clothes torn.'

'Yeah.' Determined to eat, Feeney stopped at an order table and requested a Jagger to go. 'You ought to put something in your system, Dallas, besides worry and work.'

'I'm fine. I'm not much on the club scene, but if she had it in the back of her mind to go see Leonardo, she'd have walked south and east from here. Let's check out what her most likely stop would have been.'

'Fine. Just hold on.' He made her wait until his takeout slid through the serving slot. He had the clear wrap off and the first bite in by the time they got to the car. 'Damn good stuff. Always did like Jagger.'

'Hell of a way to live forever.' She started to request a map when her car 'link beeped, signaling incoming transmission. 'Lab report,' she murmured and focused on the screen. 'Oh, goddamn it.'

'Hell, Dallas, this is a mess.' Appetite gone, Feeney stuffed the sandwich in his pocket. Both of them fell into silence.

The report was very clear. It was Mavis's skin, and only Mavis's, under the victim's nails. Mavis's prints, and only Mavis's, on the murder weapon. And it was her blood, and only hers, mixed with the victim's on scene.

The 'link beeped again, and this time a face appeared on screen. 'Prosecuting Attorney Jonathan Heartly, Lieutenant Dallas.'

'Acknowledged.'

'We're issuing an arrest warrant for Freestone, Mavis, charge of murder, second degree. Please hold for transmission.'

'Didn't waste any time,' Feeney grumbled.

7

She wanted to do it alone. Had to do it alone. She could count on Feeney to work on ferreting out any details that might weaken the case against Mavis. But the job had to be done, and she had to do it herself.

Still, she was glad when Roarke opened the door.

'I can see it in your face.' And he took her face in his hands. 'I'm sorry, Eve.'

'I have a warrant. I have to take her in, book her. There's nothing else I can do.'

'I know. Come here.' He gathered her close, held her as she burrowed her face in his shoulder. 'We'll find the piece of this that clears her, Eve.'

'Nothing I've found, nothing, Roarke, helps her. Everything makes it worse. The evidence, it's all there. The motive's there, the timing.' She drew back. 'If I didn't know her, I wouldn't have a doubt.'

'But you do know her.'

'She's going to be scared.' Frightened herself, Eve looked up the stairs, toward where Mavis would be waiting. 'The PA's office told me they wouldn't block bail, but still, she's going to need . . . Roarke, I hate to ask you—'

'You don't have to. I've already contacted the best criminal defense team in the country.'

'I can't pay you back for that.'

'Eve—'

'I don't mean the money.' She took a shuddering breath and gripped both of his hands. 'You don't really know her, but you believe in her because I do. That's what I can't pay you back for. I have to go get her.'

'You want to do it alone.' He understood, and had already convinced himself not to argue the point. 'I'll alert her lawyers. What are the charges?'

'Murder two. I'll have to deal with the media. It's certainly going to leak that Mavis and I have history.' She pulled her hands through her disordered hair. 'That may bleed over onto you.'

'Do you think that worries me?'

She nearly smiled. 'No, I guess not. This may take awhile. I'll bring her back as soon as I can.'

'Eve,' he murmured as she started up the stairs. 'She believes in you, too. There's good reason for it.'

'I hope you're right.' Bracing herself, she continued up, walked slowly down the corridor to Mavis's room, and knocked.

'Come on in, Summerset. I told you I'd come down for the cake. Oh.' Surprised, Mavis leaned back from the computer where she'd been struggling to write a new song. To cheer herself up, she'd worn a skin suit of bright sapphire and had dyed her hair to match. 'I thought it was Summerset.'

'And cake.'

'Yeah, he buzzed in and told me the cook had baked a triple chocolate fudge cake. Summerset knows I've got this weakness. I know the two of you don't get along, but he's really sweet to me.'

'That's because he keeps imagining you naked.'

'Whatever works.' She began to tap her tricolored nails on the console in a quick, nervous tattoo. 'Anyway he's been great. I guess if he thought I had my eye on Roarke, it'd be different. He's like totally devoted. You'd think Roarke was his first and only born or something instead of his boss. That's the only reason he gives you grief – well, and you being a cop doesn't help. I think Summerset has this block about cops.'

She broke off, trembled visibly. 'I'm sorry, Dallas, I'm babbling. I'm so scared. You found Leonardo, didn't you? Something's really, really wrong. He's hurt, isn't he? He's dead.'

'No, he's not hurt.' Eve crossed the room and sat on the foot of the bed. 'He came into the cop shop this morning. He had a cut on his arm, that's all. The two of you had pretty much the same idea last night. He got tanked and headed for your place, ended up cutting his arm on an empty bottle he dropped before he keeled.'

'He was drunk?' Mavis sprang up at that. 'He hardly ever drinks. He knows he can't. He told me how he does things he can't remember if he drinks too much. It scares him, and . . . To my place,' she said, eyes softening. 'That's so

112

sweet. Then he came to see you because he couldn't find me.'

'He came to see me to confess to the murder of Pandora.'

Mavis reared back as if Eve had struck her. 'That's impossible. Leonardo wouldn't hurt anyone. He's just not capable of it. He was just trying to protect me.'

'He didn't know anything about your involvement at that time. He believes he must have argued with Pandora, fought with her, then killed her.'

'Well, that's absolutely wrong.'

'So the evidence indicates.' Eve rubbed her weary eyes, kept her fingers pressed there for a moment. 'The cut on his arm came from a piece of the broken bottle. None of his blood was found at the scene, none of Pandora's was on the clothes he'd been wearing. We haven't pinned down his movements precisely as yet, but we don't have anything on him.'

Mavis missed a beat, caught up. 'Oh, then it's all right. You didn't believe him.'

'I haven't decided that, but the evidence, at this point, keeps him clear.'

'Thank God.' Mavis slid down onto the bed beside Eve. 'When can I see him, Dallas? Leonardo and I have to work things out between us.'

'That may take a little time.' Eve squeezed her eyes shut, opened them again, made herself look at Mavis. 'I have to ask you for a favor, the biggest anyone's ever asked you.'

'Is it going to hurt?'

'Yeah.' Eve watched Mavis's attempt at a smile fade away. 'I have to ask you to trust me to take care of you. To believe that I'm so good at my job that nothing, however small, will get past me. I have to ask you to remember you're my closest friend, and that I love you.'

Mavis's breath started to jerk. Her eyes stayed dry, burning dry. The saliva evaporated from her mouth. 'You're going to arrest me.'

'The lab reports came in.' She caught Mavis's hands, held them hard in hers. 'They weren't a surprise, because I knew someone had set things up. I was expecting this, Mavis. I hoped I could find something – anything – before it did, but I haven't been able to. Feeney's working on it, too. He's the best, Mavis, trust me here. And Roarke's already lined up the top defense lawyers known to man. It's just procedure.'

'You have to arrest me for murder.'

'It's murder two. That's a small break. I know it doesn't sound like one, but the PA's office isn't going to try to block bail. I'll have you back here eating cake in a few hours.'

But Mavis's mind was replaying one segment, over and over. *It's murder two. It's murder two.* 'You have to put me in a cage.'

Eve's lungs were burning, and the sensation was rapidly moving toward her heart. 'Not for long. I swear it. Feeney's working right now to get the preliminary hearing up and running. He's got plenty of markers he can pull in. By the time we've got you through booking, you'll have the hearing, the judge will set bail, and you'll be back here.'

Wearing an ident alarm to track her movements, Eve thought. Trapped in the house to avoid the stalking media. The cage would be plush and friendly, but it would still be a cage.

'You make it sound easy.'

'It's not going to be easy, but it'll be easier if you remember you've got a couple of top cops on your side. Don't waive any of your rights, okay? Any of them. And once we start this, you wait for your lawyers. Don't say anything to me you don't have to say. Don't say anything to anyone. Understand me?'

'All right.' Mavis drew her hands away, rose. 'Let's get it over with.'

Hours later, when it was done, Eve stepped back into the house. The lights were low. She hoped Mavis had taken the tranq Eve had recommended and gone to sleep. Eve already knew she wouldn't do the same.

She knew Feeney would have followed her request to pass Mavis personally over to Roarke. There had been other work to do. The press conference had been particularly hideous. As expected, questions about her friendship with Mavis had been brought up, conflict of interest hinted at. She owed the commander a great deal for the appearance he'd put in and his statement of absolute faith in his primary investigator.

The one on one with Nadine Furst had been a little easier. *All you had to do,* Eve thought glumly as she climbed the stairs, *was save a person's life, and they were happy to take your side.* The blood lust for the story might have been in Nadine's heart, but so was a sense of debt. Mavis would get fair treatment from Channel 75.

Then Eve had done something she had never believed she would do. She had voluntarily called the police psychiatrist and made an appointment to talk with Dr Mira.

Could still cancel it, she reminded herself and rubbed her gritty eyes. *Probably will cancel it.*

'You're quite late, Lieutenant, after an eventful day.'

She dropped her hands and saw Summerset step silently out of a room to her right. He was, as usual, dressed in his stiff black, his stern face set in disapproving lines. Hating her seemed to be something he did with almost as much seamless skill as he ran the household.

'Don't hassle me, Summerset.'

He stepped directly into her path. 'I had believed, though you have countless flaws, you were, at least, a competent investigator. I see now, you are not, any more than you are a competent friend to one who depended on you.'

'You really think after what I've been through tonight that you can say anything to touch me?'

'I don't believe anything touches you, Lieutenant. You're without loyalty and that makes you nothing. Less than nothing.'

'Maybe you've got a suggestion of how I could have

handled it. Maybe I should have had Roarke fire up one of his JetStars and shoot Mavis off planet to some remote little hideaway. Then she could be on the run for the rest of her life.'

'At least then she might not have wept herself to sleep.'

The arrow pierced, directly under the heart where it had been aimed. Pain shimmered through fatigue. 'Get out of my way, you bastard, and keep out of my way.' She shoved by him, but stopped herself from running. She walked into the master bedroom just as Roarke was replaying her press conference on screen.

'You did well here,' he said and rose. 'Under tremendous pressure.'

'Yeah, I'm a real pro.' She walked into the bathroom, then stood staring at herself in the mirror. She saw a woman, pale face, dark, shadowed eyes, grim mouth. And she saw beyond it to helplessness.

'You're doing everything you can,' Roarke said quietly from behind her.

'You got her good lawyers.' Ordering water cold, she leaned down, splashed it liberally over her face. 'They juggled me through Interview. I was tough. Gotta be tough. But they've got some moves on them. Next time I've got to grill a friend, I'll be sure to sign them up.'

He watched her bury her face in a towel. 'When's the last time you've eaten?'

She merely shook her head. The question had no relevance. 'The reporters were out for blood. Someone like

117

me's very juicy game. Couple of high-profile cases, I come out on top. Some of them would just love to see me take it between the eyes. Think of the ratings.'

'Mavis doesn't blame you, Eve.'

'I blame me,' she exploded, heaving the towel aside. 'I blame me, goddamn it. I told her to trust me, I told her I'd take care of things. How did I take care of it, Roarke? I arrested her, I booked her. Prints, mug shots, voice ident, all of it on file now. I put her through a horrible two-hour interview. I locked her in a cell until the lawyers you hired for her got her out on bail you posted. I hate myself.'

She broke, simply broke. Covering her face with her hands, she began to sob.

'It's about time you let go.' Briskly, he scooped her into his arms and carried her up to the bed. 'You'll feel better for it.' He kept her cradled in his arms, stroked her hair. Whenever she cried, he thought, it was a storm, a passionate tumult. Rarely were there a few easy, quiet tears for Eve. Rarely was anything easy for Eve.

'This isn't helping,' she managed.

'Yes, it is. You'll purge some of that misplaced guilt and some of the grief you're entitled to. You'll think more clearly tomorrow.'

She was down to shuddering breaths and a raging headache. 'I have to work tonight. I'm going to run some names and scenarios for probability.'

No, he thought quite calmly, *she won't.* 'Take a minute. Get something to eat.' Before she could protest, he was shifting her aside and moving to the AutoChef. 'Even your admirable system needs fuel. And there's a story I want to tell you.'

'I can't waste time.'

'It won't be wasted.'

Fifteen minutes, she thought, as the scent of something glorious wafted toward her. 'Let's make it a quick meal and a short story, okay?' She rubbed at her eyes, not sure if she was ashamed or relieved to have let the cork pop and spew out the tears. 'Sorry I blubbered on you.'

'I'm always available for blubbering.' He came toward her with a steaming omelette and a cup. He sat down, stared into her swollen, exhausted eyes. 'I adore you.'

She flushed. It seemed he was the only one who could bring embarrassed color to her cheeks. 'You're trying to distract me.' She took the plate and a fork. 'That kind of stuff always does, and I can never get my tongue around what I should say back.' She sampled the eggs. 'Maybe something like you're the best thing that ever happened to me.'

'That'll do.'

She lifted the cup, started to sip, then scowled. 'This isn't coffee.'

'It's tea, for a change. A soothing blend. I imagine you're overloaded on caffeine.'

'Maybe.' Because the eggs were fabulous and she didn't have the energy to argue, she took a sip. 'It's nice. Okay, what's the story?'

'You've wondered why I keep Summerset, even when he's . . . less than solicitous to you.'

She snorted. 'You mean even though he hates my fucking guts. Your business.'

'Our business,' he corrected.

'Anyway, I don't want to hear about him right now.'

'It's actually more about me, and an incident that you might find correlates with what you're feeling right now.' He watched her drink again, calculated he had just enough time to tell the tale. 'When I was very young, and still in Dublin on the street, I hooked up with a man and his daughter. The little girl was, well, an angel, gold and rose with the sweetest smile on either side of heaven. They ran confidence games, superbly. Short cons for the most part, bilking foolish marks and making a reasonable living. At that time, I was doing somewhat the same myself, but I liked variety, and enjoyed picking pockets and organizing floating games. My father was still alive when I met Summerset – though he didn't go by that name then – and his daughter, Marlena.'

'So, he was a con,' she said between bites. 'I knew there was something shifty about him.'

'He was quite brilliant. I learned a lot from him, and I like to think he from me. In any case, after one particularly enthusiastic beating from my dear old da, he happened to find me unconscious in an alley. He took me in. He took care of me. There was no money for a doctor, and I didn't have a medical card. What I did have was a few broken ribs, a concussion, and a fractured shoulder.'

'I'm sorry.' The image brought back others, ones that dried up the spit in her mouth. 'Life sucks.'

'It did. Summerset was a man of many talents. He had some medical training. He often used an MT disguise in his work. I wouldn't go so far as to say he saved my life. I was young and strong and used to it, but he certainly kept me from suffering needlessly.'

'You owe him.' Eve set the empty plate aside. 'I understand. It's all right.'

'No, that's not it. I owed him. I paid him back. There were times he owed me. After my father met his unmourned end, we became partners. Again, I wouldn't say he raised me, I took care of myself, but he gave me what might be considered a family. I loved Marlena.'

'The daughter.' She had to shake her head to clear it. 'I'd forgotten. Hard to picture that dried up old fart as a father. Where is she?'

'She's dead. She was fourteen. I was sixteen. We'd been together, more or less, for about six years. One of my gambling projects was turning a tidy profit, and it came to the attention and the disapproval of a small, particularly violent syndicate. They felt I was cutting into their territory. I felt I was carving out my own. They threatened. I was arrogant enough to ignore them. Once or twice they tried to get their hands on me, to teach me respect, I imagine. But I was difficult to catch. And I was gaining power, even prestige. I was certainly making money. Enough that between us we were able to buy a small, very decent flat. And somewhere along the way, Marlena fell in love with me.'

He paused, looking down at his own hands, remembering, regretting. 'I cared for her a great deal, but not as a lover. She was beautiful, and unbelievably innocent, despite the life we led. I didn't think of her romantically, but as a man – because I was a man already – might think of a perfect piece of art: romantically. Never sexually. She had different ideas, and one night she came into my room and rather sweetly, and terrifyingly, offered herself to me. I was appalled, furious, and scared to the bones. Because I was a man, and therefore, tempted.'

His lifted his gaze to Eve's again, and there was storm in them. 'I was cruel to her, Eve, and sent her away shattered. She was a child, and I devastated her. I've never forgotten the look on her face. She trusted me, believed in me, and I, by doing what was right, betrayed her.'

'The way I betrayed Mavis.'

'The way you're thinking you did. But there's more. She left the house that night. Summerset and I didn't know she was gone until the next day, the next morning when the men who wanted me sent word that they had her. They sent back the clothes she'd been wearing, and there was blood on them. For the first time in my life, and the last, I saw Summerset unable to function. I would have given them anything they demanded, done anything. I would

122

have traded myself for her without hesitation. Just as you, if you could, would trade places with Mavis now.'

'Yes.' Eve set the empty cup aside woozily. 'I'd do anything.'

'Sometimes anything comes too late. I contacted them, told them we would negotiate, begged them not to hurt her. But they had already hurt her. They had raped her and tortured her, this delightful fourteen-year-old girl who had found so much joy in life, and who was just beginning to feel what women feel. Within hours of that first contact, her body was dumped on my doorstep. They had used her as no more than a means to an end, to make a point to a competitor, an upstart. She wasn't even human to them, and there was nothing I could do to go back and change what had happened.'

'It wasn't your fault.' She reached out and took his hands. 'I'm sorry. So sorry, but it wasn't your fault.'

'No, it wasn't. It took me years to believe that, to understand and accept that. Summerset never blamed me, Eve. He could have. She was his life, and she had suffered and died because of me. But he never once blamed me.'

She sighed, closed her eyes. She knew what he was telling her, by repeating a tale that had to be a nightmare for him to relive. Neither was she to blame. 'You couldn't stop what happened. You could only control what happened after, the way I can only do everything I can to find the answers.' Wearily, she opened her eyes again. 'What did happen after, Roarke?'

'I hunted down the men who had done it, and I killed them, in as slow and as painful a method as I could devise.' He smiled. 'We each have our own way of finding solutions and justice, Eve.'

'Vigilantism isn't justice.'

'Not for you. But you'll find the solution and justice for Mavis. No one doubts it.'

'I can't let her stand trial.' Her head lolled; she snapped it back. 'I have to find . . . I need to go . . .' She couldn't even lift her weighted arm to her head. 'Damn it, Roarke, damn it, that was a tranq.'

'Go to sleep,' he murmured and gently unhooked her weapon harness and set it aside. 'Lie back.'

'Inducing chemicals on unknowing people is a violation of . . .' She slipped deeper, barely felt him unbutton her shirt.

'Arrest me in the morning,' he suggested. He undressed her, then himself, before slipping into bed beside her. 'Just sleep now.'

She slept, but even there, dreams chased her.

8

She did not wake up cheerful. She did wake alone, which was probably a wise move on Roarke's part, but she didn't surface with a smile. There were no aftereffects from the tranq, which made him a very lucky man. She woke alert, refreshed, and pissed.

The electronic memo beeping its red light on the nightstand didn't improve the mood. Nor did Roarke's smooth voice when she engaged it.

'Good morning, Lieutenant. Hope you slept well. If you're up before eight, you'll find me in the breakfast nook. I didn't want to disturb you by ordering up. You looked so peaceful.'

'Not for long,' she said between gritted teeth. She managed to shower, dress, and strap on her weapon in ten minutes flat.

The breakfast nook, as he charmingly called it, was a huge, sunny atrium off the kitchen. Not only was Roarke there, but so was Mavis. Both of them beamed blindingly as Eve strode in.

'We're going to get a couple things straight here, Roarke.'

'Your color's back.' Pleased with himself, he rose and

nipped a kiss onto the tip of her nose. 'That gray cast to your skin didn't suit you.' Then he grunted as her fist jammed into his stomach. He cleared his throat manfully. 'Your energy level's obviously up, too. Want coffee?'

'I want you to know that if you ever pull a stunt like that again, I'll . . .' She trailed off, narrowed her eyes at Mavis. 'What are you grinning at?'

'It's fun to watch. You two are so tipped over each other.'

'So tipped he's going to end up on his back checking out the ceiling if he doesn't watch out.' But she continued to study Mavis, baffled. 'You look . . . fine,' she decided.

'I am. I had a good cry, a big bag of Swiss chocolates, and then I stopped feeling sorry for myself. I've got the number-one cop in the city working on my side, the best team of lawyers a billionaire can buy, and a guy who loves me. See, I figured out that when this is all over, and it's going to work out, I'll be able to look back on it as kind of an adventure. And with all the media attention, my career's going to soar.'

Reaching up, she took Eve's hand and tugged her down on the padded bench. 'I'm not scared anymore.'

Not willing to take the words to heart, Eve looked hard and long into Mavis's eyes. 'You're really not. You're really okay. I can see it.'

'I'm fine now. I thought about it, and thought about it. When it all shakes down, it's pretty simple. I didn't kill her. You'll find out who did, and when you do, it'll all be over. Until then, I get to live in this incredible house, eat incred-

126

ible food.' She forked up a last bite of a paper-thin crepe. 'And have my name and face splashed all over the media.'

'That's one way of looking at it.' Uneasy, Eve rose to program coffee for herself. 'Mavis, I don't want you to worry or be upset, but this isn't going to be a glide through the park.'

'I'm not stupid, Dallas.'

'I didn't mean—'

'You're thinking I'm not aware of the worst that could happen. I am, but I just don't believe the worst is going to happen. From now on, I'm thinking positive, and I'm giving you that favor you asked me to give you yesterday.'

'Okay. We've got a lot of work to do. I want you to concentrate, try to remember details. Any detail, no matter how small or insignificant— What's this?' she demanded as Roarke set a bowl in front of her.

'Your breakfast.'

'It's oatmeal.'

'Exactly.'

She frowned at it. 'Why can't I have one of those crepes?'

'You can, after you eat your oatmeal.'

Eyes hot, she shoveled in a mouthful. 'We're really going to talk.'

'You guys are great together. I'm really glad I've had this chance to see it up close and personal. Not that I didn't think it was great all along, but mostly I was just jazzed that Dallas had landed a rich one.' Mavis beamed at Roarke.

'That's what friends are for.'

'Yeah, but it's so mag the way you keep her in line. Nobody ever could before.'

'Shut up, Mavis. You think, and think hard, but you don't tell me anything until you've cleared it with your lawyers.'

'They already advised me of that. I figure it's going to work just like it does when I'm trying to remember a name or where I put something. You stop thinking about it, start doing other stuff, then zip, it pops into your head. So, I'm doing other stuff, and the big one is the wedding. Leonardo said you need to do your first fitting very soon.'

'Leonardo?' Eve all but lunged out of the chair. 'You've been talking to Leonardo?'

'The lawyers cleared it. They think it's a good thing for us to resume our relationship. It adds a sympathy and romance factor in the public awareness.' Mavis leaned an elbow on the table and began to toy with the trio of earrings she'd hung in her left lobe. 'You know, they only ditched the truth detection test and hypnosis because they can't be sure what I'll remember. They mostly believe me, but they can't take chances. But they said seeing Leonardo is cool. So we need to set up that fitting.'

'I don't have time to think about fittings. Christ, Jesus, Mavis, you think I'm going to fuss with designs and flowers now? I'm not getting married until this is cleared up. Roarke understands that.'

Roarke took out a cigarette, studied it. 'No, he doesn't.'

'Now, listen—'

'No, you listen.' Mavis stood up, her bright blue hair

glinting in the sunlight. 'I'm not letting this mess screw up something this important to me. Pandora did her best to fuck with my life and Leonardo's. And she did worse by dying. She is not going to fuck with this. These plans are not on hold, Dallas, and you just better make time in your schedule for the fitting.'

She couldn't argue, not with the sheen of tears in Mavis's eyes. 'Okay, fine. Great. I'll deal with the stupid dress.'

'It's not a stupid dress. It's going to be a sensational dress.'

'That's what I meant.'

'Better.' She sniffed, sat. 'When can I tell him we'll get together for it?'

'Ah . . . listen. It's better for your case, and your fancy lawyers would back me up, if you and I aren't seen running around together. Primary investigator and defendant. It doesn't look good.'

'You mean I can't—' Mavis shut her mouth, regrouped. 'All right then, we won't go running around together. Leonardo can work here. Roarke won't mind, will you?'

'On the contrary.' He took a satisfied drag on his cigarette. 'I think it's a perfect solution.'

'One big happy family,' Eve mumbled. 'The primary, the defendant, and the tenant of the murder scene, who also happens to be the victim's former lover and the defendant's current. Are you all insane?'

'Who's to know? Roarke has excellent security. And if there's even the smallest chance that things could go wrong, I want to spend whatever time I can with Leonardo.' Mavis set her mouth in a stubborn pout. 'So that's what I'm going to do.'

'I'll have Summerset arrange for a work space.'

'Thanks. We appreciate it.'

'While you people orchestrate your mad tea party, I've got a murder to solve.'

Roarke winked at Mavis and called after Eve as she stormed away, 'What about your crepe?'

'Stuff it.'

'She's crazy about you,' Mavis commented.

'It's almost embarrassing, the way she fawns. Want another crepe?'

Mavis patted her stomach. 'Why the hell not?'

A downed circuit at Ninth and Fifty-sixth played hell with street traffic. Both pedestrians and drivers ignored the noise pollution laws and honked, shouted, and buzzed out their frustrations. Eve would have rolled up her windows to cut the din, but her temperature controls were on the fritz again.

To add to the fun, Mother Nature had decided to body slam New York with a humature of a hundred and ten. To pass the time, Eve watched the heat waves dance up from the concrete. At this rate, more than a few computer chips were going to fry by noon.

She considered taking to the air, though her control panel seemed to have developed a mind of its own. But several other harried drivers had already done so. The traffic overhead was in a nasty snarl. A couple of one-man traffic copters were trying to deal with it and instead added to the mess with the bee swarm buzz of their blades and the irritating drone of voices.

She caught herself snarling at the i love new york hologram sticker on the bumper jammed in front of hers.

The sanest idea, she decided, was to get some work done in her car.

'Peabody,' she ordered the 'link, and after a few frustrating hisses of static, it engaged.

'Peabody. Homicide.'

'Dallas here. I'm going to pick you up in front of the Cop Shop, west side. ETA, fifteen minutes.'

'Yes, sir.'

'Bring all files pertinent to the Johannsen case and the Pandora case, and be . . .' She trailed off and squinted at the screen. 'Why is it so quiet in there, Peabody? Aren't you in the bull pen?'

'Only a couple of us made it in this morning. There's a bad traffic snag on Ninth.'

Eve scanned the sea of traffic. 'Is that a fact?'

'It pays to listen to the traffic network in the morning,' she added. 'I took an alternate route.'

'Shut up, Peabody,' Eve muttered and broke transmission. She spent the next couple of minutes retrieving messages from her desk 'link, then set up a morning appointment at Paul Redford's office in midtown for an interview. She called the lab to harass them for the toxicology report on

Pandora, got the runaround, and left them with a creative threat.

She was debating whether to call Feeney and nag him when she saw a narrow break in the wall of cars. She jogged forward, cut left, squeezed through, ignoring the rude blast of horns and spearing middle fingers. Praying her vehicle would cooperate, she punched vertical. Rather than spring up, she wavered, but she did rise the minimum ten feet.

She swerved right, nipped by a jammed people glide where she caught the blur of miserable, sweaty faces, and rattled over to Seventh while her control panel warned of overload. After five blocks, the car was wheezing, but she'd cleared the worst of the jam. She set down with a teeth-rattling thud and swung toward the west entrance of Cop Central.

The dependable Peabody was waiting. How the woman managed to look cool and unperturbed in her sweltering blues, Eve didn't want to know.

'Your vehicle sounds a little rough, Lieutenant,' Peabody commented when she climbed in.

'Really? I didn't notice.'

'You sound a little rough yourself. Sir.' When Eve merely bared her teeth and started to cut across town to Fifth, Peabody dug into her kit, took out a small porta-fan, and clipped it to the dash. The blast of cool air nearly made Eve whimper.

'Thanks.'

'The temperature control on this model isn't dependable.' Peabody's face remained smooth and bland. 'But you probably haven't noticed.'

'You've got a clever mouth, Peabody. I like that about you. Give me a rundown on Johannsen.'

'The lab's still having trouble with all the elements in the powder we found. They're stalling. If they've completely analyzed the formula, they're not saying. The buzz I get from a contact I have is, Illegals is demanding priority, so there's some politicking going on. Second search found no trace of chemicals, illegal or otherwise, in the victim's body.'

'So he wasn't using,' Eve mused. 'Boomer tended to sample, but he had himself a big, fat bag of shit and didn't take a taste. What does that tell you, Peabody?'

'From the state of his flop and the statement of the lobby droid, we know he had the time and opportunity to use it. He had a history of chronic if mild abuse. Therefore, my deduction would be he knew or suspected something about the substance that put him off.'

'That would be my guess. What do you get from Casto?'

'He claims to be in the dark on this one. He's been co-operative, if not overly forthcoming, with information and theories.'

Something in the tone had Eve glancing over. 'He coming on to you, Peabody?'

Peabody kept her eyes straight forward, narrowed slightly under the bowl-cut fringe of bangs. 'He hasn't exhibited any inappropriate behavior.'

'Cut the drill, pal, that's not what I asked.'

Color snuck up under the collar of the standard-issue blues into her cheeks. 'He's indicated a certain personal interest.'

'Jesus, you sound like a cop. Is this certain personal interest reciprocated?'

'It might be considered, if I didn't suspect the subject had a much more personal interest in my immediate superior.' Peabody slid her gaze to Eve's. 'He's got a thing for you.'

'Well, he'll have to keep his thing to himself.' But she couldn't make herself completely displeased to hear it. 'My certain personal interests lie elsewhere. He's a powerful looking sonofabitch, isn't he?'

'My tongue gets all swelled up in my mouth when he looks at me.'

'Hmm.' Eve ran her own around her teeth experimentally. 'So go for it.'

'I'm not prepared to become involved in a romantic relationship at this point.'

'Hell, who said anything about relationship? Screw each other blind a couple times.'

'I prefer affection and companionship in sexual encounters,' Peabody said stiffly. 'Sir.'

'Yeah. It does make a difference.' Eve sighed. It was almost a painful effort to keep her mind from leapfrogging back to Mavis, but she tried to focus. 'I was just ragging on you, Peabody. I know what it's like when you're standing there, trying to do your job, and some guy hits you between the eyes. I'm sorry if you're uncomfortable working with him, but I need you.'

'It's not a problem.' Loosening up, Peabody smiled. 'And it's not exactly a sacrifice to look at him.' She glanced up as Eve swung toward the underground parking beneath a spearing white tower on Fifth. 'Isn't this one of Roarke's buildings?'

'Most of them are.' The electronic attendant scanned her vehicle and passed it through. 'This is his main office. It's also the New York base of Redford Productions. I've got an interview with him re the Pandora homicide.' Eve slipped into the VIP spot Roarke had arranged for her, shut down her car. 'You're not officially attached to this case, but you're officially attached to me. Feeney's up to his ass in data, and I want another set of eyes and ears. Objections?'

'None come to mind, Lieutenant.'

'Dallas,' Eve reminded her as they stepped from the car. The safety barrier blinked on, surrounding the car to protect it from dings, scratches, and theft. As if, Eve thought sourly, it didn't already have so many dings and scratches a thief would insult himself by looking twice. She strode up to the private executive elevator, entered her code, and tried not to be embarrassed. 'Saves time,' she muttered.

Peabody's eyes widened as they stepped onto thick carpeting. The car was large enough for a party of six, and boasted a lush arrangement of fragrant hibiscus. 'I'm all for saving time.'

'Thirty-fifth floor,' Eve requested. 'Redford Productions, executive offices.'

'Floor three-five,' the computer acknowledged. 'East quadrant, executive level.'

'Pandora had a small party on the night she died,' Eve began. 'Redford might be the last person to have seen her alive. Jerry Fitzgerald and Justin Young also attended, but left early after Mavis Freestone and Pandora fought. They alibi each other for the rest of the night. Redford remained with Pandora for a time. If Fitzgerald and Young are telling the truth, they're in the clear. I know Mavis is telling the truth.' She waited a beat, but Peabody made no comment. 'So we see what we can shake out of the producer.'

The elevator smoothly shifted to horizontal, gliding east. The doors opened and noise poured in.

Obviously Redford's employees liked music with their daily grind. It rocked out of recessed speakers, filled the air with energy. Two men and a woman worked at a wide circular console, chatting cheerfully into 'links, beaming at computer screens.

There appeared to be a small party in progress in the waiting area to the right. Several people milled around drinking from small cups or nibbling on tiny pastries. The sound of tinkling laughter and cocktail hour conversation underscored the lively music.

'It's like a scene from one of his movies,' Peabody said.

'Hooray for Hollywood.' Eve approached the console and took out her badge. She chose the least obsessively pert of the three receptionists. 'Lieutenant Dallas. I have an appointment with Mr Redford.'

'Yes, Lieutenant.' The man – or he might have been a god with his perfectly chiseled golden looks – smiled brilliantly. 'I'll tell him you're here. Please help yourself to some refreshments.'

'Want to chow down, Peabody?'

'Those pastries look pretty good. We could cop some on the way out.'

'Our minds are in tune.'

'Mr Redford would love to see you now, Lieutenant.' The modern-day Apollo lifted a section of the console, slipped through. 'Just let me take you to him.'

He led them through smoked glass doors where the noise switched to clashing voices. On either side of the corridor, doors were open, and men and women sat at desks, paced, or reclined on sofas, wheeling and dealing.

'How many times have I heard that plot line, JT? It's so first millennium.'

'We need a fresh face. Garboesque with Little Bo Peep innocence.'

'People don't want depth, honeypot. Give 'em a choice between the ocean and a puddle, they're going to splash in the puddle. We're all children.'

They approached a pair of double doors in sparkling silver. The guide opened them both with a dramatic sweep. 'Your guests, Mr Redford.'

'Thank you, Caesar.'

137

'Caesar,' Eve muttered. 'I was so close.'

'Lieutenant Dallas.' Paul Redford rose from behind a U-shaped workstation in the same glittery silver as his doors. The floor he crossed was smooth as glass and decorated with swirls of color. Behind him was the expected spectacular view of the city. His hand clasped Eve's with easy, practiced warmth. 'Thank you so much for agreeing to come here. I'm juggling meetings all day and it's so much more convenient for me than coming to you.'

'It's not a problem. My aide, Officer Peabody.'

The smile, as smooth and practiced as the handshake, encompassed them both. 'Please sit down. What can I offer you?'

'Just information.' Eve glanced at the seating arrangement, blinked. They were all animals: chairs, stools, sofas, all fashioned to resemble tigers, hounds, or giraffes.

'My first wife was a decorator,' he explained. 'After the divorce, I decided to keep them. They're the best memory of that time in my life.' He chose a basset hound for himself, propped his feet up on a cushion shaped like a curled cat. 'You want to talk about Pandora.'

'Yes.' If they'd been lovers, as reported, Eve decided he'd gotten over his grief quickly. A police interview apparently didn't affect him, either. He was composed, the genial host in a five-thousand-dollar linen suit and melted-butter Italian loafers.

He was, Eve mused, undoubtedly as screen friendly as any of the actors he worked with. A strong, bony face the

138

color of fresh honey was accented with a well-trimmed, glossy moustache. His dark hair was slicked back and twisted into a complicated queue that dangled to his shoulder blades.

He looked, Eve decided, like what he was: a successful producer who enjoyed his power and wealth.

'I'd like to record this, Mr Redford.'

'I'd prefer that, Lieutenant.' He leaned back into the embrace of the sad-eyed hound and folded his hands on his stomach. 'I heard you've made an arrest in this matter.'

'We have. But the investigation is ongoing. You were acquainted with the deceased, known as Pandora.'

'Well acquainted. I was considering a project with her, certainly had socialized with her on a number of occasions over the years, and when it was convenient, had sex with her.'

'Were you and the victim lovers at the time of her death?'

'We were never lovers, Lieutenant. We had sex. We did not make love. In fact, I doubt there was a man alive who ever made love to her, or attempted to. If he did, he was a fool. I'm not a fool.'

'You didn't like her.'

'Like her?' Redford laughed. 'God, no. She was the singularly most dislikable human being I've ever known. But she did have talent. Not as much as she believed, and none at all in certain areas, and yet . . .'

He lifted his elegant hands; rings sparkled: dark stones in heavy gold. 'Beauty is easy, Lieutenant. Some are born with it, others buy it. An attractive physical shell is moronically simple to come by today. It's still desired. Pleasing looks never fade from fashion, but in order to make a living from those looks, a person has to have talent.'

'And Pandora's was?'

'An aura, a power, an elemental, even animalistic ability to exude sex. Sex has always, will always sell.'

Eve inclined her head. 'Only now we license it.'

Amused, Redford flashed her a smile. 'The government needs its revenue. But I wasn't referring to the selling of sex, but of using it to sell. And we do: everything from soft drinks to kitchen appliances. And fashion,' he added. 'Always fashion.'

'And that was Pandora's particular specialty.'

'You could drape her in kitchen curtains, point her toward a runway, and reasonably intelligent people would open their credit accounts wide to have that look. She was a saleswoman. There was nothing she couldn't peddle. She wanted to act, which was unfortunate. She could never be anyone but herself, but Pandora.'

'But you were working on a project with her.'

'I was considering one where she would essentially play herself. Nothing more, nothing less. It may have worked. And the merchandizing from it . . . well, that's where the profits would have poured in. It was still in the planning stages.'

'You were at her home the night she died.'

'Yes, she wanted company. And, I suspect, wanted to rub Jerry's nose in the idea of starring in one of my films.'

'And how did Ms Fitzgerald take it?'

'She was surprised, irritated, I imagine. I was irritated myself as we were far from ready to go public. We might have had an interesting scene over it, but we were interrupted. The young woman, the fascinating young woman who arrived on the doorstep. The one you've arrested,' he said with a gleam in his eye. 'The media claim you're very close friends.'

'Why don't you just tell me what happened when Ms Freestone arrived?'

'Melodrama, action, violence. Picture this,' he said and moved his hands to form the age-old sign for a screen. 'The young, brave beauty comes to plead her case. She's been weeping, her face is pale, her eyes desperate. She will step aside, give up the man both of them want, to protect him, to do what's best for his career.

'Close up on Pandora. Her face is filled with rage, disdain, a manic energy. Christ, the beauty. It's almost evil. She won't be satisfied with sacrifice. She wants her opponent to feel pain. Emotional pain first, by the cruel names she hurls, then physical pain by striking the first blow. Now you have the classic struggle. Two women locked in combat over a man. The younger woman has love on her side, but even that isn't a match for the strength of Pandora's vengeance. Or her sharpened nails. Fur, shall we say, flies, until the two male members of our fascinated audience step in. One of them is bitten for his pains.'

Redford winced and rubbed his right shoulder. 'Pandora

sank her fangs into me as I was dragging her off. I have to say I was tempted to punch her myself. Your friend left. She tossed off some typical cliche about Pandora being sorry, but she looked more miserable than vindictive.'

'And Pandora?'

'Energized.' And so was he with the telling of the tale. 'She'd been in a dangerous mood all evening, and it was only more treacherous after the bout. Jerry and Justin bowed out, with more dispatch than grace, and I stayed behind awhile to try to bring Pandora down.'

'Did you succeed?'

'I didn't come close. She was wild then. She threatened all manner of absurdities. She was going to go after the little bitch and rip her face off. She was going to castrate Leonardo. By the time she was finished, he wouldn't be able to peddle buttons on the street corner. Not even beggars were going to wear his rags, and so on. After about twenty minutes, I gave it up. She was furious with me then for cutting the evening short, and shouted a lot of abuse after me. She didn't need me, she had bigger deals, better deals.'

'You claim to have left her at about twelve thirty?'

'That would be close.'

'And she was alone?'

'She only kept domestic droids. She didn't like people around unless she summoned them. There was no one else in the house, to my knowledge.'

'Where did you go when you left?'

'I came here; tended to my shoulder. It was a nasty bite.

I thought I'd do a little work, made some calls to the coast. Then I went to my club, used the after-hours entrance, and spent a couple of hours having a steam, a swim.'

'What time did you get to your club?'

'I'd say it was around two. I know it was well past four when I got home.'

'Did you see or speak to anyone during the hours of two and five A.M.?'

'No. One of the reasons I often use the club at those hours is for the privacy. I have my own facilities on the coast, but here, I have to make do with membership.'

'The name of your club?'

'The Olympus, on Madison.' He arched a brow. 'I see my alibi isn't without its problems. I did, however, code in and out. It's required.'

'I'm sure it is.' And she would certainly see if he had. 'Are you aware of anyone who would have wished Pandora harm?'

'Lieutenant, the list would be as long as life.' He smiled again, perfect teeth, eyes that were both amused and predatory. 'I don't happen to count myself among them, merely because she didn't matter that much to me.'

'Did you share Pandora's latest drug of choice?'

He stiffened, hesitated, then relaxed again. 'That was an excellent ploy. Non sequiturs often catch the unwary off guard. I'll state, for the record, that I never touch illegals of any kind.' But his smile was wide and easy, and told her quite plainly, he lied. 'I was aware that Pandora dabbled

143

now and again. I considered it her own business. I'd have to agree that she'd found something new, something she seemed to be overdoing. In fact, I'd come into her bedroom earlier that last evening.'

He paused a moment, as if thinking back, bringing a scene into focus. 'She'd taken a pill of some kind out of a small, beautiful little wooden box. Chinese, I think. The box,' he added with a quick smile. 'She was surprised because I was early, and shoved the box into a drawer on her vanity and locked it. I asked what she was protecting, and she said . . .' He paused again, eyes narrowed. 'What did she say? Her treasure, her fortune. No, no, something like: Her reward. Yes, I'm sure that's what she said. Then she popped the pill, chased it with champagne. Then we had sex. It seemed to me she was distracted at first, then suddenly she was wild, insatiable. I don't believe it had ever been quite that potent between us. We dressed and went down. Jerry and Justin were just arriving. I never asked her any more about it. It just didn't apply to me.'

'Impressions, Peabody?'

'He's slick.'

'So's slime.' Eve shoved her hands into her pockets as the elevator descended, toyed with loose credit tokens. 'He despised her, but he slept with her, was willing to use her.'

'I think he found her pathetic, potentially dangerous, but marketable.'

144

'And, if that marketability had waned or the danger increased, could he have killed her?'

'In a heartbeat.' Peabody stepped into the garage first. 'Conscience isn't his priority. If this deal they had were tipping the wrong way, or if she had anything to pressure him with, he'd erase her. People that smug, that controlled, tend to have a lot of violence bubbling somewhere. And his alibi sucks.'

'Yeah, it does, doesn't it?' The possibilities made Eve grin. 'We're going to check that out, right after we go by Pandora's and find her cache. Inform Dispatch,' she ordered. 'Make sure we're clear to pop locks.'

'That wouldn't stop you,' Peabody murmured, but engaged the 'link.

The box was gone. It was such a stunning letdown that Eve stood in Pandora's lavishly ornate bedroom staring down at the drawer for a full ten seconds before it fully registered it was empty.

'This is a vanity, right?'

'That's what they call it. Look at all the bottles and pots on it. Creams for this, creams for that. That's why it's called a vanity.' She couldn't help herself. Peabody picked up a jar the size of the first joint of her thumb. 'Ever Young cream. You know what this shit goes for, Dallas? Five hundred over the counter at Saks. Five hundred for a lousy half ounce. Talk about vanity.'

She set it down again, ashamed she'd been tempted, even

for an instant, to stick it in her pocket. 'You add all this stuff up, she's got ten, maybe fifteen thousand worth of enhancements.'

'Get a grip, Peabody.'

'Yes, sir. Sorry.'

'We're looking for a box. The sweepers have already done the standard here, taken in the discs from her 'links. We know she didn't get any calls that night, or make any. From here, anyway. She's pissed. She's revved. What does she do?'

Eve continued to open drawers, paw through them as she spoke. 'She drinks more, maybe, rants around the house thinking of all the things she'd like to do to the people who've ticked her off. Bastards, bitches. Who the hell do they think they are? She can have anything and anyone she wants. Maybe she comes in here and pops another pill, just to keep the energy up.'

Hopeful, though it was a plain, enameled box rather than an ornate wooden one, Eve flipped a lid. Inside was an assortment of rings. Gold, silver, gleaming porcelain, carved ivory.

'Funny place to keep jewelry,' Peabody commented. 'I mean she's got this big glass chest here for her costume, and the safe for the real stuff.'

Eve glanced up, saw her aide was perfectly serious, and didn't quite muffle the laugh. 'They're not exactly jewelry, Peabody. Cock rings. You know, you put them over it, then—'

'Sure.' Peabody shrugged, tried not to stare. 'I knew that. Just – a funny place to keep them.'

'Yeah, sure is silly to keep sex toys in a box next to the bed. Anyway, where was I? She's using, chasing the pills with champagne. Somebody's going to pay for ruining her evening. That fucker Leonardo is going to crawl, he's going to beg. She'll make him pay for screwing some worthless slut behind her back, and for letting the little bitch come around to her house – her house, goddamn it – and fuck with her.'

Eve closed a drawer, opened another. 'Her security tags her as leaving the place just after two. The door's on automatic lock. She doesn't call a car. It's at least a sixty-block walk to Leonardo's, she's in ice-pick heels, but she doesn't take a cab. There's no record of any company picking her up or dropping her. She's registered for a palm 'link, but we haven't found it. If she had it with her and made a call, either she or someone else disposed of the unit.'

'If she called her killer, he or she should have been smart enough to ditch it.' Peabody began a search of the two-level closet and managed not to hyperventilate over the racks of clothes, many with price tags still attached. 'She might have been wired on something, but no way would she walk downtown. Half the shoes in this closet aren't even scraped on the soles. She wasn't the walking kind.'

'She was wired, all right. Damned if she's taking some stinking cab. All she has to do is snap her fingers and she can have half a dozen eager slaves slathering to take her anywhere she wants to go. So she snaps them. Somebody picks her up. They go to Leonardo's. Why?'

Fascinated by the way Eve juggled Pandora's point of view with her own, Peabody stopped the search and watched Eve. 'She insists. She demands. She threatens.'

'Maybe it's Leonardo she calls. Or maybe it's somebody else. They get there, the security camera's smashed. Or she smashes it.'

'Or the killer smashes it.' Peabody pushed her way through a sea of ivory silk. 'Because he's already planning to do her.'

'Why take her to Leonardo's if he's already planning it?' Eve demanded. 'Or if it was Leonardo, why dirty your own nest? I'm not sure murder was the priority, not yet. They get there, and if Leonardo's story holds, the place is empty. He's off drinking himself into a stupor and looking for Mavis, who is drinking herself into a stupor. Pandora wants Leonardo there, she wants to punish him. She starts to wreck the place, maybe she takes out some of her rage on her companion. They fight. It escalates. He grabs the cane, maybe to defend himself, maybe to attack. She's shocked, hurt, afraid. Nobody hurts her. What the hell is this? Then he can't stop, or doesn't want to stop. She's lying there, and there's blood everywhere.'

Peabody said nothing. She'd seen the pictures of the scene. Could imagine it all happening just as Eve related.

'He's standing over her, breathing hard.' Eyes half closed, Eve tried to bring the shadowy figure into focus. 'Her blood's all over him. The smell of it's everywhere. But he doesn't panic, can't afford to panic, doesn't let himself panic. What ties her to him? The palm 'link. He takes that, pockets it. If he's smart, and he has to be smart now, he goes through her things, makes sure there's nothing that can lead to him. He wipes off the cane where he gripped it, anything else he thinks he might have touched.'

In Eve's mind it played like an old video, cloudy and full of shadows. The figure – male, female – hurrying to cover tracks, moving around the body, stepping around the pools of blood. 'Have to be quick. Someone might come back. But have to be thorough. Almost clean now. Then he hears someone coming in. Mavis. She calls out for Leonardo, rushes back, sees the body, kneels beside it. Now it's even more perfect. He knocks her out, then he curls her fingers around the cane, maybe he even gives Pandora a few extra whacks. He takes that dead hand and rakes its nails over Mavis's face, uses it to tear her clothes. He puts on something, one of Leonardo's robes, to conceal his own clothes.'

She straightened from her search of a bottom drawer and found Peabody staring at her. 'It's like you were there,' Peabody murmured. 'I want to be able to do that, to go in the way you do.'

'Walk in to a few more murder scenes, and you will. The hard part's getting out again. Where the hell is the box?'

'She could have taken it with her.'

'I don't buy that. Where's the key, Peabody? She locked this drawer. Where's the key?'

In silence, Peabody took out her field unit, requested the list of items found in the victim's purse or on her person. 'There was no key taken into evidence.'

'So he got the key, didn't he? And he came back here and took the box and anything else he needed. Let's check the security disc.'

'Wouldn't the sweepers have done that?'

'Why? She wasn't killed here. All they were required to do was verify her time of departure.' Eve walked over to the security monitor, ordered a replay for the date and time in question. She watched Pandora storm out of the house, stride quickly out of range. 'Two oh eight. Okay, let's see what shakes. Time of death was about three. Computer, advance to oh three hundred, proceed at triple real time.' She focused on the chronometer. 'Freeze image. Sonofabitch. See that, Peabody.'

'I see it, time skipped from four oh three to four thirty-five. Someone disengaged the camera. Had to do it by remote. Had to know what they were doing.'

'Someone wanted to get in bad enough, get something out bad enough, to risk it. For a box of illegals.' Her smile was grim. 'I've got a feeling dead in the gut, Peabody. Let's go hassle the lab boys.'

9

'Why you wanna give me grief, Dallas?'

Huddled in his lab coat, Chief Tech Dickie Berenski – Dickhead to those who knew and loathed him – tested a strand of pubic hair. He was a meticulous man, as well as a monster pain in the ass. Though notoriously slow in testing, his batting average in court was high enough to make him the MVP of the police and security lab.

'Can't you see I'm buried here? Jesus.' With his fussy spider fingers he adjusted the focus on his micro-goggles. 'Got us ten homicides, six rapes, a load of suspicious and unattended deaths, and too many B and Es to think about. I'm not a fucking robot.'

'Closest thing to,' Eve muttered. She didn't like coming to the lab with its antiseptic air and white walls. It was too much like a hospital, or worse, Testing. Any cop who used maximum force resulting in termination was required to undergo Testing. Her experiences with that particular intrusive routine hadn't been pleasant. 'Look, Dickie, you've had plenty of time to analyze the substance.'

'Plenty of time.' He pushed back from the counter, and his eyes behind the goggles were big and bold as an owl's.

'You and every other cop in the city figures your shit's a priority. Like we should drop every other thing and devote every minute to you. You know what happens when the temperature rises, Dallas? People go bat shit, that's what happens. All you gotta do is take them down, but me and my team, we gotta shift through every hair and fiber. It takes time.'

His voice shifted into whine and set Eve's teeth on edge. 'I've got Homicide breathing down my neck, and Illegals snapping at my heels over some goddamn bag of powder. You got the prelim.'

'I need the final.'

'Well, I haven't got it.' His flappy lips pouted as he turned back and brought the enhanced view of the hair on screen. 'I gotta finish DNA on this.'

Eve knew how to work him. She didn't like it, but she knew. 'I've got two box-seat tickets to the Yankee–Red Sox game tomorrow.'

His fingers moved slowly over the controls. 'Box seats?'

'Third-base side.'

Dickie tipped down his goggles to scan the room. Other techs were busy at their stations. 'Maybe I could get you a little more.' With one shove of his feet, he sent his chair sliding to the right until he faced another screen. Cautious, he engaged the keyboard and brought the file up manually. He tapped slowly, scanning the screen. 'Here's the problem, see? This element here.'

It was nothing but color and foreign symbols to Eve,

but she grunted as the data scrolled. The unknown, she imagined, that even Roarke's unit couldn't identify. 'That red thing?'

'No, no, no, that's a standard amphetamine. You find it in Zeus, in Buzz, in Smiley. Hell, you can get a mild derivative of that in any over-the-counter pep-up. This one.' He tapped a finger against a green squiggle.

'Okay, what is it?'

'That's the big question, Dallas. Never seen it before. The computer can't identify. My best guess is it's something from off planet.'

'That ups the stakes, doesn't it? Bringing an unknown from off planet can get you twenty years in maximum lockup. Can you tell what it does?'

'I'm working on it. It appears to have some of the same properties as an antiaging drug, and with some of the same energizers. It beats hell out of free radicals. But there's some nasty side effects when it's mixed with the other chemicals found in the powder. You got most of it in the report. Enhanced sexual drive, which is not a bad thing, but that's followed by violent mood swings. Increased physical strength hooked up to a lack of control. This shit really dances around in the old nervous system. You're going to feel terrific for a while, practically invulnerable, you'll want to fuck like a rabbit, but you won't much care if your chosen mate is interested. When the crash comes, it's going to be hard and fast and the only thing that's going to level you out is another dose. Keep taking it, keep flying up and

153

diving down, and the nervous system's going to go nutso. Then you die.'

'That's pretty much what you've given me already.'

'That's because I'm stuck on Element X. It's vegetation, I can tell you that. Similar to the sharpleaf valerian found in the Southwest. Indians used the leaves for healing. But valerian isn't toxic, and this is.'

'It's poison?'

'Taken alone and in sufficient dosage, it would be, yeah. So are a lot of herbs and plants used in medicine.'

'It's a medicinal herb.'

'I didn't say that. It's not yet identified.' He puffed out his cheeks. 'But it's likely some off planet hybrid. That's the best I've got right now. And you and Illegals hassling me isn't going to make me find the answer quicker.'

'This isn't an Illegals case, it's mine.'

'Tell them that.'

'I will. Now, Dickie, I need the toxicology on the Pandora homicide.'

'That's not my baby, Dallas. That was dumped on Suzie-Q, and it's her twenty-four hours off.'

'You're chief tech, Dickie, and I need the report.' She waited a beat. 'There are two locker room passes that go along with those box seats.'

'Yeah. Well, it never hurts to spot-check your team.' He keyed in his code, then the file. 'She secured it, good for her. Chief Tech Berenski, override security on File Pandora, ID 563922-H.'

VOICE PRINT VERIFIED.

'Display toxicology.'

TOXICOLOGY TESTS STILL IN PROGRESS. PRELIMINARY
RESULTS ON SCREEN.

'She'd been drinking a lot,' Dickie murmured. 'Top French
bubbly. Probably died happy. Looks like Dom, '55. That's
good work for Suzie-Q. Added a little happy powder to it.
Our dead girl liked to party. Looks like Zeus . . . No.' His
shoulders bowed in as they did when he was intrigued or
irritated. 'What the hell is this?'

When the computer started to detail elements, he cut it
off with an annoyed flick of the finger and began to run
the report manually. 'Something mixed up here,' he muttered.
'Something screwy.'

His fingers played over the controls like those of a well-
trained pianist giving his first recital. Slow, cautious, and
accurate. Dallas watched symbols and shapes form, disperse,
realign. And she, too, saw the pattern.

'It's the same.' Eyes steely, she looked over at the silent
Peabody. 'It's the same stuff.'

'I didn't say that,' Dickie interrupted. 'Shut up and let
me finish running this test.'

'It's the same,' Eve repeated, 'right down to that green
squiggle of Element X. Question, Peabody, what do a

high-powered model and a second-rate weasel have in common?'

'They're both dead.'

'You've answered part one correctly. Care to try for part two and double your winnings? How did they both die?'

The faintest of smiles flitted around Peabody's mouth. 'Beaten to death.'

'Now for the grand prize and part three. What connects these two seemingly unrelated murders?'

Peabody looked down at the screen. 'Element X.'

'We're on a roll, Peabody. Transmit that report to my office, Dickie. Mine,' she repeated when he glanced up at her. 'Illegals calls, you don't know any more than you knew before.'

'Hey, I can't bury data.'

'Right.' She turned on her heel. 'I'll have those tickets delivered by five.'

'You knew,' Peabody said as they took the skyglide to the Homicide sector. 'Back at the victim's apartment. You couldn't find the box, but you knew what was in it.'

'Suspected,' Eve corrected. 'A new blend, one she was proprietary about, increased sexual performance and strength.' She checked her watch. 'I got lucky. Working on both cases at the same time, having them both on my mind. I worried I was just overlapping, but then I started to wonder. I saw both bodies, Peabody. There was the same overkill, the same viciousness.'

'I don't think it was luck. I was in on both of them, too, and I was six steps behind the whole way.'

'You catch up fast.' Eve stepped off the glide to take the elevator to her level. 'Don't beat yourself up over it, Peabody. I've got more than double your time on the job.'

Peabody stepped into the glass tube, gave a disinterested glance at the city below as they climbed. 'Why did you bring me in on these?'

'You've got potential – brains and guts. That's what Feeney told me when he brought me in under him. That was Homicide, too. Two teenagers hacked to death and strewed over the skyramp at Second and Twenty-fifth. I stumbled along about six paces behind him, too. But I found my rhythm.'

'How'd you know you wanted Homicide?'

Eve stepped out of the tube, turned down the corridor toward her office. 'Because death's an insult anytime. When somebody hurries it along, that's the biggest insult of all. Let's get a couple of coffees, Peabody. I want to put this all in black and white before I take it to the commander.'

'I don't suppose we could actually eat something.'

Eve tossed a grin over her shoulder. 'I don't know what's in my AutoChef, but . . .' She trailed off as she walked in and found Casto sitting at her desk, long, denim-clad legs propped up and crossed at the ankles. 'Well, Casto, Jake T., you look right at home.'

'Been waiting for you, darlin'.' He winked at her, then flashed a killer smile at Peabody. 'Hi, there, DeeDee.'

'DeeDee?' Eve murmured, then walked over to order coffee.

'Lieutenant.' Peabody's voice was stiff as iron, but her cheeks were glowing pink.

'It's a lucky man who gets to work with a couple of cops who are not only smart but a joy to look at. Could I get a cup of that, Eve? Strong and black and sweet.'

'You can have the coffee, but I haven't got time for a consult. I have some paperwork to see to, and an appointment in a couple of hours.'

'I won't keep you.' But he didn't shift when she handed him the coffee. 'I've been trying to light a fire under Dickhead. The man's slower than a three-legged turtle. You being primary, I figured you could requisition me a sample. I've got a private lab we use now and then. They're quick.'

'I don't think we want to take this out of the department, Casto.'

'The lab's approved by Illegals.'

'I meant Homicide. Let's give Dickie a little more time. Boomer isn't going anywhere.'

'Hey, you're in charge. I'd just like to put this one behind me. Leaves a bad taste. Not like this coffee.' He closed his eyes, sighed. 'My Jesus, woman, where'd you get this? It's gold.'

'Connections.'

'Ah, that rich fiance of yours, sure.' He savored another sip. 'A man would be hard pressed to tempt you away with the offer of a cold beer and a taco.'

'Coffee's my drink, Casto.'

'Can't blame you.' He shifted his admiring gaze to Peabody. 'How about you, DeeDee? Got a taste for a cold one?'

'Officer Peabody's on duty,' Eve said when Peabody was reduced to stammers. 'We've got work to do here, Casto.'

'I'll let you get to it.' He unfolded his legs and stood. 'Why don't you give me a call when you go off duty, DeeDee? I know a place that has the best Mexican food this side of the Rio Grande. Eve, you change your mind on letting me rush that sample through, let me know.'

'Close the door, Peabody,' Eve ordered when Casto sauntered out. 'And wipe that drool off your chin.'

Appalled, Peabody lifted a hand. Finding her chin dry didn't improve her humor. 'That's not funny. Sir.'

'Cut out the "sir" Anybody who goes around answering to DeeDee loses five points on the dignity scale.' Eve dropped down in the seat recently warmed by Casto. 'What the hell did he want?'

'I thought he told us clearly enough.'

'No, that wasn't enough to bring him over here.' She leaned forward, engaged her machine. A quick test of security showed no breaches. 'If he was in here, I can't tell.'

'Why would he go into your files?'

'He's ambitious. If he could close the case ahead of me, it would look damn good. And Illegals doesn't like to share, anyway.'

'And Homicide does?' Peabody said dryly.

159

'Hell no.' She looked up, grinned. 'Let's get this report hammered out. We're going to have to request an off world toxicology expert. We better be able to back up the hole we're going to put in the budget.'

Thirty minutes later, they were summoned to the office of the chief of police and security.

Eve liked Chief Tibble. He was a big man with a bold mind and a heart that was still more cop than politician. After the stench the former chief had left behind, the city and the department had needed the kind of brisk, cold air Tibble brought with him.

But she didn't know what the hell they'd been called in for. Not until she was ushered in and saw Casto and his captain.

'Lieutenant, Officer,' Tibble gestured to chairs. In a strategic move, Eve chose one beside Commander Whitney.

'We have a little squabble to settle,' Tibble began. 'We're going to settle it quickly and finally. Lieutenant Dallas, you are primary on the Johannsen and the Pandora homicides.'

'Yes, sir, I am. I was called in to confirm identification of Johannsen's body, as he was one of my informants. In the Pandora case, I was called to the scene by Mavis Freestone, who has been charged in that case. Both files are still open and under investigation.'

'Officer Peabody is your aide.'

'I requested her as my aide and was authorized to attach her to my caseload by my commander.'

'Very well. Lieutenant Casto, Johannsen was also one of your informants.'

'He was. I was on another case when his body was taken in. I wasn't notified until later.'

'And at that time, the Illegals and Homicide departments agreed to cooperate on the investigation.'

'We did. However, recent information has come to my attention that puts both of these cases under Illegals jurisdiction.'

'They're homicides,' Eve interrupted.

'With the link of illegal substances connecting both.' Casto's easy smile flashed. 'The latest lab report shows that the substance discovered in Johannsen's room was also found in Pandora's system. This substance contains an unknown, and is not yet rated, which under Article Six, Section Nine, Code B, puts all related cases under the investigative head of Illegals.'

'Exception to which is granted with such cases that are already under investigation by another department.' Eve forced herself to take a deep breath. 'My report on these matters will be complete within the hour.'

'Exceptions are not automatic, Lieutenant.' The Illegals captain tapped his fingertips together. 'The simple fact is, Homicide doesn't have the manpower, experience, or the facilities to investigate an unknown. Illegals does. And we don't feel it was in the spirit of cooperation to hold data back from our department.'

'Your department and Lieutenant Casto will be copied when my report is complete. These are my cases—'

Whitney lifted a hand before she could spit. 'Lieutenant Dallas is primary. If these cases are linked with illegals, they are still homicides, which she has been investigating.'

'With respect, Commander,' Casto dimmed his smile, 'it's well known at Cop Central that you favor the lieutenant, and rightfully so, given her record. We requested this meeting with Chief Tibble so as to insure a fair judgment on departmental priority. I have more street contacts, and a relationship with merchants and distributors of chemicals. While working undercover, I've gained access to mills, factories, and chem-houses which the lieutenant simply doesn't have. Added to that is the fact that there is a suspect charged with the Pandora homicide.'

'A suspect who had absolutely no connection with Johannsen,' Eve broke in. 'They were killed by the same person, Chief Tibble.'

His eyes remained cool. Any approval or lack thereof was carefully masked. 'Is that your opinion, Lieutenant?'

'That's my professional judgment, sir, which I will show cause for in my report.'

'Chief, it's no secret that Lieutenant Dallas has a personal interest in the suspect charged.' The captain spoke tersely. 'It would be natural for her to want to cast a cloud over the case. How can her professional judgment remain clear when the suspect is a close friend?'

Tibble held up a finger to halt Eve's outburst. 'Commander Whitney, your opinion?'

'I will and have relied without qualification on Lieutenant Dallas's judgment. She'll do her job.'

'I agree. Captain, I don't much care for disloyalty in the ranks.' The reprimand was mild, but the aim deadly. 'Now, both departments have a valid point here on priority. Exceptions are not automatic, and we are dealing with an unknown which appears to be involved in at least two deaths. Both Lieutenant Dallas and Lieutenant Casto have exemplary records, and each, I believe, are more than competent to investigate these matters. Do you agree, Commander?'

'Yes, sir, both are excellent cops.'

'Then, I suggest they cooperate with each other instead of playing games. Lieutenant Dallas will remain primary, and as such, will keep Lieutenant Casto and his department apprised of any and all progress. Now is that it, or do I have to threaten to cut a baby in two like Solomon?'

'Get that report finished, Dallas,' Whitney muttered as they filed out. 'And next time you bribe Dickhead, do a better job of it.'

'Yes, sir.' Eve glanced down at the hand on her arm, looked up at Casto.

'Had to give it a shot. The captain, he likes those clutch RBIs.'

She didn't miss his not-so-subtle reference to baseball.

'No problem, since I'm still the one up at bat. You'll get my report, Casto.'

'Appreciate it. I'll do some more poking around on the streets. So far, nobody knows anything about a new blend. But this off planet angle might open something up. I know a couple drones in Customs who owe me.'

Eve hesitated, then decided it was time to take the term cooperation to heart. 'Try Stellar Five for a start. Pandora came back from there a couple of days before she died. I still have to backtrack and see if she did any station hopping.'

'Good. You let me know.' He smiled and the hand that was still on her arm slid down to her wrist. 'I got a feeling, now that we've aired this out, we'll make a hell of a team. Closing this one up's going to look good on both of our files.'

'I'm more interested in finding a murderer than I am in how it affects my promotion status.'

'Hey, I'm all for justice.' His dimple winked. 'But I ain't going to cry if making it pushes me closer to a captain's salary. No hard feelings?'

'No. I'd have done the same.'

'That's fine then. I might just drop around for some more of the coffee one day soon.' He gave her wrist a quick squeeze. 'And, Eve, I hope you clear your friend. I mean that.'

'I will clear my friend.' He'd taken two strides away when she admitted she couldn't resist. 'Casto?'

'Yeah, darling?'

'What'd you offer him?'

'Dickhead?' The grin was as wide as Oklahoma. 'A case of unblended scotch. He snatched at it the way a frog's tongue snatches a fly.' Casto flicked his own tongue out, winked again. 'Nobody bribes better than an Illegals cop, Eve.'

'I'll remember that.' Eve stuck her hands in her pockets, but couldn't help but grin. 'He's got style, I'll give him that.'

'And a great butt,' Peabody said before she could stop herself. 'Just an observation.'

'One I have to agree with. Well, Peabody, we won that battle. Let's go try for the war.'

By the time the report was complete, Eve's eyes were all but crossed. She sent Peabody off duty as soon as copies were transmitted to all necessary parties. She considered canceling her session with the shrink, thought of all the reasons why she could and should postpone it.

But she found herself in Dr Mira's office at the appointed time, taking in the familiar scents of herbal tea and subtle perfume.

'I'm glad you came to see me.' Mira crossed her silk-draped legs. She'd had her hair restyled, Eve noted. It was cut short and sleek rather than tucked up in a smooth roll. The eyes were the same, of course, quiet and blue and filled with ready understanding. 'You look well.'

'I'm fine.'

'I can't see how you would be, with so much going on

in your life. Professionally and personally. It must be tremendously difficult for you to have such a close friend charged with a murder you're investigating. How are you handling it?'

'I'm doing my job. By doing it, I'll clear Mavis and find out who set her up.'

'Do you find your loyalties divided?'

'No, not after I thought about it.' Eve rubbed her hands on the knees of her trousers. Damp palms were a usual side effect of her meetings with Mira. 'If I had any doubt, any doubt at all that Mavis was innocent, I'm not sure what I would do. But I don't, so the answer's clear.'

'That's a comfort to you.'

'Yeah, you could say that. I'll feel a hell of a lot more comfortable after I close the case and she's out of it. I guess I was worried when I made the appointment to see you. But I feel more in control now.'

'That's important to you. Feeling in control.'

'I can't do my job unless I know I have the wheel.'

'And in your personal life?'

'Shit, nobody grabs the wheel from Roarke.'

'He's running things then?'

'He would if you let him.' She gave a short laugh. 'He'd probably say the same about me. I guess we do a lot of juggling for the controls, end up heading in the same direction anyway. He loves me.'

'You sound surprised.'

'Nobody ever did. Not like this. It's easy to say, for some

166

people. The words. But it's not just words with Roarke. He sees inside me, and it doesn't matter.'

'Should it?'

'I don't know. I don't always like what I see there, but he does. Or at least he understands it.' And now Eve understood that this was what she'd needed to talk through. Those black, ragged edges inside her. 'Maybe it's because we both had lousy beginnings. We knew, when we should have been too young to know, how cruel people can be. How power doesn't just corrupt in the wrong hands, it mutilates. He – I never made love before him. I had sex, but I never felt anything but basic release. But I could never be . . . intimate,' she decided. 'Is that the word?'

'Yes, I think that's exactly the word. Why do you think you achieved intimacy with him?'

'He wouldn't have it any other way. Because he . . .' She felt her eyes begin to tear and blinked them dry. 'Because he opened something inside me I'd closed off. No, that had been scarred shut. Somehow, he took control of that part of me, or I let him have control of that part of me that died. That was killed when I was a child when . . .'

'You'll feel better if you say it, Eve.'

'When my father raped me.' She let out a shuddering breath and the tears didn't matter any longer. 'He raped me, and he violated me, and he hurt me. He used me like a whore when I was too small and too weak to stop him. He would hold me down, or tie me up. He would hit me until I could hardly see, or he would hold his hand over my mouth so that I couldn't scream. And he would push himself into me, and ram himself into me until the pain was almost as obscene as the act. And there was no one to help me, and nothing to do but wait for the next time.'

'Do you understand that you weren't to blame?' Mira asked gently. *When an abscess was finally lanced,* she thought, *one had to carefully, thoroughly, slowly, squeeze out all the poison.* 'Not then, not now, not ever?'

Eve used the back of her hand to wipe her cheeks dry. 'I wanted to be a cop. Because cops have control. They stop the bad guys. It seemed simple. After I was a cop for a while, I began to see that there are some who always prey on the weak and the innocent.' Her breath steadied. 'No, it wasn't my fault. It was his, and the fault of the people who pretended not to see or to hear. But I still have to live with it, and it was easier to live with it when I didn't remember.'

'But you've been remembering for a long time, haven't you?'

'Bits and pieces. Everything before I was found in the alley when I was eight was just bits and pieces.'

'And now?'

'More pieces, too many pieces. And it's clearer, closer.' She rubbed a hand over her mouth, deliberately lowered it to her lap again. 'I can see his face. I didn't used to be able to see his face. During the DeBlass case last winter –

I guess there were enough similarities there to click. Then there was Roarke, and it all started to come back clearer and faster. I can't stop it.'

'Is that what you want?'

'I'd wipe those eight years out of my mind if I could.' She said it viciously, felt it viciously. 'They have nothing to do with now. I don't want them to have anything to do with now.'

'Eve, as horrible as those eight years were, and as obscene, they formed you. They helped build your strength, your compassion for the innocent, your complexity, your resilience. Remembering, and dealing with those memories, won't change what you are. I've often recommended you agree to autohypnosis. I no longer do. I believe your subconscious is letting these memories surface at its own pace.'

If that were so, Eve wanted the pace to slow, to let her breathe. 'Maybe there are some things I'm not ready to remember. Still, it doesn't stop. There's a dream that keeps coming back. Just lately and constantly. There's a room, a filthy room with this dull red light blinking in the window. Off and on. There's a bed. It's empty, but it's stained. I know it's blood. A lot of blood. I see myself curled in the corner on the floor. There's more blood. I'm covered with it. I can't see my face, it's toward the wall. I can't see clearly at all, but it has to be me.'

'Are you alone?'

'I think so. I can't tell. I only see the bed, the corner,

and that light blinking off and on. There's a knife on the floor beside me.'

'There weren't any stab wounds on you when you were found.'

Eyes hollow and haunted lifted to Mira's. 'I know.'

10

Eve expected the cold blast of Summerset's disapproval when she walked into the house. She was used to it. She couldn't explain what perverse streak she'd developed when she found herself disappointed that he didn't greet her at the door with some snide comment.

She stepped into the parlor off the foyer, engaged the wall sensor. 'Where is Roarke?'

ROARKE IS IN THE GYMNASIUM, LIEUTENANT. DO YOU WISH TO CONTACT?'

'No. Disengage.' She'd go see him herself. A good sweaty workout might be just what she needed to clear her mind.

She took the stairs behind the faux panel in the hallway, descended a level, and cut through the pool area with its black-bottomed lagoon and tropical greenery.

There was a whole world down here, she thought. *Another of Roarke's worlds.* The lush pool with an overhead that could simulate starlight, sunshine, or moonbeams at the flick of a control; the holoroom where hundreds of games could be accessed to while away a slow night; a Turkish bath; an isolation tank; the target range; a small theater; and a meditation lounge superior to any offered in the pricey health spas on or off planet.

Toys, she supposed, for the rich. Or Roarke might call them survival tools – a necessary means of relaxation in a world that moved faster every day. He balanced relaxation and work better than she – Eve could admit that. Somehow he had found the key to enjoying what he had while protecting it and gathering more.

She'd learned quite a bit from Roarke over the past few months. One of the most important lessons was that there were times she had to push aside all the worries, the responsibilities, even the thirst for answers, and just be Eve.

That was what she thought of now as she slipped into the gym and coded the door to lock behind her.

He wasn't a man to stint on his equipment, nor was he one to take the easy way and pay to have his body sculpted, his muscles toned, his organs flushed. Sweat and effort were as important to him as the gravity bench, the aqua track, or the resistance center. Because he was a man who appreciated tradition, his personal gym was also stocked with old-fashioned free weights, incline benches, and a virtual reality system.

He was using the first of those now, doing long, slow curls as he watched a monitor flash with some sort of schematic and spoke to someone on a head 'link.

'Security's a priority at the resort, Teasdale. If there's a flaw, find it. And fix it.' He frowned at the screen, switched fluidly from curls to extensions. 'You'll simply have to do better. If you're going to have cost overruns, you'll have to justify them to me. No, I didn't say excuse them to me, Teasdale. Justify them. Have a report transmitted to my office by oh nine hundred on planet time. Disengage.'

'You're tough, Roarke.'

He glanced around as the screen went dark, smiled at her. 'Business is war, Lieutenant.'

'The way you play it, killer. If I were Teasdale, I'd be trembling in my gravity boots right now.'

'That's the idea.' He set the weights down to take off the headset and put it aside. She watched him switch to the resistance center, set a program, and start on leg presses. Absently, she picked up a weight, worked on her triceps, and kept watching him.

The black sweatband gave him a warrior look, she thought. And the dark, sleeveless T-shirt and shorts showed off very attractive muscles and skin gleaming with honest sweat. She watched those muscles bunch, that sweat bead, and she wanted him.

'You're looking pleased with yourself, Lieutenant.'

'Actually, I'm pleased with you.' She angled her head, let her gaze skim over him. 'That's quite a body you've got there, Roarke.'

His brow winged up as she strolled over, reached down to test his biceps. 'Tough guy.'

He grinned up at her. She was in a mood, he could see.

He just wasn't sure what mood it was. 'Want to see how tough?'

'Think I'm afraid of you?' With her eyes still on his, she stripped off her weapon harness, hung it over one of the bars. 'Come on.' She walked over to a mat, curled her fingers in challenge. 'See if you can take me down.'

Still prone, he studied her. There was something in her eyes other than challenge, he noted. If he wasn't mistaken, it was lust. 'Eve, I'm covered with sweat.'

She sneered. 'Coward.'

He winced. 'Let me grab a shower, then—'

'Chicken. You know, some men are still stuck in the mind-set that a woman can't go toe to toe on a physical level. Since I know you're above that, I can only assume you're afraid I'll whip your ass.'

That did it. 'End program.' Slowly he sat up and reached toward a stack of towels. He mopped his face. 'Wanna fight? I'll give you time to warm up.'

Her blood was already pumping. 'I'm warm enough. Standard hand to hand.'

'No punching,' he said as he stepped onto the mat. At her derisive snort, he narrowed his eyes. 'I'm not hitting you.'

'Right. Like you could get past my—'

He came in fast, caught her off balance, and sent her skidding on her butt. 'Foul,' she muttered and swung up to the balls of her feet.

'Oh, now there're rules. Just like a cop.'

They crouched, circled each other. He feinted, she stepped in. For ten interesting seconds, they grappled, her hands sliding off his slick skin. His quick leg hook would have worked if she hadn't anticipated and gone in low. Using leverage and a quick twist of her body, she flipped him over.

'Now we're even.' She crouched again as he got to his feet, shook back his hair.

'Okay, Lieutenant, I'm going to stop holding back.'

'Holding back, my butt. You were—'

He almost caught her again, certainly would have taken her down if she hadn't realized with seconds to spare that his strategy was to distract her with insults. She evaded and turned into his move. Then, when their faces were close, their bodies straining, she pulled out her best weapon.

She slid a hand between his legs, cupped gentle fingers over his balls. He blinked in surprise, in delight. 'Well, then,' he murmured and lowered his lips to within an inch of hers before she switched her grip.

He didn't even have time to curse as he went sailing. He landed with a thud, and she was on him, a knee pressed to his crotch, his shoulders pinned by her hands.

'You're down, pal. And out.'

'Talk about fouls.'

'Don't be a sore loser.'

'It's hard to argue with a woman when she's got her knee on my ego.'

'Good. Now I'm going to have my way with you.'

'Are you?'

'Damn right. I won.' She cocked her head and reached down to strip off his shirt. 'Cooperate and I won't have to hurt you. Uh-uh.' When he reached for her, she gripped his hands and pushed them back to the mat. 'I'm in charge here. Don't make me get out the cuffs.'

'Hmm. An interesting threat. Why don't you—' His words trailed off as her mouth came down on his, hard and hot. Instinctively, his hands flexed under hers, wanting to touch, to take. But he understood she wanted something else, something more. So he would let her find it.

'I'm going to take you.' She bit down on his lip, sending an edge of lust razoring through his gut. 'Do whatever I want to you.'

His mind was already spinning, his breath clogging. 'Be gentle with me,' he managed, and felt warmth twine with the heat when she laughed.

'Dream on.'

She was rough – quick, demanding hands, impatient, restless lips. He could all but feel the wildness of her need vibrate from her, shimmer into him with some reckless energy that seemed to feed on itself. If she wanted control, he would give it to her. Or so he thought. But somewhere during her onslaught of his system, he simply lost the choice.

She scraped her teeth over him, down him, until the muscles he had toned trembled helplessly. His vision wavered when she took him into her mouth, worked him hard, fast, so that he had to fight every instinct or explode.

'Don't you hold back on me.' She nipped his thigh, slid her way back up his torso while her hand replaced her mouth. 'I want to make you come.' She sucked his tongue into her mouth, bit, released. 'Now.'

She watched his eyes go opaque seconds before she felt the orgasm rip through him. Her laugh was shaky with power as she assaulted his ear. 'I won again.'

'Jesus. Christ Jesus.' He managed, barely, to wind his arms around her. He was weak as a baby, and tangled with embarrassment at his complete loss of control was a giddy delight. 'I don't know whether to apologize or thank you.'

'Save it. I haven't finished with you yet.'

He nearly chuckled, but she was nibbling her way around his jaw and sending fresh signals to his battered system. 'Darling, you'll have to give me a minute.'

'I don't have to do anything.' She was drunk on pleasure, energized by her own power. 'You just have to take it.'

Straddling him, she pulled her shirt over her head. Watching him, she skimmed her hands up her own torso, over her breasts and down again. Saliva pooled in his mouth. Smiling, she took his hands and brought them to her. With a sigh, she let her eyes close.

His touch was familiar now, yet always fresh. Constantly arousing. His fingers played over her, teasing her nipples until they were hot and on the point of pain, then tugging until there was an answering clutch in her center.

Obliging them both, she arched back as he reared up to cover her with his mouth. She cupped his head, let herself become steeped in the sensations – the scrape of teeth on sensitized flesh that ran from tender to brutal, the flex and release of his fingers on her hips, the slick slide of flesh against flesh and the hot, ripe smell of sweat and sex. And when she urged his mouth back to hers, the explosive taste of reckless lust.

He made a sound caught between a groan and an oath when she pulled away. She rose quickly, delighted to find herself shaky on her feet, her body heavy with need. She didn't have to tell him it had never been – she had never been like this with anyone but him. He knew it already. Just as she had come to know that he found more with her, somehow with her, than with anyone else.

She stood over him, no longer trying to level her breathing, no longer shocked by the shudders that coursed through her. She toed off her shoes, unhooked her trousers, let them fall away.

Heat swamped her as his eyes skimmed up, then down, then up again to her face. She'd never thought much about her body. It was a cop's body, and had to be strong, resilient, flexible. With Roarke she'd discovered how wonderful those aspects could be for a woman. Trembling a little, she planted a knee on either side of him, then leaned forward to lose herself in the giddy pleasure of mouth on mouth.

'I'm still in charge,' she whispered as she rose up.

With his eyes burning into hers, he smiled. 'Do your worst.'

She lowered herself to him, took him into her slowly, torturously. And when he was deep, when her body went rigid, bowed back, she let out a shuddering sob as the first glorious orgasm rippled through her. Greedy, she lunged forward again, gripped his hands with hers, and began to ride.

Explosions burst in her head, in her blood. Behind her closed eyes, riotous colors danced, and there was nothing inside her but Roarke and a desperate need for more of him – still more of him. Climax slammed into climax, slapping her up before she was able to float down again. The grinding ache in her was met, then built again until at last her body slid limply down to his. She buried her face against his throat and waited for sanity to return.

'Eve?'

'Huh?'

'My turn.'

She blinked groggily as he rolled her onto her back. It took her a second to realize he was still hard inside her. 'I thought you'd – we'd—'

'You had,' he murmured. He watched fresh, stunning pleasure flicker over her face as he moved inside her. 'Now you just have to take it.'

She started to laugh, but it ended on a moan. 'We'll kill each other if we keep this up.'

'I'll risk it. No, don't close your eyes. See me.' He

watched those eyes glaze as he quickened the pace, heard her strangled cry as he drove himself deeper, deeper inside her.

Then they were both bucking, plunging, her hands grappling for purchase, his hips thrusting harder. Her eyes went blank and wild. He covered her mouth ruthlessly with his and swallowed her scream.

They were tangled together, like two boxers down for the count and gasping for air. He'd slid slightly down her body, and found that though her breast was handy to his lips, he didn't have the energy to take advantage of it.

'I can't feel my toes,' she realized. 'Or my fingers. I think I broke something.'

It occurred to him that he was probably cutting off most of her air and her circulation. With an effort, he reversed their positions. 'Better?'

She took a long, wheezing gulp of air. 'I think.'

'Did I hurt you?'

'Huh?'

He tipped her head up and studied her foolish, blank-eyed grin. 'Never mind. You finished with me yet?'

'For the moment.'

'Thank God.' He dropped back down and concentrated on breathing.

'Jesus, we're a mess.'

'Nothing like sticky, sweaty sex to remind you you're human. Come on.'

'Come on where?'

'Darling.' He skimmed a kiss over her damp shoulder. 'You need a shower.'

'I'm just going to sleep here for the next couple of days.' She curled up, yawned. 'You go ahead.'

He shook his head. Gathering his strength, he shoved her aside, got to his feet. After a deep breath, he reached down and hauled her up over his shoulder. 'Oh sure, take advantage of a dead woman.'

'Dead weight,' he muttered and crossed the gym to the changing area. He shifted her more securely, then stepped onto the tile. With a wicked grin, he turned around so that her face would encounter the full force of one of the crisscrossing sprays. 'Sixty-three degrees, maximum spray.'

'Sixty—' It was all she had time for. The rest of her words were lost in screams and curses that echoed off the shining tiles.

She wasn't dead weight now, but a wriggling, wet, desperate woman. He clamped down hard, roaring with laughter as she sputtered and swore at him.

'Ninety-two,' she shouted. 'Ninety fucking two degrees. Now.'

When the spray pumped hot, she managed to catch her breath. 'I'll kill you, Roarke. The minute I thaw out.'

'It's good for you.' He set her carefully on her feet and offered her the soap. 'Clean up, Lieutenant. I'm starving.'

So was she. 'I'll kill you later,' she decided. 'After I eat.'

★　　★　　★

Within the hour, she was showered, satisfied, dressed, and attacking a two-inch sirloin. 'You know, I'm only marrying you for sex and food.'

He sipped a deep red wine and watched her plow through the meal. 'Of course.'

She nipped into a shoestring fry. 'And because you have a beautiful face.'

Unruffled, he only grinned. 'That's what they all say.'

Those weren't the reasons, but good sex, good food, and a beautiful face could certainly mellow a mood. She smiled at him. 'How's Mavis?'

He'd been waiting for her to ask, but he had known she'd needed to get something out of her system first. 'She's fine. She and Leonardo are having a kind of reunion in her suite tonight. You can talk to them in the morning.'

Eve looked down at her plate as she cut into the steak again. 'What do you think of him?'

'I think he's desperately, almost pathetically in love with our Mavis. And since I have some experience with that emotion, I have sympathy for his situation.'

'We can't verify his movements on the night of the murder.' She picked up her wine. 'He had motive, he had means, and very likely opportunity. There's no physical evidence linking him to the crime, but the crime took place in his apartment, and the weapon was his.'

'So you see him killing Pandora, then setting the scene so that Mavis takes the blame?'

'No.' She set her wine down again. 'It would just be

easier if I could.' Eve tapped her fingers on the table, then picked up her glass again. 'Do you know Jerry Fitzgerald?'

'Yes. We're acquainted.' He waited a beat. 'No, I've never slept with her.'

'I didn't ask.'

'Just simplifying.'

She shrugged and took another sip. 'My impressions are smart, ambitious, clever, and tough.'

'Your impressions are usually accurate. I wouldn't argue with them.'

'I don't know a lot about the modeling game, but I've been doing some research. At Fitzgerald's level, it's pretty high stakes. Money, prestige, media. Having top bill on a show that's being anticipated as much as Leonardo's is worth big credits, full-blown coverage. She'll step right into Pandora's shoes on it now.'

'If his designs click, it could be worth a considerable amount to be the top endorser,' Roarke agreed. 'But it's still speculative.'

'She's involved with Justin Young, and she admitted that Pandora was trying to lure him back.'

Roarke considered. 'Difficult for me to imagine Jerry Fitzgerald going into a murderous rage over a man.'

'She'd more likely have one over a stylist,' Eve admitted, 'but there's more.'

Briefly, she told him of the connection between Boomer's data and death and the new blend found in Pandora's system.

'We can't find her cache. Someone else went after it, and knew where to look.'

'Jerry's come out publicly against illegals. Of course, that's publicly,' Roarke added. 'And you're dealing with profit here, not partying.'

'That's my theory. A new blend like this, quickly addictive, potent, has the potential for a great deal of profit. The fact that it's eventually lethal won't stop its distribution or its use.'

She pushed her half-eaten steak aside, a gesture that had Roarke frowning. When she didn't eat, she was worried. 'It seems to me like you have a lead you can get your teeth into, Eve. A lead that steers far wide of Mavis.'

'Yeah.' Restless, she rose. 'A lead that doesn't point to anyone else. Fitzgerald and Young alibi each other. The security discs confirm their whereabouts at the time of death. Unless, of course, one or both of them got around security. Redford doesn't have an alibi, or doesn't have one without big holes, but I can't tie him. Yet.'

That she wanted to seemed very clear to Roarke. 'What were your impressions?'

'Callous, ruthless, self-interested.'

'You didn't like him.'

'No, I didn't. He was slick, smug, confident he could handle some city cop without straining his brain cells. And he volunteered information, just like Young and Fitzgerald did. I don't trust volunteers.'

The way the mind of a cop worked was a marvel, he

184

mused. 'You'd trust him more if you'd had to pry information out of him.'

'Sure.' It was one of the basic rules, for her. 'He was anxious to feed me Pandora's drug use. So was Fitzgerald. And all three of them were almost happy to tell me they didn't like her.'

'I don't suppose you'd consider they were simply being honest.'

'When people are that open, especially to a cop, there's usually another layer underneath. I'm going to do some more digging on them.' She circled back, sat again. 'Then there's the Illegals cop I'm butting heads with.'

'Casto.'

'Yeah. He wants the cases, took it well enough when he lost the stab, but it's not going to be share and share alike with him. He wants a captaincy.'

'And you don't?'

Her gaze shifted coolly to his. 'When I've earned it.'

'And, of course, you'll be sharing and sharing alike cheerfully with Casto in the meantime.'

Her lips curved. 'Shut up, Roarke. The point is, I have to link Boomer's death with Pandora's solidly. I have to find the person or persons who connect them, who knew them both. Until I do, Mavis is facing a murder trial.'

'As I see it, you have two avenues to explore.'

'Which are?'

'The glittery road to haute couture and the gritty road to the streets.' He took out a cigarette, lighted it. 'Where did you say Pandora had been before she got back on planet?'

'Starlight Station.'

'I have some interests there.'

'What a surprise,' she said dryly.

'I'll ask a few questions. The people in the circle Pandora exploited don't respond terribly well to badges.'

'If I don't get the right answers, I may have to go there myself.'

Something in her tone alerted him. 'Problem?'

'No, no problem.'

'Eve.'

She pushed away from the table again. 'I've never been off planet.'

Bemused, he stared. 'Never? As in never?'

'Not everybody just goes popping off into orbit whenever they get an itch. There's plenty to keep most of us busy right here.'

'There's nothing to be afraid of,' he said, reading her perfectly. 'Space travel is safer than driving in the city.'

'Bullshit,' she said under her breath. 'I didn't say I was afraid. If I have to do it, I'll do it. I'd just rather not, that's all. The closer I'm able to keep this to home, the faster I'll have Mavis out of it.'

'Umm-hmm.' Interesting, he thought, to discover his stalwart lieutenant had a phobia. 'Why don't we see what I can find out for you?'

'You're a civilian.'

'Unofficially, of course.'

She looked back at him, saw amused understanding, and sighed. 'Fine. I don't suppose you've got an off planet flora expert you can lend me while you're at it.'

Roarke picked up his wine again, smiled. 'As a matter of fact . . .'

11

The case was going in too many directions at once, Eve decided. The best course was the most familiar. She took to the streets. And she took to them alone.

She'd left Peabody with a pile of data to check, buzzed Feeney for an update, but she headed out solo.

She didn't want to make small talk, didn't want anyone looking too closely. She'd had a bad night and was well aware it showed.

The nightmare had been one of the worst so far. It had squeezed her by the throat, battered her awake in a sweaty, whimpering mess. Her only relief had been that dawn had been breaking when it had reached its peak. And she'd been alone in bed with Roarke already up and in the shower.

If he'd heard her or seen her, she'd never have gotten past him. Perhaps it had been misplaced pride, but she'd used every tactic at her disposal to avoid him, then had left him a quick memo before slipping out of the house.

She'd avoided Mavis and Leonardo as well, and had only run into Summerset long enough to have been granted one of his freezing looks.

She'd turned away from that and had walked out. There was a sick knowledge inside her that she was turning away from a great deal more.

Work was the answer, or so she hoped. Work she understood. She pulled up in front of the Down and Dirty Club in the East End and got out of the car.

'Hey there, white girl.'

'How's it passing, Crack?'

'Oh, without much hassle.' He grinned at her, a giant of a black man with a face seamed with tattoos. His rocket launcher chest was partially covered with a feathered vest that hung past his knees and added flair to the loincloth of neon pink he sported. 'Gonna be another hot one this day.'

'Got time to go inside and cool me off with a drink?'

'Might be, for you, sweet butt. You taking Crack's advice and turning in your badge to shake your talent in the Down and Dirty?'

'Not in this lifetime.'

He laughed, patting his gleaming belly. 'Don't know why it is I got a liking for you. You come on in, wet your whistle, and tell Crack what's rocking down.'

She'd been in worse clubs, and would be eternally grateful she'd been in better. The stale smells from the night hung still: incense, bad perfumes, liquor, smoke from dubious leaves, unwashed bodies, and casual sex.

It was too early for even the most dedicated partier. Chairs were overturned onto tables, and she could see where someone had made a careless pass with a mop over the sticky floor. Substances she didn't care to identify had been left behind.

Still, the bottles behind the main bar gleamed in the colored lights. On the stage to the right, a dancer draped in pink net practiced a routine to the blare of simulated brass.

A jerk of Crack's huge head had the domestic droid and the dancer wandering off. 'What's your pleasure, white girl?'

'Coffee, black.'

Crack lumbered behind the bar, still grinning. 'Gotcha. How 'bout a drop or two of my special reserve in that coffee?'

Eve lifted a shoulder. When in Rome. 'Sure.'

She watched him program the coffee, then uncode a cabinet where he took out a bottle fit for a Genie. And, leaning on the cloudy bar, smelling the smells, she relaxed a little. She knew why she had a liking for Crack, a nighthawk she barely knew but understood. He was part of a world she'd wandered in most of her life.

'Now, whatcha doing in this nasty place, honey pot? Being a cop?'

'Afraid so.' She sampled the coffee, sucked in her breath. 'Jesus, some reserve.'

'Only for my favorite people. It skims under the legal limit.' He winked. 'Just. What you want Crack to do for you?'

'Did you know Boomer? Carter Johannsen. Small-time player. Data hound.'

'I know Boomer. He's meat now.'

'Yeah, that's right. Somebody slaughtered him. You ever do business with him, Crack?'

'He come in now and then.' Crack preferred his reserve straight up. He sipped, then smacked his tattooed lips in appreciation. 'Sometimes he flush, sometimes not. He liked to watch the show and talk the shit. Not much harm in old Boomer. Heard he got his face erased.'

'That's right. Who'd want to do that?'

'He pissed somebody off bad, I'd say. Boomer, he had big ears. If he popped a few, he had a big mouth, too.'

'When did you see him last?'

'Hell, now, hard to remember. Few weeks, anyway. Seems to me he came through one night with a pocket full of credits. Bought himself a bottle, a few tabs, and a privacy room. Lucille went with him. No, not Lucille, shit. Was Hetta. All you white girls look alike,' he said with a wink.

'Did he tell anyone how he came to have full pockets?'

'Mighta told Hetta, he was blissed out enough. Seems she picked up some more tabs for him. He wanted to stay happy. She said something about how old Boomer was going to be an entrepreneur or some horseshit like. We had ourselves a laugh over it, then he come out and got up onstage naked. We had a bigger laugh. Dude had the most pitiful cock you ever seen.'

191

'So he was celebrating a deal.'

'That'd be my take. We got busy. I had to crack a few heads, toss out some bodies. I remember how I was out on the street, and he come rushing out. I grabbed hold, just fooling. He didn't look happy no more, he looked piss-your-pants scared.'

'He say anything?'

'Just shook himself loose and took off running. Last time I saw him, as I recollect.'

'Who spooked him? Who'd he talk to?'

'Can't tell you that, sweet face.'

'Did you see any of these people here that night?' Eve took photos out of her bag, spread them out. Pandora, Jerry, Justin, Redford, and because it was necessary, Mavis and Leonardo.

'Hey, I know these two. Fancy-face models.' His wide fingers traced lovingly over Pandora and Jerry. 'The redhead, she come in now and then, trolling for partners, looking to score. Could be she was here that night, but can't say for certain sure. These others aren't on our guest list, so to speak. Least I can't make 'em.'

'Did you ever see the redhead with Boomer?'

'He wasn't her pick. She liked them big, stupid, and young. Boomer was just stupid.'

'What do you hear about a new blend on the streets, Crack?'

His big face went blank, closed off. 'Don't hear nothing.'

Friendly only went so far, she knew. Silently, Eve took out credits, laid them on the bar. 'Hearing improved?'

He studied the credits, then looked back at her face. Recognizing the tactic negotiations, she added to them. The credits slid across the bar and disappeared.

'Some rumblings recent, maybe, about some new shit. High powered, good long buzz, tough on the credit balance. Heard it called Immortality. None's come passing this way, not yet. Most people 'round here can't afford designer. They'll have to wait for the knockoff, and that takes a few months more.'

'Did Boomer talk about it?'

'Is that what he was into?' Speculation shifted into Crack's eyes. 'He never flapped to me about it. Like I said, I heard some rumblings pass through. It's getting good advance hype, chemi-heads are jazzed over it, but I ain't heard anybody had a taste. It's good business,' he said with a smile. 'You got a product, a new one, you get the clientele wired up, hungry. Then when it hits, they'll pay. They'll pay big.'

'Yeah, good business.' She leaned forward. 'Don't try a sample, Crack. It's fatal.' When he started to blow that off, she put a hand on his beefy arm. 'I mean literally. It's poison, slow-acting poison. If there's anyone you care about who uses, you warn them off this shit, or you won't have them very long.'

He studied her face. 'No jive here, white girl? This ain't cop talk?'

'No jive, no cop talk. A regular user's got about five years before it overloads the nervous system and takes him out.

That's straight, Crack. And whoever's manufacturing it knows it.'

'Hell of a way to make a profit.'

'Isn't it just. Now, where can I find Hetta?'

Crack blew out a breath, shook his head. 'Nobody gonna believe it if I tell 'em, anyhow. Not the ones already hungry.' He looked back at Eve, focused. 'Hetta? Shit, I don't know. Ain't seen her in weeks. These girls come and go, work one joint, go on to the next.'

'Last name?'

'Moppett. Hetta Moppett, rented a room over on Ninth last I heard, around a hundred and twentieth. Anytime you want to take up where she left off, sugarpuss, just let me know.'

Hetta Moppett hadn't paid her rent in three weeks, nor had she shown her skinny little ass. This, according to the building super, who also informed Eve that Ms Moppett had forty-eight hours to come up with back rent or her property was forfeit.

Eve listened to his angry yammering as she hoofed it up the stairs in the miserable three-floor walk-up. She had his master code in hand, and was certain he'd already used it as she unlocked Hetta's door.

It was a single room, narrow bed, dingy window, with a few attempts at homey with the frilly pink curtain and cheap shiny pink pillows. Eve did a quick toss, turned up an address log, a credit book with over three thousand in deposit, some framed photographs, and an expired driver's license that listed Hetta's last address in Jersey.

The closet was half full, and from the scarred suitcase on the top shelf, Eve judged it to be all Hetta had. She ran the 'link, made a dupe of all the calls on disc, then copied the license.

If Hetta had gone on a trip, she'd taken no more with her than walking-around credits, the clothes on her back, and her club companion's license.

Eve wasn't betting on it.

She called the morgue from her car 'link. 'Run the Jane Does,' she ordered. 'White, blond, twenty-eight, about a hundred and thirty pounds, five foot four. Transmitting copy of driver's license holo.'

She was barely three blocks away, heading to Cop Central, when the answer came in.

'Lieutenant, we got a possible match. Need dental, DNA, or prints to verify. Our possible can't be identified by hologram.'

'Because?' Eve asked, but she already knew.

'She doesn't have enough face left.'

The prints matched. The primary assigned to the Jane Doe handed Hetta over to Eve without a backward glance. In her office, Eve stared down at the three files.

'Sloppy work,' she muttered. 'Moppett's prints were on file from her companion's license. Carmichael could have ID'd her weeks ago.'

'I'd say Carmichael wasn't much interested in a Jane Doe,' Peabody commented.

Eve reined in the anger, flicked a glance up at Peabody. 'Then Carmichael's in the wrong business, isn't she? We've got links here, Peabody. From Hetta to Boomer, Boomer to Pandora. What probability did you get when you ran them, asked if they were killed by the same hand?'

'Ninety-six point one.'

'Okay.' Eve's stomach jittered with relief. 'I'm taking all of this to the PA, doing a tap dance. I may be able to talk them into dropping charges on Mavis. At least until we gather more evidence. If they don't . . .' She looked Peabody dead in the eye. 'I'm leaking it to Nadine Furst for broadcast. That's a code violation, and I'm telling you because as long as you're attached to me and this case, you can be held equally responsible. You're risking a possible reprimand if you stay. I can have you reassigned before this goes down.'

'I would consider that action a reprimand, Lieutenant. An undeserved one.'

Eve said nothing for a moment. 'Thanks. DeeDee.'

Peabody winced. 'Don't call me DeeDee.'

'Fine. Take everything we have over to EDD, hand deliver personally to Captain Feeney. I don't want this data transmitted through channels, at least not until I talk to the PA, then try a little solo investigation.'

She saw the light go on in Peabody's eyes and smiled. She could remember what it was like to be new and have your first shot. 'Go over to the Down and Dirty Club where

Hetta worked, tell Crack, he's the big one. Believe me, you won't miss him. Tell him you're mine, tell him Hetta's a corpse. See what you can get out of him, out of anybody. Who she hung with, what she might have said about Boomer that last night, who else she spent time with. You know the drill.'

'Yes, sir.'

'Oh, and Peabody.' Eve slipped the files into her bag and rose. 'Don't go in uniform, you'll scare the natives.'

The PA smashed Eve's hopes in ten minutes flat. She continued to argue for another twenty, but it was all spinning wheels. Jonathan Heartly agreed that there was a likely connection in the three homicides. He was an agreeable man. He admired her investigative work, her deductive powers, and her organized presentation of same. He admired any cop who did the job in an exemplary fashion and kept his office's conviction rate high.

But he, and the prosecutor's office, were not prepared to drop the charges against Mavis Freestone. The physical evidence was too strong, and the case, at this point, too solid to warrant a backpedal.

He would, however, keep his door open. When and if Eve had another suspect, he would be more than willing to listen to her case.

'Puss head,' Eve muttered as she slammed into the Blue Squirrel. She spotted Nadine immediately, already in a booth and grimacing over the menu.

'Why the hell does it always have to be here, Dallas?' Nadine demanded the minute Eve dropped down across from her.

'I'm a creature of habit.' But the club wasn't the same, she noted, not without Mavis standing onstage screeching out her incomprehensible lyrics in her latest, eye-popping costume. 'Coffee, black,' Eve ordered.

'I'll have the same. How bad can it be?'

'Just wait for it. Are you still smoking?'

Nadine glanced around, uneasy. 'This isn't a smoking booth.'

'Like they're going to say something in a joint like this. Give me one, will you?'

'You don't smoke.'

'I'm hoping to develop bad habits. You want the two bucks?'

'No.' Keeping an eye out, just in case anyone she knew was around, Nadine took out two cigarettes. 'You look like you could use something a little stronger.'

'This'll do.' She leaned over so that Nadine could light it, took one puff. Hacked. 'Jesus. Let me try that again.' She drew in smoke, felt her head spin, her lungs revolt. Annoyed, she crushed it out. 'That's disgusting. Why do you do that?'

'It's a developed taste.'

'So's eating dog shit. And speaking of dog shit.' Eve slid her coffee from the serving slot and took one brave sip. 'So, how've you been?'

'Good. Better. I've been doing things I didn't used to

think I had time for. It's funny how a near death experience makes you realize not making time is wasting time. I heard Morse has been found competent to stand trial.'

'He's not crazy. He's just a killer.'

'Just a killer.' Nadine ran a finger along her throat where a knife had once drawn blood. 'You don't figure being the latter makes him the former.'

'No, some people just like killing. Don't dwell on it, Nadine. It doesn't help.'

'I've been trying not to. I took a few weeks, spent some time with my family. That helped. It also reminded me that I love my job. And I'm good at it, even though I folded—'

'You didn't fold,' Eve interrupted impatiently, 'you were drugged, you had a knife to your throat, and you were scared. Put it behind you.'

'Yeah. Right. Well.' She blew out smoke. 'Anything new on your friend? I wasn't really able to tell you how sorry I am that she's in trouble.'

'She's going to be all right.'

'I'd bank on you seeing to that.'

'That's right, Nadine, and you're going to help me. I've got some data for you from an unidentified police source. No, no recorders, write it down,' Eve ordered as Nadine reached in her bag.

'Whatever you say.' Nadine dug deeper, found a pad and a pen. 'Shoot.'

'We have three separate homicides, and evidence points to one killer. The first, Hetta Moppett, part-time dancer and licensed club companion, was beaten to death on May 28, at approximately two A.M. The majority of blows were delivered to her face and head in such a manner as to obliterate her features.'

'Ah,' Nadine said and left it at that.

'Her body was discovered, without identification, at six the next morning and tagged as a Jane Doe. At the time of her murder, Mavis Freestone was standing on that stage behind you, belting her guts out in front of about a hundred and fifty witnesses.'

Nadine's brow shot up, and she smiled. 'Well, well. Keep going, Lieutenant.'

So she did.

It was the best she could do for the moment. When the broadcast hit, it was doubtful whether anyone in the department would have to guess who the unnamed source was. But they wouldn't be able to prove it. And Eve would, for Mavis, if not for herself, lie without a qualm if and when she was questioned.

She put in a few more hours at Cop Central, had the miserable job of contacting Hetta's brother, the only next of kin who could be tracked down, and informing him that his sister was dead.

After that cheerful interlude, she went back over every scrap of forensic evidence the sweepers had sucked up at the Moppett murder scene.

There was no doubt that she had been killed where she'd

been found. The murder had been a clean, probably a quick hit. A shattered elbow had been the only defensive wound. No murder weapon had yet been found.

No murder weapon on Boomer either, she mused. A few broken fingers, the added finesse of the broken arm, the shattered kneecaps – all prior to death. That, she had to assume, was torture. Boomer had had more than information, he'd had a sample, and the formula, and the killer had wanted both.

But Boomer had hung tough there. The killer, for whatever reason, hadn't had the time or wanted to take the risk to go to Boomer's flop and toss it.

Why had Boomer been dumped in the river? To buy time, she speculated. But the ploy hadn't worked, and the body had been found and ID'd quickly. She and Peabody had been at the flop within hours of the discovery and had bagged and tagged the evidence.

So, on to Pandora. She knew too much, wanted too much, proved an unstable business partner, threatened to talk to the wrong people. Any of the above, Eve mused and rubbed her hands over her face.

There'd been more rage in her death, more of a fight, more of a mess. Then again, she was hopped on Immortality. She wasn't some foolish club dancer caught in an alley, or a pitiful weasel who knew more than he should. Pandora was a powerful woman, with a sharp mind and an ambitious bent. And, Eve remembered, well-developed biceps.

Three bodies, one killer, and one link between them. And the link was money.

She ran all suspects through her computer, checking normal credit transactions. The only one who was hurting was Leonardo. He was in debt up to his gold eyeballs, and then some.

Then again, greed had no credit balance. It was the property of the rich as well as the poor. She dug a little deeper, and found that Redford had been busy juggling funds. Withdrawals, deposits, more withdrawals. Electronic transfers had been bouncing from coast to coast and to neighboring satellites.

Interesting, she thought, and more interesting still when she hit on a transfer from his New York account direct into that of Jerry Fitzgerald in the amount of a hundred and twenty-five thousand.

'Three months ago,' Eve murmured, rechecking the date. 'That's a lot of money between friends. Computer scan for any and all transfers from this account to any and all accounts under the name of Jerry Fitzgerald or Justin Young in the past twelve months.'

Scanning. No transfers recorded.

'Scan for transfers from any and all accounts under the name of Redford to previously requested accounts.'

Scanning. No transfers recorded.

'Okay, okay, let's try this. Scan for transfers from any and all accounts under the name of Redford to any and all accounts under the name Pandora.'

SCANNING. TRANSFERS AS FOLLOWS:

TEN THOUSAND FROM NEW YORK CENTRAL ACCOUNT TO NEW YORK CENTRAL ACCOUNT, PANDORA, 2/6/58. SIX THOUSAND FROM NEW LOS ANGELES ACCOUNT TO NEW LOS ANGELES SECURITY, PANDORA, 3/19/58. TEN THOUSAND FROM NEW YORK CENTRAL ACCOUNT TO NEW LOS ANGELES SECURITY, PANDORA, 5/4/58. TWELVE THOUSAND FROM STARLIGHT STATION BONDED TO STARLIGHT STATION BONDED, PANDORA, 6/12/58.

NO OTHER TRANSFERS RECORDED.

'Well, that oughta do it. Was she bleeding you, pal, or was she dealing for you?' Eve wished fleetingly for Feeney, then went after the next layer herself. 'Computer, scan previous year, same data.'

While the computer worked, she programmed coffee and speculated on scenarios.

Two hours later, her eyes were sore, her neck screaming, but she had more than enough to warrant another interview with Redford. She had to settle for his E-service, but did have the pleasure of requesting his presence at Cop Central at ten the following morning.

After leaving memos for Peabody and Feeney, she decided to call it a day.

It didn't do her mood much good to discover a memo from Roarke on her car 'link.

'You've been out of touch, Lieutenant. I had something come up that requires my presence. I'll be in Chicago by the time you get this, I imagine. I may have to stay over tonight, unless I can clear this little mess up quickly. You can reach me at the River Palace if you need to, otherwise, I'll see you tomorrow. Don't stay up working half the night. I'll know.'

With an annoyed flick, she switched off memo mode. 'What the hell else am I supposed to do?' she demanded. 'I can't sleep when you're not there.'

She swung through the gates, and saw with some hope that lights were blazing everywhere. He'd canceled the meeting, fixed the problem, missed his transportation. Whatever, she thought, he was home. She walked in the door with a welcoming smile on her face and followed the sound of Mavis's laughter.

There were four people having drinks and canapes in the parlor, but none of them was Roarke. *Quick observation powers, Lieutenant,* Eve thought glumly, then took a moment to scan the room before she was noticed.

Mavis was still laughing, and dressed in what only she would consider at-home wear. Her red skin suit was studded with silver stars and covered with a sheer emerald sweep shirt left loose and open. She teetered on six-inch ice-pick heels as she cuddled Leonardo. He had one arm wrapped around her, and the other hand was fisted around a glass filled with something clear and fizzy.

A woman munched on canapes, eating them with a speed and precision to rival a factory droid stamping out computer chips. Her hair was in short corkscrew curls, with each twist a different jewel tone. Her left earlobe was encased in silver hoops that draped a twisted chain around and under her pointed chin to her other ear where it was affixed with a single thumb-size stud. There was a tattoo of a rosebud along the side of her thin, pointed nose. Over electric blue eyes, her brows were sharp Vs of royal purple.

Which matched, Eve saw in amazement, the micro-size suspendered playsuit that ended in cuffs just south of her crotch. The suspenders were strategically placed over bare breasts to cover the nipples. The breasts were the size of farm-grown cantaloupes.

Beside her, a man with what appeared to be a map tattooed on his bald pate watched the action through rose-tinted glasses and guzzled what Eve deduced to be some of Roarke's vintage white. His party clothes consisted of baggy shorts that hung to bony knees and a chest plate of patriotic red, white, and blue.

She considered, seriously, sneaking upstairs unobserved and locking herself in her office.

'Your guests,' Summerset said in dismissive tones from behind her, 'have been waiting for you.'

'Look, pal, they're not my—'

'Dallas!' Mavis squealed it, and leaped dangerously across the room in her fashionable stilts. She caught Eve in a tipsy bear hug that nearly felled them both. 'You're so late. Roarke had to go somewhere, and he said it was all right if Biff and Trina came by. They've been dying to meet you.

Leonardo will fix you a drink. Oh, Summerset, the goodies are just mag. You're so sweet.'

'I'm delighted you're enjoying them.' He beamed at her. There was no other description for the bright, moony look that shot out of his stony face before he faded back into the hall.

'Come on, Dallas, join the party.'

'Mavis, I've really got a lot of work—' But Eve was already being dragged into the parlor.

'Can I get you a drink, Dallas?' Leonardo offered her a sad, puppy dog smile. Eve crumbled.

'Sure. Fine. A glass of wine.'

'Absolutely extraordinary wine. I'm Biff.' The man with the map on his head offered a slim, delicate hand. 'It's an honor to meet Mavis's champion, Lieutenant Dallas. You're absolutely right, Leonardo,' he continued with his eyes intense behind the rosy lenses. 'The bronze silk is perfect for her.'

'Biff is a fabric expert,' Mavis explained in a voice that continued to bubble and froth. 'He's worked with Leonardo for just ever. They've been plotting your trousseau.'

'My—'

'And this is Trina. She's going to do your hair.'

'She is?' Eve felt the blood drain out of her head and into her feet. 'Oh well, I don't . . .' Even women with little vanity can panic when faced with a stylist boasting rainbow curls. 'I don't really think—'

'Gratis,' Trina announced in a tone that was the vocal equivalent of rusted iron. 'When you clear Mavis, I'm giving you free hair consultations and styling for the rest of your life.' She grabbed a handful of Eve's hair and squeezed. 'Good texture. Good weight. Bad cut.'

'Here's your wine, Dallas.'

'Thanks.' She needed it. 'Listen, it's nice to meet you, but I've got some work I have to get to.'

'Oh, but you can't.' Mavis latched onto Eve's arm like a leech. 'Everyone's here to start doing you.'

Now the blood flowed out of her toes. 'Doing what to me?'

'We're all set up upstairs, too. Leonardo's work space, Trina's, Biff's. All the other worker bees will be buzzing around by tomorrow.'

'Bees?' Eve managed. 'Buzzing.'

'For the show.' Cold sober, and less likely to assume welcome, Leonardo patted Mavis's arm to try to restrain her enthusiasm. 'Little dove, Dallas might not want the house full of people at this point. I mean . . .' He dodged around the investigation. 'With the wedding so close.'

'But it's the only way we can be together and finish the designs for the show.' The plea naked in her eyes, Mavis turned back to Eve. 'You don't mind, do you? We won't be in the way. Leonardo just has so much to do. Some of the designs have to be altered now because . . . because Jerry Fitzgerald is going to be the headliner.'

'Different coloring,' Biff put in. 'Different body type. From Pandora,' he finished, saying the name they had been avoiding.

'Yeah.' Mavis's smile went bright and fixed. 'So it's a lot of extra work, and Roarke said it was all right. The house is so big and everything. You won't even know they're all here.'

People, Eve thought, scurrying in and out. Security nightmares. 'Don't worry about it,' she said. She would.

'I told you it would be all right,' Mavis said, planting a kiss on Leonardo's chin. 'And I promised Roarke I wouldn't let you bury yourself tonight, Dallas. You're going to sit back and be pampered. We're getting pizza.'

'Oh goodie. Mavis—'

'Everything's working out,' Mavis went on, almost desperately, her fingers tightening on Eve's arm. 'On Channel 75 they were talking about this new lead, and these other murders, a drug connection. I didn't even know the other people who got whacked. I didn't even know them, Dallas, so it's going to come out that it was somebody else. And it's all going to be over.'

'It's going to take a little time yet, Mavis.' Eve stopped, felt her heart drop at the flickers of panic in Mavis's eyes, worked up a smile. 'Yeah, it's all going to be over. Pizza, huh? I could use some.'

'Great. Mag. I'm going to find Summerset and tell him we're ready for it. Take Dallas up and show her, okay?' She darted out.

'It really lifted her,' Leonardo said quietly. 'That news report. She needed a lift. The Blue Squirrel let her go.'

'Let her go?'

'Bastards,' Trina muttered around a canape.

'Management decided it wasn't in their best interest to have an accused murderer headlining. It shook her bad. I had the idea to take her mind off it this way. I'm sorry, I should have cleared it with you first.'

'No, it's fine.' Eve took another sip of wine and braced herself. 'Let's go do me then.'

12

It wasn't so bad, Eve decided. Not when compared to the riots of the Urban Wars, the torture chambers of the Spanish Inquisition, a test ride on the XR-85 moon jet. And she was a cop, a ten-year vet, used to facing danger.

She was certain her eyes wheeled like a panicked horse's when Trina tested her cropping sheers.

'Hey, maybe we could just—'

'Leave it to the experts,' Trina said. Eve nearly whimpered with relief when she set the shears down again. 'Let's see about this.'

She approached, unarmed, but Eve watched warily.

'I've got a hair consult program.' Leonardo looked up from the long table, covered with fabrics where he and Biff muttered together. 'Full morphing capabilities.'

'I don't need a stinking program.' To prove it, Trina caught Eve's face in her firm, wide hands. Eyes narrowed, she began to move up then around Eve's head, over the jaw, up the cheekbones. 'Decent bone structure,' she approved. 'Who do you use?'

'For what?'

'Face sculpting.'

'God.'

Trina paused, snickered, then let out an ear-blasting laugh, the tone of a rusted tuba. 'I like your cop, Mavis.'

'She's the best,' Mavis said drunkenly. She perched on a nearby stool, studying herself in the triple mirrors. 'Maybe you could do me, too, Trina. The lawyers suggested I go for a more sedate look. You know, brunette or something.'

'Fuck that.' Trina pressed her thumbs under Eve's jaw to lift it. 'I've got some new shit that'll blast any judge out of his robe, cutie. Bordello pink with silver tipping. Just on the market.'

'Oh yeah.' Mavis flipped her sapphire locks back and considered.

'What I could do for you with a little highlighting.'

Eve's blood ran cold. 'Just the cut, right? We're just snipping a little.'

'Yeah, yeah.' Trina pushed Eve's head onto her chest. 'This color a gift from God, too?' She chuckled to herself, yanked Eve's head back, and dragged all the hair away from her face. 'The eyes are good. The brows could use a little work, but we can fix that.'

'Give me some more wine, Mavis.' Eve shut the eyes that were good, and told herself whatever happened, it would grow back.

'Okay, wet down.' Trina whirled the chair and its reluctant occupant to a porta-sink, tipped it back until Eve's neck was braced in the padded slot. 'Close your eyes and enjoy, honey. I give the best shampoo and head massage in the business.'

There was something to be said for that. The wine or Trina's clever fingers mellowed Eve's mood toward some twilight world of relaxation. Dimly she heard Leonardo and Biff arguing over their preferences of crimson satin or scarlet silk for evening pajamas. The music Leonardo had programmed was something classical with sobbing piano arpeggios, and the scent of crushed flowers filled the air.

Why had Paul Redford told her about the Chinese box and the illegals? If he'd gone back for them himself, had them in his possession, why would he want their existence known?

Double bluff? A ploy? Maybe there had never been a box to begin with. Or he knew it was gone already so . . .

Eve didn't stir until something cold and sticky was slapped on her face. Then she yelped.

'What the hell—'

'A Saturnia facial.' Trina glopped on more dun-colored goo. 'Clear out your pores like a vacuum. It's a crime to neglect your skin. Mavis, get out the Sheena, will you?'

'What's the Sheena – never mind.' With one final shudder, Eve closed her eyes and surrendered. 'I don't want to know.'

'Might as well have the full treatment.' Trina slicked more mud under Eve's jaw, quick fingers working up. 'You're tight, honey. Want me to plug in a nice VR program for you?'

'No, no. This is about as fanciful as I can handle, thanks.'

'Okay. Want to tell me about your man?' Briskly, Trina tugged open the robe Eve had been ordered to wear and clamped her mud coated hands on Eve's breasts. When Eve's eyes popped open, fired, she laughed. 'Don't you worry, I'm not into females. Your man's going to love your tits when I'm done with them.'

'He likes them just fine now.'

'Yeah, but Saturnia's breast smoother is top of the line. They'll feel like rose petals. Take my word. Is he a nibbler or a sucker?'

Eve just closed her eyes again. 'I'm not even here.'

'There you go.'

She heard water run, then Trina was back and rubbing something into her hair that smelled appealingly of vanilla.

People paid for this, Eve reminded herself. Huge amounts that put gaping holes in their credit accounts.

People were obviously insane. She kept her eyes stubbornly closed as something warm and wet was laid over her mud-covered breasts, her face. Conversations went on cheerfully around her. Mavis and Trina discussed various beauty aids, Leonardo and Biff consulted over line and color.

Very insane, Eve thought, then let out a groan as her feet were massaged. They were dipped in something hot and oddly pleasant. She heard the crackle of something, felt her feet being lifted, covered. Then her hands received the same treatment.

She tolerated it, tolerated even the quick buzz of something around her eyebrows. And felt heroic when she heard Mavis laugh easily and flirt with Leonardo.

She had to keep Mavis's spirits up, she thought. It was as vital as every step in the investigation. It wasn't enough to represent the dead.

She squeezed her eyes tighter when she heard the snip of Trina's shears, felt the light tugs, the comb through. Hair was just hair, she told herself. Appearances didn't matter.

Oh Jesus, don't let her scalp me.

She forced her mind to focus on work, ran through questions she would ask Redford in the morning, considered his possible answers. It was likely she would be called to the commander's office about the news leak. She would deal with that.

She needed a conference with both Feeney and Peabody. It was time to see if any of the data the three of them had dug up would dovetail. She'd go back to the club, have Crack turn her on to some of the regulars. Someone might have seen whoever had spooked Boomer that night. And if that same person had talked to Hetta—

She jerked when Trina adjusted the chair to recline and began to scrub off the mud. 'She'll be ready for you in five,' Trina told an impatient Leonardo. 'I don't rush my genius.' She grinned down at Eve. 'You've got decent skin. I'm going to leave some samples with you. Use them, you'll keep it decent.'

Mavis peered down and Eve began to feel like a patient

on an operating table. 'You did a wonderful job on the eyebrows, Trina. They look so natural. All she needs to do is dye her lashes. They don't even need a lengthener. And don't you think that dimple in her chin is mag?'

'Mavis,' Eve said wearily. 'I don't want to have to hit you.'

Mavis only grinned. 'Pizza's here. Have a bite.' She stuffed some in Eve's mouth. 'Wait till you see your skin, Dallas. It's gorgeous.'

Eve only grunted. The hot cheese had seared the roof of her mouth, but it also stirred juices. She risked choking and took the rest of the slice while Trina bound up her hair in a silver turban.

'It's thermal,' Trina told her as she shot the chair back up. 'I've got a root and shaft penetrator on it.'

Eve eyed the reflection. Maybe her skin did look dewy, and at a wary stroke of her fingers, it certainly felt smooth. But she couldn't see even a single strand of hair. 'I've got hair under there, right? My hair?'

'Sure you do. Okay, Leonardo. She's yours for twenty minutes.'

'At last.' He beamed. 'Take off the robe.'

'Oh, look—'

'Dallas, we're all professionals. You have to try on the foundation for the wedding dress. It will certainly need a few adjustments.'

She'd already been felt up by a stylist, Eve decided. Why not stand naked in a roomful of people? She shrugged out of the robe.

Leonardo came at her with something white and sleek. Before she could do much more than squeak, he had it around her torso and snugged at her back. His big hands reached under the material, fussily adjusted her breasts. Bending down, he drew a swatch of material between her legs, secured it, stepped back.

'Ah.'

'Holy hell, Dallas. Roarke's tongue's going to land on his feet when he gets you down to that.'

'What the hell is it?'

'A variation on the old Merry Widow.' With quick nips and tucks, Leonardo perfected the fit. 'I call it a Curvaceous. Added a bit of lift under the breasts for you. Yours are quite nice, but this line adds more contour. Just a touch of lace, a few pearls. Nothing too ornate.' He turned her to face the mirror.

She looked sexy, curvy. Ripe, Eve realized with some amazement. The material had a faint gleam to it, as though it was damp. It nipped at her waist, molded her hips, and, she had to admit, lifted her bustline to new, fascinating heights.

'Well . . . I guess . . . for, you know, wedding nights.'

'For any nights,' Mavis said dreamily. 'Oh, Leonardo. Are you going to make me one?'

'I already have, in Rascal Red satin. Now, Dallas, does it pinch anywhere? Rub?'

'No.' She couldn't get over it. It should have been torturous, but it was as comfortable as a sprint suit. Experimentally she bent, twisted. 'It's just sort of there.'

'Excellent. Biff found the material at a little cottage shop on Richer Five. Now the dress. It's only basted, so we take care. Lift your arms, please.'

He slipped it over her, let it float down. The material was stunning. Eve could see that, even when it was streaked with tailor's marks. It seemed perfect to her, the sleek column, the snug sleeves, the simple line, but Leonardo creased his brow and tugged at the material, folded, bunched.

'The neckline works, yes. Where is the necklace?'

'Huh?'

'The copper and stone necklace. Didn't I tell you to ask for it?'

'I can't just tell Roarke I want a necklace.'

Leonardo sighed, turned Eve around, and exchanged a look with Mavis. He nodded, then tested the line at Eve's hips.

'You've lost weight,' he accused.

'No, I haven't.'

'Yes, at least two pounds.' He clucked his tongue. 'I won't take it in yet. See that you put them back on.'

Biff marched over and held a bolt of material next to her face. With a nod, he marched away, muttering into his notebook.

'Biff, would you show her the other designs while I note the adjustments to the gown?'

With a flourish, Biff switched on a wall monitor. 'As you can see, Leonardo has taken both your lifestyle and your body line into consideration with these designs. This simple day suit is perfect for a corporate lunch, a press conference, unrestricted, yet *tres, tres* chic. The material we're using is a blended linen with just a whisper of silk. The color is citrine with trim of garnet.'

'Uh-huh.' It looked like a nice, simple suit to Eve, but it was a jolt to see the computer-generated image of herself modeling it. 'Biff?'

'Yes, Lieutenant?'

'Why do you have a map tattooed on your head?'

He smiled. 'I have a very poor sense of direction. Now this next design continues the theme.'

She viewed a dozen. They blurred together in her mind. Rayspan in citrus lemon, Breton lace with velvet, classic black silk. Every time Mavis oohed or aahed, Eve ordered recklessly. What was being in debt for the rest of her life compared to her closest friend's peace of mind?

'That'll keep you two busy awhile.' The minute Leonardo slipped the dress back off, Trina bundled Eve into the robe. 'Let's take a look at the crowning glory.' After unwinding the turban, she pulled a wide forked comb out of her twirling curls and began to pick, smooth, and fluff.

Eve's initial relief that she had hair to be fussed with faded quickly as she stared directly at a snaking pink spring. 'Who does your hair, Trina?'

'Nobody touches me but me.' She winked. 'And God. Take a look.'

Braced for the worst, Eve turned. The woman in the mirror was definitely Eve Dallas. At first she thought it had all been some elaborate joke, and nothing had been done at all. Then she looked closer, stepped closer. Gone were the wild tufts and stray spikes. Her hair was still casually cropped, unstructured, but it seemed to have a shape after all. And certainly it hadn't had that pretty shine before. It followed the lines of her face nicely, the fringe of bangs, the curve at the cheeks. And when she shook her head it fell back into place obediently.

Eyes narrowed, she raked fingers through it and watched it tumble back. 'Did you put blond in it?'

'Nope. Natural highlights. Brought them out with Sheena, that's all. You got deer hair.'

'What?'

'Ever seen a deer hide? It's got all those colors from russet, brown, gold, even touches of black. That's what you've got there. God's been good to you. Trouble is, whoever's been doing you must have been using hedge trimmers and no highlight puncher, either.'

'It looks good.'

'Damn right it does. I'm a genius.'

'You look beautiful.' Suddenly, Mavis put her face in her hands and wept. 'You're getting married.'

'Oh, Christ, don't do that, Mavis. Come on.' Feeling helpless, Eve gave her encouraging pats on the back.

'I'm so drunk, and I'm so happy. And I'm so scared. Dallas, I lost my job.'

'I know, baby. I'm sorry. You'll get another one. A better one.'

'I don't care. I don't care. I'm not going to care. We're going to have the most mag wedding, aren't we, Dallas?'

'You bet.'

'Leonardo's making me the most rocking dress. Let's show her, Leonardo.'

'Tomorrow.' He came over, scooped her into his arms. 'Dallas is tired.'

'Oh, yeah. She needs to rest.' Mavis let her head loll on his shoulder. 'She works too hard. She's worried about me. I don't want her to worry, Leonardo. Everything's going to be fine, isn't it? It's going to be fine.'

'Just fine.' Leonardo sent Eve one last uneasy look before he carried Mavis off.

Eve watched them go, sighed. 'Fuck.'

'Like that sweet little thing could bash anybody's face in.' Trina scowled as she gathered up her tools. 'I hope Pandora's burning in hell.'

'You knew her?'

'Everybody in the business knew her. Loathed her ever-fucking guts. Right, Biff?'

'She was born a bitch, died a bitch.'

'Did she just use, or did she deal?'

Biff slanted a look at Trina, then shrugged. 'She never dealt in the open, but you'd hear talk now and again that she was always well supplied. The buzz was she was an Erotica junkie. She liked sex, and she might deal to her partner of choice.'

'Were you ever her partner of choice?'

He smiled. 'Romantically, I prefer men. They're less complicated.'

'How about you?'

'I prefer men, too – same reason. So did she.' Trina picked up her kit. 'Last runway gig I had, the gossip was she was mixing business and pleasure. Had some guy she was bleeding. She was flashing a lot of new glitters. Pandora liked to decorate her body with real rock, but she didn't like to pay for it. People figured she'd made some deal with a source.'

'Got a name on the source?'

'Nope, but she was on her palm 'link between changes all day. That was about three months ago. I don't know who she was talking to, but at least one of the calls was intergalactic, because she got royally pissed at the delay.'

'Did she always carry a palm 'link?'

'Everybody in fashion and beauty does, honey. We're just like doctors.'

It was close to midnight when Eve settled down at her desk. She couldn't face the bedroom, preferred the suite she used for privacy and work. She programmed coffee, then forgot to drink it. Without Feeney, she had no choice but to go a roundabout route to try to trace a three-month-old intergalactic call from a palm 'link she didn't have.

After an hour, she gave up and crawled onto the sleep chair. She'd take a nap, she told herself. Set her mental alarm for five A.M.

Illegals, murder, and money, she thought. *They went together. Pin down the source,* she thought groggily. *Identify the unknown.*

Who were you hiding from, Boomer? How did you get your hands on a sample and the formula? Who broke your bones to get them back?

The image of his battered body flashed into her mind and was ruthlessly shut off. She didn't need to drift into sleep with that loop playing.

It might have been a better choice than the show she ended with.

The dirty red light was flashing. Over and over through the window. SEX! LIVE! SEX! LIVE!

She was only eight, but her mind was quick. She wondered if people would pay to see dead sex. Lying on her bed, she watched the light blink. She knew what sex was. It was ugly, it was painful, it was frightening. It was inescapable.

Maybe he wouldn't come home tonight. She'd stopped praying that he would forget where he'd left her or fall down dead in some handy ditch. He always came back.

But sometimes, if she was very, very lucky, he would be too drunk, too buzzed to do more than stumble to the bed and snore. Those nights, she would shiver with relief and huddle in the corner to sleep.

She still thought about escape. Of finding a way out of the locked door, or down the five stories. If the night was very bad, she imagined just jumping from the window. The flight down would be quick, and then it would be over.

He wouldn't be able to hurt her then. But she was too much a coward to jump.

She was only a child, after all, and tonight she was hungry. And she was cold because he had broken the temperature control in one of his rages and it was stuck on full air.

She padded toward the corner of the room, the excuse for a kitchenette. Experienced, she pounded the drawer first, to send any roaches scattering. She found a chocolate roll inside. The last one. He would probably beat her for eating the last one. Then again, he would beat her anyway, so she might as well enjoy it.

She bolted it like an animal, wiped her mouth with the back of her hand. Hunger churned still. A further search turned up a hunk of moldy cheese. She didn't want to think what had been nibbling on it. Carefully, she took a knife, began to shear off the nasty edges.

Then she heard him at the door. In her panic, she dropped the knife. It clattered to the floor as he came in.

'What are you doing, little girl?'

'Nothing. I woke up. I was just going to get a drink of water.'

'Woke up.' His eyes were glazed, but not glazed enough, she saw without hope. 'Missing your daddy. Come give your daddy a kiss.'

She couldn't breathe. Already she couldn't breathe and

223

the place between her legs where he would hurt her began to throb in painful fear. 'I have a stomachache.'

'Oh? I'll kiss it better.' He was grinning as he crossed to her. Then the grin faded. 'You've been eating without asking again, haven't you? Haven't you?'

'No, I—' But the lie, and the hope to evade both died as his hand swiped hard over her face. Her lip split, her eyes watered, but she barely winced. 'I was going to fix some cheese. A snack for when you—'

He hit her again, hard enough to make stars explode inside her head. She went down this time, and before she could scramble up, he was on her.

Screams, her screams, because his fists were hard and merciless. Pain, blinding, numbing pain that was nothing beside the fear. The fear because however horrible, this would not be the worst he did to her.

'Daddy, please. Please, please.'

'Have to punish you. You never listen. Never fucking listen. Then I'll give you a treat. A nice big treat, and you'll be a good girl.'

His breath was hot on her face and somehow smelled like candy. His hands tore at her already tattered clothes, poking, squeezing, invading. His breathing changed, a change she knew and feared. It became shallow, greedy.

'No, no, it hurts, it hurts!'

Her poor young flesh resisted. She batted at him, screaming still, was driven beyond fear to claw. His cry of rage bellowed out. He twisted her arm back. She heard the dry, hideous sound of her own bone snapping.

'Lieutenant. Lieutenant Dallas.'

The scream ripped from her throat and she came to, swinging blindly. In wild panic she scrambled up, her own legs tangling and taking her to the floor in a heap.

'Lieutenant.'

She reared away from the hand that touched her shoulder, huddled back as sobs and screams knotted in her throat.

'You were dreaming.' Summerset spoke carefully, his face impassive. She might have seen the realization in his eyes if her own hadn't been clouded with memory. 'You were dreaming,' he repeated, approaching her as he would a trapped wolf. 'You had a nightmare.'

'Stay away from me. Go away. Stay away.'

'Lieutenant. Do you know where you are?'

'I know where I am.' She got the words out between quick gulps of air. She was freezing, boiling, and couldn't stop the tremors. 'Go away. Just go away.' She made it as far as her knees, then covered her mouth and rocked. 'Get the hell out of here.'

'Let me help you to the chair.' His hands were gentle, but firm enough to keep hold when she tried to shove him away.

'I don't need help.'

'I'm going to help you to your chair.' As far as he was concerned, she was a child now, a wounded one who needed care. As his Marlena had been. He tried not to think if his child had begged as Eve had begged. After he put her in the chair, he went to a chest, drew out a blanket. Her teeth were chattering and her eyes were wide with shock.

'Be still.' The order was brisk as she began to push up. 'Stay where I've put you and be quiet.'

He turned on his heel, striding into the kitchen alcove and the AutoChef. There was sweat on his brow and he dabbed at it with a handkerchief as he ordered a soother. His hand was shaking. It didn't surprise him. Her screams had chilled him to the bone and brought him to her suite at a dead run.

They'd been a child's screams.

Steadying himself, he carried the glass to her. 'Drink it.'

'I don't want—'

'Drink it, or I'll pour it down your throat, with pleasure.'

She considered knocking it out of his hand, then embarrassed them both by curling into a ball and whimpering. Giving up, Summerset set the drink aside, tucked the blanket more securely around her, and went out with the object of contacting Roarke's personal physician.

But it was Roarke himself he met on the landing.

'Summerset, don't you ever sleep?'

'It's Lieutenant Dallas. She's—'

Roarke dropped his briefcase, grabbed Summerset by the lapels. 'Has she been hurt? Where is she?'

'A nightmare. She was screaming.' Summerset lost his usual composure and dragged a hand over his hair. 'She won't cooperate. I was about to call your doctor. I left her in her private suite.'

As Roarke pushed him aside, Summerset grabbed his arm. 'Roarke, you should have told me what had been done to her.'

Roarke merely shook his head and kept going. 'I'll take care of her.'

He found her curled up tight, trembling. Emotions warred through him, anger, relief, sorrow, and guilt. He battled them back and lifted her gently. 'It's all right now, Eve.'

'Roarke.' She shuddered once convulsively, then curved into him as he settled back in the chair with her on his lap. 'The dreams.'

'I know.' He pressed a kiss to her damp temple. 'I'm sorry.'

'They come all the time now, all the time. Nothing stops them.'

'Eve, why didn't you tell me?' He tipped her head back to look at her face. 'You don't have to go through this alone.'

'Nothing stops them,' she repeated. 'I couldn't not remember anymore. And now I remember all of it.' She rubbed the heels of her hands over her face. 'I killed him, Roarke. I killed my father.'

13

He looked into her eyes, felt the tremors that still shook her. 'Darling, you had a nightmare.'

'I had a flashback.'

She had to be calm, had to be to get it all out. To be calm and rational, she had to think like a cop, not like a woman. Not like a terrorized child.

'It was so clear, Roarke, that I can still feel it on me. Still feel him on me. The room in Dallas where he'd lock me. He'd always lock me in wherever he took me. Once I tried to get away, to run away, and he caught me. After that, he always got rooms high up, and locked the door from the outside. I never got to go out. I don't think anyone even knew I was there.' She tried to clear her raw throat. 'I need some water.'

'Here. Drink this.' He picked up the glass Summerset had left beside the chair.

'No, it's a tranq. I don't want a tranq.' She let air in and out of her lungs. 'I don't need one.'

'All right. No, I'll get it.' He shifted her, rose, caught the doubt in her eyes. 'Just water, Eve. I promise.'

Accepting his word, she took the glass he brought back

and drank gratefully. When he sat on the arm of the chair, she stared straight ahead and continued.

'I remember the room. I've been having part of this dream for the past couple of weeks. Details were beginning to stick. I even went to see Dr Mira.' She glanced over. 'No, I didn't tell you. I couldn't.'

'All right.' He tried to accept that. 'But you're going to tell me now.'

'I have to tell you now.' She took a breath, brought it all into her mind as she would any crime scene. 'I was awake in that room, hoping he'd be too drunk to touch me when he came back. It was late.'

She didn't have to close her eyes to see it: the filthy room, the blink of the red light through the dirty windows.

'Cold,' she murmured. 'He'd broken the temperature control, and it was cold. I could see my breath.' She shivered in reaction. 'But I was hungry, too. I got something to eat. He never kept much around. I was hungry all the time. I was cutting the mold off some cheese when he came in.'

The door opening, the fear, the clatter of the knife. She wanted to get up, pace off the nerves, but wasn't sure her legs were ready to support her.

'I could see right away that he wasn't drunk enough. I could see. I remember what he looked like now. He had dark brown hair and a face gone soft from drinking. He might have been handsome once, but that was gone. Broken capillaries in his face, in his eyes. He had big hands. Maybe it was just because I was small, but they seemed awfully big.'

Roarke lifted his hands to her shoulders, began to massage the tension. 'They can't hurt you now. Can't touch you now.'

'No.' *Except in the dreams,* she thought. *There was pain in dreams.* 'He got mad because I'd been eating. I wasn't supposed to take anything without asking.'

'Christ.' He tucked the blanket more securely around her because she was still shivering. And found he wanted to feed her, anything, everything, so she would never think about hunger again.

'He started hitting me, and hitting me.' She heard her voice hitch, made the effort to level it. *It's just a report now,* she told herself. *Nothing more.* 'Knocked me down and hit me. My face, my body. I was crying and screaming, begging him to stop. He tore my clothes and rammed his fingers in me. It hurt, horribly, because he'd raped me the night before and I was still hurting from that. Then he was raping me again. Panting in my face, telling me to be a good girl and raping me. It felt like everything inside me was tearing. The pain was so bad I couldn't take it anymore. I clawed at him. I must have drawn blood. That's when he broke my arm.'

Roarke stood abruptly, paced away, jabbed the mechanism to open the windows. He needed air.

'I don't know if I blacked out, maybe for a minute, I think. But I couldn't get past the pain. Sometimes you can.'

230

'Yes,' he said dully. 'I know.'

'But it was so enormous. Black, greasy waves of pain. And he wouldn't stop. The knife was in my hand. It was just there, in my hand. I stabbed him with it.' She let out a shuddering breath as Roarke turned to her. 'I stabbed him, and kept stabbing him. Blood was everywhere. The raw, sweet smell of it. I crawled out from under him. He might have been dead already, but I kept stabbing him. Roarke, I can see myself, kneeling, the hilt in my hand, blood past my wrists, splattered on my face. And the pain, the rage pounding at me. I just couldn't stop.'

Who would have? he wondered. *Who could have?*

'Then I pulled myself into the corner to get away from him, because when he got up, he'd kill me. I passed out or just zoned, because I don't remember anything else until it was daylight. And I hurt − I hurt so bad, everywhere. I got sick. Really sick, and when I was finished, I saw. I saw.'

He reached down for her hand, and it was like ice, thin, brittle ice. 'That's enough, Eve.'

'No, let me finish. I have to finish.' She pushed the words out as though she were shoving rocks off her heart. 'I saw. I knew I'd killed him, and they'd come for me, put me in a cage. A dark cage. That's what he'd always told me they did if you weren't good. I went in the bathroom and washed off all the blood. My arm − my arm was screaming, but I didn't want to go in a cage. I put on some clothes and I put everything else that was mine in a bag. I kept imagining he was going to get up and come for me, but he stayed dead. I left him there. I started walking. It was early, early in the morning. Hardly anyone was out. I threw away the bag, or I lost it. I can't remember. I walked a long way, then I went into an alley and hid until night.'

She rubbed a hand over her mouth. She could remember that, too, the dark, the stench, the fear overriding even pain. 'Then I walked more, and kept walking until I couldn't walk anymore. I found another alley. I don't know how long I stayed there, but that's where they found me. By then, I didn't remember anything – what had happened, where I was. Who I was. I still don't remember my name. He never called me by my name.'

'Your name's Eve Dallas.' He cupped her face in his hands. 'And that part of your life is over. You survived it, you overcame it. Now you've remembered it, and it's done.'

'Roarke.' Looking at him, she knew she had never loved anyone more. Never would. 'It's not. I have to face what I've done. The reality of it, and the consequences. I can't marry you now. Tomorrow I have to turn in my badge.'

'What insanity is this?'

'I killed my father, do you understand? There has to be an investigation. Even if I'm cleared, it doesn't negate the fact that my application for the academy, my records, are fraudulent. As long as the investigation is ongoing, I can't be a cop, and I can't marry you.' Steadier, she rose. 'I have to pack.'

'Try it.'

His voice was low, dangerous, and it stopped her. 'Roarke, I have to follow procedure.'

'No, you have to be human.' He strode to the door and slammed it shut. 'Do you think you're walking out on me, on your life, because you defended yourself against a monster?'

'I killed my father.'

'You killed a fucking monster. You were a child. Are you going to stand there, look me in the face, and tell me that child was to blame?'

She opened her mouth, closed it. 'It's not a matter of how I see it, Roarke. The law—'

'The law should have protected you!' With visions dancing evilly in his head, he snapped. He could all but hear the tight wire of control break. 'Goddamn the law. What good did it do either one of us when we needed it most? You want to chuck your badge because the law's too fucking weak to care for its innocents, for its children, be my guest. Throw your career away. But you're not getting rid of me.'

He started to grab her by the shoulders, then dropped his hands. 'I can't touch you.' Shaken by the violence that spewed up in him, he stepped back. 'I'm afraid to put my hands on you. I couldn't stand it if being with me reminded you of what he did.'

'No.' Appalled, it was she who reached out. 'No. It doesn't. It couldn't. There's nothing but you and me when you touch me. It's just that I have to handle this.'

'Alone?' It was, he realized, the most bitter of words. 'The way you had to handle the nightmares alone? I can't go back and kill him for you, Eve. I'd give everything I have and more if I could do that one thing. But I can't. I won't let you deal with this without me. That's not an option for either of us. Sit down.'

'Roarke.'

'Please, sit down.' He took one cleansing breath. She wouldn't listen to anger, he decided. Nor, from him, to reason. 'Do you trust Dr Mira?'

'Yes, I mean—'

'As far as you trust anyone,' he finished. 'That'll do.' He walked over to her desk.

'What are you doing?'

'I'm going to call her.'

'It's the middle of the night.'

'I know what time it is.' He engaged the 'link. 'I'm willing to abide by her advice on this. I'm asking you to do the same.'

She started to argue but found no solid ground. Weary, she dropped her head into her hands. 'All right.'

She stayed there, barely listening to Roarke's quiet voice, the murmured responses. When he came back to her, he reached out a hand. She stared at it.

'She's on her way. Will you come downstairs?'

'I'm not doing this to hurt you or make you angry.'

'You've accomplished both, but that's not the main issue here.' He took her hand and drew her to her feet. 'I won't

234

let you go, Eve. If you didn't love me or want me or need me, I would have to. But you do love me and want me. And though you still have difficulty with the concept, you need me.'

I won't use you, she thought, but she said nothing as they went downstairs.

It didn't take Mira long. In her usual manner, she arrived promptly and perfectly groomed. She greeted Roarke serenely, took one look at Eve, and sat.

'I'd love a brandy, if you wouldn't mind. I believe the lieutenant should join me.' As Roarke saw to the drinks, she looked around the room. 'What a perfectly lovely home. It feels happy.' She smiled, cocked her head. 'Why, Eve, you've changed your hair. It's very flattering.'

Baffled, Roarke stopped, stared. 'What have you done to it?'

Eve lifted a shoulder. 'Nothing, really, just . . .'

'Men.' Mira took her brandy, swirled. 'Why do we bother? When my husband fails to notice a change, he always says it's because he adores me for me, not for my hair. I usually let him get away with it. Now then.' She sat back. 'Can you tell me?'

'Yes.' Eve repeated everything she'd told Roarke. But it was the cop's voice now, cool, composed, detached.

'It's been a difficult night for you.' Mira skimmed her gaze over Roarke. 'For both of you. It might be hard to believe that it will begin to be better now. Can you accept that your mind was ready to deal with this?'

'I suppose. The memories started coming more clearly, more often after that—' She closed her eyes. 'A few months ago I answered a domestic disturbance call. I was too late. The father was on Zeus. He'd hacked the little girl to death before I got in. I terminated him.'

'Yes, I remember. The child, she might have been you. Instead, you survived.'

'My father didn't.'

'And how does that make you feel?'

'Glad. And uneasy, knowing I have that much hate in me.'

'He beat you. He raped you. He was your father and you should have been safe with him. You weren't. How do you believe you should feel about that?'

'It was years ago.'

'It was yesterday,' Mira corrected. 'It was an hour ago.'

'Yes.' Eve looked down at her brandy and squeezed the tears back.

'Was it wrong to defend yourself?'

'No. Not to defend. But I killed him. Even when he was dead, I kept killing him. This – blinding hate, uncontrollable rage. I was like an animal.'

'He had treated you like an animal. Made you an animal. Yes,' she said at Eve's shudder. 'More than stealing your childhood, your innocence, he stripped you of your humanity. There are technical terms for a personality capable of doing what he did to you, but in simple English,' she said in her cool tones, 'he was a monster.'

Mira watched Eve's eyes dart to Roarke, linger, drop away.

'He took your freedom,' she continued, 'and your choices, marked you, branded you, defiled you. You weren't human to him, and if the situation hadn't changed, you might never have been more than an animal if you had survived at all. And yet, after you escaped, you made yourself. What are you now, Eve?'

'A cop.'

Mira smiled. She'd expected exactly that answer. 'And then?'

'A person.'

'A responsible person?'

'Yeah.'

'Capable of friendship, loyalty, compassion, humor. Love?'

Eve looked at Roarke. 'Yes, but—'

'Was the child capable?'

'No, she – I was too afraid to feel. All right, I've changed.' Eve pressed a hand to her temple, surprised and relieved to find the headache drumming there was easing. 'I've made myself into something decent, but that doesn't override the fact that I killed. There has to be an investigation.'

Mira arched a brow. 'Naturally, you can instigate one if finding your father's identity is important to you. Is it?'

'No, I don't give a damn about that. It's procedure—'

'Excuse me.' Mira held up a hand. 'You want to instigate an investigation into the death of this man by your hand when you were eight years old?'

'It's procedure,' Eve said stubbornly. 'And requires my automatic suspension until the investigative team is satisfied. It's also best if my personal plans are put on hold until the matter is resolved.'

Sensing Roarke's fury, Mira flicked him a warning glance and watched him win the bitter battle for control. 'Resolved in what manner?' she asked reasonably. 'I don't want to presume to tell you your job, Lieutenant, but we're talking about a matter that took place some twenty-two years ago.'

'It was yesterday.' Eve found some hollow pleasure in tossing Mira's words back at her. 'It was an hour ago.'

'Emotionally, yes,' Mira agreed, unruffled. 'But in practical terms, and legal ones, more than two decades. There will be no body or physical evidence to examine. There are, of course, the records of your condition when you were found, the abuse, the malnutrition and neglect, the trauma. Now, there is your memory. Do you feel your story will change during interview?'

'No, of course not, but . . . It's procedure.'

'You're a very good cop, Eve,' Mira said gently. 'If this matter came across your desk, exactly as it is, what would be your professional and objective direction? Before you answer, be careful, and be honest. There's no point in punishing yourself, or that innocent, misused child. What would you do?'

'I'd . . .' Beaten, she set down the snifter and pressed her hands to her eyes. 'I'd close it.'

'Then close it.'

'It's not up to me.'

'I'll be happy to take this up with your commander, in private, give him the facts and my personal recommendation. I think you know what his decision would be. We need people like you to serve and protect, Eve. There's a man here who needs you to trust him.'

'I do trust him.' She braced herself to look over at Roarke. 'I'm afraid of using him. It doesn't matter what other people think about the money, about the power. I don't want to ever give him reason to think I ever could or ever would use him.'

'Does he think it?'

She closed a hand around the diamond hanging between her breasts. 'He's too much in love with me to think it now.'

'Well, I'd say that's lovely. And before much longer, you might figure out the difference between depending on someone you love and trust and exploiting their strengths.' Mira rose. 'I'd tell you to take a sedative and tomorrow off, but you'll do neither.'

'No, I won't. I'm sorry to have dragged you away from home in the middle of the night.'

'Cops and doctors, we're used to it. You'll talk with me again?'

She wanted to refuse, to deny – as she had spent years refusing and denying. But that time, Eve realized, was over. 'Yes, all right.'

On impulse, Mira laid a hand on Eve's cheek and kissed her. 'You'll do, Eve.' Then she turned to Roarke and extended her hand. 'I'm glad you called me. I have a personal interest in the lieutenant.'

'So do I. Thank you.'

'I hope you'll invite me to the wedding. I'll see myself out.'

Roarke walked over, sat beside Eve. 'Would it be better for you if I gave away my money, my properties, tossed aside my companies, and started from scratch?'

Whatever she'd been expecting, it hadn't been this. She gaped at him. 'Would you?'

He leaned forward, kissed her lightly. 'No.'

The laugh that bubbled out surprised her. 'I feel like an idiot.'

'You should.' He linked his fingers with hers. 'Let me help take the pain away.'

'You've been doing that since you walked in the door.' With a sigh, she rested her brow on his. 'Tolerate me, Roarke. I'm a good cop. I know what I'm doing when the badge is on. It's when I take it off I'm not so sure of my moves.'

'I'm a tolerant man. I can accept your dark spaces, Eve, just as you accept mine. Come on, let's go to bed. You'll sleep.' He brought her to her feet again. 'And if you have nightmares, you won't hide them from me.'

'No, not anymore. What is it?'

Eyes narrowed, he combed his fingers through her hair.

'You did change it. Subtly, but charmingly. And there's something else . . .' He rubbed a thumb over her jawline.

Eve wiggled her eyebrows, hoping he'd noticed their new improved shape, but he only continued to stare at her. 'What?'

'You're beautiful. Really quite beautiful.'

'You're tired.'

'No, I'm not.' He leaned in, closed his mouth over hers softly in a long, lingering kiss. 'At all.'

Peabody was staring, and Eve decided not to notice. She had coffee, and anticipating Feeney's arrival had even come up with a basket of muffins. The shades were open to her own spectacular view of New York with its spearing skyline behind the lush green of the park.

She supposed she couldn't blame Peabody for gaping.

'I really appreciate you coming here instead of to Cop Central,' Eve began. She knew she wasn't running at full capability yet, just as she knew Mavis couldn't afford for her to take any down time. 'I want to get some of this business squared away before I clock in. As soon as I do, I imagine Whitney will call me up. I need ammunition.'

'No problem.' Peabody knew there really were people who lived like this. She'd heard of it, read of it, seen it on screen. And there was nothing particularly fabulous about the lieutenant's rooms. They were nice, certainly – plenty of space, good furnishings, excellent equipment.

But the house. Jesus, the house. It went beyond the

category of mansion into that of fortress, or maybe even castle. The green lawns, flowering trees, and fountains. There were all the towers, the sparkle of stone. That was before you were brought inside by a butler and blown away by marble and crystal and wood. And space. So much space.

'Peabody?'

'What? Sorry.'

'It's all right. The place is pretty intimidating.'

'It's incredible.' She swung her gaze back to Eve. 'You look different here,' she decided, then narrowed her eyes. 'You do look different. Hey, you got your hair cut. And the eyebrows.' Intrigued, she leaned closer. 'A skin job.'

'It was just a facial.' Eve caught herself just before she squirmed. 'Can we get down to it now, or do you want the name of my consultant?'

'Couldn't afford it,' Peabody said cheerfully. 'But you look good. You want to start pumping up since you're getting married in a couple weeks.'

'It's not a couple weeks, it's next month.'

'Guess you haven't noticed that it's next month now. You're nervous.' Amusement flitted around Peabody's mouth. 'You never get nervous.'

'Shut up, Peabody. We've got homicide here.'

'Yes, sir.' Slightly ashamed, Peabody swallowed the smirk. 'I thought we were killing time until Captain Feeney arrived.'

'I've got a ten o'clock interview with Redford. I don't

have time to kill. Give me the rundown of your progress at the club.'

'I have my report.' Back in the saddle, Peabody took a disc out of her bag. 'I arrived at seventeen thirty-five, approached the subject known as Crack, and identified myself as your aide.'

'What did you think of him?'

'An individual,' Peabody said dryly. 'He suggested I would make a good table dancer, as I appeared to have strong legs. I told him it wasn't an option at this time.'

'Good one.'

'He was cooperative. In my judgment, he was angry when I informed him of Hetta's death, and the means. She hadn't worked there long, but he said she was good-natured, efficient, and successful.'

'In those words.'

'In the vernacular, Dallas. His vernacular, which is quoted in my report. He did not observe who she spoke with after the incident with Boomer as the club was crowded and he was busy.'

'Cracking heads.'

'Exactly. He did, however, point out several other employees and regulars who might have seen her with someone. I have their names and their statements. None noticed anything peculiar or out of the ordinary. One client believed he observed her going into one of the private booths with another man, but he didn't recall the time, and his description is vague. "A tall dude."'

'Terrific.'

'She clocked out at oh two fifteen, which was more than an hour earlier than her habit. She told one of the other companions that she'd made over her quota and was calling it a night. Flashed a fistful of credits and cash. Bragged about a new customer who believed in paying for quality. That was the last time she was seen at the club.'

'Her body was found three days later.' Frustrated, Eve pushed away from the table. 'If I'd gotten the case sooner, or if Carmichael had bothered to dig . . . Well, that's done.'

'She was well liked.'

'Did she have a partner?'

'No one serious or long term. Those kind of clubs discourage dating the customers on the outside, and apparently Hetta was a real pro. She did move around from club to club, but so far, I haven't hit on anything. If she worked anywhere the night she died, there's no record of it.'

'Did she use?'

'Socially, casually. Nothing heavy, according to the people I spoke with. I checked her sheet, and other than a couple of old possession charges, she was clean.'

'How old?'

'Five years.'

'Okay, keep on it. Hetta's yours.' She glanced over as Feeney strolled in. 'Glad you could join us.'

'Hey, traffic's murder out there. Muffins!' He pounced. 'How's it going, Peabody?'

'Good morning, Captain.'

'Some digs, huh? New shirt, Dallas?'

'No.'

'Look different.' He poured coffee while she rolled her eyes. 'Found our snake tattoo. Mavis hit Ground Zero at about two, bought herself a Screamer and a table dancer. Talked to the guy myself last night after I bounced to it. He remembers her. Said she was way out of orbit, and chugging them back. He offered her a list of accepted services, but she passed and staggered out.'

Feeney sighed, sat. 'If she crawled into any other clubs, she didn't use credit. I've got nothing after her totaling out from Ground Zero at two forty-five.'

'Where's Ground Zero?'

'About six blocks from the murder scene. She'd been moving steadily down and across town from the time she left Pandora and walked into ZigZag. She went into five other clubs between, Screamers all the way, mostly triples. I don't know how she stayed on her feet.'

'Six blocks,' Dallas murmured. 'Thirty minutes before the murder.'

'I'm sorry, kid. It doesn't make it look any better for her. Now, the security discs. Leonardo's scanner was busted up at ten on the night in question. Lots of complaints about kids whacking outside cameras in that area, so it's likely that's how it went down. Pandora's security was turned off using the code. No fiddling, no sabotage. Whoever went in knew how to get in.'

'Knew her, knew the setup.'

'Had to,' Feeney agreed. 'I can't find any blips on the discs from Justin Young's building security. I've got them going in about one thirty, and her going out again at ten or twelve the next day. Nothing in between. But . . .' He paused for effect. 'He's got a back door.'

'What?'

'Domestic entrance, through the kitchen to a freight elevator. No security on the freight. It goes to six other floors and the garage. Now, the garage has security, and so do the other floors. But . . .' Another pause. 'You can also take it to the rear utility, ground floor. The maintenance area, and security's very spotty there.'

'Could they have gotten out unobserved?'

'Could have.' Feeney slurped coffee. 'If they knew the building, the system, and if they were careful to time the exit to avoid the sweep in maintenance.'

'Could put a different light on their alibis. Bless you, Feeney.'

'Yeah, well. Send money. Or just give me these muffins.'

'They're yours. I think we'll have to talk to our young lovers again. We've got some interesting players here. Justin Young used to sleep with Pandora and is now intimately involved with Jerry Fitzgerald who is one of Pandora's associates and her top rival for queen of the runway. Both Fitzgerald and Pandora are after a screen career. Enter Redford, producer. He's interested in working with Fitzgerald, has worked with Young, and is sleeping with Pandora. All four of these people are partying at Pandora's, at her invitation on the night she's killed. Now, why would she want them there, her rival, her ex-lover, and the producer?'

'She liked drama,' Peabody put in. 'She enjoyed friction.'

'Yeah, true. She also liked causing discomfort. I wonder if she had something she wanted to rub their faces in. They were all very calm in interview,' she recalled. 'Very composed, very easy. Let's see if we can shake them up.'

Eve glanced over as the panel between her offices and Roarke's slid open.

'It wasn't secured,' he said as he stopped on the threshold. 'I'm interrupting.'

'It's all right. We just need to finish up.'

'Hey, Roarke.' Feeney toasted him with a muffin. 'Ready to strap on the old ball and chain? Just a joke,' he muttered when Eve scalded him with a look.

'I think I'll continue to hobble along well enough.' He glanced at Peabody, lifted a brow.

'Sorry. Officer Peabody, Roarke.'

At Eve's introduction, he smiled, crossed the room. 'The efficient Officer Peabody. It's a pleasure.'

Struggling not to goggle, she accepted the hand he offered. 'Nice to meet you.'

'If I could steal the lieutenant for just a moment, I'll get out of your way.' He laid a hand on Eve's shoulder, squeezed. When she rose to go with him, Feeney snorted.

'You're going to swallow your tongue, Peabody. Why is it just because a man's got the face of a devil and the body of a god, women get all glassy-eyed?'

'It's hormonal,' Peabody muttered, but she continued to watch Roarke and Eve. She'd developed an interest in relationship games recently.

'How are you?' Roarke asked.

'I'm fine.'

He cupped Eve's chin, dipped his thumb lightly in its dent. 'I believe you're working at it. I have some meetings in midtown this morning, but I thought you'd want this.' He handed her a card, one of his own, with a name and address scrawled on the back. 'It's the off planet expert you asked about. She'll make time for whatever you need. She already has the sample you gave to me, but would like another. Cross-testing, I believe she called it.'

'Thanks.' Eve slipped the card into her pocket. 'Really.'

'The reports from Starlight Station—'

'Starlight Station?' It took her a moment. 'Christ, I forgot I asked you. My mind's not cued.'

'It has a great deal to do just now. In any case, my sources tell me Pandora did quite a bit of socializing this last trip – which is usual. There didn't seem to be anyone in particular she was interested in. At least not for more than one night.'

'Shit, is it always sex?'

'With her it was a priority.' He smiled when Eve's eyes narrowed and speculated. 'And, as I said before, our short liaison was a long time ago. She did, however, make a number of calls, all on her pocket 'link. She never used the resort's system.'

'No outside record,' Eve mused.

'That would be my take. She was on assignment, and did her job with her usual flair. There's some talk about the way she bragged about a new product she was going to endorse, and a video.'

Eve grunted and filed the data away. 'I appreciate the time.'

'Always happy to support our local police. We have an appointment with the florist at three. Can you make it?'

She shuffled obligations in her head. 'If you can squeeze it in, so can I.'

Not willing to risk it, he took her logbook out of her pocket and programmed the appointment himself. 'I'll see you there.' He lowered his head, watched her eyes shift toward the table across the room. 'I doubt this will diminish your authority,' he murmured, then pressed his lips softly to hers. 'I love you.'

'Yeah, well.' She cleared her throat. 'Okay.'

'Poetry.' Amused, he skimmed a hand through her hair, kissed her again to fluster her. 'Officer Peabody, Feeney.' With a nod, he stepped back into his office. The panel slid shut behind him.

'Wipe that stupid grin off your face, Feeney. I've got a drop-off for you.' She pulled the card back out of her pocket as she went back to the table. 'I need you to take a sample of the powder we took from Boomer's to this flora expert. Roarke's cleared it. She's not a police and security attache, so keep it low profile.'

'Can do.'

'I'll be checking in with her later today on her progress. Peabody, you're with me.'

'Yes, sir.'

Peabody waited until she was in Eve's car before she spoke. 'I guess it's a lot of work for a cop to juggle personal relationships.'

'Tell me about it.' *Grill suspect, lie to commanding officer, hassle lab tech. Order bridal bouquet. Jesus.*

'But if you're steady, you know, careful, it doesn't have to bog down your career.'

'If you ask me, cops are a bad bet. But what do I know?' In a nervous rhythm, she tapped her fingers on the wheel. 'Feeney's been married since the dawn of time. The commander has a happy home. Others do it.' She blew out a breath. 'I'm working on it.' It struck her as she drove through the gates. 'You got a personal thing going, Peabody?'

'Maybe. I'm thinking about it.' She rubbed her hands on her pants, linked them, pulled them apart.

'Anybody I know?'

'Actually.' Peabody shifted her feet. 'It's Casto.'

'Casto?' Eve headed crosstown to Ninth, swung around a commuter tram. 'No shit. When did this happen?'

'Well, I ran into him last night. That is, I caught him shadowing me, so—'

'Shadowing you?' Quickly, Eve rammed the car to auto. It shuddered, whined, then chugged. 'What the hell are you talking about?'

'He's got a good nose. He sniffed out we were digging at a lead. I was pretty steamed when I tagged him, then I had to admit, I'd have done the same thing.'

Eve tapped her fingers on the wheel, thought about it. 'Yeah, so would I. Did he try to pump you?'

Peabody flushed deep red, stuttered.

'Jesus, Peabody, I didn't mean—'

'I know, I know. I'm not used to this, Dallas. I mean I like men, sure.' She brushed at her bangs, checked the collar of her stiff uniform shirt. 'I've been around some, but men like Casto – you know, like Roarke.'

'They fry the circuits.'

'Yeah.' It was a relief to be able to lay it out to someone who would understand. 'He did try to slide some data out of me, but he took it well enough when I wouldn't give. He knows the route. The chief says interdepartmental cooperation, and we pretty much ignore it.'

'You think he's got something of his own?'

'He might. He made the rounds at the club just like I did. That's how I tagged him first. Then, when I left, he followed me. I led him around for awhile, just to see what he'd do.' Her smile spread. 'And I backtracked him. You should have seen his face when I came up behind him and he knew he'd been nailed.'

'Good work.'

'We got into it a little. Territory, and all that. Then we, well, we had a drink, agreed to put the cop routine on hold. It was nice. We have a lot of common ground, outside

251

the job. Music and films and stuff. Hell, oh Jesus, I slept with him.'

'Oh.'

'I know it was stupid. But, well, I did.'

Eve waited a moment. 'So, how was it?'

'Wow.'

'That good, huh?'

'Then this morning, he said maybe we could have dinner or something.'

'So, it sounds pretty normal to me.'

Sober-eyed again, Peabody shook her head. 'Guys like that aren't attracted to me. I know he's got a thing for you—'

Eve's hand shot up. 'Hold on, playback.'

'Come on, Dallas, you know he does. He's attracted to you. He admires your skill, your mind. Your legs.'

'You're not going to tell me you and Casto discussed my legs.'

'No, but your mind came up. Anyway, I don't know if I should take this any farther. I've got to concentrate on my career, and he's steeped in his. When this case is resolved, we'll lose the connection.'

Hadn't Eve thought the same when Roarke had hit her between the eyes? It should have been true. It usually was. 'You're attracted to him, you like him, you find him interesting to be around.'

'Sure.'

'And the sex was good.'

'The sex was incredible.'

'Then, as your superior, Peabody, my advice is, go for it.'

Peabody smiled a little, then looked out the window. 'Maybe I'll think about it.'

14

Eve was pleased with her timing. She clocked into Cop Central at 9:55, went directly to Interview. By avoiding her office, she avoided any messages from Commander Whitney demanding her presence. She hoped by the time she had to face him, she'd have the buffer of new information.

Redford was prompt, she had to give him that. And he was as sleek and unruffled as he'd been the first time she'd seen him.

'Lieutenant, I hope this won't take long. It's a very inconvenient time.'

'Then we'll get started right away. Have a seat.' She closed and secured the door behind her.

Interview wasn't the most pleasant of atmospheres. It wasn't meant to be. The conference table was small, the chairs hard, the walls unadorned. The mirror was obviously two-way glass and meant to intimidate. She went directly to her recorder, engaged, and recited the necessary data.

'Mr Redford, you are entitled to counsel or a representative at Interview.'

'Are you reading me my rights, Lieutenant?'

'If you request I do so, I'll oblige. You are not charged,

but you are entitled to counsel when being questioned in a formal interview. Do you wish counsel?'

'Not at this time.' He flicked a speck of lint from his sleeve. Gold winked at his wrist in the form of a cuff bracelet. 'I'm more than willing to cooperate with this investigation, as I've proven by coming here today.'

'I'd like to replay your previous statement so that you have the opportunity to add, delete, or change any portions thereof.' She slipped the labeled disc into the slot. With mild impatience in his eyes, Redford listened.

'Do you wish to stand by that statement, as given?'

'Yes, it's as accurate as I can remember.'

'Very well.' Eve replaced the disc and folded her hands. 'You and the victim were sexual partners.'

'That's correct.'

'This was not an exclusive arrangement.'

'Not at all. Neither of us wished it to be.'

'Did you on the night of the murder engage with the victim in the use of illegals?'

'No.'

'Did you, at any other time, engage with the victim in the use of illegals?'

He smiled. When he angled his head, she caught more gold, threaded through the sleek queue twisting to his shoulder blades. 'No. I didn't share Pandora's affection for substances.'

'Did you have the victim's security code for her town house in New York?'

'Her security code.' His brow furrowed. 'I might have it. Probably.' For the first time he appeared uneasy. Eve could all but see his mind weighing his answer and the consequences. 'I imagine she gave it to me at one time or another to simplify matters when I visited her.' Composed again, he took out his notebook, keyed in data. 'Yes, I have it here.'

'Did you use her code to gain access to her home on the night of her murder?'

'A domestic let me in. There wasn't any need for it.'

'No, there wouldn't have been. Before her murder. Are you aware that her security code also engages and disengages her video system?'

Caution flickered in his eyes again. 'I'm not sure I follow you.'

'With the code, which you state is in your possession, the outside security camera can be deactivated. That camera was deactivated for a period of approximately one hour after the murder. During that period, Mr Redford, you state you were at your club. Alone. During that period, someone who knew the victim, who was in possession of her code, who was aware of the workings of her home and security, deactivated the system, entered the house, and it would seem, took something from the house.'

'I would have no reason to do any of those things. I was at my club, Lieutenant. I keyed in and out.'

'A member can key in and out without ever going in.' She watched his face harden. 'You saw an ornate, possibly

256

Chinese antique box, from which you state the victim took a substance and ingested it. You further state that she then locked the box away in the vanity of her bedroom. This box has not been found. Are you sure this box existed?'

There was ice now, but beneath it, just around the edges of it, she thought she caught something else. Not panic, not yet. But wariness, and worry.

'Are you certain the box you described existed, Mr Redford?'

'I saw it.'

'And the key?'

'The key?' He reached for a pitcher of water. His hand was still steady, Eve noted, but that mind was working overtime. 'She wore it on a chain, a gold chain, around her neck.'

'No chain or key was recovered on the body or at the scene.'

'Then it would follow that the murderer took it, wouldn't it, Lieutenant?'

'Did she wear the key openly?'

'No, she—' He stopped, the muscles in his jaw twitching. 'Very good, Lieutenant. As far as I am aware, she wore it under her clothes. But, as I have stated, I am not the only one who was invited to see Pandora without clothing.'

'Why were you paying her?'

'I beg your pardon?'

'Over the past eighteen months, you transferred over three hundred thousand dollars into the victim's credit accounts. Why?'

His eyes went blank, but Eve saw, for the first time, fear behind them. 'Certainly what I do with my money is my own business.'

'No, it's not. Not when it's murder. Was she blackmailing you?'

'That's absurd.'

'Plays for me. She had something on you, something dangerous, embarrassing, something she enjoyed holding over you. She nibbled away, demanding little payments here and there, and some not so little. I imagine she was the type to flaunt that kind of power, to enjoy it. A man could get tired of that. A man could begin to realize there was only one way to end it. It wasn't the money, really, was it, Mr Redford? It was the power, the control, and that enjoyment she rubbed in your face.'

His breathing deepened raggedly, but his face remained still. 'I would say that Pandora was not above blackmail, Lieutenant. But she had nothing on me, and I would not tolerate threats.'

'What would you do about them?'

'A man in my position can afford to ignore quite a bit. In my business, success is much more important than gossip.'

'Then why did you pay her? For sex?'

'That's insulting.'

'No, I suppose a man in your position wouldn't have to pay for sex. Still, it might add a certain twist to the excitement. Do you ever frequent the Down and Dirty Club on the East End?'

'I don't frequent the East End, and I certainly don't frequent a second-rate sex club.'

'But you know what it is. Were you ever there with Pandora?'

'No.'

'Alone?'

'I said I hadn't been there.'

'Where were you on June tenth, at approximately two A.M.?'

'What is this?'

'Can you verify your whereabouts on that date and time?'

'I don't know where I was. I don't have to answer that.'

'Were your payments to Pandora business payments, gifts?'

'Yes, no.' He fisted his hands under the table. 'I believe I'd like to consult with counsel now.'

'Sure. Your choice. We will break this interview to allow subject to exercise his right to consult counsel. Disengage.' She smiled. 'You'd better tell them all you know. You'd better tell someone. And if you're not in this alone, I'd advise you to start thinking seriously about rolling over.' She pushed back from the table. 'There's a public 'link outside.'

'I have my own,' he said stiffly. 'If you could show me to a room where I can make my call privately.'

'No problem. Come with me.'

Eve managed to avoid Whitney by transmitting an update and steering clear of her desk. She snagged Peabody and headed out.

'You shook Redford. You really shook him.'

'That was the idea.'

'It was the way you kept coming at him from different angles. Everything straight down the line at first, then pow. You tripped him up with the club.'

'He'll get his balance back. I still have the payment he made to Fitzgerald to pitch at him, but he'll be more prepared. This reprieve with his lawyers.'

'Yeah, and he won't underestimate you again. You think he did it?'

'I think he could have. He hated her. If we can link him to the drugs . . . we'll see.' So many angles to explore, Eve thought, and time was racing – racing toward Mavis's pretrial hearing. If she didn't have something solid within the next couple of days . . . 'I want that unknown ID'd. I want to know the source. We find the source, we follow it.'

'Is that when you're going to bring Casto in? That's a professional inquiry.'

'He'd have better contacts. I'll share the wealth once we have the unknown nailed.' Her 'link beeped, and she winced. 'Shit, shit, shit. I know that's Whitney. I can feel it.' She blanked her face and answered. 'Dallas.'

'What the hell are you doing?'

'Sir, checking a lead. I'm en route to the lab.'

'I left orders for you to be in my office at oh nine hundred.'

'I'm sorry, Commander, I didn't receive that transmission. I haven't been to my desk. If you've received my report, you'll see that I've been tied up in interview this morning. Subject is currently consulting counsel. I believe—'

'Cut the tap dance, Lieutenant. I spoke with Dr Mira a few minutes ago.'

Her skin seemed to ice over, go stiff. 'Sir.'

'I'm disappointed in you, Lieutenant.' He spoke slowly, his eyes hard on hers. 'That you would consider wasting the department's time and manpower on such a matter. We have no intention nor desire to investigate formally, or to launch any informal inquiries into the incident. This matter is closed, and will remain closed. Is that understood, Lieutenant?'

Emotions swirled: relief, guilt, gratitude. 'Sir, I . . . Yes. Understood.'

'Very well. The leak to Channel 75 has caused major problems here.'

'Yes, sir.' Snap back, she ordered herself. Think of Mavis. 'I'm sure it has.'

'You are aware of departmental policy on unauthorized leaks to the media.'

'Well aware.'

'How is Ms Furst?'

'I thought she looked quite well on screen, Commander.'

He scowled, but there was a glint in his eye. 'You stay on the balls of your feet, Dallas. And you be here, my office, eighteen hundred. We have a fucking press conference.'

'Good dodge,' Peabody congratulated. 'And all truth, except that you told him we were en route to the lab.'

'I didn't say which lab.'

'What was that other business? He seemed pretty steamed over it. Have you got something else going on? Does it hook with this?'

'No, it's old business. Dead business.' Grateful to have gotten through it, Eve glided toward the gate of Futures Laboratories and Research, a subsidiary of Roarke Industries. 'Lieutenant Dallas, NYPSD,' she announced into the scanner.

'You are expected, Lieutenant. Please proceed to Blue parking facility. Leave your vehicle and take transport C to the East complex, sector six, level one. You will be met.'

They were met by a lab droid, an attractive brunette with milk-white skin, clear blue eyes, and a security badge that identified her as Anna-6. Her voice was as melodious as church bells.

'Good afternoon, Lieutenant. I hope you had no trouble finding us.'

'No, we didn't.'

'Very good. Dr Engrave will see you in the solarium. It's very pleasant there. If you'd follow me.'

'That's a droid,' Peabody murmured to Eve, and Anna-6 turned, smiled beautifully.

'I'm a new, experimental model. There are only ten of us at this stage, all in use here, at this complex. We hope to be on the market within six months. The research behind us is very extensive, and unfortunately the cost is still prohibitive for most general markets. We hope that larger industries will find the expense worthwhile until we can be cost-effectively mass produced.'

Eve cocked a head. 'Has Roarke seen you?'

'Of course. Roarke approves all new products. He was very involved in the design.'

'I bet he was.'

'Through here, please,' Anna-6 continued, turning into a long, arched corridor in hospital white. 'Dr Engrave has found your specimen highly interesting. I'm sure you will find her very helpful.' She stopped by a mini wall screen and coded in a sequence. 'Anna-6,' she announced. 'Accompanied by Lieutenant Dallas and aide.'

The tiles parted, opening up into a large room filled with flora and lovely artificial sunlight. There was the tinkle of running water and the lazy drone of contented bees.

'I will leave you here and return to lead you out. Please request any refreshment you might like. Dr Engrave often forgets to offer.'

'Go smile someplace else, Anna.' The testy voice seemed to come from a clump of ferns. Anna-6 merely smiled, stepped back, and let the tiles click together. 'I know droids have their place, but damned if they don't make me itchy. Over here, in the spirea.'

Warily, Eve stepped to the ferns, and through. There, kneeling in rich black dirt, was a woman. Her graying hair was scooped up in a messy knot, her hands reddened and soiled. Coveralls that might have once been white were stained with too many streaks to identify. She looked up, and her plain, narrow face proved to be as filthy as her clothes.

'I'm checking my worms. Trying out a new breed.' She held up a clump of dirt that wiggled.

'Very nice,' Eve decided and was faintly relieved when Engrave buried the busy clump.

'So, you're Roarke's cop. Always figured he'd choose one of those fussy purebreds with the skinny necks and big boobs.' She pursed her lips as she looked Eve over. 'Glad he didn't. Trouble with purebreds is, they need constant pampering. Give me a good hybrid any day.'

Engrave wiped her dirty hands on her dirty clothes. When she rose, she proved to be about five feet tall. 'Digging around with worms is good therapy. More people should try it, then they wouldn't need drugs to get through the day.'

'Speaking of drugs . . .'

'Yes, yes, over here.' She started off at marching pace, then began to slow, to meander. 'Need some pruning here. More nitrogen. Underwatered. Root bound.' She paused beside spearing green leaves, trailing vines, explosive blooms. 'It's gotten to the stage they pay me to garden. Nice work if you can get it. Know what this is?'

Eve looked at a purple trumpet-shaped bloom. She was pretty sure, but wary of a trap. 'A flower.'

'Petunia. Hah. People have forgotten the charm of the traditional.' She stopped by a sink, washed some of the dirt off her hands, left more under her short ragged nails. 'Everybody wants exotic nowadays. Bigger, better, different. A good bed of petunias will give a lot of pleasure for little care. You plant them, don't expect them to be something they're not, and enjoy. They're simple, don't wither up on you if you look cross-eyed. A good bed of petunias means something. Well then.'

She hoisted herself onto a stool in front of a workbench crowded with garden tools, pots, papers, an AutoChef that blinked on empty, and a top-of-the-line computer system.

'That was an interesting bag of tricks you sent over with that Irishman. Who knew his petunias, by the way.'

'Feeney's a man of many talents.'

'Gave him a nice flat of pansies for his wife.' Engrave engaged the computer. 'Already ran analysis on the sample Roarke brought by. Sweet-talked me into putting a rush on it. Another Irishman. God love 'em. Believe in crossing my *t*'s on something like this. The fresh sample gave me more to work with.'

'Then you have the results—'

'Don't rush me, girl. It only works with good-looking Micks. And I don't like working for cops.' Engrave smiled widely. 'They don't appreciate the art of science. Bet you don't even know your periodic table, do you?'

'Listen, Doctor—' To Eve's relief the formula flashed on screen. 'Is this unit controlled?'

'It's passkeyed, don't you worry. Roarke said it was top security. I've been off the turnip truck longer than you've been alive.' She brushed Eve off with one grimy hand, gestured toward the screen with the other. 'Now, I don't have to go into the basic elements here. A child could make them, so I assume you've ID'd them.'

'It's the single unknown—'

'I know the drill, Lieutenant. Here's your little problem.' She highlighted a series of factors. 'You haven't tagged it from this formula, because they coded it. What you got here's just a bunch of jibberish. It's what you've got here.' Reaching over, she took a small slide dusted with powder. 'Even your top labs would have a tough time fining this down. It looks like one thing, it smells like another. And when it's all blended together as it is in this form, it's the reaction that changes the mix. You know much about chemistry?'

'Do I have to?'

'If more people understood—'

'Dr Engrave, I want to understand murder. You tell me what it is, and let me go from there.'

'Impatience is another problem with people today,' Engrave huffed, then took out a small covered dish. Inside were a few drops of milky liquid. 'Since you don't give a rat's skinny ass, I won't tell you what I did. We'll leave it that I ran some tests, did some basic chemistry, and separated your unknown.'

'Is that it?'

'In its liquid form, yes. I bet your lab tech told you it was some form of a valerian – southwest U.S. native species.'

Eve looked over. 'And?'

'He'd be close, but no cigar. It's a plant, all right, and valerian was used in the grafting of the specimen. This is nectar, the substance that seduces the birds and bees and makes the world go round. This nectar is not from any native species.'

'Not native to the U.S.'

'Not native anywhere. Period.' She reached over, picked up a potted plant, and set it down with a thud. 'This is your baby.'

'It's pretty,' Peabody said, leaning closer to the lush frilled-edged blooms that varied from creamy white to royal purple. She sniffed, closed her eyes, and sniffed deeper. 'God, it's wonderful. It's like . . .' Her head swam. 'Strong.'

'You bet your ass it's strong. That's enough or you'll be buzzed for an hour.' Engrave shoved the plant clear.

'Peabody?' Eve took her arm, shook. 'Snap out of it.'

'It's like taking a full glass of champagne in one gulp.' She pressed a hand to her temple. 'It's wonderful.'

'An experimental hybrid,' Engrave explained. 'Code name Immortal Blossom. This one is fourteen months old, and it's never stopped blooming. They were grafted in the Eden Colony.'

'Sit down, Peabody. The nectar from this is what we're looking for?'

'By itself the nectar is potent and causes a reaction in bees not unlike drunkenness. They have the same sort of reaction to overripe fruit, windfall peaches for example, where the juice is highly concentrated. Unless the intake is controlled, it's been found that the bees OD on the nectar. They just can't get enough of it.'

'Addicted bees?'

'You could say that. Basically, they don't want to go fucking the other flowers because they're so seduced by this one. Your lab didn't hook into it because the hybrid's on the horticultural colonies' restricted list, and puts it under Galactic Customs' jurisdiction. The colony is working to alleviate this problem with the nectar, as it puts a world of hurt on the potential for export.'

'So the Immortal Blossom is a controlled specimen.'

'For the moment. There are some medicinal uses, and particularly cosmetic ones. Ingestion of the nectar can cause a luminescence to the skin, a rejuvenation of elasticity, and an appearance of youth.'

'But it's poison. Long-term use undermines the nervous system. Our lab confirmed that.'

'So's arsenic, but fine ladies once took it in small doses to make their skin whiter, clearer. Beauty and youth are desperate matters for some.' Engrave shrugged her bony shoulders in dismissal. 'In combination with the other elements in this formula, this nectar is an activator. The result is a highly addictive chemical that causes increased energy and strength, sexual desire, and the feeling of renewed youth. And since uncontrolled, these hybrids will propagate like rabbits, it has the potential to be produced cheaply and in great bulk.'

'They'll propagate in on planet conditions?'

'Absolutely. The Eden Colony produces vegetation, flora, and plant life for on planet conditions.'

'So you get a few plants,' Eve mused. 'A lab, the other chemicals.'

'And you've got yourself an illegal with mass appeal. Pay up,' Engrave said with a sour smile, 'be strong, be beautiful, be young and sexy. Whoever came up with this formula knew his chemistry and his human nature and understands the beauty of profit.'

'Fatal beauty.'

'Oh sure, four to six years of regular use will take you down. Your nervous system will just give out. But in four to six years, you'll have a hell of a time, and somebody's going to make big, fat credits.'

'How do you know so much about this – what, Immortal Blossom – if its cultivation is limited to the Eden Colony?'

'Because I'm the top in my field, I do my homework, and my daughter happens to be head beekeeper on Eden. A licensed lab, such as this, or a horticulture expert can, with limitations, import a specimen.'

'You mean we've already got some of these down here, on planet?'

'Mostly replicas, harmless simulations, but some of the genuine article. Regulated – for indoor, controlled use only. Now, I've got roses to graft. Take the report and the two samples to your bright boys at Cop Central. If they can put it all together from that, they ought to be hanged anyway.'

'You all right, Peabody?' Cautious, Eve kept a firm hand on Peabody's arm as she opened the car door.

'Yeah, just really relaxed.'

'Too relaxed to drive,' Eve noted. 'I was going to have you drop me off at the florist. Plan B, we swing by and get you something to eat to counteract your flower sniffing, then you take the samples and Engrave's report by the lab.'

'Dallas.' Peabody let her head rest against the seat back. 'I really feel wonderful.'

Cautious, Eve eyed her. 'You're not going to kiss me or anything?'

Peabody slanted her a look. 'You're not my type. Anyway, I don't feel particularly sexy. Just good. If taking that stuff is anything like smelling that flower, people are going to go crazy for it.'

'Yeah. Someone's already gone crazy enough to kill three people.'

Eve dashed into the florist shop. She had twenty minutes on the outside if she was going to track down her other suspects, badger them, get back to the station to file her report, and make the press conference.

She spotted Roarke loitering near a display of small, flowering trees.

'Our floral consultant is waiting for us.'

'Sorry.' She wondered why anyone would want trees that were less than a foot tall. They made her feel like a freak. 'I'm backed up.'

'I just walked in myself. Was Dr Engrave helpful?'

'And then some. She's quite a character.' She followed him under a trellis of fragrant vines. 'I got a load of Anna-6.'

'Ah, the Anna line. I think it's going to be a hit.'

'Especially with teenage boys.'

Roarke laughed and urged her through. 'Mark, this is my fiancee, Eve Dallas.'

'Ah, yes.' He looked like everyone's favorite uncle when he extended a hand, and his grip was like an arm wrestler's on a dare. 'Let's see what we can do for you. Weddings are such a complicated business, and you haven't left me much time.'

'He didn't give me a hell of a lot, either.'

Mark laughed, patted his silvery hair. 'Sit, relax, have a little tea. I have a great deal to show you.'

She didn't mind really, Eve decided. She liked flowers. She just hadn't known there were so damn many of them. And after five minutes, her head began to swim with orchids and lilies, roses and gardenias.

'Simple,' Roarke decided. 'Traditional. No simulations.'

'Yes, of course. I have some holograms that may spark some ideas. You're having it outdoors, so I might suggest arbors, wisteria. Very traditional, and with a lovely, old-fashioned fragrance.'

Eve studied the holograms, tried to envision herself standing under an arbor with Roarke, exchanging vows. Her stomach jittered. 'What about petunias?'

Mark blinked. 'Petunias?'

'I like petunias. They're simple, and they don't pretend to be what they're not.'

'Yes, certainly. Quite charming. Perhaps backed with a bank of lilies. As to color . . .'

'Do you carry Immortal Blossoms?' she asked on impulse.

'Immortals.' Mark's eyes brightened. 'They're quite a specialty item. Difficult to import, of course, but very hardy and spectacular in baskets. I have several simulations.'

'We don't want simulations,' Eve reminded him.

'I'm afraid they can only be exported in small amounts, and then only to licensed florists and horticulturists. And only for indoor use. As your ceremony is outdoors—'

'Do you sell many?'

'Very rarely, and only to other licensed horticulture experts. I do have something just as lovely—'

'You have records of those sales? Can you get me a list of names? You're on the net for world delivery, aren't you?'

'Naturally, but—'

'I need to know everyone who ordered Immortals during the past two years.'

When Mark sent him a baffled look, Roarke ran his tongue around his teeth. 'My fiancee is an avid gardener.'

'Yes, I see. It may take a few moments to access. You want everyone.'

'Everyone who placed an order to the Eden Colony for Immortals during the last two years. You can start with the States.'

'If you'll just wait then, I'll see what I can do.'

'I like the arbor idea,' Eve announced, springing up when Mark left them. 'Don't you?'

Roarke rose, put his hands on her shoulders. 'Why don't you let me handle the floral arrangements? I'll surprise you.'

'I'll owe you one.'

'Indeed you will. You can start paying me back by remembering we're attending Leonardo's showing on Friday.'

'I knew that.'

'And by remembering to access your three weeks' leave for our honeymoon.'

'I thought we said two.'

'We did. Now you owe me one. Would you like to tell me why you have this sudden fascination with a flower from the Eden Colony? Or do I just assume that you found your unknown.'

'It's the nectar. It does a lot to tie the three homicides together. If I can just get a break.'

'I hope this is what you're looking for.' Mark came back in with a sheet of paper. 'It wasn't as difficult as I'd feared. There haven't been many orders for Immortals. Most importers are satisfied with simulations. There are a few problems with the actual specimen.'

'Thank you.' Eve took the page, skimmed down the list.

'Gotcha,' she murmured then whirled to Roarke. 'I have to go. Buy lots of flowers, boatloads of flowers. Don't forget the petunias.' She charged out, pulling her communicator. 'Peabody.'

'But – but the bouquet. The bridal bouquet.' Confused, Mark turned to Roarke. 'She hasn't chosen.'

Roarke watched her fly out. 'I know what she likes,' he said. 'Often better than she does.'

15

'Nice to have you back, Mr Redford.'

'This is becoming an unfortunate habit, Lieutenant.' Redford took his seat at the interview table. 'I'm expected in New Los Angeles in a few hours. I trust you won't inconvenience me long.'

'I believe in backing up my data. Wouldn't want anything or anyone to slip through the cracks.'

She glanced toward the corner where Peabody stood, looking her officious best in full uniform. On the other side of the glass, Eve knew, Whitney and the prosecutor watched every move. She nailed it down here, or very likely, she'd be nailed herself.

She took her seat, nodded to the hologram of Redford's chosen counsel. Obviously, neither Redford nor his attorney believed the situation was serious enough to warrant an in-the-flesh representation. 'Counselor, you have the transcript of your client's statements?'

'I do.' The pinstriped, tough-eyed image folded his manicured hands. 'My client has cooperated fully with you and your department, Lieutenant. We agree to this interview only to finalize the matter.'

You agreed to it because you don't have a choice, she thought, but kept her face bland. 'Your cooperation is noted, Mr Redford. You have stated that you were acquainted with Pandora, that you had a casual and intimate relationship.'

'That's correct.'

'Were you also involved in any business dealings with her?'

'I produced two direct-to-home screen videos in which Pandora played a part. Another was under consideration.'

'Were these projects successful?'

'Moderately.'

'And outside of these projects, did you have any other business dealings with the deceased?'

'None.' A faint smile touched his mouth. 'Other than a small speculative investment.'

'A small speculative investment?'

'She claimed to have been laying groundwork for her own fashion and beauty line. Of course, she needed backers and I was intrigued enough to invest.'

'You gave her money?'

'Yes, over the course of the last year and a half, I invested just over three hundred thousand.'

Found a way to cover your ass, Eve noted, and leaned back in her chair. 'What's the status of this fashion and beauty line you claim the deceased was implementing?'

'It has no status, Lieutenant.' He lifted his hands, let them fall. 'I was duped. It wasn't until after her death that I discovered there was no line, no other backers, no product.'

'I see. You're a successful producer, a money man. You must have asked her for a prospectus, figures, expenses, projected earnings. Perhaps a sample of the products.'

'No.' His mouth tightened as he looked down at his hands. 'I did not.'

'You expect me to believe that you just handed her money for a projected line you had no information on?'

'It's embarrassing.' He lifted his eyes again. 'I have a reputation in the business, and if this information gets out, that reputation would certainly suffer.'

'Lieutenant,' the counselor interrupted. 'My client's reputation is a valuable asset. This asset will be damaged if this data goes beyond the parameters of this investigation. I can and will secure a gag order on this portion of his statement to protect his interests.'

'Go right ahead. This is quite a story, Mr Redford. Now, do you want to tell me why a man with your reputation, your assets, would commit three hundred thousand dollars to an investment that didn't exist?'

'Pandora was a persuasive woman, a beautiful one. She was also clever. She skirted around my request for projections and figures. I justified the continued payments because I felt she was an expert in the field.'

'And you didn't learn of her duplicity until after her death.'

'I made some inquiries – contacted her business agent, her representative.' He puffed out his cheeks and nearly succeeded in looking sheepish. 'No one knew anything about the line.'

'When did you make these inquiries?'

He hesitated for a heartbeat. 'This afternoon.'

'After our interview? After I questioned you on the payments?'

'That's correct. I wanted to insure there was no mix-up of any kind before I answered your questions. On advice of counsel, I contacted Pandora's people and discovered I'd been conned.'

'Your timing is . . . very skillful. Do you have any hobbies, Mr Redford?'

'Hobbies?'

'A man with your type of high-pressure job, your . . . assets, must need some sort of release. Stamp collecting, computer doodling, gardening.'

'Lieutenant,' the counselor said with weariness. 'The relevance?'

'I'm interested in your client's leisure time. We've established how he spends his business time. Perhaps you speculate on investments as a release valve.'

'No, Pandora was my first mistake and will be my last. I don't have time for hobbies, or the inclination for them.'

'I know what you mean. I had someone tell me today that more people should plant petunias. I can't imagine spending time digging in dirt and fussing with flowers. Not that I don't like them. You like flowers?'

'They have their place. That's why I have a staff to deal with them.'

'But you're a licensed horticulturist.'

'I—'

'You applied for a license and were granted one three months ago. Just about the time you made a payment to Jerry Fitzgerald in the amount of a hundred and twenty-five thousand. And two days before, you placed an order for an Immortal Blossom from the Eden Colony.'

'My client's interest in flora has no relevance in this matter.'

'It has plenty,' Eve shot back, 'and this is an interview, not a trial. I don't need relevance. Why did you want an Immortal?'

'I – it was a gift. For Pandora.'

'You went to the considerable time, trouble, and expense to secure a license, then purchased a controlled species at considerably more expense, as a gift for a woman you occasionally had sex with. A woman who over the last eighteen months bled you for over three hundred thousand dollars.'

'That was an investment. This was a gift.'

'This is bullshit. Save your objections, Counselor, they're duly noted. Where's the flower now?'

'In New L.A.'

'Officer Peabody, arrange to confiscate.'

'Now, just a damn minute.' Redford scraped back his chair. 'That's my property, paid for.'

'You falsified data on your license. You illegally purchased a controlled species. It will be confiscated, and you will be charged appropriately. Peabody?'

'Yes, sir.' Smothering a smirk, Peabody took out her communicator and made the contact.

'This is obvious harassment.' The counselor scowled. 'And these petty charges are ridiculous.'

'Oh, I'm just getting started. You knew about the Immortal Blossom, knew it was a necessary element to create the drug. Pandora was going to make big money on that drug. Was she trying to cut you out?'

'I don't know what you're talking about.'

'Did she turn you on to it, give you enough tastes to addict? Maybe she held it back then, until you wanted to beg for it. Until you wanted to kill her.'

'I never touched it,' Redford exploded.

'But you knew about it. You knew she had it. And there were ways of getting more. Did you decide to cut her out instead? Bring Jerry in? You bought the plant. We'll find out if you had the substance analyzed. With the plant, you could manufacture your own. You wouldn't need her. You couldn't control her, either, could you? She'd want more money, more of the drug. You found out it was fatal, but why wait five years? With her out of the way, you'd have a clear field.'

'I didn't kill her. I was through with her, I had no reason to kill her.'

'You went to her house that night. You went to bed with her. She had the drug. Did she taunt you with it? You'd already killed twice to protect yourself and your investment, but she was still in the way.'

'I killed no one.'

She let him shout, let the counselor spout his objections and threats. 'Did you follow her to Leonardo's that night, or did you take her?'

'I was never there. I never touched her. If I was going to kill her, I'd have done it in her own house when she threatened me.'

'Paul—'

'Shut up, just shut up,' Redford spat at his counsel. 'She's trying to pin murder on me, for Christ's sake. I argued with her. She wanted more money, a lot more money. She made sure I saw her supply of the drug, how much she had at her personal disposal. It was worth a fortune. But I'd already had it analyzed. I didn't need her, and I told her so. I had Jerry to endorse the line when it was ready. She was furious, threatened to ruin me, to kill me. It gave me great pleasure to walk out on her.'

'You planned to manufacture and distribute the illegal yourself?'

'As a topical,' he said, dabbing his mouth with the back of his hand. 'Once it was ready. It was irresistible. The money. Her threats meant nothing, do you understand? She couldn't ruin me without ruining herself. And that, she would never do. I was finished with her. And when I heard she was dead, I opened a bottle of champagne and toasted her killer.'

'Very nice. Now let's start again.'

After Eve turned Redford over to booking, she stepped into the commander's office.

'Excellent work, Lieutenant.'

'Thank you, sir. I'd rather be booking him for murder than drug charges.'

'That may come.'

'I'm counting on it. Prosecutor.'

'Lieutenant.' He'd risen when she'd come in, and continued to stand. His manners were well known in and out of the courtroom. Even when he went in for the kill, he did so with panache. 'I admire your interview techniques. I'd love to have you on the witness stand in this matter, but I don't believe it will come to trial. Mr Redford's attorney has already contacted my office. We'll negotiate.'

'And on the murder?'

'We don't have enough to tie him. No physical evidence,' he went on before she could protest. 'And motive . . . you've proven he had the means to his end before her death. It's still more than possible that he's guilty, but we have quite a bit more work to do to justify charges.'

'You justified charging Mavis Freestone.'

'On overwhelming evidence,' he reminded her.

'You know she didn't do it, Prosecutor. You know that the three victims in this matter are tied together.' She looked toward Casto who lounged in a chair. 'Illegals knows it.'

'I have to go with the lieutenant on this,' Casto drawled. 'We've investigated the aspect of Freestone being involved with the substance known as Immortality, found no connection between her and the drug or either of the other victims. She had some splotches on her record, but they're old, and minor. You ask me, the lady was in the wrong place at the wrong time.' He offered Eve a smile. 'I have to throw my weight with Dallas and recommend the charges against Mavis Freestone be dropped pending further investigation.'

'Your recommendation is noted, Lieutenant,' the prosecutor said. 'The prosecutor's office will take it into consideration as we review all current data. At this point, our belief that these three homicides are linked still falls short of solid proof. Our office is, however, willing to agree to Ms Freestone's representative's recent request for testing, re truth detection, auto hypnosis, and VR recreation. The results will weigh heavily in our decision.'

Eve let out a long, slow breath. It was a concession, and a big one. 'Thank you.'

'We're on the same team, Lieutenant. And now we'd all best keep that in mind and coordinate our stand before this press conference.'

As they prepped, Eve moved over to Casto. 'I appreciate what you did.'

He shrugged it off. 'It was my professional opinion. I hope it helps your friend. Ask me, Redford's guilty as homemade sin. Either he whacked them himself or paid to have it done.'

She wanted to latch onto that, but shook her head slowly. 'Professional hits. Seems sloppy for pros, too personal. Still, thanks for adding the weight.'

'You can consider it payback if you want for handing me one of the biggest illegals cases of the decade. Once

283

we clean it up and go public with the Immortality drug and the busts, I'm going to get me a set of captain's bars.'

'Then congratulations in advance.'

'I'd say that goes for both of us. You're going to nail down these homicides, Eve, then we'll both be sitting pretty.'

'I'll nail them down all right.' She lifted a brow when he brushed a hand over her hair.

'I like it.' With a quick smile he tucked his hands in his pockets. 'You damned sure you gotta get married?'

Angling her head, she smiled back. 'I hear you're having dinner with Peabody.'

'She's a jewel, all right. I've got a weakness for strong women, Eve, and you'll have to forgive me if I'm a little disappointed in the timing here.'

'Why don't I try to be flattered instead?' She caught Whitney's signal and sighed. 'Oh hell, here we go.'

'Makes you feel like a big meaty bone, don't it?' Casto murmured as the doors opened to a horde of reporters.

They got through it, and Eve would have considered it a good day's work if Nadine hadn't ambushed her in the underground lot.

'This area's off limits to unauthorized personnel.'

'Give me a break, Dallas.' Still lounging on the hood of Eve's car, Nadine grinned. 'How about a lift?'

'Channel 75's out of my way.' When Nadine only continued to smile, Eve swore and uncoded the doors. 'Get in.'

'You look good,' Nadine said casually. 'Who's the stylist?'

'Friend of a friend. I'm tired of talking about my hair, Nadine.'

'Okay, let's talk about murder, drugs, and money.'

'I just spent forty-five minutes talking about that.' Eve flashed her badge at the security camera and bumped out to the street. 'I believe you were there.'

'What I saw was a lot of dancing and dodging. What's that squeaking noise?'

'My well-tuned vehicle.'

'Oh yeah, you got hit with budget cuts again, didn't you? Damn shame. Anyway, what's this business about a new line of inquiry?'

'I'm not at liberty to discuss that aspect of the ongoing investigation.'

'Uh-huh. What's this buzz about Paul Redford?'

'Redford has, as stated in the press conference, been charged with fraud, possessing a controlled specimen, and intent to manufacture and distribute an illegal.'

'And where does that tie to Pandora's murder?'

'I'm not at liberty to—'

'All right, shit.' Nadine flopped back in the seat, scowled at the traffic clogging the roadway. 'How about a trade?'

'Maybe. You first.'

'I want an exclusive interview with Mavis Freestone.'

Eve didn't bother to answer. She just snorted.

'Come on, Dallas, let her tell her side of it to the public.'

'Screw the public.'

'Can I quote you? You and Roarke have her surrounded. Nobody can get to her. You know I'll be fair.'

'Yeah, we have her surrounded. No, no one can or will get to her. And you'd probably be fair, but she's not talking to the media.'

'Is that her decision, or yours?'

'Back off, Nadine, unless you want to try public transportation from here.'

'Just relay my request. That's all I'm asking, Dallas. Just let her know I'm interested in letting her tell her story on air.'

'Fine, now change the channel.'

'All right. I got an interesting little tidbit from the gossip station anchor this afternoon.'

'And you know how I live to hear the details of the lives of the rich and ridiculous.'

'Dallas, face it, you're about to become one of them.' At Eve's furious grimace, Nadine laughed. 'Christ, I love needling you. It's so easy. Anyway, word is that the hot couple of the last couple months is split city.'

'I'm agog.'

'You may be when I tell you that hot couple consists of Jerry Fitzgerald and Justin Young.'

Eve's interest level rose enough to have her reconsidering swinging into a bus stop and ditching her passenger. 'Do tell.'

'There was a very public scene today at the rehearsal for Leonardo's showing. Apparently our lovebirds got physical. Blows were exchanged.'

'They hit each other?'

'More than love taps, according to my source. Jerry retired to her dressing room. She has the star's dressing room now, by the way, and Justin left in a huff and with a puffy eye. A few hours later, he was in Maui, partying with another blonde. Also a model. A younger model.'

'What were they fighting about?'

'No one's sure. Sex is thought to have reared its ugly head. She accused him of cheating on her, he did the same. She wasn't going to stand for it. Neither was he. She didn't need him anymore, he didn't need her right back.'

'That's interesting, Nadine, but it doesn't mean anything.'
But the timing, Eve thought. *Oh, the timing.*

'Maybe it does, maybe it doesn't. But it's funny, people in the public eye like that, both of them media personalities losing it in front of an audience. I'd have to say they were pretty wired up or putting on a hell of a show.'

'Like I said, it's interesting.' Eve pulled up at the security gates of Channel 75. 'This is your stop.'

'You could take me to the door.'

'Take a tram, Nadine.'

'Listen, you know you're going to look into what I just told you, so how about matching some data. Dallas, you and I have a history here.'

That was true enough. 'Nadine, things are balanced on a very thin line right now. I can't afford to tip it.'

'I won't go on air with anything until you give me the go ahead.'

Eve hesitated, then shook her head. 'I can't. Mavis is too important to me. Until she's in the clear, solid, I can't risk it.'

'Is she heading toward the clear? Come on, Dallas.'

'Off the record, the prosecutor's office is reconsidering the charges. But they're not dropping them, not yet.'

'Have you got another suspect? Redford? Is he your new prime?'

'Don't push me on this, Nadine. You're almost a friend.'

'Hell. Let's do this. If anything I've told you, or pass on later regarding this adds to your case, you pay back.'

'I'll feed you, Nadine, as soon as it's cleared.'

'I want a one-on-one with you, ten minutes before any info hits the media.'

Eve leaned over, opened Nadine's door. 'See you.'

'Five minutes. Goddamn it, Dallas. Five lousy minutes.'

Which meant, Eve knew, hundreds of ratings points and thousands of dollars. 'I can do five – if and when. I can't promise you more.'

'It'll be when.' Satisfied, Nadine got out, then leaned on the door. 'You know, Dallas, you just don't miss. It'll be when. You've got a knack for the dead and the innocent.'

The dead and the innocent, Eve thought with a shudder as she drove away. She knew that too many of the dead were the guilty.

There was moonlight drizzling through the sky window over the bed when Roarke shifted away from Eve. It was a new experience for him, the nerves before, during, after lovemaking. There were dozens of reasons, or so he told himself as she curled against him, as was her habit. The house was full of people. Leonardo's motley team had taken over an entire wing with their mania. He had several projects and deals at varying stages of development, business he was determined to close before the wedding.

There was the wedding itself. Surely a man was entitled to be a bit distracted at such a time.

But he was, at least with himself, a brutally honest man. There was only one reason for the nerves. That was the image that continually leapt into his mind of Eve, battered and bloodied and broken.

And the terror that by touching her he might bring it all back, turn something beautiful into the beastly.

Beside him she stirred, then pushed herself up to look down at him. Her face was still flushed, her eyes dark. 'I don't know what I'm supposed to say to you.'

He trailed a finger along her jaw. 'About?'

'I'm not fragile. There's no reason for you to treat me as if I'm wounded.'

His brows drew together, the annoyance self-directed. He hadn't realized he was that transparent, even with her. And the sensation didn't sit well. 'I don't know what you mean.' He started to get up, with the idea of pouring a drink he didn't want, but she took a firm grip on his arm.

'Avoidance isn't your usual style, Roarke.' It worried her.

'If your feelings have changed because of what I did, what I remembered—'

'Don't be insulting.' He snapped it out, and the temper kindling in his eyes was a great relief to her.

'What am I supposed to think? This is the first time you've touched me since that night. It was more like nursing than—'

'You have a problem with tenderness?'

He was clever, she thought. Calm or aroused, he knew how to turn things to his own favor. She kept her hand on his arm, her eyes level with his. 'Do you think I can't tell you're holding back? I don't want you to hold back. I'm fine.'

'I'm not.' He jerked his arm free. '*I'm* not. Some of us are a little more human, need a little more time. Leave it alone.'

His words were a sharp slap on a naked cheek. She nodded once, slid down into bed, and turned away from him. 'All right. But what happened to me when I was a child wasn't sex. It was an obscenity.' She closed her eyes tight and willed herself to sleep.

16

When her 'link beeped, it was barely dawn. Eyes still closed, Eve reached out. 'Block video. Dallas.'

'Dallas, Lieutenant Eve. Dispatch. Probable homicide, male, rear of 19 One hundred eighth Street. Proceed immediately.'

Nerves churned in Eve's stomach. She wasn't on rotation, shouldn't have been called. 'Cause of death?'

'Apparent beating. Victim not yet identified due to facial injuries.'

'Acknowledged. Goddamn it.' She threw her legs over the side of the bed and blinked when she saw Roarke was already up and getting dressed. 'What are you doing?'

'Taking you to a murder scene.'

'You're a civilian. You don't have any business at a murder scene.'

He merely shot her a look as she tugged on jeans. 'Your vehicle is in repair, Lieutenant.' He had some small satisfaction of hearing her mutter oaths as she remembered. 'I'll drive you. Drop you,' he qualified. 'On my way to the office.'

'Suit yourself.' She shrugged on her weapon harness.

★   ★   ★

It was a miserable neighborhood. Several buildings were decorated with vicious graffiti, broken glass, and the tattered signs the city used to condemn them. Of course, people still lived in them, huddled in filthy rooms, avoiding the patrols, blissing out on whatever substance offered the most kick.

There were neighborhoods like it all over the world, Roarke thought as he stood in the thin sunlight behind the police barricade. He had grown up in one not so different, though it had been three thousand miles across the Atlantic.

He understood the life here, the despair, the deals, just as he understood the violence that had led to the result Eve was even now examining.

As he watched her, along with the derelicts, the sleepy street whores, the miserably curious, he realized he understood her as well.

Her movements were brisk, her face impassive. But there was pity in her eyes as they studied what had once been a man. She was, he thought, capable, strong, and resilient. Whatever wounds she had, she would live with. She didn't need him to heal, but to accept.

'Not your usual milieu, Roarke.'

Roarke glanced down as Feeney stepped up beside him. 'I've been to worse.'

'Haven't we all.' Feeney sighed and took a wrapped Danish out of his pocket. 'Breakfast?'

'I'll pass. You go ahead.'

Feeney downed the pastry in three whopping bites. 'Better go see what our girl's up to.' He walked through the barricade, tapping his chest where his badge was fixed to settle the nervous uniforms guarding the scene.

'Lucky the media hasn't come in yet,' he commented.

Eve flicked a glance up. 'Not much interest in a murder in this neighborhood – at least not until the how leaks.' Her clear-coated hands were already smeared with blood as she knelt beside the body. 'Got the pictures?' At the nod from the video tech, she slid her hands under the body. 'Let's turn him over, Feeney.'

He'd fallen, or had been left facedown, and had leaked a great deal of blood and brains from the fist-sized hole in the back of his head. The flip side wasn't any prettier.

'No ID,' Eve reported. 'Peabody's inside the building doing door to door, see if we can come up with anyone who knows him or saw anything.'

Feeney shifted his gaze to the rear of the building. There were a couple of windows, filthy glass heavily grilled. He skimmed the concrete yard where they crouched. There was a recycler, broken, a grab bag of garbage, junk, rusted metal.

'Not much of a view,' he commented. 'We tag him yet?'

'I took prints. One of the uniforms is running them now. Weapon's already bagged. Iron pipe tossed under the recycler.' Eyes narrowed, she studied the body. 'He didn't leave a weapon with Boomer or Hetta Moppett. It's obvious why he left one at Leonardo's. Now he's playing with us,

Feeney, tossing it where a blind frog would hop to it. What do you make of this guy?' She snapped a finger under a wide, neon-pink suspender.

Feeney grunted. The corpse was decked out in full fashion. Pegged knee shorts in rainbow stripes, moon glow T-shirt, expensive beaded sandals.

'Had money to waste on bad clothes.' Feeney studied the building again. 'If he lived here, he wasn't putting it into real estate.'

'Dealer,' Eve decided. 'Midlevel. You live here because your business is here.' She rose, smearing blood from her hands onto her jeans, as a uniform approached.

'Got a match, Lieutenant. Victim is ID'd as Lamont Ro, aka Cockroach. He's got a long sheet. Mostly under Illegals. Possession, manufacturing with intent, a couple of assaults.'

'Anybody use him? He weasel for anyone?'

'That data didn't come up.'

She glanced at Feeney who acknowledged the silent request with a grunt. He'd dig and find out. 'Okay, let's bag him and ship him. I want a tox report. Let the sweepers in here.'

Her gaze skimmed the scene again and landed on Roarke. 'I need a ride, Feeney.'

'Can do.'

'I'll just be a minute.' She headed to the barricade. 'I thought you were going to the office.'

'I am. Are you done here?'

'A few more things. I can catch a ride with Feeney.'

'You're looking for the same murderer here.'

She started to tell him that was police business, then shrugged. The media would have its greedy hands on it within the hour. 'Seeing as his face has been turned into jelly, it's a pretty good bet. I've got to—'

She whirled around at the screams. Long, screeching wails that could have drilled holes in steel. She saw the woman, big, naked but for a pair of red panties, burst out of the building. She mowed over two uniforms who'd been sipping coffee, bowled them down like duckpins and streaked toward what was left of Cockroach.

'Oh, fucking A,' Eve muttered and raced to intercept. Less than a yard from the body, she leaped and took the woman down in a flying tackle that had them both making painful acquaintance with the concrete.

'That's my man.' The woman flopped like a two-hundred-pound fish, beat at Eve with meaty hands. 'That's my man, you cop bitch.'

In the interest of order, of preserving the scene, and of self-preservation, Eve brought her fist up hard under the woman's pudgy jaw.

'Lieutenant. You all right, Lieutenant?' Both uniforms reached down to help Eve off the unconscious woman. 'Jesus, she came out of nowhere. Sorry—'

'Sorry?' Jerking away, Eve scalded them both. 'Sorry? You miserable brain-dead assholes. Another two seconds, and she'd have contaminated the scene. Next time you're assigned to something bigger than traffic detail, you keep your stupid hands off your dicks. Now, see if you can manage to call the MTs and have them take a look at that idiot woman. Then you get her some clothes and take her into holding. Can you handle that?'

She didn't bother to wait for an answer but started limping off. Her jeans were torn, her own blood mixing with the dead man's, and her eyes were still flashing when they met Roarke's. 'What the hell are you grinning at?'

'It's always a delight to watch you work, Lieutenant.' Abruptly, he caught her face in his hands and crushed his mouth to hers in a kiss potent enough to stagger her back on her heels. 'No holding back,' he said as she blinked at him. 'Have the MT's take a look at you, too.'

It was several hours later when she received the summons to Whitney's office. With Peabody beside her, Eve took the skywalk.

'I'm sorry, Dallas. She shouldn't have gotten past me.'

'Jesus, Peabody, let it go. You were in another part of the building when she made her run.'

'I should have realized one of the other tenants would inform her.'

'Yeah, we all need to keep our crystal ball polished. Look, the upshot is, she didn't do any more than put another couple dents in me. Casto call in yet?'

'He's still in the field.'

'Is he still in *your* fields?'

Peabody's mouth twitched. 'We were together last night.

We were just going to have dinner, but one thing led to another. I swear, I haven't slept like that since I was a kid. Who knew great sex was such a terrific soother.'

'I could have told you.'

'Anyway, he got a call just after mine came in. My take is, he'll know who the victim is, maybe be able to help.'

Eve grunted. They weren't kept waiting in Whitney's outer office, but shown straight in. He pointed to chairs. 'Lieutenant, I realize your written report is on the way, but I prefer a verbal rundown on this latest homicide.'

'Yes, sir.' She relayed the address and description of the murder scene, the name and description of the victim, along with details of the weapon found, the wounds, the ME's determination of time of death. 'Peabody's initial door to door didn't turn up anything useful, but we will follow that up with a second pass. The woman who was living with the victim was of some help.'

Whitney lifted his brows. Eve was still wearing her stained shirt and torn jeans. 'I'm told you had a bit of trouble there.'

'Nothing to speak of.' Eve had already decided the tongue lashing she'd given would do. There was no need to layer on punishment with official reprimands. 'She's a former licensed street companion. Didn't have the credits to renew. She's also a user. By applying a little pressure in that area, we were able to get her to tell us something of the victim's movements last night. According to her statement, they were together in the apartment until about oh one hundred.

They'd had some wine and a little Exotica. He claimed he had to go, had a deal to close. She took some Download, passed out. As the ME puts the time of death at approximately oh two hundred in his prelim, it jibes.

'Evidence indicates the victim was killed where he was found early this morning. It also strongly indicates that the victim was taken out by the same person who killed Moppett, Boomer, and Pandora.'

She took time for a breath and continued to speak formally. 'Mavis Freestone's movements during the time of this murder can be accounted for by the primary and others.'

Whitney said nothing for a moment, but kept his eyes on Eve's face. 'This office does not believe that Mavis Freestone is in any way connected with this murder, nor does the office of the prosecuting attorney. I have Dr Mira's preliminary analysis of Ms Freestone's testing.'

'Testing?' Formality forgotten, Eve sprang up. 'What do you mean her testing? That wasn't scheduled until Monday.'

'It was rescheduled,' Whitney said calmly. 'And has been completed as of thirteen hundred hours.'

'Why wasn't I informed?' Uncomfortable memories of her own experiences with Testing roiled in her stomach. 'I should have been there.'

'It was in the best interest of all parties involved that you were not.' He held up a hand. 'Before you lose your temper and risk insubordination, let me tell you that Dr Mira clearly states in her report that Ms Freestone passed all testing. The truth detector indicates her veracity in her statements. As to the other elements, Dr Mira feels that the subject is highly unlikely to have exhibited the extreme violence with which Pandora was killed. Leaving out the hundred-credit words, Dr Mira recommends the charges against Ms Freestone be dropped.'

'Dropped.' The backs of Eve's eyes burned as she sat again. 'When?'

'The prosecutor's office is taking Dr Mira's report under advisement. Unofficially, I can tell you that unless other data come to light that disproves her analysis, the charges will be withdrawn on Monday.' He watched Eve block most of a shudder, approved her control. 'The physical evidence is strong, but outweighed at this point by Mira's report and the evidence gathered in the investigation of the allegedly connected deaths.'

'Thank you.'

'I didn't clear her, Dallas, nor have you, but you've come damn close. Get the bastard, and soon.'

'I intend to.' Her communicator beeped. She waited for Whitney's nod before she answered. 'Dallas.'

'Got your damn rush order.' Dickie scowled at her. 'Like I got nothing else to do.'

'Whine later. What have we got?'

'Your latest corpse had a nice ride on Immortality before he bought it. Just before, is my guess. Don't think he had time to enjoy it.'

'Transmit the report to my office,' she said and cut

him off before he could complain. She was smiling as she rose this time. 'I have this thing I have to go to tonight, and I think I might be able to tie a few things up.'

Chaos, panic, and tattered nerves seemed to be as much a part of a high-fashion runway show as needle-thin models and glitzy fabrics. It was intriguing and amusing to watch the players assume their roles. The pouty-lipped mannequin who found fault with every accessory, the rabbit-faced dresser who wore glinting needles and pins in a tuft of her hair, the stylist who swept down on models like a soldier pumped for battle, and the hapless creator of all the glitz who stood by amid the swirl, wringing his huge hands.

'We're running behind. We're running behind. I need Lissa out in the cotton swirler in two minutes. The music's on pace, but we're running behind.'

'She'll be there. Jesus, Leonardo, get a grip.'

It took Eve a moment to recognize the stylist. Trina's hair was in sharp ebony spikes that could gouge an eye at three paces. But the voice gave her away, and Eve watched, letting herself be elbowed back by another frantic dresser as Trina glopped something that looked distressingly like come onto a streaked mane before squishing it into a smooth cone shape.

'What are you doing there?' A man with owl eyes and a knee-length cape bore down on Eve like a snapping terrier. 'Get out of those clothes, for God's sake. Don't you know Hugo's out front?'

'Who's Hugo?'

The man made a sound like escaping gas and reached out to tug off Eve's T-shirt.

'Hey, buddy, you want to keep those fingers?' She smacked them away and glowered at him.

'Get naked, get naked. We're running out of time.'

Threats made no dent and he snatched at the snap of her jeans. She considered decking him, then pulled out her shield instead. 'You can back off, or I can haul your ass in for assaulting an officer.'

'What are you doing here? We have our license. We paid our revenue. Leonardo, there's a cop here. I simply can't be expected to deal with police.'

'Dallas.' Mavis hurried over, varicolored fabric draped over her arm. 'You're really in the way here. Why aren't you out front? Christ, why are you still dressed like that?'

'I didn't have time to go back and change.' Absently Eve tugged at her stained shirt. 'Are you all right? I didn't know they'd rescheduled your tests, or I'd have been there.'

'I got through it. Dr Mira was mag, but let's just say I'm glad it's over. I don't want to talk about it,' she said quickly, and looked around the disordered and crowded space. 'At least not now.'

'Okay. I want to see Jerry Fitzgerald.'

'Now? The show's already started. It's timed down to the last microsecond.' With the skill of a veteran, Mavis swayed

301

out of the path of a pair of long-legged models. 'She has to concentrate, Dallas. This pace is murder.' Cocking her head, she tuned into the music. 'Her next cue is in less than four minutes.'

'Then I won't keep her long. Where?'

'Dallas, Leonardo is—'

'Where, Mavis?'

'Back there.' Waving one frantic hand, she turned over one layer of fabric to a passing dresser. 'In the star's room.'

Eve managed to dodge, shift, and spin her way through the milling crowd to a door marked prominently with Jerry's name. She didn't bother to knock but pushed it open and saw the woman in question being squeezed into a gold lame tube.

'I'm not going to be able to breathe in this. A skeleton couldn't breathe in this.'

'You shouldn't have eaten that pate, dearie,' the dresser said implacably. 'Just suck it in.'

'An interesting look,' Eve commented from the doorway. 'Makes you look like a fairy wand.'

'It's one of his retro shots. Early twentieth-century glamour. I can't fucking move.'

Eve came closer, narrowed her eyes at Jerry's face. 'The cosmetician did a nice job. I can't see any bruises.' And she would check with Trina to see if there'd been any bruises to cover. 'I heard Justin Young gave you a couple of shots.'

'Bastard. Hitting me in the face before a big show.'

'I'd say he pulled his punch. What did you fight about, Jerry?'

'He thought he could diddle with some little chorus dancer. Not on my time.'

'Time's the interesting factor, isn't it? When did he start his diddling?'

'Listen, Lieutenant, I'm a little pressed here, and walking out on the runway with a scowl on my face is going to ruin the presentation. Let's just say, Justin's history.'

Despite her claims to the contrary, Jerry moved with quick agility through the door. Eve stayed where she was, listening to the burst of applause as Jerry made her entrance. In six minutes flat, she was back being peeled out of the gold lame.

'How'd you find out about it?'

'Trina. Hair, for God's sake! Christ, you're persistent. I got wind of it, that's all. And when I called him on it, he denied it. But I could tell he was lying.'

'Uh-huh.' Eve considered liars as Jerry stood, arms out. Trina transformed her ebony swing of hair into a complicated twist of curls with a hand-held heater. Sheer white silk with rainbow trimming was slipped over her arms. 'He didn't stay in Maui long.'

'I don't give a shit where he is.'

'He flew back to New York last night. I checked the shuttles. You know, Jerry, it's odd. That timing thing again. Last time I saw you two, you were all but joined at the hip. You went with him to Pandora's, went home with him that night. You were still there in the morning. The word I get is he accompanied you to your fittings, rehearsals. Doesn't seem like he'd have much time to boff a chorus dancer.'

'Some men work fast.' She offered a hand so the dresser could clasp on a half dozen jangling bracelets.

'A public fight, plenty of witnesses, even some handy media coverage. You know, on the face of things, it makes your dual alibis hold more water. If I was the kind of cop to believe in the face of things.'

Jerry turned to the mirror to check the line of her costume. 'What do you want, Dallas? I'm working here.'

'Me, too. Let me tell you how I see it, Jerry. You and your pal had a little deal going with Pandora. But she's greedy. It looks like she's going to screw you and your partners. A handy thing happens. Mavis comes in, there's a fight. For a sharp woman like you, that could spark an idea.'

Jerry picked up a glass, knocked back the sparkling sapphire contents. 'You've already got two suspects, Dallas. Who's being greedy now?'

'Did the three of you discuss it? You, Justin, and Redford? You and Justin go off and solidify an alibi. Redford doesn't. Maybe he's not as smart. Maybe you were supposed to back him up, too, but you didn't. He takes her to Leonardo's. You're waiting. Did things get out of hand then? Which one of you picked up the cane?'

'This is ludicrous. Justin and I were at his place. Security verifies that. If you want to accuse me of something, bring a warrant. Until then, back off.'

'Were you and Justin smart enough not to contact each other since the fight? I don't think he's got your control, Jerry. In fact, I'm banking on it. We'll have the transmission records by morning.'

'So what if he called me? So what?' Jerry raced to the doorway as Eve strolled away. 'It doesn't prove anything. You've got nothing.'

'I've got another dead body.' Eve paused, looked back. 'I don't suppose either one of you are going to alibi each other for last night, are you?'

'Bitch.' Incensed, Jerry heaved the glass, catching a hapless dresser in the shoulder. 'You're not hanging anything on me. You've got nothing.'

As the noise and confusion of backstage rose to a new level, Mavis shut her eyes. 'Oh, Dallas. How could you? Leonardo needs her for ten more changes.'

'She'll do her job. She wants the spotlight too much not to. I'm going to find Roarke.'

'He's out front,' Mavis said wearily as Leonardo rushed over to soothe his star. 'Don't go out there looking like that. Put this on. It's already been run. Without the over-dress and the scarves, no one will recognize it.'

'I'm just going to—'

'Please. It would mean a lot if you were wearing one of his designs out front. It's a simple line, Dallas. And I'll find some shoes that fit you somewhere.'

Fifteen minutes later, with her torn clothes stuffed in her bag, Eve spotted Roarke in the front row. He was applauding politely as a trio of large-breasted models jiggled wildly in transparent rompers.

'Great. Just what we want to see women wearing when they walk down Fifth.'

Roarke lifted a shoulder. 'Actually, a great many of his designs are very attractive. And I wouldn't mind seeing you in that number on the right.'

'Keep dreaming.' She crossed her legs and the flow of black satin over them whispered in response. 'How long do we have to stay?'

'Until the bitter end. When did you buy this?' He ran a fingertip over the narrow straps draped over her biceps.

'I didn't. Mavis made me put it on. It's one of his without the frills.'

'Keep it. It suits you.'

She only grunted. Her torn jeans suited her mood a great deal better. 'Ah, here comes the diva.'

Jerry glided out, and at each step of her dainty glass shoes, the runway exploded into color. Eve paid little attention to the billowing balloon skirt and sheer bodice that caused such a furor of approval from the attendees. She watched Jerry's face, and only her face as fashion critics murmured busily into their recorders and dozens of buyers ordered frantically from their porta-links.

Jerry's face was serene as she waved aside dozens of muscular young men who prostrated themselves in front of her. She sold the outfit with graceful twists and turns and clever choreography that had her stepping nimbly onto a pyramid of hard male bodies.

The crowd applauded. Jerry posed, then aimed icy blue eyes at Eve.

'Ouch,' Roarke murmured. 'I'd say that was a direct hit. Is there something I should know?'

'She'd like to rip my face off,' Eve said mildly. 'My mission has been a success.' Satisfied, she sat back and prepared to enjoy the rest of the show.

'Did you see? Dallas, did you see?' After a quick pirouette, Mavis threw her arms around Eve. 'At the finale they actually stood up for him. Even Hugo.'

'Who the hell is Hugo?'

'He's only the biggest name in the business. He cosponsored the show, but that was with Pandora. If he'd pulled out – well, he didn't, thanks to Jerry stepping in. Leonardo's on his way. He can pay back his debts. The orders are already pouring in. He'll have his own showroom now, and in a few months, there will be Leonardo's everywhere.'

'That's great then.'

'Everything's working out.' Mavis fussed with her face in the mirror of the ladies' lounge. 'I have to find another gig, and I'll wear his designs exclusively. Things are going to go back to the way they should be. They are, aren't they, Dallas?'

'They're heading that way. Mavis, did Leonardo go to Jerry Fitzgerald, or the other way around?'

'For the show? He went to her originally. Pandora suggested it.'

Wait, Eve thought, *how did I miss this step?* 'Pandora wanted him to ask Jerry to model in his show?'

'It was just like her.' On impulse, Mavis took out a tube and removed her lip dye. She studied her naked mouth a moment, then chose a container of Berry Crush. 'She knew Jerry wouldn't play second lead, not to her, even though there was a lot of good buzz about the designs. So asking her was a kind of dig, you know. She could say yes, and take the backseat, or say no and miss being in one of the hottest shows of the season.'

'And she said no.'

'Made out like she had previous commitments. Saving face. But the minute Pandora was out of the picture, she called Leonardo and offered to fill in.'

'How much will she make?'

'For the show? She'll get about a mil, but that's nothing. The headliner gets to pick her fashions at a wholesaler's discount, an endorsement fee for each wearing. Then there's the media clause.'

'Which is?'

'Well, the big models get it to go on the fashion channels, the talk channels and all that. They get to pump up the designs and get paid for the appearances. Exposure and big bucks for the next six months, with an option to renew. She could rake in five, six mil plus bennies from this one appearance.'

'Nice work if you can get it. She profits in excess of six million from Pandora's death.'

'You could look at it that way. It's not as if she was hurting before, Dallas.'

'Maybe not. But she sure as hell isn't hurting now. She'll put in an appearance at this postshowing party?'

'Sure. She and Leonardo are the stars. We'd better get out there if we want any food. Those fashion critics are like hyenas. They don't even leave bones.'

'You've been around Jerry and the others for a while now,' Eve began as they made their way back to the ballroom. 'Anybody using?'

'Jesus, Dallas.' Uncomfortable, Mavis shrugged. 'I'm not a weasel.'

'Mavis.' Eve tugged her into an alcove resplendent with potted ferns. 'Don't take that line with me. Is anyone using?'

'Hell, sure, there's some shit around. Poppers mostly, and a lot of Zero Appetite. It's a tough business, and not all the low-tier models can afford body sculpting. You've got a few illegals filtered through, but it's mostly over the counter.'

'Jerry?'

'She's into health shit. That drink she guzzles. She smokes a little, but it's some special blend for soothing nerves. I've never seen her use anything dicey. But . . .'

'But?'

'Well, she's real territorial about her stuff, you know? Couple of days ago one of the other girls wasn't feeling well. Dragging from a late night. She started to cop a taste of Jerry's blue juice, and Jerry went nuts. Wanted to have her fired.'

'Interesting. Wonder what's in it.'

'Some vegetable extract. She claims it's made up for her metabolism. She made some noise about going on the market with it, endorsing.'

'I need a sample. I haven't got enough for a search or confiscation warrant.' She paused, considered, smiled. 'But I think I know how to fix that. Let's go party.'

'What are you going to do? Dallas.' Doubling her pace, Mavis caught up with Eve's long strides. 'I don't like that look in your eye. Don't cause any trouble. Please, come on. It's Leonardo's big night.'

'I bet a little more media coverage will increase his sales.'

She stepped into the ballroom where the crowd was gyrating on the dance floor or huddled around the tables of food. Spotting Jerry, Eve started over. Roarke caught her eye and crossed to her.

'Suddenly you look like a cop.'

'Thanks.'

'I'm not sure it was a compliment. Are you about to cause a scene?'

'I'm going to do my best. Want to keep your distance?'

'Not on your life.' Intrigued, he took her hand and walked with her.

'Congratulations on a successful show,' Eve began, edging aside a fawning critic to stand face to face with Jerry.

'Thank you.' Jerry raised a glass of champagne. 'But from

what I've seen, you're not exactly a fashion expert.' She sent Roarke a melting look. 'Though you do appear to have excellent taste in men.'

'Better than yours. Did you hear Justin Young was spotted at the Privacy Club tonight with a redhead? A redhead who bore a remarkable resemblance to Pandora.'

'You lying bitch. He wouldn't—' Jerry caught herself, hissed gently through her teeth. 'I told you, I don't care who he sees or what he does.'

'Why would you? It's true though, isn't it, that after a certain number of sessions, body sculpting and facial enhancements don't completely fight reality. I suppose Justin wanted a taste of youth. Men are such pigs.' Eve accepted a glass of champagne from a roving waiter and took a sip. 'Not that you don't look wonderful. For your age. Those harsh stage lights just tend to make a woman look . . . mature.'

'Fuck you.' Jerry dashed the contents of her glass in Eve's face.

'Thought that would do it,' Eve murmured as she blinked her stinging eyes. 'That's assaulting an officer. You're under arrest.'

'Take your hands off me.' Incensed, Jerry shoved Eve back.

'Add resisting arrest. This must be my lucky night.' In two quick moves, Eve had Jerry's arm twisted up and behind her back. 'We'll just call a uniform to take you in. It shouldn't take you long to make bail. Now, behave so I can read you your rights on the way out.' She shot Roarke a sunny smile. 'I won't be long.'

'Take your time, Lieutenant.' He plucked up Eve's champagne and drank it himself. He gave her ten minutes, then wandered out of the ballroom.

She was standing at the hotel entrance, watching Jerry being loaded into a cruiser.

'What was that for?'

'I needed to buy some time and some probable cause. The suspect showed violent tendencies and a nervous manner, indicative of drug use.'

Cops, Roarke thought. 'You pissed her off, Eve.'

'That, too. She'll be out almost before they get her in. I've got to move.'

'Where?' he demanded as they hurried around the ballroom to the backstage area.

'I need a sample of that stuff she likes to drink. The assault gives me clearance – if we bend things a little. I want it analyzed.'

'You honestly think she's using illegals that blatantly?'

'I think people like her – like Pandora and Young and Redford – are incredibly arrogant. They've got money, looks, a certain amount of power and prestige. It makes them feel above the law.' She sent him a look as she slipped into Pandora's dressing room. 'You have the same tendencies.'

'Thank you so much.'

'Lucky for you, I came along to keep you on the straight and narrow. Watch the door, will you? If she's got a quick lawyer, I'm not going to have time to finish this.'

'The straight and narrow, naturally,' Roarke commented and stationed himself at the door as she searched the room.

'Christ, there's a fortune in cosmetic enhancements.'

'It is her business, Lieutenant.'

'Vanity's costing her several hundred K a year, I'd say, just on the topicals. Christ knows what she spends in ingestives and sculpting. If I could just find a little of that nice powder.'

'You're looking for Immortality?' He let out a laugh. 'She may be arrogant, but she doesn't look stupid.'

'Maybe you're right.' She opened the door of a friggie and smiled. 'But she's got a container of that drink in here. A locked container.' Pursing her lips, Eve looked toward Roarke. 'I don't suppose you could . . .'

'Veer from the straight and narrow.' He sighed, walked over, and studied the lock on the clear bottle. 'Sophisticated. She's not taking any chances with it. The bottle's unbreakable from the look of it.' His fingers played over the lock mechanism as he spoke. 'Find me a nail file, a hair clip, something like that, will you?'

Eve pushed through the drawers. 'Will this do?'

Roarke frowned at the tiny pair of manicure scissors. 'Close enough.' He jiggled the lock with the points, finessed, and stepped back. 'There you are.'

'You're awfully good at that.'

'Just a small, insignificant talent, Lieutenant.'

'Right.' She dug in her bag, pulled out an evidence

holder. She filled it with a couple of ounces. 'That should be more than enough.'

'Would you like me to relock it? It would only take a moment.'

'Don't bother. We can swing by the lab on the way.'

'On the way to?'

'To where I've got Peabody staked out. Justin Young's back door.' She started out, flicking him a smile. 'You know, Roarke, Jerry was right about one thing. I have pretty good taste in men.'

'Darling, your taste is impeccable.'

17

Being hooked up with a rich man had a number of disadvantages in Eve's mind, but it had one overwhelming plus. That was food. On the way back across town she managed to stuff herself to bursting with chicken Kiev from the fully stocked AutoChef in his car.

'Nobody has chicken Kiev in their car unit,' she said with her mouth full.

'They do if they run around with you. Otherwise you'd live off soy burgers and irradiated powdered eggs.'

'I hate irradiated powdered eggs.'

'Exactly.' It pleased him to hear her chuckle. 'You're in a rare old mood, Lieutenant.'

'It's coming together, Roarke. They'll drop charges on Mavis by Monday morning, and by then I'll have the bastards. It was all money,' she said and dabbed up grains of wild rice with her fingers. 'Fucking money. Pandora was the connection to Immortality, and those three high flyers wanted their share.'

'So they lured her to Leonardo's and killed her.'

'Leonardo's was probably her idea. She wasn't letting go there, and she was revved to fight. Gave them the perfect opportunity and setting. Mavis walking in was just icing. They'd have left Leonardo hanging by his balls, otherwise.'

'Not to question your quick, agile, and suspicious mind, but why not just whack her in an alley? If you're right, they'd done it before.'

'So they wanted some staging this time.' She moved her shoulders. 'Hetta Moppett was a potential loose end. One of them confronted her, likely questioned her, then got rid of her. Better not to chance whatever Boomer had let slip during sex.'

'Then Boomer came next.'

'He knew too much, had too much. It's not likely he knew about all three of them. But he'd nailed at least one, and when he spotted that one in the club, he went underground. They managed to get him out, tortured him, killed him. But they didn't have time to go back and get the stuff.'

'All for profit?'

'For profit, and if that analysis comes out the way I think it will, for Immortality. Pandora was on it, no question. My take is that whatever Pandora had or wanted, Jerry Fitzgerald wanted to have more. You've got a drug that makes you look good, younger, sexier. It could be worth a fortune to her professionally. Not to mention her ego.'

'But it's lethal.'

'That's what they say about smoking, but I've seen you light up some tobacco.' She arched a brow at him. 'Unprotected sex was lethal during the latter half of the

316

twentieth century. Didn't stop people from fucking strangers. Guns are lethal, but we spent decades getting them off the street. Then—'

'Point taken. Most of us think we're going to live forever. Did you do testing on Redford?'

'We did. He's clean. Doesn't mean his hands are any less bloody. I'm going to lock the three of them away for the next fifty years.'

Roarke eased the car to a stop at a light, turned to look at her. 'Eve, are you after them for murder, or for messing with the life of your friend?'

'The results are the same.'

'Your feelings aren't.'

'They hurt her,' she said tightly. 'They put her through hell. Forced me to help them put her through it. She lost her job, and a lot of her confidence. They're going to pay for that.'

'All right. I only have one thing to say.'

'I don't need criticisms on procedure from a guy who pops locks like you, pal.'

He took out a handkerchief, dabbed at her chin. 'The next time you start to say you have no family,' he began quietly, 'think again. Mavis is yours.'

She started to speak, reevaluated. 'I'm doing my job,' she decided. 'If I get some personal pleasure out of it, what's wrong with that?'

'Not a thing.' He kissed her lightly, then turned left.

'I want to go around the back of the building. Take a right at the next corner, then—'

'I know how to get around the back of that building.'

'Don't tell me you own that one, too.'

'All right, I won't tell you. And by the way, if you had asked me about the security setup at Young's place, I could have saved you – or I should say Feeney – a little time and trouble.' When she huffed, he smiled. 'If I get some personal pleasure out of owning large chunks of Manhattan, what's wrong with that?'

She turned to stare out of the window so he couldn't see her smirk.

For Roarke, it seemed, there would always be a table at the most exclusive restaurant, front row seats at the current hit play, and a convenient parking place on the street. He glided in and killed the engine.

'You don't, I trust, expect me to wait here.'

'What I expect doesn't usually hold water with you. Come on, but try to remember you're a civilian. I'm not.'

'That's something I never forget.' He code locked the car. It was a good neighborhood, but the car was worth an easy six months' rent in even the most exclusive of units in the building. 'Darling, before we shift into the official mode, what do you have on under that dress?'

'A device designed to drive men wild.'

'It's working. I don't believe I've ever seen your butt move quite that way.'

'It's a cop's butt now, ace, so watch it.'

'I am.' He smiled, gave it a nice solid smack. 'Believe me. Good evening, Peabody.'

'Roarke.' Her face bland, as if she hadn't heard a word, Peabody stepped out from the shrubbery. 'Dallas.'

'Any sign of—' Eve went into a defensive crouch as the shrubbery rustled, then swore as Casto came out grinning. 'Goddamn it, Peabody.'

'Now, don't blame DeeDee. I was with her when your call came in. She wouldn't have been able to shake me. Interdepartmental cooperation, Eve?' Still smiling, he extended a hand. 'Roarke, a pleasure to meet you. Jake Casto, Illegals.'

'So I gathered.' Roarke's brow cocked as he noted Casto take in the black satin that slithered over Eve's body. In the manner of men or unfriendly male dogs, Roarke showed his teeth.

'Nice dress, Eve. You mentioned something about taking a sample to the lab.'

'Do you always listen in on another cop's transmissions?'

'Well . . .' He stroked his chin. 'The call came through at a particular moment, you see. I'd have had to be deaf not to catch it.' He sobered. 'You figure you got Jerry Fitzgerald with a dose of Immortality?'

'We'll have to wait for the analysis.' She shifted her attention to Peabody. 'Is Young in there?'

'That's confirmed. A check with security shows him coming in about nineteen hundred. He hasn't been out since.'

'Unless he took the back way.'

'No, sir.' Peabody allowed herself a small smile. 'I called

his 'link when I arrived, and he answered. I apologized for the wrong contact.'

'He's seen you.'

Peabody shook her head. 'Men like that don't remember underlings. He didn't make me, and there's been no movement in this area since my arrival at twenty-three thirty-eight.' She gestured over, up. 'His lights are on.'

'So we wait. Casto, you could make yourself useful and stake out the front entrance.'

He flashed a grin. 'Trying to get rid of me?'

Her eyes lit in response. 'Yep. We could get technical. As primary on the Moppett, Johannsen, Pandora, and Ro homicides, I have full authority on coordinating investigations. Therefore—'

'You're a tough woman, Eve.' He sighed, shrugged, sent Peabody a wink. 'Keep a light burning for me, DeeDee.'

'I'm sorry, Lieutenant,' Peabody began formally when Casto moved off. 'He overheard the transmission. As there was no way to prevent him from coming to the scene on his own, it seemed more productive to enlist his aid.'

'It doesn't seem to be a problem.' When her communicator beeped, she shifted aside. 'Dallas.' She listened a moment, lips curving, then nodded. 'Thanks.' She started to slip the unit into her pocket, then remembered she didn't have a pocket, and dropped it into her bag. 'Fitzgerald's sprung, own recognizance. Not surprising she'd get OR over a little tussle at a fashion party.'

'If the lab results fall,' Peabody said.

'If. We wait on that.' She glanced at Roarke. 'This could be a long night. You don't have to hang. Peabody and Casto can drop me when we're done.'

'I like long nights. A moment of your time, Lieutenant.' With a firm hand on her arm, Roarke led her a few paces away. 'You didn't mention you had an admirer in Illegals.'

She ran a hand through her hair. 'Didn't I?'

'The kind of admirer who'd like to nibble his way up your extremities.'

'That's an interesting way of putting it. Look, he and Peabody are an item at the moment.'

'That doesn't stop him from licking his chops over you.'

She gave a quick snorting laugh, then catching the look in Roarke's eye, she sobered and cleared her throat. 'He's harmless.'

'I don't think so.'

'Come on, Roarke, it's just one of those little testos-terone games you guys play.' His eyes were still gleaming and caused something to jitter, not unpleasantly, in her stomach. 'You're not, like, jealous?'

'Yes.' It was demeaning to admit it, but he was a man who did what had to be done.

'Really?' The jittery feeling turned into a nice warm spread of pleasure. 'Well, thanks.'

There was no point in sighing. Certainly no point in giving her a quick shake. Instead, he dipped his hands in his pockets and inclined his head. 'You're welcome. Eve, we're going to be married in a few days.'

The jittering started again, big time. 'Yeah.'

'If he keeps looking at you like that, I'm going to have to hurt him.'

She smiled, patted his cheek. 'Down, boy.'

Before she could do more than chuckle, he'd snagged her wrist, leaned in close. 'You belong to me.' Her eyes fired, her teeth bared. The show of temper had him relaxing immediately. 'It goes both ways, darling, but in case you haven't noticed, it seems only fair to tell you, I'm very territorial over what's mine.' He kissed her snarling mouth. 'I do love you, Eve. Ridiculously.'

'It's ridiculous all right.' To settle her temper, she tried a long, slow breath. 'Look, not that I figure you deserve any explanation, but I'm not interested in Casto, or anybody else. And, as it happens, Peabody's gone over him. So just shut down your thrusters.'

'Done. Now, would you like me to go back to the car and get some coffee?'

She angled her head. 'Is that a cheap bribe to smooth this over?'

'I'll remind you that my blend of coffee isn't cheap.'

'Peabody takes hers light. Hold it.' She grabbed his arm, tugged him back toward the bushes. 'Wait for it,' Eve murmured as a car shot down the street. It squealed to a halt, did a fast vertical to squeeze into a top-level parking spot. Impatient maneuvering knocked bumpers. A woman in shimmering silver strode down the ramp to the sidewalk.

'There's our girl,' Eve said quietly. 'She didn't waste any time.'

'You called it, Lieutenant,' Peabody commented.

'Looks like. Now why would a woman who has recently gone through an uncomfortable, inconvenient, and potentially embarrassing situation, run straight to a man she's just broken up with, accused of cheating, and who popped her in the face? All in public.'

'Sadomasochistic tendencies?' Roarke suggested.

'I don't think so,' Eve said, appreciating him. 'It's S and M all right, but it stands for sex and money. And lookie here, Peabody, our heroine knows the back way in.'

With one careless glance over her shoulder, Jerry headed straight for the maintenance entrance, keyed in a code, and disappeared inside.

'I'd say she's done that before.' Roarke laid a hand on Eve's shoulder. 'Is that enough to break their alibi?'

'It's a damn good start.' Reaching in her bag, she took out surveillance goggles. She strapped them on, adjusting the power as she focused on Justin Young's windows. 'Can't see him,' she murmured. 'No one's in the living area.' She shifted her head. 'Bedroom's empty, but there's a flight bag open on the bed. A lot of doors closed. No way to get a view of the kitchen and rear entrance from here, damn it.'

She put her hands on her hips and kept scanning. 'There's a glass of something on the table by the bed, and a light playing. I'd say his bedroom screen's on. There she is now.'

Eve's lips stayed curved as she watched Jerry storm into

the bedroom. The goggles were powerful enough to give her a clear close-up of undiluted fury. Jerry's mouth was moving. She reached down, plucked off her shoes, heaved them.

'Temper, temper,' Eve murmured. 'She's calling for him, throwing things. Enter the young hero, stage left. Well, I've got to say, he's built.'

With her own goggles in place, Peabody let out a low hum of agreement.

Justin was buck naked, his skin beaded with water, his gilded hair sleeked with it. Apparently Jerry was unimpressed. She raged at him, shoved while he held up his hands, shook his head. The argument grew heated, dramatic, Eve mused, with lots of arm gestures, tossing heads. Then it changed tones abruptly. Justin was tearing off Jerry's ten-thousand-dollar silver gown as they fell on the bed.

'Aw, isn't that sweet, Peabody? They're making up.'

Roarke tapped Eve's shoulder. 'I don't suppose you have another pair of them.'

'Pervert.' But since it seemed only fair, she tugged the goggles off, handed them to him. 'You may be called as a witness.'

'How? I'm not even here.' He slipped the goggles on, adjusted them. After a moment, he shook his head. 'They're not terribly imaginative, are they? Tell me, Lieutenant, do you spend much time watching fornication during surveillance?'

'There's nothing much a human being can do to another I haven't watched.'

Recognizing the tone, he slipped the goggles off, handed them back. 'It's a miserable job. I'd have to agree that murder suspects aren't entitled to privacy.'

She jerked a shoulder and readjusted the goggles. It was imperative to find the humor again. She knew some cops got off peeking into bedroom windows, and misuse of the goggles was rampant on all levels. She considered them a tool, an important one, no matter how often their use was challenged in the courts.

'Looks like the finale,' she said blandly. 'I have to appreciate their speed.'

Justin, levered on his elbows, plunged into her. With her feet planted firmly on the mattress, Jerry pumped her hips to meet him. Their faces shone with sweat, and tightly closed eyes added twin expressions of agony and delight. When he collapsed on her, Eve started to speak.

She held her tongue as Jerry's arms came up, cuddled. Justin nuzzled Jerry's neck. They held each other, stroking, cheek brushing cheek.

'I'll be damned,' Eve muttered. 'It's not just sex. They care.'

More than the animal lust, the very human affection was difficult to watch. They separated briefly, sat up together with legs companionably tangled. He smoothed her tangled hair. She turned her face into the palm of his hand. They began to talk. From the expressions on their faces, the tone was serious, intense. At one point, Jerry lowered her head, weeping.

Justin kissed her hair, her brow, then got up and crossed the room. From a minifriggie, he took a slim glass bottle and poured a glass of dark blue liquid.

His face was grim as she snatched it from his hand, downed it in one quick gulp.

'Health drink, my ass. She's using.'

'Just her,' Peabody put in. 'He's not having any.'

Justin drew Jerry from the bed and with an arm around her waist, led her out of the bedroom, out of vision.

'Keep scanning, Peabody,' Eve ordered. She tugged down the goggles so that they hung around her neck. 'She's on the edge about something. And I don't think it's over our little shoving match. The pressure's gotten to her. Some people aren't natural-born killers.'

'If they're trying to distance themselves from each other, add more strength to their alibi, it was risky for her to come here tonight.'

Eve nodded as she looked at Roarke. 'She needed him. Addictions come in all forms.' As her communicator signaled, Eve reached into her bag. 'Dallas.'

'Rush, rush, rush.'

'Dickie, give me good news.'

'An interesting mix, Lieutenant. Other than a few additions to take it to liquid, add pretty color, and a mildly fruity taste, you've got yourself a match. All the elements from the powder previously analyzed are in there, including nectar from the Immortal Blossom. It is, however, a less potent mix, and when ingested by mouth—'

326

'That's all I need. Transmit full report to my office unit, stat, copy Whitney, Casto, and the prosecutor.'

'Want me to tie a nice red bow around it, too?' he said sourly.

'Don't be such a shit, Dickie. You'll get your fifty-yard-line seats for arena ball.' She broke transmission, grinned. 'Call for a search and confiscate warrant, Peabody. Let's go take them down.'

'Yes, sir. Ah, Casto?'

'Tell him we're coming around front. Illegals will get its share.'

It was five A.M. by the time they'd waded through the official paperwork and finished the first round of interviews. Fitzgerald's lawyers had insisted on a six-hour break, minimum. With no choice but to comply, Eve ordered Peabody off duty until eight and swung by her own office.

'Didn't I tell you to go get some sleep?' she asked when she saw Roarke kicked back at her desk.

'I had some work.'

Frowning, she glanced at the monitor on her desk unit. The intricate blueprints had her hissing. 'This is police property. Tampering with police property can get you eighteen months under home security.'

'Would you hold off on the arrest? I'm nearly finished. East wing view, all levels.'

'I'm not kidding, Roarke. You can't use my 'link for personal business.'

'Hmm. Note to adjust recreational center C. Square footage insufficient. Transmit all memos and amended dimensions, CFD Architectural and Design, FreeStar One office. Save to disc, and disengage.' He slipped the disc out, tucked it into his pocket. 'You were saying?'

'This unit is programmed for my voice print. Just how did you get it operational?'

He only smiled. 'Really, Eve!'

'All right, don't tell me. I don't want to know, anyway. Couldn't you have done this at home?'

'Certainly. But then I wouldn't have had the pleasure of taking you home and making you get a few hours' sleep.' He rose. 'Which is what I'm about to do now.'

'I'm going to catch a nap in the lounge.'

'No, you were going to sit here combing through evidence and doing probability scans until your eyes fell out.'

She could have denied it. It wasn't very hard to lie under most circumstances. 'I just have a couple of things I want to put into order.'

He tilted his head. 'Where's Peabody?'

'I sent her home.'

'And the inestimable Casto?'

Recognizing the trap, but not the escape route, Eve shrugged. 'I think he went with her.'

'Your suspects?'

'They've got a minimum break coming.'

'And so,' he said, taking her arm, 'do you.' She started to

tug away, but he continued to march her out into the hall. 'I'm sure everyone appreciates your new interview look, but I imagine you'd do a better job of it after a nap, a shower, and a change of clothes.'

She looked down at the black satin gown. She'd completely forgotten she had it on. 'I've probably got a pair of jeans in my locker.' When he was able to bundle her into the elevator with little effort, she realized she was flagging. 'Okay, okay. I'll go home and catch a shower, maybe some breakfast.'

And, Roarke thought, *at least five hours' sleep.*

'How'd it go in there?'

'Hmm?' She blinked, shook herself alert. 'Not too much progress. Didn't expect it on the first round. They're sticking tight to their original story and claiming the drug was planted. We've got enough for an enforced drug test on Fitzgerald. Her lawyers are making a lot of noise over it, but we'll get it.'

She yawned hugely. 'We'll use that to finesse data out of her, if not an outright confession. We'll triple team them on the next round.'

Roarke led her out the breezeway to the visitors' lot where he'd parked. She was walking, he noted, with the intense care of a woman deeply drunk. 'They won't stand a chance,' he said as they approached his car. 'Roarke, disengage locks.'

He opened the door, all but folded her into the passenger seat.

'We'll shift off. Casto's a good interviewer.' Her head lolled back on the seat. 'Gotta give him that. Peabody's got potential. She's tenacious. We'll keep the three of them in separate rooms, keep changing interviewers on them. I'm betting on Young to fall first.'

Roarke eased out of the lot, headed for home. 'Why?'

'The bastard loves her. Love messes you up. You make mistakes 'cause you're worried, protective. Stupid.'

He smiled a little, brushed her hair back from her face, and she dropped steeply into sleep. 'Tell me about it.'

18

If recent behavior was any example of what it was like to have a husband, Eve told herself it couldn't be half bad. She'd been coddled into bed, which she was forced to admit had been for the best, and had been awakened five unremembered hours later by the scent of hot coffee and fresh waffles.

Roarke had already been up, dressed, and poring over some vital business transmission.

It did irk her from time to time that he seemed to get by on less sleep than a normal human, but she didn't mention it. That sort of comment would only gain her a smirk.

It was to his benefit that he didn't point out that he was taking care of her. Knowing it was weird enough without having him crow over it.

So she headed toward Cop Central, rested, well fed, and in her newly repaired vehicle, which in under five blocks decided to surprise her with a new foible. Her speed indicator shot straight into red, though she was sitting dead still in a traffic snarl.

WARNING, she was told pleasantly. ENGINE OVERLOAD

IN FIVE MINUTES AT CURRENT SPEED. PLEASE REDUCE
VELOCITY OR SWITCH TO AUTO OVER.

'Bite me,' she suggested, not so pleasantly, and drove the
rest of the way with the constant cheerful advice to reduce
velocity or blow up.

She wasn't going to let it affect her mood. The nasty
black-hearted thunderclouds rolling in and sending air
traffic scrambling didn't bother her. The fact that it was
Saturday, a week before her wedding, and she was in for
a long, hard, potentially brutal day at work didn't diminish
her pleasure.

She strode into Cop Central, her smile fixed and grim.

'You look ready to gnaw raw meat,' Feeney commented.

'The way I like it best. Any additional data?'

'Let's take the long way. I'll fill you in.'

He detoured to a sky glide, nearly empty at midday. The
mechanism stuttered a bit, but carried them upward.
Manhattan receded to a pretty toy town of crisscrossing
avenues and brightly colored vehicles.

Lightning cracked the sky with an accompanying boom
of thunder that shook the glass enclosure. Rain poured
through the crack in gleeful buckets.

'Just made it.' Feeney peered down, watched pedestrians
scramble like maddened ants. An airbus blatted its horn and
skidded past the glass with inches to spare. 'Jesus.' Feeney
slapped a hand to his jumping heart. 'Where do those
fuckers get their license?'

'Anybody with a pulse can drive those sky cloggers. You couldn't get me in one with a laser blast.'

'Public transportation in this city's a disgrace.' He took out a bag of candied nuts to calm himself. 'Anyway, your hunch on the calls from Maui panned out. Young called Fitzgerald's place twice before he hopped a shuttle back. He ordered the showing on screen, too. Full two hours.'

'Got any security of his place on the night Cockroach bought it?'

'Young came in, with his flight bag, about six A.M. His shuttle got in at midnight. No data on how he spent the missing six hours.'

'No alibi. He had plenty of time to get from the terminal to the murder scene. Can we place Fitzgerald?'

'She was at the ballroom until a little past twenty-two thirty. Rehearsals for last night's do. Didn't show up at her place until oh eight. She made plenty of calls: her stylist, her masseuse, her body sculptor. Spent four hours yesterday at Paradise, getting herself buffed and polished. Young, he spent the day talking with his agent, his business manager, and . . .' Feeney smiled a little. 'A travel consultant. Our boy was interested in a trip for two to the Eden Colony.'

'I love you, Feeney.'

'I'm a lovable kind of guy. Picked up the sweeper's reports on my way in. Nothing we can use on Young's place or Fitzgerald's. The only trace of illegals was in the blue juice. If they've got more, they're keeping it elsewhere. No logs or records of any transactions, no sign of formulas. I've still got the hard drives to diddle with, see if they hid anything in them. But if you ask me, those two aren't high-tech geniuses.'

'No, Redford would probably know more about that. We've got more than murder and trafficking here, Feeney. If we can get the stuff classified as poison and pin them with prior knowledge of its lethal qualities, we'll have full-scale racketeering and conspiracy to slaughter.'

'Nobody's used conspiracy to slaughter since the Urban Wars, Dallas.'

The glide ground to a halt. 'I think it has a nice ring.'

She found Peabody waiting outside the interview area. 'Where's the rest of our party?'

'Suspects are in conference with their attorneys. Casto's getting coffee.'

'Okay, contact the conference rooms. Their time's up. Any word from the commander?'

'He's on his way in. He wants to observe. The PA's office will participate via 'link.'

'Good. Feeney's going to oversee the recordings on all three subjects. I don't want any slipups when this business comes to trial. You take Fitzgerald for the first round, Casto's on Redford. I want Young.'

She signaled when she spotted Casto coming toward them juggling a tray of coffee. 'Feeney, fill them in on the additional data. Use it wisely,' she added and copped a cup of coffee. 'We'll switch teams in thirty minutes.'

She slipped into her interview area. The first sip of miserable eatery coffee made her smile. It was going to be a good day.

'You can do better than that, Justin.' Eve was revving up, had barely hit her stride. It was hour three of interview.

'You asked me what happened. The other cops asked me what happened.' He took a drink of water. He was well off his stride, and faltering. 'I told you.'

'You're an actor,' she pointed out, all friendly smiles. 'A good one. All the reviews say so. I read one just the other day that said you can make a bad line sing. I don't hear music here, Justin.'

'How many times do you want me to go over the same ground?' He looked toward his lawyer. 'How long do I have to do this?'

'We can stop the interview process at any time,' his lawyer reminded him. She was a sharp-looking blonde with killer eyes. 'You're under no obligation to make any further statements.'

'That's right,' Eve chimed in. 'We can stop. You can go back to holding. You're not going to make bail on the illegals charges, Justin.' She leaned forward, made sure his eyes focused on hers. 'Not while there are four counts of murder hanging over you.'

'My client has not been charged with any crime other than suspicion of possession.' The lawyer peered down her needle-straight nose. 'You don't have a case here, Lieutenant. We all know it.'

'Your client's dangling over the edge of a very steep cliff. We all know that. Want to take the fall alone, Justin? That doesn't seem very fair to me. Your friends are answering questions right now.' She lifted her hands, spread her fingers. 'What are you going to do if they roll over on you?'

'I didn't kill anyone.' He flicked his gaze toward the door, toward the mirror. He knew he had an audience, and for once he didn't know how to play the crowd. 'I never even heard of those other people.'

'But you knew Pandora.'

'Of course I knew Pandora. Obviously I knew her.'

'You were there, at her house on the night she died.'

'I've said so, haven't I? Look, Jerry and I went to her house, at her invitation. We had a few drinks, that other woman came around. Pandora got obnoxious, and we left.'

'How often do you and Ms Fitzgerald use the unsecured entrance at your building?'

'It's just a matter of privacy,' he insisted. 'If you had media hounding you every time you tried to take a piss, you'd understand.'

Eve knew exactly what that was like and smiled toothily. 'Funny, neither of you seemed to be particularly shy of media exposure. In fact, if I were a cynic, I'd have to say the two of you exploited it. How long has Jerry been on Immortality?'

'I don't know.' His eyes shifted to the mirror again, as if he was hoping a director would say 'cut' and end the scene. 'I told you I didn't know what was in that drink.'

'You had a bottle in your bedroom, but you didn't know the contents. Never took a taste of it?'

'I never touched it.'

'That's funny, too, Justin. You know, it seems to me if something was in my friggie, I'd be tempted to sample it. Unless I knew it was poison, of course. You know Immortality's a slow poison, don't you?'

'It doesn't have to be.' He stopped himself, breathed hard through his nose. 'I don't know anything about it.'

'An overload on the nervous system, slow acting, but lethal all the same. You poured Jerry a drink, handed it to her. That's murder.'

'Lieutenant—'

'I'd never hurt Jerry,' he exploded. 'I'm in love with her. I'd never hurt her.'

'Really? Several witnesses claim you did just that a few days ago. Did you or did you not strike Ms Fitzgerald in the backstage area of the Waldorf's Royal Ballroom on July second?'

'No, I— We lost our tempers.' The lines were tangling in his head. He couldn't remember his cue. 'It was a misunderstanding.'

'You hit her in the face.'

'Yes – no. Yes, we were arguing.'

'You were arguing, so you punched the woman you love, knocking her off her feet. Were you still violently angry with her when she came to your apartment last night? When you poured her a glass of slow-acting poison?'

'I tell you, it's not poison, not like you mean. I wouldn't hurt her. I was never angry with her. I couldn't be.'

'You were never angry with her. You never hurt her. I believe you, Justin.' Eve soothed her voice, leaned forward again, laid a kind hand over his trembling one. 'You never hit her, either. You staged it all, didn't you? You're not the kind of man who strikes the woman he loves. You staged it, just like one of your performances.'

'I didn't – I—' He looked up helplessly into Eve's eyes, and she knew she had him.

'You've done a lot of action videos. You know how to pull a punch, how to fake one. That's what you did that day, isn't it, Justin? You and Jerry pretended to fight. You never laid a hand on her.' Her voice was gentle, full of understanding. 'You're not a violent kind of guy, are you, Justin?'

Torn, he pressed his lips together, looked at his lawyer. She held up a hand to hold off more questions and leaned close to Justin's ear.

Keeping her face bland, Eve waited. She knew the pickle they were in. Did he admit to the staging, making himself into a liar, or did he cop to punching his lover, showing his capabilities for violence? It wasn't a steady wire to cross.

The lawyer shifted back and folded her hands. 'My client and Ms Fitzgerald were playing a harmless game. Foolish, admittedly, but it isn't a crime to pretend to fight.'

'No, it isn't a crime.' Eve felt the first crackle, weakening the back of their alibi. 'Neither is going off to Maui and

338

pretending to play house with another woman. It was all make believe, wasn't it, Justin?'

'We just – I suppose we didn't take time to think it all through. We were worried, that's all. After you picked up Paul, we wondered if you'd shoot for us. We were all there that night, so it seemed logical.'

'You know, that's just what I thought.' She beamed a friendly smile. 'It's a very logical step.'

'We both had important projects going. We couldn't afford what's happening right now. We thought if we pretended to split up, it would add weight to our alibi.'

'Because you knew the alibi was weak. You had to figure we'd fall to the fact that either of you, or both of you, could have left the apartment undetected on the night of Pandora's murder. You could have gone to Leonardo's, killed her, and slipped back home without any security breach.'

'We didn't go anywhere. You can't prove we did.' His shoulders straightened. 'You can't prove anything.'

'Don't be too sure. Your lover's an Immortality junkie. You had possession of the drug. How did you get it?'

'I – someone gave it to her. I don't know.'

'Was it Redford? Did he hook her, Justin? You must hate him, if he did. The woman you love. She started dying, Justin, the first time she took a sip.'

'It's not poison. It's not. She told me that was just Pandora's way of keeping it for herself. Pandora didn't want Jerry to benefit from the drink. The bitch knew what it could do for Jerry, but she wanted—' He broke off, heeding his lawyer's sharp warning a little too late.

'What did she want, Justin? Money? A lot of money? You? Did she taunt Jerry? Did she threaten you? Is that why you killed her?'

'No. I never touched her. I tell you I never touched her. We argued, all right? We had an ugly scene after Leonardo's woman left that night. Jerry was upset. She had a right to be, after everything Pandora said. That's why I took her out, had a few drinks, calmed her down. I told her not to worry, that there were other ways of getting a supply.'

'What other ways?'

His breath heaved in and out. Frantically, he shook off his lawyer's restraining hand. 'Shut up,' he snapped at her. 'Just shut up. What the hell good are you doing me? She'll have me in a cage for murder before she's finished. I want to cut a deal. Why aren't you cutting a deal here?' He scrubbed the back of his hand over his mouth. 'I want to deal.'

'We'll have to talk about that,' Eve said calmly. 'What have you got to offer me?'

'Paul,' he said and shuddered out a breath. 'I'll give you Paul Redford. He killed her. The bastard probably killed them all.'

Twenty minutes later, Eve paced the conference room. 'I want Redford to stew for a while. Let him wonder how much they've told us.'

'Not getting much out of the lady.' Casually, Casto

propped his feet on the table, crossed his ankles. 'She's tough. Showing signs of withdrawal – dry mouth, trembling, occasional lack of focus – but she's sticking.'

'She hasn't had a fix in what – over ten hours. How long do you figure she can last?'

'Don't know enough.' Casto spread his hands. 'She could ice it out, come out the other side, or she could be a sloppy puddle of tapioca in another ten minutes.'

'Okay, so we don't count on her breaking.'

'Redford was showing a few cracks,' Peabody put in. 'He's scared boneless. His lawyer's the hard-ass. If we had him alone for five minutes, he'd crack like a walnut.'

'That's not an option.' Whitney studied the hard copy of the most recent interviews. 'You'll have Young's statement to pressure him with.'

'It's weak,' Eve muttered.

'You'll have to make it look stronger. He claims Redford first introduced Fitzgerald to Immortality about three months ago, suggested a partnership.'

'And according to our fair-haired boy, it was all going to be legal and aboveboard.' Eve gave a derisive grunt. 'Nobody's that fucking naive.'

'I don't know,' Peabody murmured. 'He's cross-eyed over Fitzgerald. I'd say she could have convinced him it was a straight deal. Research and development, a new line of beauty and youth aids carrying Fitzgerald's name.'

'And all they had to do was edge out Pandora.' Casto smiled. 'The money would roll in.'

'It still comes down to profit. Pandora was in the way.' Eve dropped into a seat. 'The others were in the way. Maybe Young's just an innocent schmuck, maybe not. He's pointed at Redford, but what he hasn't figured out yet is that he could be fingering Fitzgerald at the same time. She told him enough for him to plan a trip to the Eden Colony, hoping the two of them could finesse a specimen of their own.'

'You've got your illegals conspiracy,' Whitney pointed out. 'If Young shakes off the rest, he'll have his deal. You've still got a way to go for murder. At this point, his testimony isn't going to hold much weight. He believes Redford did Pandora. He gives us motive. We can establish opportunity. But there's no physical evidence, no witnesses.'

He rose. 'Get me a confession, Dallas. The PA's putting on the pressure. They're dropping charges on Freestone Monday. If they don't have something else to feed the media, we're all going to look like assholes.'

Casto took out a penknife, began trimming his nails as Whitney left the room. 'Christ knows we wouldn't want the PA to look like an asshole. Shit, they want it all laid out on a platter, don't they?' His eyes lifted to Eve's. 'Redford's not going to cop to murder, Eve. He'll go down for the drug. Hell, it's almost fashionable, but he's not going to swing to four homicides. We've only got one hope to pin on.'

'Which is?' Peabody wanted to know.

'That he didn't do it alone. We crack one of the others, we crack him. My money's on Fitzgerald.'

'Then you take her.' Eve blew out a breath. 'I'll work Redford. Peabody, take Redford's picture. Go back to the club, go back to Boomer's place, to Cockroach's, to Moppett's. Show the damn thing to everybody. I need one lousy make.'

She scowled as the 'link beeped, and she engaged it. 'Dallas, don't bother me.'

'It's always lovely to hear your voice,' Roarke said implacably.

'I'm in conference.'

'So am I. I'm leaving for FreeStar in thirty minutes.'

'You're going off planet? But . . . well, have a good trip.'

'It can't be avoided. I should be back within three days. You know how to contact me.'

'Yeah, I know.' She wanted to say things, foolish things, private things. 'I'm going to be pretty tied up myself for a while,' she said instead. 'See you when you get back.'

'You might check your office, Lieutenant. Mavis has been trying to reach you most of the day. It appears you've missed your last fitting. Leonardo is . . . distraught.'

Eve did her best to ignore Casto's quick chuckle. 'I've got other things on my mind.'

'Don't we all? Find a minute to deal with him, darling. For my sake. Let's get all those people out of our house.'

'I wanted to boot them out days ago. I thought you liked having all those people around.'

'And I thought he was your brother,' Roarke murmured.

'What?'

343

'Old joke. No, Eve, I don't like having all those people around. They are, in a word, maniacs. I found Galahad cowering under the bed just now. Someone has covered him with beads and tiny red bows. It's mortifying, for both of us.'

She bit down on her tongue to hold back the snort of laughter. Roarke wasn't looking amused. 'Now that I know they're driving you crazy, I feel better. We'll move them along.'

'Do that. Oh, and I'm afraid there might be a few details for next Saturday you'll have to handle while I'm gone. Summerset has the memos. My transport's waiting.' She watched him signal to someone off screen, then his eyes locked back on hers. 'See you in a few days, Lieutenant.'

'Yeah.' The screen went blank as she muttered. 'Bon fucking voyage.'

'Well, hell, Eve. If you need to run off to your dress-maker, or take your cat to therapy, Peabody and I can handle this minor matter of murder.'

Eve's lips stretched in a vicious smile. 'Bite me, Casto.'

Despite his many annoying qualities, Casto had solid instincts. Redford wasn't going to break any time soon. Eve worked him hard and had the mild satisfaction of pinning him on the illegals charges, but a confession to multiple murder just wasn't happening.

'Let's see if I've got this straight.' She rose. She needed to stretch her legs. She poured coffee. 'It was Pandora who told you about Immortality. And that was?'

'As I said, about a year and a half ago, perhaps a little more.' He was iced down now, totally in control. The illegals charges could be dealt with, particularly from the angle he'd chosen. 'She came to me with a business proposition. Or so she termed it. She claimed to have access to a formula, something that would revolutionize the beauty and health industry.'

'A beauty aid. And she didn't mention the illegal or the dangerous qualities.'

'Not at that time. She needed backing to start the line. One she intended to launch under her name.'

'Did she show you the formula?'

'She did not. As I told you before, she strung me along, made promises. Admittedly, it was poor judgment on my part. I was sexually addicted to her, a weakness she exploited. At the same time, the business aspect seemed to have merit. She was using the product in tablet form. And the results were impressive. I could see that it made her look younger, more fit. It increased her energy and her sexual drive. Marketed correctly, a product such as that would generate enormous profit. I wanted the money for some commercially risky projects.'

'You wanted the money, so you continued to pay her, little dribs and drabs, without being fully informed.'

'For a time. I did grow impatient and made demands. She made more promises. I began to suspect that she intended to go out on her own or that she was working with someone else. Using me. So I took a sample for myself.'

'Took a sample?'

He took his time answering, as if he was still crafting the words. 'I took her key while she was sleeping and unlocked the box where she kept the tablets. I, in the interest of protecting my investment, took a few to have them analyzed.'

'And when did you steal the drug, in the interest of protecting your investment?'

'Theft is not established,' the lawyer interrupted. 'My client had paid, in good faith, for the product.'

'Okay, we'll rephrase. When did you decide to take a more active interest in your business investment?'

'About six months ago. I took the samples to a contact I have in chemical analysis and paid him for a private report.'

'And learned . . .'

Redford paused to study his fingers. 'I learned that the product did indeed have the properties Pandora had promised. However, it was addictive, which pushed it automatically into the illegals category. It was also potentially lethal when taken regularly over a long period of time.'

'And being a righteous man, you counted your losses and pulled out of the deal.'

'Being righteous is not a legal requirement,' Redford said mildly. 'And I had an investment to protect. I decided to do some research to see if the unacceptable side effects could be diminished or eradicated. I believe we accomplished that, or nearly.'

'So you used Jerry Fitzgerald as a guinea pig.'

'That was a miscalculation. Perhaps I was overeager as

Pandora continued to push for more money and made statements that indicated she was about to go public with the product. I wanted to beat her to it, and knew that Jerry would be the perfect spokeswoman. She agreed, for a fee, to try the product my people had refined. In a liquid form. Science makes mistakes, Lieutenant. The drug was still, as we learned too late, highly addictive.'

'And fatal?'

'It seems. The process has been slowed, but yes, I'm afraid there is still the potential for physical harm in the long term. A possible side effect I warned Jerry of several weeks ago.'

'Before or after Pandora discovered you were trying to ace her out?'

'I believe it was after, just after. Unfortunately, Jerry and Pandora ran into each other at a function. Pandora made some comments about her former relationship with Justin. From what I gather, and this is secondhand, Jerry tossed the business deal we had made in Pandora's face.'

'And Pandora didn't take kindly to it.'

'She was, naturally, furious. Our relationship was rocky at best by that time. I had already procured a specimen of the Immortal Blossom, determined to delete all side effects from the formula. I had no intention, Lieutenant, of releasing a dangerous drug to the public. My records will substantiate that.'

'We'll let Illegals handle that one. Did Pandora threaten you?'

'Pandora lived for threats. One became accustomed to

them. I felt I was in a good position to ignore them, even to counter them.' He smiled now, more confident. 'You see, if she had gone forward, knowing what properties were contained in the formula, I could have ruined her. I had no reason to harm her.'

'Your relationship was rocky, yet you went to her home that night.'

'In hopes that we could come to some compromise. That's why I insisted that Justin and Jerry be present.'

'You had sex with her.'

'She was a beautiful, desirable woman. Yes, I had sex with her.'

'She had tablets of the drug in her possession.'

'She did. As I told you, she kept them in a box in her vanity.' His smile came back. 'I told you about the box and the tablets because I assumed, correctly, that an autopsy would show traces of the drug. It seemed wise to be forthcoming. I did nothing but cooperate.'

'Easy to cooperate if you knew I wouldn't find the tablets. After she was dead, you went back for the box. Protecting your investment. If there was no product but yours, no competitor, how much more profit there would be.'

'I did not go back to her home after I left. I had no reason to. My product was superior.'

'Neither of those products would have made the market, and you knew it. But on the street, hers would have hit big, bigger than your refined, watered down, and most likely more expensive version.'

'With more research, more testing—'

'More money? You'd already put over three hundred thousand in her hands. You'd gone to the considerable expense to procure a specimen, paid for the research and testing to date, paid Fitzgerald. I imagine you were becoming a little anxious to see some profit. How much did you charge Jerry for a fix?'

'Jerry and I had a business arrangement.'

'Ten thousand a delivery,' Eve interrupted, and watched the point strike home. 'That's the amount she transferred three times over a two-month period to your account on Starlight Station.'

'An investment,' he began.

'You addicted her, then you hosed her. That makes you a dealer, Mr Redford.'

The lawyer went into his spin routine, turning a drug deal into a profit-and-loss arrangement between investment partners.

'You needed contacts. Street contacts. Boomer was always a sucker for a credit in the hand. But he got carried away, liked to test the product. How did he get the formula? That was sloppy of you.'

'I don't know anyone by that name.'

'You saw him flapping his lips at the club. Making a big deal of himself. When he went into a privacy room with Hetta Moppett, you couldn't be sure how much he'd told her. But when he saw you, and he ran, you had to act.'

'You're on the wrong beam, Lieutenant. I don't know these people.'

'Maybe you killed Hetta in panic. You didn't really mean to, but when you saw she was dead, you had to cover it up. That's where the overkill came in. Maybe she told you something before she died, maybe she didn't, but you had to get to Boomer then. I'd say you were enjoying it now, the way you messed him up, tortured him before you finished him. But you got a little overconfident, and didn't get to his flop to search it before I did.'

She pushed away from the table, took a turn around the room. 'Now you've got big problems. The cops have a sample, they have the formula, and Pandora's getting out of hand. What choice do you have?' She put her hands on the table, leaned in close. 'What can a man do when he sees his investment and all those future profits going into the sewer?'

'My business with Pandora was finished.'

'Yeah, you finished it. Taking her to Leonardo's was smart. You're a smart man. She was already wired over Mavis. If you do her at his place, it's going to look like he'd had enough. You'd have to do him, too, if he was there, but you had a taste for it now. He's not there, so it's easier. Easier still when Mavis walks in and you can set her up.'

Redford's breathing was a bit forced, but he was holding. 'The last time I saw Pandora, she was alive, vicious, and eager to punish someone. If Mavis Freestone didn't kill her, my guess would be Jerry Fitzgerald.'

Intrigued, Eve angled back to her chair, leaned back. 'Really? Why?'

'They despised each other, were in direct competition, now more than ever. On top of everything else, Pandora was angling to lure Justin back. That was something Jerry wouldn't tolerate. And . . .' He smiled. 'It was Jerry who put the idea of going to Leonardo's for a showdown into Pandora's head.'

This is a new one, Eve thought and cocked a brow. 'Is that so?'

'After Ms Freestone left, Pandora was edgy, angry. Jerry seemed to enjoy that, and the fact that the young woman had gotten a few shots in. She egged Pandora on. Said something to the effect that if she was Pandora, she wouldn't tolerate being humiliated that way, and why didn't she go straight over to Leonardo's and show him who was in charge. There was another little dig about Pandora not being able to hold onto a man, then Justin hustled Jerry out.'

His smile widened. 'They despised Pandora, you see. Jerry for obvious reasons, and Justin because I'd told him that the drug was Pandora's doing. Justin would do anything to protect Jerry. Absolutely anything. I, on the other hand, had no emotional attachment to any of the players. It was just sex with Pandora. Just sex, Lieutenant, and business.'

Eve rapped on the door where Casto was interviewing Jerry. When he poked his head out, she shifted her gaze, studied the woman at the table. 'I need to talk to her.'

'She's running down, running out. Not going to get too much out of her today. Lawyer's already making noises about a break.'

'I need to talk to her,' Eve repeated. 'How have you been handling her this round?'

'Tough line, hard-ass.'

'Okay, I'll downgrade.' Eve slipped into the room.

She could still feel pity, she realized. Jerry's eyes were jittery and shadowed. Her face was drawn, and her hands shook as they ran over it. Her beauty was fragile now, and haunted.

'You want some food?' Eve asked in a quiet voice.

'No.' Jerry's gaze bounced around the room. 'I want to go home. I want Justin.'

'We'll see if we can arrange a visit. It'll have to be supervised.' She poured water. 'Why don't you drink a little of this, take a minute?' She covered Jerry's hands with her own on the glass, lifted it to the trembling lips. 'This is rough on you. I'm sorry. We can't give you anything to counteract the crash. We don't know enough yet, and whatever we gave you might be worse.'

'I'm all right. It's nothing.'

'It sucks.' Eve slipped into a seat. 'Redford got you into this. He verified that.'

'It's nothing,' she said again. 'I'm just tired. I need a little of my health drink.' She looked hopefully, pitifully at Eve. 'Can't I have a little, just to gear back up?'

'You know it's dangerous, Jerry. You know what it's doing

to you. Counselor, Paul Redford has stated on record that he introduced Ms Fitzgerald to the illegal, under the pretense of a business venture. It is our assumption that she was unaware of its addictive qualities. We have no intention, at this time, of charging her with use.'

As Eve had hoped, the lawyer relaxed visibly. 'Well, then, Lieutenant, I'd like to arrange for my client's release and her admission into rehab. Voluntary admission.'

'Voluntary admission can be arranged. If your client can cooperate for a few more minutes, it would help me in closing the charges on Redford.'

'If she cooperates, Lieutenant, all illegals charges will be dropped?'

'You know I can't promise that, Counselor. I will, however, recommend leniency on the charges of possession and intent to distribute.'

'And Justin? You'll let him go?'

Eve looked back at Jerry. Love, she thought, was an odd burden. 'Was he involved in the business transaction?'

'No. He wanted me to pull out. When he found out that I was . . . dependent, he pushed me to go into rehab, to stop taking the drink. But I needed it. I was going to stop, but I needed it.'

'The night Pandora died, there was an argument.'

'There was always an argument with Pandora. She was hateful. She thought she could get Justin back. The bitch didn't care about him. She just wanted to hurt me. To hurt him.'

'He wouldn't have gone back to her, would he, Jerry?'

'He hated her as much as I did.' She lifted her beautifully manicured nails to her mouth, started to gnaw. 'We're glad she's dead.'

'Jerry—'

'I don't care,' she exploded with a wild look to her cautioning lawyer. 'She deserved to die. She wanted everything, never cared how she got it. Justin was mine. I would have been headliner at Leonardo's show if she hadn't found out I was interested. She went out of her way to seduce him, to have me cut out so that she could take the job. It would have been my job, it should have been my job all along. Just like Justin was mine. Like the drug was mine. It makes you beautiful and strong and sexy. And every time anyone takes it, they'll think of me. Not of her, of me.'

'Did Justin go with you to Leonardo's that night?'

'Lieutenant, what is this?'

'It's a question, Counselor. Did he, Jerry?'

'No, of course not. We – we didn't go there. We went out for drinks. We went home.'

'You taunted her, didn't you? You knew how to play her. You had to be sure she'd go hunt down Leonardo. Did Redford contact you, tell you when she'd left?'

'No, I don't know. You're confusing me. Can't I have something? I need my drink.'

'You were using it that night. It made you strong. Strong enough to kill her. You wanted her dead. She was always in your way. And her tablets were stronger, more effective than your liquid. Did you want them, Jerry?'

'Yes, I wanted them. She was getting younger in front of my eyes. Thinner. I have to watch every fucking bite I take, but she . . . Paul said he might be able to get them from her. Justin told him to back off, to stay away from me. But Justin doesn't understand. He doesn't understand how it makes you feel. Immortal,' she said with a horrible smile. 'It makes you feel immortal. For God's sake, just one drink.'

'You slipped out of the back that night, went to Leonardo's. What happened then?'

'I can't. I'm confused. I need something.'

'Did you pick up the cane and hit her? Did you keep hitting her?'

'I wanted her dead.' On a sob, Jerry laid her head on the table. 'I wanted her dead. For God's sake help me. I'll tell you anything you want to hear if you just help me.'

'Lieutenant, anything my client says under physical and mental duress is inadmissible.'

Eve studied the weeping woman and reached for the 'link. 'Get the MT's in here,' she ordered. 'And arrange for hospital transport for Ms Fitzgerald. Under guard.'

19

'What do you mean you're not charging her?' His eyes went dark with shock and temper as Casto erupted, 'You got a fucking confession.'

'It wasn't a confession,' Eve corrected. She was tired, dead tired and sick of herself. 'She'd have said anything.'

'Jesus Christ, Eve. Jesus Christ.' In an attempt to walk off fury, Casto paced up and down the antiseptic tiled corridor of the health center. 'You aced her.'

'The hell I did.' Wearily, Eve rubbed at a headache in her left temple. 'Listen to me, Casto, the shape she was in, she'd have told me she personally drove nails into the palms of Christ if I'd promised her a fix. I charge her on the basis of that, her lawyers will tear it apart in pretrial.'

'You're not worried about pretrial.' He passed the tight-lipped Peabody on his stride back to Eve. 'You went for the jugular, just like a cop's supposed to in a murder case. Now you've gone soft. You're fucking sorry for her.'

'Don't tell me what I am,' Eve said evenly. 'And don't tell me how to run this investigation. I'm primary, Casto, so back the hell off.'

He measured her. 'You don't want me to go over your head with this decision.'

'Threats?' She angled her body up on the balls of her feet, like a boxer ready to dance. 'You go ahead and do what you have to do. My recommendation stands. She gets treatment, though Christ knows how much good that's going to do her in the short term, then we reinterview. Until I'm satisfied she's coherent and capable of judgment, she won't be charged.'

Eve could see he was making an effort to pull himself back. And she could see it was costing him. She didn't give a damn.

'Eve, you've got motive, you've got opportunity, you've got the personality capacity tests. She's capable of the crimes in question. She was, at her own admission, under the influence and predisposed to hate Pandora's guts. What the fuck do you want?'

'I want her to look me in the eye, clear in the eye, and tell me she did them. I want her to tell me how she did them. Until then, we wait. Because I'll tell you something, hotshot. No way she acted alone. No fucking way she did all of them with her own pretty hands.'

'Why? Because she's a woman?'

'No, because money isn't her big pull. Passion is, love is, envy is. So maybe she did Pandora in a fit of jealous rage, but I don't buy her doing the others. Not without help. Not without a push. So we wait, we reinterview, and we get her to finger Young and/or Redford. Then, we have it all.'

'I think you're wrong.'

'So noted,' she said briskly. 'Now, go file your interdepartmental complaint, take a walk, or blow it out your ass, but get out of my face.'

His eyes flickered, the temper in them ripe and ready. But he stepped back. 'I'm going to go cool off.'

He stormed off, with barely a glance at the silent Peabody.

'Your pal's running a little low on charm this evening,' Eve commented.

Peabody could have said the same went for her commanding officer, but she held her tongue. 'We're all under a lot of pressure, Dallas. This bust means a lot to him.'

'You know what, Peabody? Justice means a little more to me than a pretty gold star on my record or some fucking captain's bars. And if you want to go run after lover boy and stroke his ego, no one's stopping you.'

Peabody's jaw twitched, but her voice was even. 'I'm not going anywhere, Lieutenant.'

'Fine, just stand here and look martyred because I—' In midtirade, Eve stopped, sucked in her breath. 'I'm sorry. You're a goddamn handy target at the moment, Peabody.'

'Is that part of my job description? Sir.'

'You always have a fine comeback. I could learn to hate you for that.' Calmer, Eve laid a hand on her aide's shoulder. 'I am sorry, and I'm sorry to put you in a tight spot. Duty and personal emotions never mix well.'

'I can handle it. He was wrong to come at you that way,

Dallas. I can understand how he feels, but it doesn't make him right.'

'Maybe not.' Eve leaned against the wall and closed her eyes. 'But he was right about one thing, and it's eating at me. I didn't have the stomach for what I did to Fitzgerald in interview. I didn't have the stomach while I was doing it, while I was hearing myself hammer at her, twist her up when she was suffering. But I did it, because that's my job, and going for the jugular when the prey's wounded is exactly what I'm supposed to do.'

Eve opened her eyes and stared hard at the door behind which Jerry Fitzgerald was mildly sedated. 'And sometimes, Peabody, the job just fucking sucks.'

'Yes, sir.' For the first time, Peabody reached out and touched a hand to Eve's arm. 'That's why you're so good at it.'

Eve opened her mouth, surprised when a laugh popped out. 'Goddamn, Peabody, I really like you.'

'I like you, too.' She waited a beat. 'What's wrong with us?'

Cheered a little, she slung an arm around Peabody's sturdy shoulders. 'Let's go get something to eat. Fitzgerald's not going anywhere tonight.'

On that, Eve's instincts proved to be wrong.

The call woke her at a little before four A.M., out of a deep and thankfully dreamless sleep. Her eyes were gritty, her tongue thick from the wine she'd indulged in to be marginally sociable with Mavis and Leonardo. She managed a croak as she answered the 'link.

'Dallas. Christ, doesn't anyone ever sleep in this town?'

'I often ask myself the same question.' The face and voice on the 'link were vaguely familiar. Eve struggled to focus, to roll through her memory discs.

'Doctor . . . hell, Ambrose?' It slid back, layer by layer. Ambrose, spindly female, mixed race, head of chemical rehab at the Midtown Rehabilitation Center for Substance Addiction. 'You still there? Is Fitzgerald coming around?'

'Not exactly. Lieutenant, we have a problem here. Patient Fitzgerald is dead.'

'Dead? What do you mean dead?'

'As in deceased,' Ambrose said with a bland smile. 'As a homicide lieutenant, I imagine you're familiar with the term.'

'How, damn it? Did her nervous system give out, did she jump out a fucking window?'

'As near as we can determine, she overdosed herself. She managed to get her hands on the sample of Immortality we were using to determine the proper treatment for her. She took all of it, in combination with a few of the other goodies we have stashed here. I'm sorry, Lieutenant, she's gone. We can't bring her back. I'll fill you in on the details when you and your team arrive.'

'Damn right you will,' Eve snapped and broke transmission.

Eve viewed the body first, as if to ensure herself there hadn't been a horrible mistake. Jerry had been laid on the bed, her color-coded hospital gown draped to midthigh. Sky blue for addict, first stage treatment.

She was never going to get to stage two.

Her beauty was back, oddly eerie, in the bone-white face. The shadows were gone from under her eyes, the strain from around the mouth. Death was the ultimate calmer, after all. There were faint burn marks on her chest where the resuscitating team had worked on her, a light bruising on the back of her hand where the IV had pinched. Under the doctor's wary eye, Eve examined the body thoroughly, but found no signs of violence.

She'd died, Eve supposed, as happy as she would ever be.

'How?' Eve demanded shortly.

'The combination of Immortality and, as far as we can determine by what's missing, doses of morphine and synthetic Zeus. Autopsy will confirm.'

'You keep Zeus here, in a rehab?' The idea had Eve scrubbing her hands over her face. 'Jesus.'

'For research and rehabilitation,' Ambrose said tightly. 'Subjects addicted need a slow, supervised withdrawal period.'

'So where the hell was the supervision, Doctor?'

'Ms Fitzgerald was sedated. She was not expected to regain full consciousness until eight A.M. My hypothesis would be that, as we don't fully understand the properties of Immortality as yet, what was left in her system counteracted the sedative.'

'So she got up, marched herself down to your drug hold, and helped herself.'

'Something of the kind.' Eve could all but hear Ambrose's teeth grinding.

'What about security, the nursing staff? Did she turn herself invisible and walk right by them?'

'You can check with your own officer on duty about security, Lieutenant Dallas.'

'Be sure I will, Dr Ambrose.'

Ambrose gnashed her teeth again, then sighed. 'Listen, I don't want to hang the mess on your uniform, Lieutenant. We had a disruption here a few hours ago. One of our violent tendencies attacked his ward nurse, got out of his restraints. We had our hands full for a few minutes, and the uniform pitched in. If she hadn't, the ward nurse would very likely be standing at the Pearly Gates with Ms Fitzgerald right now instead of dealing with a broken tibia and some cracked ribs.'

'You've had a busy night, Doctor.'

'Not one I want to repeat any time soon.' She dragged her fingers through curly, rust-colored hair. 'Listen, Lieutenant, this center has an excellent reputation. We help people. Losing one, this way, makes me feel every bit as shitty as you. She should have been asleep, damn it. And that uniform wasn't away from her post for more than fifteen minutes.'

'Timing again.' Eve looked back at Jerry and tried to shrug off the weight of guilt. 'What about your security cameras?'

'We don't have any. Lieutenant, can you imagine how

many media leaks we'd have if we had recordings of patients, some of whom are prominent citizens? We're bound by privacy laws here.'

'Great, no security discs. Nobody sees her take her last walk. Where's the drug hold where she OD'd?'

'This wing, one level down.'

'How the hell did she know that?'

'That, Lieutenant, I can't tell you. Any more than I can explain how she unkeyed the lock, not only on the door, but on the holds themselves. But she did. The night watch found her on his sweep. The door was open.'

'Unlocked or open?'

'Open,' Ambrose confirmed. 'As were two holds. She was on the floor, dead as Caesar. We tried the usual resuscitations, of course, but it was more for form than from hope.'

'I'll need to talk to everyone in this wing – patients as well as staff.'

'Lieutenant—'

'Fuck privacy laws, Doctor. I'm overriding them. I want your night watch as well.' Pity jangled Eve's nerves as she re-covered the body. 'Did anyone come in, try to see her? Did anyone call to check her condition?'

'Her ward nurse will have that information.'

'Then let's start with her ward nurse. You round up the rest of them. Is there a room I can use for interview?'

'You can use my office, such as it is.' Ambrose looked back at the body, hissed between her teeth. 'Beautiful woman. Young, with fame and fortune at her fingertips. Drugs heal,

Lieutenant. They extend life and the quality of it. They eradicate pain, soothe a troubled mind. I work hard to remember that when I see what else they can do. If you ask me, and you're not, she was headed here the first time she sipped that pretty blue juice.'

'Yeah, but she got here a lot faster than she was supposed to.'

Eve strode out of the room, spotted Peabody in the corridor. 'Casto?'

'I contacted him. He's on his way.'

'It's a goddamn mess, Peabody. Let's do what we can to mop it up. See that this room . . . Hey, you.' She saw the officer she'd left on guard at the end of the hallway. Her finger pointed like an arrow. She could see that it hit its mark by the way the uniform winced before she blanked her face and started toward her commanding officer.

Eve blew off some steam giving the uniform a dressing down. She didn't have to know Eve would recommend no disciplinary action be taken. Let her sweat.

In the end, when she was sweating and pale, Eve studied the nasty bruising scrape on the officer's collarbone. 'The VT give you that?'

'Sir, before I restrained him.'

'Have it seen to, for Christ's sake. You're in a health center. And I want this door secured. You got that this time? Nobody in, nobody out.'

'Yes, sir.' She snapped to attention, looking, Eve thought, pathetically like a whipped puppy. Barely old enough to buy a beer at a street stall, Eve mused with a shake of her head.

'Stand your watch, Officer, until I order your relief.'

She spun away, gesturing for Peabody to follow.

'You ever get that pissed off at me,' Peabody said in her mild voice, 'I'd prefer a bare-knuckled punch in the face to a tongue lashing.'

'So noted. Casto, glad you decided to join us.'

His shirt was rumpled, as if he'd tossed on the first thing that had come to hand. Eve knew the routine. Her own shirt looked as if it had been balled in someone's pocket for a week. 'What the hell happened here?'

'That's what we're going to find out. We're setting up in Dr Ambrose's office. We'll question the relevant staff one at a time. For the patients we're likely going to be required to do a room to room. Everything on record, Peabody, starting now.'

In silence, Peabody took out her recorder, clipped it to her lapel. 'On record, sir.'

Eve nodded to Ambrose, then followed her through re-inforced glass doors, down a short hallway, and into a small, cluttered office.

'Dallas, Lieutenant Eve. Questioning of possible witnesses in the death of Fitzgerald, Jerry.' She checked her watch for time and date and recorded them. 'Also present are Casto, Lieutenant Jake T., Illegals Division, and Peabody, Officer Delia, temporary attache to Dallas. Questioning to take place in the office of Dr Ambrose, Midtown

Rehabilitation Center for Substance Addictions. Dr Ambrose, please send in the ward nurse. And stand by, Doctor.'

'How the hell did she die?' Casto demanded. 'Her system just give out? What?'

'In a manner of speaking. I'll fill you in as we go.'

He started to speak, then controlled himself. 'Can we get some coffee in here, Eve? I haven't had my fix.'

'Try that.' She jerked her thumb at a battered AutoChef, then took her place behind the desk.

It didn't get much better. By midday, Eve had personally questioned every staff member on duty in the wing, with nearly the same results each time. The VT in room 6027 had gotten out of his restraints, attacked his ward nurse, and all hell had broken loose. From what she could gather, people had poured down the hallway like a river, leaving Jerry's room unattended for anywhere from twelve to eighteen minutes.

More than enough time, Eve supposed, for a desperate woman to flee. But how did she know where to find the drug she craved, and how did she gain access to it?

'Maybe some of the staff were talking about it in her room.' Casto shoveled in veggie pasta on their midday break in the center's eatery. 'A new blend always creates a big buzz. It's not much of a stretch to figure that the ward nurse or a couple of orderlies were gossiping about it. Fitzgerald obviously wasn't as sedated as anyone thought.

She hears them, and when she sees her chance, goes for it.'

Eve chewed over the theory and a forkful of grilled chicken hash. 'I can buy that. She had to hear it somewhere. And she was desperate, and smart. I can buy that she'd figure a way to get down to it undetected. But how the hell did she get past the locks? Where'd she get the code?'

He fumbled there and scowled down at his meal. A man wanted meat, damn it. Good red meat. And these pussy health centers treated it like poison.

'Could she have gotten a master code somewhere?' Peabody speculated. She was sticking to green leaf salad, undressed, with the idea of shaving off a couple of pounds. 'Or a code breaker.'

'Then where is it?' Eve shot back. 'She was stone dead when they found her. The sweepers didn't find any master code in the room.'

'Maybe the frigging door was open when she got there.' Disgusted, Casto shoved his plate aside. 'That's the kind of luck we've been having.'

'That's a little too serendipitous for me. Okay, she hears a discussion about Immortality, how it's being kept in the drug hold for research. She's in acute withdrawal, with whatever they've plugged into her smoothing out the worst of the raw edges. But she needs it. Then, like a gift from God, there's a commotion outside. I don't like gifts from God,' Eve muttered. 'But we'll run with it for now. She gets up, the guard's gone, and she's out of there. She gets down to the drug hold, though I can't see a couple of orderlies discussing directions to it. Still, she got there, we've established that. But getting in . . .'

'What are you thinking, Eve?'

She lifted her gaze to Casto's. 'That she had help. That somebody wanted her to get to it.'

'You think one of the staff led her down there so she could help herself?'

'It's a possibility.' Eve shrugged off the doubt in Casto's voice. 'A bribe, a promise, a fan. And when we go through everyone's records, we might hit on something that indicates a weak link. In the meantime—' She broke off as her communicator sounded. 'Dallas.'

'Lobar, sweeper. We found something interesting in the disposal hold down here, Lieutenant. It's a master code, and its got Fitzgerald's prints all over it.'

'Bag it, Lobar. I'll be down shortly.'

'That explains a lot,' Casto began. The transmission perked up his appetite enough for him to dig into the pasta again. 'Somebody helped her, like you said. Or she copped it from one of the nurses' stations during the confusion.'

'Clever girl,' Eve murmured. 'Very clever girl. Times it all like clockwork, goes down, unkeys what she wants, then takes the additional time to ditch the master. She sure was thinking clearly, wasn't she?'

Peabody drummed her fingers on the table. 'If she took a hit of the Immortality first – and it seems likely she would, it probably jolted her back on full. She probably realized she could be caught there, with the master. If she ditched it, she could claim she'd wandered off, that she was confused.'

'Yeah.' Casto flashed her a smile. 'That works for me.'

'Then why stay?' Eve demanded. 'She'd had her fix. Why didn't she make a run for it?'

'Eve.' Casto's voice was quiet, sober, as were his eyes. 'There's a possibility we haven't touched on here. Maybe she wanted to die.'

'A deliberate OD?' She had thought of it, didn't like what it did to her stomach muscles. Guilt descended like a clammy mist. 'Why?'

Understanding her reaction, he laid a hand briefly over hers. 'She was trapped. You had her. She had to know she was going to spend the rest of her life in a cage – in a cage,' he added, 'with no access to the drug. She'd have gotten old, lost her looks, lost everything that mattered most to her. It was a way out, a way to die young and beautiful.'

'Suicide.' Peabody picked up the threads and wove them. 'The combination she took was lethal. If she was clear-headed enough to get into the hold, she would have been clear-headed enough to know that. Why face the scandal, imprisonment, another withdrawal if you could go out quick and clean?'

'I've seen it happen,' Casto added. 'In my line, it's not unusual. People can't live with the drug, can't live without it. So they take themselves out with it.'

'No note,' Eve said stubbornly. 'No message.'

'She was despondent, Eve. And like you said, desperate.' Casto toyed with his coffee. 'If it was an impulse, something she felt she had to do and do quick, she might not have wanted to think long enough to leave a message. Eve, nobody forced her. There's no sign of violence or struggle on the body. It was self-induced. It may have been an accident, it may have been deliberate. You're not likely to fully determine which.'

'It doesn't close the homicides. No way she acted alone.'

Casto exchanged a look with Peabody. 'Maybe not. But the fact is that the influence of the drug may explain that she did just that. You can hammer away at Redford and Young for a while. Christ knows, neither one of them should get off clean in this. But you're going to have to close this thing sooner or later. It's done.' He set his cup down. 'Give yourself a break.'

'Well, this is cozy.' Justin Young stepped up to the table. His eyes, hollow and red-rimmed, fastened on Eve. 'Nothing spoils your appetite, does it, you bitch?'

As Casto started to rise, Eve lifted a finger, signaling him down. She shoved pity aside. 'Your lawyers manage to spring you, Justin?'

'That's right, all it took was Jerry dying to push them into granting bail. My lawyer tells me that with these latest developments – that's just how the fucker phrased it – with these latest developments, the case is all but closed. Jerry's a multiple murderer, a drug addict, a dead woman, and I'm all but in the clear. Handy, isn't it?'

'Is it?' Eve said evenly.

'You killed her.' He leaned forward on the table, the slap of his hands rattling cutlery. 'You might as well have rammed a knife in her throat. She needed help, understanding, a little compassion. But you kept hacking away at her until she fell to pieces. Now she's dead. Do you understand that?' Tears began to swim in his eyes. 'She's dead and you get a nice big star next to your name. Bagged yourself a mad killer. But I've got news for you, Lieutenant. Jerry never killed anyone. But you did. This isn't over.' He swept an arm across the table, sending dishes to the floor in a mess of broken crockery and spilled food. 'No way in hell is this over.'

She let out a long breath as he walked away. 'No, I guess it's not.'

20

She'd never known a week to move so fast. And she felt brutally alone. Everyone considered the case closed, including the PA's office and her own commander. Jerry Fitzgerald's body was reduced to ashes, her final interview logged.

The media went into its usual frenzy. Top level model's secret life. The killer beneath the perfect face. Quest for immortality leaves a trail of death.

She had other cases, certainly had other obligations, but she spent every free minute reviewing the case, picking through evidence, and trying out new theories until even Peabody told her to give it up.

She tried to juggle the few little details on the wedding Roarke had asked her to see to. But what the hell did she know about caterers, wine selections, and seating charts? In the end, she swallowed her pride and dumped the whole mess on a sneering Summerset.

And was told, in didactic tones, that a wife of a man in Roarke's position would have to learn basic social skills.

She told him to shove it, and they both went off, well

satisfied, to do what they did best. Under it all, Eve was almost afraid they were beginning to like each other.

Roarke wandered from his office into Eve's. And shook his head. They would be married the next day. In less than twenty hours. Was the bride-to-be fussing with her wedding gown, bathing herself in fragrant oils and perfumes, daydreaming about her life to come?

No, she was hunched over her computer, muttering at it, her hair tousled from constant raking with her fingers. There was a stain on her shirt where she'd spilled coffee. A plate holding what might have once been a sandwich had been set on the floor. Even the cat avoided it.

He walked up behind her, saw, as he had expected to see, the Fitzgerald file on screen.

Her tenacity fascinated him, and yes, allured him. He wondered if she had allowed anyone else to see that she suffered over Fitzgerald's death. If she'd been able, she would have hidden it even from him.

He knew the guilt was there, and the pity. And the duty. All would push her, chain a part of her to the case. It was one of the reasons he loved her, that huge capacity for emotion strapped into a logical, restless mind.

He started to bend down to kiss the crown of her head just as she lifted it. They both swore when her head connected hard with his jaw.

'Christ Jesus.' Torn between amusement and pain, Roarke

dabbed at the blood on his lip. 'You make romance a dangerous business.'

'You shouldn't sneak up behind me that way.' Frowning, she rubbed the top of her head. It was just one more spot to throb. 'I thought you and Feeney and a few of your hedonistic friends were going out to rape and pillage.'

'A bachelor's party is not a Viking invasion. I have some time yet before the barbarism begins.' He sat down on the corner of her desk and studied her. 'Eve, you need a break from this.'

'I'm going to be taking a three-week one, aren't I?' she hissed as he only lifted his brows patiently. 'Sorry, I'm being bitchy. I can't get past this, Roarke. I've put it aside a half dozen times this past week, but I keep coming back.'

'Say it aloud. Sometimes it's helpful.'

'Okay.' She shoved back from the desk, narrowly missed stepping on the cat. 'She could have gone to the club. Some of the fancy people slum at that kind of place.'

'Pandora did.'

'Exactly. And they did run with the same basic crowd. So yeah, she could have gone to the club, she could have seen Boomer there. She might even have had a contact tell her he was in. This is all supposing that she knew him, which is not firmly established. And was working with him, or through him. She sees him there, realizing he's mouthing off. He's a loose end, someone who's outlived his useful- ness and is now a liability.'

'So far that's logical.'

374

She nodded, but didn't stop pacing. 'Okay, he spots her after he comes out of the privacy room with Hetta Moppett. Jerry has to worry now what he's said. He could have bragged, even puffed up his own connection to impress the woman. Boomer's smart enough to know he's in trouble, takes off, goes underground. Hetta's the first victim. She's got to go because she might know something. She's taken out quick, brutally, so it looks like a random rage hit. Her ID's taken. That means it'll take longer to trace her, connect her with the club and Boomer. If anyone cared to connect her, which was unlikely.'

'Except they didn't count on you.'

'There's that. Boomer's got a sample, he's got the formula. He had quick hands when he wanted them, and a skill for larceny. Judgment wasn't his strong suit. Maybe he pressed for more money, a larger cut of the whole. But he was good at his job. Nobody knew he was a weasel but a handful of people connected to NYPSD.'

'And those who did wouldn't have known how seriously and personally you take a partnership.' He cocked his head. 'Under most circumstances, I'd say his death would have been chalked off to a soured drug deal, a revenge hit by one of his associates, and left at that.'

'True enough, but Jerry didn't move quick enough. We found the stuff at Boomer's, started to work on that angle. At the same time, I get a first-hand look at Pandora at work. You know the story there, and you've heard the rundown on the circumstances on the night of her death.

Pinning Mavis with the crime was a stroke of luck, good and bad. It gave Jerry time, presented her with a convenient scapegoat.'

'A scapegoat who just happened to be near and dear to the primary's heart.'

'That's the bad luck. How many times am I going to walk into a case and know the most likely suspect is absolutely innocent? Despite all the evidence, despite everything? It's just not going to happen.'

'I don't know. It did with me a few months ago.'

'I didn't know, I felt. After awhile, I knew.' She jammed her hands in her pockets, ripped them out again. 'With Mavis I knew, from the get go, I knew. So I approached the entire case from a different angle. Now I see three potential suspects, all, as it turns out, with motive, with opportunity, and with means. One of those suspects, I begin to believe, is addicted to the very drug that started the ball rolling. Just when you think it's safe to start assuming, a dealer on the East End is taken out. Same MO. Why? That's a sticking point, Roarke, one I can't clean up. They didn't need Cockroach. The odds of Boomer trusting him with any data on this are so long they reach through the stratosphere. But he's taken out, and there are traces of the drug in his system.'

'A ploy.' Roarke took out a cigarette and lighted it. 'A distraction.'

For the first time in hours, she grinned. 'That's what I like about you. Your criminal mind. Toss in a red herring to confuse the issue. Leave the cops straining to find a logical connection with Cockroach. In the meantime, Redford's manufacturing a variety of Immortality on his own, he's given it to Jerry. Along with a hefty fee. But he got that back by bleeding her for every bottle of it from then on. A smart businessman, he's gone to the trouble, taken the risk of procuring a specimen from the Eden Colony.'

'Two,' Roarke said and had the pleasure of seeing that intense face go blank.

'Two what?'

'He ordered two. I swung by Eden on my way back on planet, had a talk with Engrave's daughter. I asked if she could find the time to do some cross-checking. Redford ordered his first specimen nine months ago, using another name and a forged license. But the ID numbers are the same. He had it shipped to a florist on Vegas II, one with a dubious reputation for dealing in contraband flora.' He paused to tap his ash into a marble bowl. 'I'd say it was sent from there to a lab, where the nectar was distilled.'

'Why the hell didn't you tell me before?'

'I'm telling you now. It was just confirmed five minutes ago. You can probably contact security on Vegas II and have the florist questioned.'

She was swearing as she pounded to her 'link, gave orders for just that.

'Even if they crack him, it'll take weeks to cut through the bureaucracy and have him transported on planet so I can have a go at him.' But she rubbed her hands together, anticipating it. 'You might have mentioned you were doing this.'

'If it came to nothing, you wouldn't be disappointed. Instead, you have to be grateful.' His eyes sobered. 'Eve, this doesn't change the situation overmuch.'

'It means Redford was working on his own longer than he wanted us to know about. It means—' She broke off and dropped into a chair. 'I know she could have done it, Roarke. On her own. She could slip out of Young's apartment without detection. She could have left him sleeping, come back, cleaned up. Every fucking time. Or he could have known. He'd go to the wall for her, and he's an actor. He'd toss Redford to the wolves in a heartbeat, but not if it implicated Jerry.'

She lowered her head to her hands a moment, fingers rubbing hard over her brow. 'I know she could have done it. I know she could have seen a window of opportunity and gotten into the drug hold. She might have decided to end it her way, it suits her personality. But it just doesn't feel right.'

'You can't blame yourself for her death,' Roarke said quietly. 'For the obvious reason that you aren't to blame, and also a reason you'll accept, guilt clouds logic.'

'Yeah. I know.' She rose again, restless. 'I've been off my stride with this one. Mavis, remembering about my father. I've missed details, overlapped where it wasn't necessary. All these distractions.'

'Including the wedding?' he suggested.

She managed a weak smile. 'I've tried not to think too much about that. Nothing personal.'

'Consider it a formality. A contract, if you like, with a few trimmings.'

'Have you considered that a year ago we didn't even know each other? That we're living in the same house, but for a good deal of the time we're on two different steps? That all this . . . stuff we feel for each other might not really be the sort of thing that holds up in the long stretch?'

He looked at her steadily. 'Are you going to piss me off the night before we're married?'

'I'm not trying to piss you off, Roarke. You brought it up, and since it has been one of the distractions, I'd like to clear it up. These are reasonable questions and deserve reasonable answers.'

His eyes went dark. She recognized the warning and braced herself for the storm. Instead, he rose, spoke with such icy calm she nearly shuddered. 'Are you backing out, Lieutenant?'

'No. I said I'd do it. I just think we should . . . think,' she said lamely, and hated herself.

'Well, you think then, find your reasonable answers. I have mine.' He glanced at his watch. 'And I'm running late. Mavis is waiting downstairs for you.'

'For what?'

'Ask her,' he said with the slightest edge to his voice as he walked out.

'Damn it.' She kicked the desk with enough force to have Galahad eyeing her maliciously. She kicked it again because pain had some rewards, then limped out to go find Mavis.

An hour later, she found herself being dragged into the Down and Dirty Club. She'd suffered through Mavis's orders to change her clothes, to do something about her hair, her face. Even her attitude. But when the music and noise hit her like a roundhouse punch, she balked.

'Jesus, Mavis. Why here?'

'Because it's nasty, that's why. Bachelor parties are supposed to be nasty. Christ, look at that guy onstage. His cock's big enough to drill spikes. Good thing I asked Crack to save us an A table. The place is sardine city, and it's barely midnight.'

'I have to get married tomorrow,' Eve began, finding it a handy excuse for the first time.

'That's the point. Jesus, Dallas, loosen up. Hey, there's our party.'

Eve was used to shocks. But this was a doozy. It was a bit more than credulity could bear to see a table directly under a cock swinger crowded by Nadine Furst, Peabody, a woman who she thought was probably Trina, and, dear God Almighty, Dr Mira.

Before she could close her mouth, Crack swooped up behind her and hoisted her off her feet. 'Hey there, skinny white girl. Gonna party tonight. Got you a bottle of champagne on the house.'

'You've got any champagne in this joint, pal, I'll chew the cork.'

'Hell, it sparkles. What you want?' He gave her a quick spin, to the vocal appreciation of the crowd, caught her midair, and thumped her down in a seat at the table. 'Ladies, y'all enjoy yourselves now, or I'm gonna hear about it.'

'You have such interesting friends, Dallas.' Nadine puffed on a cigarette. No one was going to worry about tobacco restrictions in there. 'Have a drink.' She lifted a bottle of unknown substance, poured some into what looked like a fairly clean glass. 'We're way ahead of you.'

'I had to get her to change.' Mavis hipped her way into a seat. 'She bitched all the way.' Then Mavis's eyes filled. 'She only did it for me.' She took Eve's drink, swilled it down. 'We wanted to surprise you.'

'You did. Dr Mira. It is Dr Mira, isn't it?'

Mira smiled brilliantly. 'It was when I walked in. I'm afraid I'm a little fuzzy on details at this point.'

'We gotta have a toast.' Rocky on her pins, Peabody used the table for balance. She managed to raise her glass without spilling more than half its contents on Eve's head. 'To the best fucking cop in the whole stinking city, who's gonna marry the sexiest sumbitch I, personally, have ever laid eyes on, and who, because she's so goddamn smart, has seen to it that I'm perman'ly attached to Homicide. Which is where any half-blind asshole could tell you I belong. So there.' She downed the rest of her drink, fell backward into her chair, and grinned foolishly.

'Peabody,' Eve said and flicked a finger under her eyes. 'I've never been more touched.'

'I'm shit faced, Dallas.'

'The evidence points to it. Can we get any food in here that doesn't promise ptomaine? I'm starved.'

'The bride to be wants to eat.' Still sober as a nun, Mavis bolted to her feet. 'I'll take care of it. Don't get up.'

'Oh, and Mavis.' Eve jerked her down, murmured in her ear. 'Get me something nonlethal to drink.'

'But, Dallas, it's a party.'

'And I'm going to enjoy it. I really am, but I want to be clear-headed tomorrow. It's important to me.'

'That's so sweet.' Weeping again, Mavis lowered her face to Eve's shoulder.

'Yeah, I'm a regular sugar substitute.' On impulse she jerked Mavis around and kissed her square on the mouth. 'Thanks. Nobody else would have thought of this.'

'Roarke did.' Mavis mopped at her eyes with the glittering fringe swinging from her sleeve. 'We worked it out together.'

'He would, wouldn't he?' Smiling a little, Eve took another dubious look at the naked bodies gyrating on stage. 'Hey, Nadine.' She topped off the reporter's glass. 'The guy up there with the red tail feathers has his eye on you.'

'Oh, yeah?' Nadine looked blearily around.

'Dare you.'

'Dare me what? To get up there? Shit, that's nothing.'

'Then do it.' Eve leaned over, grinned in her face. 'Let's see some action.'

'You think I won't.' Rising, Nadine teetered, righted herself. 'Hey, hot stuff,' she shouted to the closest dancer. 'Give me a hand up.'

The crowd loved her, Eve decided. Especially when Nadine got into the spirit and stripped down to purple underwear. Eve sighed into her mineral water. She sure knew how to pick her friends. 'How's it going, Trina?'

'I'm having an out of body experience. I think I'm in Tibet.'

'Uh-huh.' Eve cast a look at Dr Mira. The way the woman was cheering, Eve was afraid she'd leap up onstage herself. She didn't think either one of them wanted that vision in their memory logs. 'Peabody.' She had to jab her fingers into Peabody's arm to get even a vague reaction. 'Let's get some more food here.'

Peabody grunted. 'I could do that.'

Following her gaze, Eve watched Nadine in a crotch grind with a seven-foot black in body paint. 'Sure you could, pal. You'd bring the house down.'

'It's just that I've got this little pouch.' She staggered, and Eve caught her neatly by the arm. 'Jake called it my jelly belly. I'm saving up to have it sucked.'

'Just do some more abs. Don't go for the vacuum.'

'It's heditary.'

'Hereditary.'

'Right.' She swayed and bobbled as Eve steered her

through the crowd. 'Everybody in my family's got one. Jake likes 'em skinny. Like you.'

'Screw him, then.'

'Did.' Peabody giggled, then leaned heavily on a serving bar. 'Screwed our brains out. That's not what does it, though, you know that, Evie.'

Eve sighed. 'Peabody, I don't want to punch a fellow officer when she's impaired. So don't call me Evie.'

'Right. Know what does it?'

'Food,' she ordered from the server droid. 'Any kind and lots of it. Table three. What does what, Peabody?'

'What does it. It. What you and Roarke got, that's what does it. Connection. Inside connections. Sex is just the extra.'

'Sure. You and Casto having problems?'

'Nope. Just don't have much connection now that the case is closed.' Peabody shook her head and lights exploded in front of her eyes. 'Jesus, I'm plowed. Gotta use the john.'

'I'll go with you.'

'I can do it myself.' With some dignity, Peabody nudged Eve's hand from her arm. 'I don't care to vomit in front of a superior officer, if it's all the same to you.'

'Suit yourself.'

But Eve watched her like a hawk as she toddled across the floor. They'd been at it nearly three hours, she judged. And though fun was fun, she was going to get some food into her little playmates and see that they all got transport home.

Smiling, she leaned on the bar herself, watching Nadine, still wearing purple briefs, sitting at the table having an earnest discussion with Dr Mira. Trina had her head on the table now and was probably communing with the Dalai Lama.

Mavis, eyes shining, was onstage, screeching out an impromptu number that had the dance floor rocking.

Damn it, she thought as she felt her throat burn. She loved the whole snockered lot of them. Peabody included, she decided, and opted to take a short peek into the toilet to make sure her aide hadn't passed out or drowned.

She made it nearly halfway across the club before she was grabbed. As it had been happening on and off all evening as hopeful clubgoers trolled for partners, she started to shake off good-naturedly.

'Try again, ace. Not interested. Hey!' The quick pinch on her arm annoyed more than hurt. But her vision was already wavering as she was muscled through the hooting crowd and shoved into a privacy room.

'Goddamn it, I said I wasn't interested.' She started to reach for her badge, missed her pocket completely. At a gentle nudge, she spilled backward onto a narrow bed.

'Take a rest, Eve. We have to talk.' Casto dropped down next to her and crossed his feet at the ankles.

Roarke wasn't in a partygoing mood, but as Feeney had gone to some trouble to create a monstrously hedonistic atmosphere, he played his part. It was a hall of sorts, crowded with men, many of whom were surprised to find themselves participating in such a pagan ritual. Still, Feeney, with his electronic expertise, had ferreted out some of Roarke's closer business associates, and none had wanted to risk offending someone of Roarke's stature with a refusal.

So there they were, the rich, the famous, and the scrambling, pressed into a badly lit room with life-size screens flickering with naked bodies in various, imaginative acts of sexual frenzy, a trio of live strippers already entertainingly naked, and enough beer and whiskey to sink the Seventh Fleet and all its crew.

Roarke had to admit it had been a nice gesture and was doing his best to live up to Feeney's expectations as a man on his final night of freedom.

'There you are, boy-o, another whiskey for you.' After several of the Irish himself, Feeney had slipped comfortably into the brogue of the country he'd never seen – that indeed his great-great-grandparents had never set foot on. 'Up the rebels, eh?'

Roarke cocked a brow. He himself had been born in Dublin and had spent most of his youth wandering its streets and alleys. Yet he couldn't claim the sentimental attachment Feeney did for a land and its rebellions. '*Slainte*,' he said to please his friend, and sipped.

'There's a lad. Now you see here, Roarke, the ladies among us are for looking purposes only. No touching for you now.'

'I'll do my best to restrain myself.'

386

Feeney grinned and slapped Roarke on the back hard enough to stagger him. 'She's a prize, isn't she? Our Dallas.'

'She's . . .' Roarke scowled into his whiskey. 'Something,' he decided.

'Keep you on your toes, she will. Keeps them all on their toes. Got a mind like a fucking shark. You know, focused on one thing till the thing's done. Tell you straight, this last case had her bug-shit.'

'She hasn't let it go,' Roarke murmured, and smiled coolly when a naked blonde sidled up to rub her hands up his chest. 'You'll have better luck with that one,' he told her, gesturing to a glaze-eyed man in charcoal gray pinstripes. 'He owns Stoner Dynamics.'

When she looked blank, Roarke gently disengaged the hands that were gliding cheerfully toward his crotch. 'He's loaded.'

She shimmied off, leaving Feeney gazing wistfully after her. 'I'm a happily married man, Roarke.'

'So I've been told.'

'It's lowering to admit I'm not but a little tempted to give a pretty young thing like that a quick ride in a dark room.'

'You're a better man for it, Feeney.'

'That's the truth.' He sighed, low and long, then veered back to the former topic. 'Dallas goes off for a few weeks, she'll put this aside, get on with the next.'

'She doesn't like losing, and she thinks she has.' He tried to dismiss it. Damn if he wanted to spend the night before

387

his wedding picking apart a homicide. With a muttered curse, he steered Feeney to a quiet corner. 'What do you know about that dealer who got hit in the East End?'

'Cockroach. Not much to know. Dealer, fairly slick, fairly stupid. It's amazing how many of them are both. Stuck to his own turf. Liked a quick, easy profit.'

'Was he a weasel, too? Like Boomer?'

'Usta weasel. His trainer retired last year.'

'What happens when a trainer retires?'

'Another one takes on the weasel, or he's let go. Didn't find any new trainer for Cockroach.'

Roarke started to shrug it off, but it kept niggling. 'The cop who retired? Did he work with anybody?'

'What d'you think? I got memory chips in my head?'

'Yes.'

Flattered, Feeney preened. 'Well, as a matter of fact, I recall he was partnered with an old pal of mine. Danny Riley. That was back in, oh, forty-one. Seems like he cruised with Mari Dirscolli for a few years to about forty-eight. Might be forty-nine.'

'Never mind,' Roarke muttered.

'Then he teamed with Casto a couple years.'

Roarke's attention snapped back. 'Casto? Was he partnered with Casto while he was Cockroach's trainer?'

'Sure, but only one leg of a team works as trainer.' Course,' Feeney murmured as his brow furrowed. 'Usual procedure is to take over your partner's contacts. No record Casto did. He had his own weasels.'

Roarke told himself it was his own prejudice, his own ridiculous knee-jerk jealousy. He didn't give a damn. 'Not everything's locked into record. You don't find it coincidental that two weasels who worked close to Casto got hit, both of them with connections to Immortality?'

'We aren't saying Casto had Cockroach. And it's not that coincidental. You're dealing with illegals here, you got overlaps.'

'What other connection have you found that links Cockroach to the other murders, other than Casto?'

'Jesus, Roarke.' He ran a hand over his face. 'You're as bad as Dallas. Look, a lot of Illegals cops end up with abuse problems. Casto's clean to the bone. Never had a trace in any of his testing. He's got a good rep, he's coming up for captaincy, and it's no secret he wants it. He's not going to go messing around with this kind of shit.'

'Sometimes a man is just a little bit tempted, Feeney, and sometimes he gives in. You want to tell me it would be the first time an Illegals cop made a few credits on the side?'

'No.' Feeney sighed again. He was sobering up with this kind of talk. And he didn't like it. 'There's nothing to pin on him, Roarke. Dallas was working with him. If he was a wrong cop, she'd have smelled it. She's like that.'

'She's been distracted. Off stride,' Roarke murmured, remembering her own words. 'Think it through, Feeney, no matter how fast she moved on this, she always seemed to be one step off. If someone had known her moves, they might have anticipated her. Especially someone who thinks like a cop.'

'You don't like him because he's almost as pretty as you,' Feeney said sourly.

Roarke let that pass. 'How much can you dig up on him tonight?'

'Tonight? Jesus, you want me to dig shit up on another cop, go into personal records, because he had a couple of weasels knocked? And you want me to do it tonight?'

Roarke put a hand on Feeney's shoulder. 'We can use my unit.'

'You'll make a good pair,' Feeney muttered as Roarke steered him through the crowd. 'Both a couple of sharks.'

Eve's vision wavered as if she'd suddenly stepped over her head into a tankful of water. Through the ripple, she saw Casto, could smell the faint scent of soap and sweat on his skin. But she couldn't home in on what he was doing there.

'What's going on, Casto? We get a call?' Blankly, she looked around for Peabody, saw the shimmering red drapes that were supposed to add sensuality to a room designed for quick, cheap sex. 'Wait a minute.'

'Just relax.' He didn't want to give her another dose, not in addition to what she'd been drinking at her hen party. 'The door's locked, Eve, so you can't go anywhere. You've got a nice buzz on to make it easier all around.' He pushed a satin-edged pillow behind his back. 'It would have been easier still if you'd just let go. But you didn't.

You won't. Jesus Christ, I can't believe you put the hammer on Lilligas.'

'Who – what?'

'The florist on Vegas II. That's cutting it too damn close. I've been using the bastard myself.'

Her stomach tilted nastily. When she tasted bile at the back of her throat, she leaned forward, stuck her head between her knees and concentrated on breathing in and out.

'Downloads make some people nauseous. We'll go with something else next time.'

'I missed you.' She tried to focus on keeping the heavy, greasy food she'd celebrated with instead of liquor from spewing back up. 'I fucking missed you.'

'Yeah.' He knew she wasn't speaking out of sentiment. 'You weren't looking for another cop. Hey, why should you? And you had your own worries. Broke the rules, Eve. You know the primary is never, ever supposed to get personally involved. You were too worried about your friend. I admire that, really, even if it is stupid.'

He took her by the hair, dragged her head back. After a quick check of her pupils, he decided the initial dose would hold her for a while. He didn't want to risk overdosing her. Not until he'd finished.

'And I do admire you, Eve.'

'You sonofabitch.' Her voice slurred over her thickened tongue. 'You killed them.'

'Each and every one.' Relaxed, he crossed his feet at the

391

ankles. 'It's been hard to hold it all back, I've got to admit. Rough on the ego not to be able to show a woman like you what a smart man can accomplish. You know, Eve, I was a little worried when I learned you were in charge of Boomer.' He reached out, ran a fingertip from her chin down between her breasts. 'I thought I could charm you. Gotta admit you were attracted.'

'Get your hand off me.' She slapped out at it, missed by several inches.

'Your depth perception's off.' He chuckled. 'Drugs mess you up, Eve. Take it from me. I see it every shitty day on the streets. Got sick of seeing it. That's how it started. All those fancy dudes making their fancy profits and never getting their manicures sticky. Why not me?'

'For money.'

'What else is there? I fell into the Immortality connection a couple years back. It was like kismet. Early days then, took my time, did my homework, used a source on the Eden Colony to slip me a sample. Poor old Boomer ferreted it out – my connection from the Eden Colony.'

'Boomer told you.'

'Sure he did. He had something in the Illegals market, he came to me. Didn't know I was already in on it, not then. I kept it under wraps. I didn't know Boomer had a copy of the fucking formula. Didn't know he was holding out, hoping for a nice big chunk.'

'You killed him. You broke him to pieces.'

'Not until it was necessary. I never do anything until

it's necessary. It was Pandora, you see, that beautiful bitch.'

Eve listened, fighting to bring her brain and motor skills back into mesh while Casto spun her a tale of sex, power, and profit.

Pandora had spotted him at the club. Or they'd spotted each other. She'd liked the idea that he was a cop, and the kind of cop he was. He'd be able to get his hands on lots of goodies, wouldn't he? And for her, he'd been happy to do so. He'd been enchanted with her, obsessed, and yes, addicted. No harm in admitting that now. His mistake had been to share his information about Immortality with her, to listen to her ideas for cashing in. Huge profits, she'd predicted. More money than they could spend in three lifetimes. And youth, beauty, great sex. She'd become addicted to the drug quickly, always hungered for more, and she had used him to get it.

But she had been useful, too. Her career, her fame, had made it easy for her to travel, to carry more of what was then being manufactured exclusively on Starlight Station in a little private lab.

Then he'd discovered she'd brought Redford in on the deal. He'd been furious with her, but she'd been able to string him along with sex and promises. And the money, of course.

But things had started to go wrong. Boomer had pushed for money, had pocketed a bag of the drug in powder form.

'I should have been able to handle him. Little wart. Trailed him here. He was flying, running his mouth, tossing the credits I'd given him to keep him quiet around like candy. I couldn't know what he'd said to that damn whore.' Casto shrugged. 'You figured that out yourself. Right scenario, Eve, wrong person. I had to take her out. I was in too deep for mistakes by then. She was just a whore.'

Eve leaned her head back against the wall. Her head had nearly stopped spinning now. She thanked God the dose had been light. Casto was on a roll. She could keep him talking. If she couldn't get the hell out on her own, someone was going to come looking for her soon.

'Then you went after Boomer.'

'I couldn't go to his flop and drag him out. My face is too well known around there. I gave him a little time, then I contacted him. Told him we'd be able to deal. We needed him in on our side. He was stupid enough to buy it. Then I had him.'

'You messed him up first. You didn't kill him quick.'

'I had to find out how much he'd let out, who he might have talked to. He didn't deal well with pain, our Boomer. Spilled his guts. I found out about the formula. Really pissed me off. I wasn't going to mess up his face like the hooker's, but I lost it. Plain and simple. Got emotionally involved, you could say.'

'You're a cold bastard,' Eve muttered, making her voice weak and blurry.

'Now that's just not true, Eve. You ask Peabody.' He grinned, gave her breast a quick tweak that sent fury and rage cycling to her gut. 'I went for DeeDee when I realized you weren't

394

going to take a nibble. Too wrapped up in that rich Irish bastard to take a look at a real man. And DeeDee, bless her, was ripe for plucking. Never could get much out of her on what you were up to, though. DeeDee's got good cop all over her. Slip a little help into her wine, though, she gets more cooperative.'

'You drugged Peabody?'

'Now and then, just to pump her for any details you might have left out of your official report. And to keep her sleeping pretty when I had to go out at night. She was an airtight alibi. Anyway, you know about Pandora. That went pretty much as you had figured, too. Only I was staking out her place that night. Scooped her up the minute she came storming out. She wanted to go to that designer's. We'd pretty much finished up our sexual relationship by then. Just business now. I figured why not take her? I knew she was working to cut me out of the whole deal. She wanted it all. She didn't think she needed some street cop hanging on, even if he was the one to give her the damn stuff to begin with. She knew about Boomer, too. But that didn't bother her. What did she care about some dirty alley croucher? And she never thought, never considered that I'd hurt her.'

'But you did.'

'I took her where she wanted to go. I'm not really sure if I was going to do it then, but when I saw the security camera smashed, it seemed like a sign. Then the place was empty. Just her and me. They'd hang it on the dressmaker, right? Or on the little lady she'd had a fight with. So I hit her. The first strike took her down, but she was up again. That shit made her strong and mean. I had to keep hitting her, and hitting her. Fucking blood flying. Then she was down for good. Your little friend came in, and you know the rest.'

'Yeah, I know the rest. You went back and took the box with the tabs. Why did you take her palm 'link?'

'She always used it to call me. She might've recorded the numbers.'

'Cockroach?'

'Just something extra in the mix. To confuse things. Cockroach was always willing to sample a new product. You were hammering away, and I wanted a hit where I was well alibied, just in case. So I had DeeDee.'

'You got to Jerry, too, didn't you?'

'Easy as a walk on the beach. Get one of the VT's stirred up with a quick buzz, wait for the chaos. I had a reviver for Jerry, brought her around and had her out of there before she knew what was happening. I promised her a fix, and she cried like a baby. Morphine first so she wouldn't get any idea about not cooperating. Then Immortality, then a dash of Zeus. She died happy, Eve. Thanking me.'

'You're a humanitarian, Casto.'

'No, Eve, I'm a selfish man looking out for number one. And I'm not ashamed of it. I've got twelve years on the streets, wading through blood, vomit, and come. I've paid my dues. This drug's going to give me everything I've ever wanted. I'll take my captaincy, and with that kind of connection, I'll feed profits from the drug into a nice numbered account for four or five years, then I'll retire to a tropical island and sip mai tais.'

He was winding down now, she could tell it from the tone of his voice. The excitement, the arrogance had cooled to practicality. 'You'll have to kill me first.'

'I know that, Eve. It's a damn shame. I all but handed you Fitzgerald, but you just wouldn't let it be.' With what might have been affection, he brushed a hand over her hair. 'I'm going to make it easy on you. I've got something here that'll take you down gently. You won't feel anything.'

'That's damn considerate of you, Casto.'

'I owe you that much, honey. Cop to cop. If you'd let it lay, after your friend got off, but you wouldn't. I wish things had been different, Eve. I had a real taste for you.' He leaned close, so close she felt his breath waft over her lips as though he were indeed about to taste her.

Slowly, she lifted her lashes, looking through them into his face. 'Casto,' she said softly.

'Yeah. Just relax now. Won't take long.' He reached for his pocket.

'Fuck you.' She brought her knee up hard. Her depth perception was still slightly skewed. Rather than connecting with his groin she knocked solidly into his chin. He went backward off the bed, and the pressure injector in his hand skittered over the floor.

They both dived for it.

★   ★   ★

'Where the hell is she? She wouldn't have walked out on her own party.' Mavis tapped her spiked heels impatiently as she continued to scan the club. 'And she's the only one of us still sober.'

'Ladies' room?' Nadine suggested, half-heartedly tugging her blouse over her lacy bra.

'Peabody's checked twice. Dr Mira, she wouldn't have made a run for it, would she? I know she's nervous, but—'

'She's not the running kind.' Though her head was still revolving, Mira struggled to keep her speech coherent. 'We'll look around again. She's here somewhere. It's just so crowded.'

'Still looking for the bride?' Grinning widely, Crack lumbered up. 'Looks like she just wanted a last ride. The dude over there saw her slip into one of the privacy rooms with a cowboy type.'

'Dallas?' Mavis snorted at the thought of it. 'No way.'

'So, she's celebrating.' Crack lifted his shoulders.

'Got plenty more rooms, ladies, if you got an itch.'

'Which room?' Peabody demanded, sober now that she'd thrown up everything in her stomach including, she was sure, a good portion of the lining.

'Number five. Hey, you want a gang bang, I can round up some nice young boys for you. All sizes, all shapes, all colors.' He shook his head as they marched off, and decided that he'd better go along to keep the peace.

★   ★   ★

Eve's fingers slipped off the injector, and the elbow to her cheekbone sent pain grinding down her face and into her teeth. Still, she had first blood, and the shock of finding her ready to fight had shaken him.

'You should have given me a bigger dose.' She followed up the statement with a short-armed punch to his windpipe. 'I wasn't drinking tonight, asshole.' She managed to roll him over. 'I'm getting married tomorrow.' She punctuated this by bloodying his nose. 'That was for Peabody, you bastard.'

He caught her in the ribs and winded her. She felt the injector pass over her arm and heaved up by the hips to kick. She would never know if it was blind luck, her lack of depth perception, or his own miscalculation, but he dodged to avoid the gut thrust, and her feet, coming up like pistons, caught him square in the face.

His eyes rolled back in his head; his head hit the floor with an ominous and satisfying thud.

Still, he'd managed to get more of the drug into her. She crawled, drifting in the sensation of swimming through thick, golden syrup. She made it to the door, but the lock and its key code appeared to be twelve feet above her grasping hand.

Then the door burst open and all hell broke loose.

She felt herself lifted, patted down. Someone was ordering in no-nonsense tones that she be given air. Giggles bubbled up in her. She was flying now, was all she could think.

'Bastard killed them,' she kept saying. 'Bastard killed them all. I missed it. Where's Roarke?'

Her eyelids were pulled back and she would have sworn her eyeballs rolled like fiery little marbles. She heard the words 'health center' and began to fight like a tiger.

Roarke descended the stairs, a grim set to his mouth. He knew Feeney was still upstairs, huffing and blowing, but he was convinced. A business deal of the size of Immortality's potential required an expert and an inside connection. Casto filled both those bills.

Eve might not want to hear it, either, so he wouldn't mention it. Yet. Feeney would have three weeks to poke around while they were on their honeymoon. If there was indeed going to be a honeymoon.

He heard the door open and angled his chin. They were going to have this out once and for all, he determined. Here and now. He took two more steps, then was down the rest of them in a dead run.

'What the hell happened to her? She's bleeding.' There was blood in his own eye as he snatched a limp Eve from the arms of a seven-foot black in a silver loincloth.

As everybody began talking at once, Mira clapped her hands like a schoolteacher in a room of rowdy students. 'She needs a quiet room. The MTs treated her for the drug, but she'll have some residual effects. And she wouldn't let them deal with the cuts and bruises.'

Roarke's face went stony. 'What drug?' His gaze latched on Mavis. 'Where the hell did you take her?'

'Not her fault.' Still glassy-eyed, Eve wrapped her arms around Roarke's neck. 'Casto. It was Casto, Roarke. Know that?'

'As a matter of fact—'

'Stupid – stupid to miss it. Sloppy. Can I go to bed now?'

'Take her upstairs, Roarke,' Mira said calmly. 'I can tend to her. Believe me, she'll be fine.'

'I'll be fine,' Eve agreed as she floated up the stairs. 'I'll tell you everything. I can always tell you, can't I? 'Cause you love me, you sap.'

There was only one piece of information Roarke wanted at the moment. He laid Eve on the bed, took a good look at her bruised cheek and swollen mouth. 'Is he dead?'

'Nope. I just beat the hell out of him.' She smiled, caught the look in his eye, and shook her head slowly. 'Nuh-uh, no way. Don't even think about it. We're getting married in a couple hours.'

He smoothed the hair back from her face. 'Are we?'

'I figured it out.' It was hard to concentrate, but it was important. She lifted her hands, cupped his face to keep it in focus. 'It's not a formality. And it's not a contract.'

'What is it?'

'It's a promise. It's not so hard to promise to do something you really want, anyway. And if I'm lousy at being a wife, you'll just have to live with it. I don't break my promises. And there's this one other thing.'

He could see her slipping, and shifted slightly so that Mira could tend the cut on her cheek. 'What other thing, Eve?'

'I love you. Sometimes it makes my stomach hurt, but I kind of like it. Tired now, come to bed. Love you.'

He eased back to let Mira get on with her tending. 'It's all right for her to sleep?'

'Best thing for her. She'll be fine when she wakes up. Maybe a little hungover, which seems unfair since she didn't drink anything. She said she wanted a clear head for tomorrow.'

'Did she?' She didn't look calm when she slept, he noted. She never did. 'Will she remember any of that? What she was telling me?'

'She may not,' Mira said cheerfully. 'But you will, and that should do the job.'

He nodded and stepped back. She was safe again. One more time safe. He glanced over at Peabody. 'Officer, can I count on you to fill me in on the details?'

Eve did have a hangover, and wasn't pleased about it. Her stomach was tied in greasy knots, and her jaw was sore. Between Mira and Trina's wizardry with cosmetics, the bruises didn't show. As brides went, she supposed, studying herself, she was passable.

'You look mag, Dallas.' Mavis sighed and took a slow turn around Leonardo's finest hour. The dress sleeked down, as it was meant to, the bronze tone adding warmth to Eve's skin, the lines highlighting her long, lean form. Its very simplicity made the statement that it was the woman within who counted.

'The garden's packed with people,' Mavis went on cheerily as Eve's stomach roiled. 'Did you look out the window?'

'I've seen people before.'

'There was media doing flybys earlier. I don't know whose button Roarke pushed, but they've stopped.'

'Goodie.'

'You're all right, aren't you? Dr Mira said you shouldn't have any dangerous aftereffects, but—'

'I'm fine.' It was only partly a lie. 'Having it closed, knowing all the facts, the truth makes it easier.' She thought of Jerry and suffered. She looked at Mavis, the glowing face, the silver-tipped hair, and smiled. 'You and Leonardo still planning to cohabitate?'

'At my place, temporarily. We're looking for bigger digs, one where he'll have room to work. And I'm going to start making the club rounds again.' She took a box from the bureau, handed it over. 'Roarke sent this up for you.'

'Yeah?' Opening it, Eve felt twin tugs of pleasure and alarm. The necklace was perfect, of course. Two drapes of twisted copper studded with colored stones.

'I happened to mention it.'

'I bet you did.' With a sigh, Eve draped it on, then fastened the long matching drops to her ears. And looked, she thought, like a stranger. A pagan warrior.

'There's one more thing.'

'Oh, Mavis, I can't stand one more thing. He's got to understand that I—' She broke off as Mavis turned from the long white box on the table, took out a sweeping spray of white flowers – petunias. Simple, backyard-variety petunias.

'He always knows,' she murmured. All the muscles in her stomach loosened, all the nerves died away. 'He just knows.'

'I guess when somebody understands you that way, that, you know, intimately, it makes you pretty lucky.'

'Yeah.' Eve took the flowers, cradled them. The reflection in the mirror didn't look like a stranger. It looked, she thought, like Eve Dallas on her wedding day. 'Roarke's going to swallow his tongue when he gets a load of me.'

She laughed, grabbed Mavis's arm, and rushed out to make her promises.

Read an extract from

INDULGENCE IN DEATH

The new J.D. Robb thriller,

out now

It was good to be home. Driving downtown to Cop Central through ugly traffic, blasting horns, hyping ad blimps, belching maxi-buses just put her in a cheerful mood.

Vacations were great, but to Eve's mind New York had it all and a bag of soy chips.

The temperature might have been as brutal as a tax audit with sweaty waves of heat bouncing off concrete and steel, but she wouldn't trade her city for any place on or off planet.

She was rested, revved and ready for work.

She rode the elevator up from the garage, shuffling over as more cops squeezed in on every floor. When she felt the oxygen supply depleting, she pried her way out to take the glides the rest of the way up.

It smelled like home, she thought—cop, criminal, the pissed off, the unhappy, the resigned. Sweat and bad coffee merged together in an aroma she wasn't sure could be found anywhere but a cop shop.

And that was fine with her.

She listened to a beanpole of a man in restraints mutter his mantra as a pair of uniforms muscled him up the glide.

Fucking cops, fucking cops, fucking cops.

It was music to her ears.

She stepped off, angled toward Homicide, and spotted Jenkinson, one of her detectives, studying the offerings at Vending with a hopeless expression.

"Detective."

He brightened slightly. "Hey, Lieutenant, good to see you."

He looked as if he'd slept in his clothes, for a couple days.

"You pull a double?"

"Caught one late, me and Renicke." He settled on something that looked like a cheese danish if you were blind in one eye. "Just wrapping it up. Vic's in a titty bar over on Avenue A, getting himself a lap dance. Asshole comes in, starts it up. The titty doing the lap dance is his ex. Gives her a couple smacks. The guy with the hard-on clocks him. Asshole gets hauled out. He goes home, gets his souvenir Yankee's ball bat, lays in wait. Vic comes out, and the asshole jumps him. Beat the holy shit of out of him and left his brains on the sidewalk."

"High price for a lap dance."

"You're telling me. Asshole's stupid, but slippery." Jenkinson ripped the wrapping off the sad-looking danish, took a resigned bite. "Leaves the bat and runs. We got wits falling out of our pockets, got his prints, got his name, his address. Slam fucking dunk. He doesn't go home and make our lives easier, but what he does, a couple hours after, is go to the ex's. Brings her freaking flowers he dug up out of a sidewalk planter deal. Dirt's still falling off the roots."

"Classy guy," Eve observed.

"Oh yeah." He downed the rest of the danish. "She won't let him in—stripper's got more sense—but calls it in while he's crying and banging on the door, and dumping flower dirt all over the hallway. We get there to pick him up, and what does he do? He jumps out the freaking window end of the hall. Four flights up. Still holding the damn flowers and trailing dirt all the way."

He shifted to order coffee with two hits of fake sugar. "Got the luck of God 'cause he lands on a couple chemi-heads doing a deal down below—killed one of them dead, other's smashed up good. But they broke his fall."

Deeply entertained, Eve shook her head. "You can't make this shit up."

"Gets more," Jenkinson told her, slurping coffee. "Now we got to chase his ass. I go down the fire escape—and let me tell you smashed chemi-heads make one hell of a mess—Renicke goes out the front. He spots him. Asshole runs through the kitchen of an all-night Chinese place, and people are yelling and tumbling like dice. This fucker is throwing shit at us, pots and food and Christ knows. Renicke slips on some moo goo something, goes down. Hell no, you can't make this shit up, LT."

He grinned now, slurped more coffee. "He heads for this sex joint, but the bouncer sees this freaking blood-covered maniac coming and blocks the door. The guy—the bouncer's built like a tank—so the asshole just bounces off him like a basketball off the rim, goes airborn for a minute and plows right into me. Jesus. Now I've got blood and chemi-head brains on me, and Renicke's hauling ass over, and he's covered with moo goo. And this asshole starts yelling police brutality. Took some restraint not to give him some.

"Anyway." He blew out a breath. "We're wrapping it up."

Was it any wonder she loved New York?

"Good work. Do you want me to take you off the roll?"

"Nah. We'll flex a couple hours, grab some sleep up in the crib once the asshole's processed. You look at the big picture, boss? All that, over a pair of tits."

"Love screws you up."

"Fucking A."

She turned into the bullpen, acknowledged "heys" from cops finishing up the night tour. She walked into her office, left the door open. Detective-Sergeant Moynahan had, as she'd expected, left her desk pristine. Everything was exactly as it had been when she'd walked out her office door three weeks before, except cleaner. Even her skinny window sparkled, and the air smelled vaguely—not altogether unpleasantly—like the woods she'd walked through in Ireland.

Minus the dead body.

She programmed coffee from her AutoChef and with a satisfied sigh, sat at her desk to read over the reports and logs generated during her absence.

Murder hadn't taken a holiday during hers, she noted,

but her division had run pretty smooth. She moved through closed and open cases, requests for leave, overtime, personal time, reimbursements.

She heard the muffled clump that was Peabody's summer airboots, and glanced up as her partner stepped into the open doorway.

"Welcome home! How was it? Was it just mag?"

"It was good."

Peabody's square face sported a little sun-kiss, which reminded Eve her partner had taken a week off with her squeeze, EDD ace McNab. She had her dark hair pulled back in a short but jaunty tail, and wore a thin, buff-colored jacket over cargo trousers a few shades darker. Her tank matched the airboots in a bright cherry red.

"It looks like DS Moynahan kept things oiled while I was gone."

"Yeah. He sure dots every i, but he's easy to work with. He's solid, and he knows how to ride a desk. He steers clear of field work, but he had a good sense of how to run the ship. So, what did you get?"

"A pile of reports."

"No, come on, for your anniversary. I know Roarke had to come up with something total. Come on," Peabody insisted when Eve just sat there. "I came in early just for this. I figure we've got nearly five before we're officially on the clock."

True enough, Eve thought, and since Peabody's brown eyes pleaded like a puppy's, she held up her arm, displayed the new wrist unit she wore.

"Oh."

The reaction, Eve thought, was perfect. Baffled surprise, severe disappointment, the heroic struggle to mask both.

"Ah, that's nice. It's a nice wrist unit."

"Serviceable." Eve turned her wrist to admire the simple band, the flat, silver-toned face.

"Yeah, it looks it."

"It's got a couple of nice features," she added as she fiddled with it.

"It's nice," Peabody said again, then drew her beeping communicator out of her pocket. "Give me a sec, I . . . hey, it's you." Mouth dropping, Peabody jerked her head up. "It's got a micro-com in it? That's pretty mag. Usually they're all fuzzy, but this is really clean."

"Nano-com. You know how the vehicle he rigged up for me looks ordinary?"

"Ordinary leaning toward ugly," Peabody corrected. "But nobody gives it a second look or knows that it's loaded, so . . . Same deal?"

Automatically Peabody dug out her 'link when it signalled, then paused. "Is that you? It got full communication capability? In a wrist unit that size?"

"Not only that, it's got navigation, full data capabilities. Total data and communications—he programmed it with all my stuff. If I had to, I could access my files on it. Water proof, shatter proof, voice command capabilities. Gives me the ambient temp. Plus it tells time."

Not to mention he'd given her a second with the exact

same specs—only fired with diamonds. Something she'd wear when she suited up for fancy.

"That is so utterly iced. How does it—"

Eve snatched her wrist away. "No playing with it. I haven't figured it all out myself yet."

"It's just like the perfect thing for you. The abso perfect thing. He really gets it. And you got to go to Ireland and Italy and finish it up at that island he's got. Nothing but romance and relaxation."

"That's about it, except for the dead girl."

"Yeah, and McNab and I had a really good time—what? What dead girl?"

"If I had more coffee I might be inclined to tell you."

Peabody sprang toward the AutoChef.

Minutes later, she polished off her own cup and shook her head. "Even on vacation you investigated a homicide."

"I didn't investigate, the Irish cop did. I consulted—unofficially. Now, my serviceable yet frosty wrist unit tells me we're on duty. Scram."

"I'm scramming, but I want to tell you about how McNab and I took scuba lessons, and—"

"Why?"

"I don't know, but I liked it. And how I did these interviews on Nadine's book, which is still number one in case you haven't been checking. If we don't catch a case, maybe we can have lunch. I'll buy."

"Maybe. I've got to catch up."

Alone, she considered it. She wouldn't mind hanging for

lunch, she realized. It would be a kind of bridge between vacation and the job, screwing around and the routine of work.

She didn't have any meetings scheduled, no actives on her plate. She'd need to go over some of the open cases with the teams assigned, touch base with Moynahan, mostly to thank him for his service. Other than that—

She scanned the next report, answering her 'link. "Lieutenant Dallas, Homicide."

Dispatch, Dallas, Lieutenant Eve.

So much, she thought, for bridges.

Jamal Houston died with his chauffeur's hat on behind the wheel of a limo of glittery gold, long and sleek as a snake. The limo had been tidily parked in a short-term slot at LaGuardia.

Since the crossbow bolt angled through Jama's neck and into the command pad of the wheel, Eve assumed Jamal had done the parking.

With her hands and boots sealed, Eve studied the entry wound. "Even if you're pissed off you missed your transpo, this is a little over-the-top."

"A crossbow?" Peabody studied the body from the other side of the limo. "You're sure?"

"Roarke has a couple in his weapons collection. One of them fires these bolts like this. One question is just why someone had a loaded crossbow in a limo to begin with."

Houston, Jamal, she mused, going over the data they'd

already accessed, black male, age forty-three, co-owner of Gold Star transportation service. Married, two offspring. No adult criminal. Sealed juvie. He'd been six feet one inch and one-ninety and wore a smart and crisp black suit, white shirt, red tie. His shoes were shined like mirrors.

He wore a wrist unit as gold as the limo and a gold star lapel pin with a diamond winking in the center.

"From the angle, it looks like he was shot from the right rear."

"Passenger area is pristine," Peabody commented. "No trash, no luggage, no used glasses or cups or bottles, and all the slots for the glassware are filled, so the killer and/or passenger didn't take any with him. Everything gleams, and there are fresh—real—white roses in these little vases between the windows. A selection of viewing and audio and reading discs all organized by alpha and type in a compartment, and they don't look like they've been touched. There are three full decanters of different types of alcohol, a friggie stocked with cold drinks, and a compact AutoChef. The log there says it was stocked about sixteen hundred, and it hasn't been accessed since."

"The passenger must not have been thirsty, and didn't want a snack while he didn't listen to music, read or catch some screen. We'll have the sweepers go over it."

She circled the car, slid in beside the body. "Wedding ring, pricey wrist unit, gold star with diamond pin, single gold stud in his ear lobe." She worked her hand under the body, tugged out a wallet.

"He's got plastic, and about a hundred-fifty cash, small bills. It sure as hell wasn't robbery." She tried to access the dash comp. "It's passcoded." She had better luck with the 'link, and listened to his last transmission, informing his dispatcher he'd arrived at LaGuardia with his passenger for the pick-up, and suggesting the dispatcher call it a night.

"He was supposed to pick up a second passenger." Eve considered. "Picked up the first, second passenger coming in, transpo on time according to this communication. So he parks, and before he can get out to open the door for passenger one, he takes one in the neck. Time of death and the 'link log are only a few minutes apart."

"Why does somebody hire a driver to go to the airport, then kill him?"

"There's got to be a record of who hired the service, where they were picked up. One shot," Eve murmured. "No muss, but a lot of fuss. Add in what you'd call an exotic weapon."

She took a memo book from his pocket, his personal 'link, breath mints, a cotton handkerchief. "He's got a pick-up listed here at the Crystler Building, ten-twenty p.m. AS to LTC. Passenger initials. No full name, no full addy. This is just his back-up. Let's see if we can find anyone who saw anything—ha ha—get crime scene in here. We'll go check in with the company first."

**Random hits, thrill kills and murders
with a taste for the finer points
in life – and death . . .**

INDULGENCE IN DEATH
Available now.